CW01597008

Bristol

Written

By

Casper Parks

Copyright 2012© Casper Parks all rights reserved.

Prayerful thanks for the blessing of an imagination.

Novels by Casper Parks
Perceptional Threshold
Ages Past
Coming From Darkness

Sign-up for information on upcoming novels
Visit www.casperparks.com

Without limiting, the rights under copyright reserved above no part of this publication may be reproduced, stored in or introduced into a retrieval system, or transmitted in any form, or by any means electronic, mechanical, photo copying, recording, or otherwise, without prior written permission of both the copyright owner and the above publisher. This is a work of fiction, names, characters, places, and incidents either are product of the author's imagination or used fictitiously, and any resemblance living or dead, business establishments, events, or locales is entirely coincidental. Scanning, uploading, and distributions of this book via the internet or via any other means without permission of the author and publisher are illegal and punishable by law. Please purchase only authorized electronic editions, and do not participate in or encourage piracy of copyrighted materials. Support of the author's rights is greatly appreciated.

Copyright 2012, © Casper Parks all rights reserved.
Copyright © Cover Art by RavenandBlack
SelfPubBookCovers.com

Part One

Soul Lost At Sea

1

Resolved to delay death, Carl Ver Haven staggered through vestibules of darkened oblivion. A short distance away, a doorway opened and bled light into the darkness. Distorted corridors wrenched and tilted upward, slowing his forward trek. Mustered by shear willpower, he forged onward. Claustrophobic, he stretched into a swimmer's dive and propelled through the passage and into the light.

As Carl's soul rebounded to life, his shackled legs jittered against the wooden deck. Cumbersome chains bolted to a bulkhead restricted his movements. Metal clamps around his ankles chilled his shinbones. Shackled wrists weighted his near lifeless hands against the deck, and a metal band padlocked around his neck had rubbed his skin raw.

Sluggish, he shook free remnants of his passage to perdition and back. Through silted bruised eyes, he surveyed nearby surroundings. He remained a prisoner onboard the Tea Clipper, Lady Beth. Perhaps, the nightmare was a better place. On his next venture among dark passages, he vowed to find a doorway leading to a place of peace and rest.

Low whimpers from inside of a wire-mesh-crate caught his attention. Inside the crate was a gift from the Manchu Dynasty for the President of the United States. As a private joke on a former Commanding Officer, Carl had named the dog Bristol.

During a brief layover at the Hawaiian Islands, he had learned Lincoln won the election. Having once met Lincoln, he knew of the family's love for pets. Bristol's fate now lay in the hands of a cabin boy named Kern.

Carl recounted recent months that led him to this finial hellish destiny. He had booked passage on the Lady Beth at Hong Kong. Before reaching China, the Lady Beth had taken cargo at India, and had a week layover at Limmen Bight Australia before sailing toward the Hawaiian Islands. Two weeks ago, they had left Hawaii and bound for San Francisco.

A gray blur of a rat scurried across Carl's leg and vanished between crevasses of stacked burlap bags stuffed with rice.

Directly behind the, rat an orange tomcat skidded across the deck then extended his claws and braked to a halt.

The cat's tattered ears lay tight as his tail polished the deck. After a low hiss sliced mildew-tainted air, he gracefully jumped on top of the burlap bags, crouched low then focused on the crevasses and waited for the rat to reappear.

Carl estimated the rat was foot long not including its long thick leathery tail. He muttered, "And in Texas they brag about the size of their cattle." He scarcely had strength to chuckle at the thought. Given how large the rat was, he reckoned the tomcat lacked common sense.

Again, his thoughts drifted in cadence with the ship against ocean swells. Eleven days after departing the Hawaiian Islands, they encountered an ill-tempered storm that rocked the ship for two days.

For the past day, they had sought refuge inside the eye of the storm and drifted aimlessly. Encompassed by the tranquil eye an uneasy calm had settled onboard ship. Although no longer fighting to remain afloat against twenty-foot swells, the crew had not returned to torturing him. Instead, they rested and prepared to fight the storm, again.

It was only a matter of time until venturing back into the wrath of the sea. Captain La Horn was tedious at keeping schedules. This delay hoisted his foul temper, matching that of the storm.

He reflected on his journey to the Chinese cities of Shanghai, Canton, Amoy and Thaiping as a representative from the United States government.

Carl considered global conquests by both French and English and their shady commerce dealings. He was primarily on a fact-finding mission, confirming the depth of France and England's involvement in the opium trade. Moreover, learn if England was honoring the Tientsin Treaty with the Manchu Dynasty.

In route to China, he had a week layover at New Zealand. There, he learned local Maori Tribes were at war with British Colonists. With the United States divided over issues at home, he doubted President Lincoln, Congress, or the Senate had time to consider turmoil overseas. In truth, none in Washington posed a genuine interest with affairs abroad. His trip was more of a political gesture.

After the Lady Beth left Hawaii, Bristol had alerted him to an unseen cargo. Curious, Carl jimmied open a crate and discovered opium concealed among of tea bags. Among the cargo, an unusually large number of gunpowder kegs.

He had decided to wait until reaching San Francisco, and learn where the shipment was delivered and to whom, and why all the secrecy. Opium was legal in the United States unless a local village, town or city passed laws making it illegal.

Powder kegs onboard likely a result of supply and demand, due to the pending conflict between Northern and Southern States. Including gunpowder, he had planned to include a mention of opium in his report to Lincoln. It appeared that opium dealers were looking for new markets to sell their addictive Black Tar.

Along the coast of China, Carl had witnessed firsthand the devastating effects of the drug on people's lives. Beyond the report, he planned to do nothing and hoped Americans had enough commonsense to avoid the deadly addiction.

First mate Caleb had caught him resealing the crate. La Horn suspected him as a spy and ordered torture to extract the truth. Throughout various Indian Campaigns, Carl came across brutal people both Indian and white alike however, none like these barbaric sea hounds.

Splinters of bamboo jammed beneath his fingernails continued to irritate him. They had broken his front teeth at the roots and probed open nerve endings with a thin wire. Pain was execrating.

Violent emotions gushed from a dark place he thought long ago dead. These former Buccaneers were illegitimate bastards of the devil. If given a chance he would set the ship afire, leaving them at the mercy of the sea.

Overhead a hatch creaked open and poured overcast daylight into the ship's belly. Wooden steps chattered beneath bare feet as the cabin boy tromped downward. They all needed killing, except Kern who was innocent of wrongdoing.

The hatch fell partly closed behind Kern, filtering daylight into miniature spotlights across the worn deck. Kern's sun stained blond hair and shined beneath scattered rays of light.

Kern squatted, tipped a canteen against Carl's perched lips and smiled. At age thirteen, his piercing blue eyes should have sparkled with wonderment, awe, and an innocent exploration in pursuit of life. A rigidity belonging to a seasoned killer had hardened his young eyes.

Suddenly, gale force winds ushered massive waves against the ship haul. Timber creaked and moaned opposed to reentering the storm.

Kern steadied himself and advised, "As ya can tell, captain's putting us back amidst the fray." His tone lifted, ridiculing La Horn's thick French accent. "Storm or no storm we'll remain on schedule. Hell or high water this cargo is being delivered on time, sooner if at all possible. We're losing money here!"

Carl smirked at Kern's imitation of La Horn. He swallowed another swig of water, then pushed the canteen away and insisted, "Boy, you outta be saving this for yourself. I'm three-quarters dead as it is."

Chains clattered as Carl tapped the side of his head and said, "Betwixt body and soul there's a nasty argument going on inside. They simply haven't agreed upon a time to give-up the ghost. Remember everything I told you, boy…"

Kern peered through long locks of hair that dangled across his forehead and stood his ground. "At least call me something other than boy before ya croak." A silly sneer crinkled his cheeks. He enjoyed imitating accents as if trying to find one that suited him. Teasing, he flexed a bicep and mocked Carl's southern accent. "This boy's libel to show ya' what he's made of, and pop ya' betwixt both eyes."

Carl pondered Kern's true accent and was unable to place it with certainty. He had noted a guess at Kern's origin inside a personal journal. Evidently, Kern was a recent addition as a crewmember aboard the Lady Beth. He drew a breath and exhaled, "Boy didn't your pa ever teach ya any manners?"

"The name is Kern, and you'd be best to recollect it."

Carl smirked and reminded him, "So you've said a dozen or more times, already." Then, he nodded at the wooden and wire-mesh crate that housed the dog. "Promise me, you'll look after Bristol. A boy and dog is like a partnership, take of him and he will take care of you." From inside of the crate, Bristol whimpered acknowledging he had heard his name.

Kern glimpsed over his shoulder at the crate, then stared at the overhead hatch and risked sitting. He crisscrossed his legs and whispered, "I know why Captain La Horn hasn't let old slant eyed Cookie skin Bristol for dinner. Captain said, since the dog was trained to sniff-out opium, Bristol was of use. Sniff out the competition is what he said."

Knife like, Kern sliced a hand across his throat. "Guessing put em out of business is what he really meant." He struggled to pronounce, "Monopolies the market' is what Caleb said."

As Carl smirked, his dried lips cracked and bled. "You mean monopolize?"

"That's what I said… Monopolize." Kern nailed the word and offered another swig of water. Carl tipped the canteen for himself this time and wiped his perched lips.

Kern nodded. "Don't ya' worry none about Bristol. Been taking care of him since they leg ironed ya… And I'll keep taking care of him." Again, he eyed the crate and felt sorry for the dog. "Don't reckon Bristol cares much for this storm, he's looking more sickly than usual."

Carl licked his chapped lips giving them moister and tasted his own blood. "Most dogs don't take to the sea very well, he'll be fine once he gets back on land. Remember what I told you."

Kern deepened his voice, trying to sound older. "Since I was knee-high to a spider been taking care of myself. Like I said, ya don't need to worry none for me."

Carl wanted to ask why knee-high to a spider and not a grasshopper. However, he acknowledged the lad's resolve. "Aye, I reckon not. Like a game of poker, you bluffed your way across this vast ocean. All the way from Australia to Hong Kong, to Hawaii and nearly San Francisco. Seriously, I doubt you know where you're headed in life."

Stout faced, Kern thumb his chest. "I know this much... Once we make port, this boy ain't headed back out to sea anytime soon. No sir, not me, no way, no how. I'm a land-lover through and through. Once back on dry land, I'm going to take these feet of mine on a long walkabout. Visit all them places ya been bragging about. I wanna see that big old White House Bristol'll be living at."

Lady Beth's haul murmured as she reentered the storm and rode against mammoth waves. Overhead beams vibrated, scattering a sandstorm of dust into the air. Carl buckled forward, clinched his stomach and hacked a dark glob from his lungs. Bleeding to death internally was not how he had expected to die. He always believed a bullet would lead to his final demise.

Carl cleared his throat, placed a hand on Kern's knee and gave it a strong squeeze. "I suspect you're on the run from something or other. Some people claim you can't run from your problems. Here and now is not one of those cases. Once ashore, get away from these people as quick and as far as you can. They'll spoil those joys life's laid-out for you to discover. Run and never look back. These people aren't a very good reflection of society. There are decent people in the world - you've just not met them yet…"

Kern leaned close and whispered, "Never-ya' mind about me. Like I just said, I'm planning on a walkabout." He spread an assuring smile. "Right after I deliver your journal and Bristol as promised, first."

Graceful, Kern got to his feet. His sturdy sea legs glided with the rising and falling deck beneath him. He rested a hand on a knife-handle sheathed at his waist, gazed at the overhead hatch and said, "I'd best be getting back above deck before they start wondering what I'm up to down here."

"Don't be leaving just yet," Carl said, then slipped an amulet from around his neck and tangled it outward. "Got me no son to pass it on down, so I want you to have it..."

Desire lit Kern's blue eyes, yet he hesitated to reach for it.

Carl insisted, "Don't be shy. Day before yesterday, I saw you eyeing it." He rattled the amulet, setting it into a spin and repeated, "Here take."

Kern fought an urge to take it and shook his head. "Someday, you'll have a son. Probably a right nice one, who'll take after ya."

Carl's eyes watered. "If'n I were to have a son, I'd hope he'd be a lot like you - honorable and just." His tone shifted to urgency. "I'll be having no son, a fight between body and soul is near over. I'm not allowing La Horn and his bunch to have the pleasure of seeing this body shed its last breath."

Again, Carl dangled the amulet. "Take it before Fat Sam gets his spongy hands on it after I'm dead and gone to the hereafter. Consider it as payment for looking after Bristol."

Kern took the amulet and stared at an array of star patterns molded into the metal. At the center of the amulet, a hooded man held a tall hooked walking stick. The metal amulet was amazingly lightweight. Without lifting his eyes, he asked, "What's it mean?"

Weak, Carl grinned. "Willing to take an oath of secrecy?"

Kern nodded, ready to learn shrouded mysteries La Horn's crew was unable to extract from Carl.

Guarded, Carl bestowed the secret meaning of imagery on the amulet. "It's an ethos called the Herdsmen. It symbolizes an organization I am part of... After I fail to show-up, sure as rainfalls from the sky, they will be looking for me. My parting this world won't go unnoticed. La Horn will be brought to justice."

Kern examined detailed artwork engraved on the amulet. He had no idea what ethos meant, and thought perhaps small lettered words on the amulet explained it. Given Carl's ailing condition, he decided not to ask how to pronounce the words and what they meant.

Kern drew a breath, slid the silver chain over his head and dropped the amulet beneath his baggy hemp shirt. Pending the loss of a friend he vowed, "I'll tell none of it."

An ill-mannered voice bellowed from above deck, "Boy get your arse up here! We're running against high-seas and you are needed on deck!"

Kern cringed and labored a polite smile. Steadfast, he held back tears. In recent seasons, he had witnessed Death's reach for others. Again, he sensed Death nearby, this time for his new friend. It seemed as of late, anyone he befriended or who had befriended him died shortly afterwards.

Carl glimpsed upward and advised, "Best do as they say for the time-being, keep playing that game of poker. At least until you reach San Francisco then make your move and run." He hacked another dark glob from deep inside. Bloody-goo slobbered across his chin and dripped onto his lap. He wiped his face and cleared his throat. "Kern my friend, I will miss you."

Kern swallowed, then turned to conceal his tears and trotted up the creaking steps. At the top board, he glimpsed downward and into the front hold. He wanted to tell Carl things kept secret and unload a life of despair. Carl was dying sure as can be, and did not need to hear a life of despair and heartaches. He pushed the hatch upward and vanished into a gray mist of overcast skies.

Seconds before the hatch slammed closed a gust of ocean fresh salt air rushed cool against Carl's face. He was grateful for a last fresh breath before shedding his mortal shell. There was unfinished business in life, people he wished to bid farewell, apologize for wrongs done, and a woman he had failed to tell how much he loved her.

It was time to go.

A peace swept over him, washing away regrets and concerns. As he greeted Death with open arms his legs, feet, hands and head involuntarily twitched.

The storm drowned Bristol's howling wail keeping it from penetrating upper decks. Outside the tempest raged-on, offering no moment of solitude in respect for a man passing to the afterlife.

A lifetime of experiences bound together inside of his leather journal now laid the hands of a cabin boy, Kern.

2

Kern stood aft, his hand clasped around the amulet hanging at chest level. Moments ago, crewmembers had tossed Carl's personal belongings overboard and returned to their chores. Saddened, he watched Carl's trunk and field office cases bob amid the Lady Beth's wake.

Taking on water, both field case and trunk tilted partly beneath the water. A minute later, it slipped beneath rolling waves and disappeared. His heart sank to depths of despair. Other than Carl's amulet, personal journal, gun and shoulder holster, and Bristol, all evidence the man had been onboard now rested at the ocean bottom.

He wished La Horn had waited until the weather broke to dispose of Carl's body. Three days ago during the storm and to avoid the stench of a decaying corpse, they had tossed Carl's corpse overboard. A day later, the storm altered course and headed south while they were bound for where east meets west.

"East meets west," Kern thought warmly of the phrase Carl had used when describing California. His thoughts fell to the many times Mister Ver Haven and himself had passed time onboard ship. Ver Haven insisted Kern discarded the pretense of mister, and call him by first name. As Carl wove tails of California, Kern imagined a land full of life and bursting with excitement.

Thrills of a new life where east meets west fell-away. Reflections flowed across boundless waves toward Australia and vague memories of his deceased parents. His father was a former sailor from a state called Maine in America, his British mother once part of an Australian Penal Colony.

Months after his father was murdered, his mother had succumbed to a high fever. Kern believed a broken heart had snatched her will to live. Since boarding the Lady Beth, cryptic memories of his father's murder teased him. He was uncertain what triggered earlier childhood memories. Was it his escape to his father's homeland of America, or something about La Horn and Caleb?

Kern's thoughts drifted to a nomadic Australian Aboriginal Clan known as the Namra. After his parents had died, the Clan had raised him as one of their own and taught him to survive among the wilds of Kakadu. It was a harsh land experiencing six seasonal weather cycles known as Gunemeleng, Gudjewg, Banggereng, Yegg, Wurrgeng and Gurrang. Only when the Fire Season Wurrgeng scorched the earth did they leave their region of Kakadu.

The Clan existed in what they perceived as Dreamtime. His years spent with the Clan were a time of fantasy. Emotions surged as he recalled events that forever separated him from the Clan. Months ago when the Fire Season Wurrgeng consumed dense vegetation, an armed white man hunting party had murdered Clan members for sport.

The Clan was compelled to seek refuge among the inferno of Wurrgeng. Walls of flames had separated him from the Clan. Perched on a high cliff above the flames, Kern had witnessed remaining his clan family parish at the hands of evil white hunters.

It was an oddly dressed white man who had saved Kern's life. Kern suspected the man was an American in the wrong place at the wrong time. By giving his life, the stranger had proven not all white men were evil.

As customary for Kern's Clan, he had buried him seated upright, making it easier to stand if the man decided to go for a walkabout. Traditionally, a deceased Clan member's spear was stuck in the ground at the head of the grave, so that if the dead rose his spear was there for him. The stranger had carried guns instead of a spear, so Kern had stuck the man's rifle in the ground.

For weeks afterward, Kern had wandered aimlessly across the wilderness. He had stumbled into the former British Penal Colony of Limmen Bight, wearing nothing more than a loincloth. It had not taken long to relearn the English language. In addition, he learned the ways of the streets quickly.

At the present, Kern was on the run for having killed a man. Self-defense made no difference. He had killed a lawman. Unjustly, a local magistrate had issued a warrant calling for Kern's arrest. Authorities had tacked on lampposts and walls throughout Limmen Bight, posters of his likeness with words *Dead or Alive for murder*.

The lawman was forcing street children to steal. Kern had refused to steal. Setting an example of what happened to those who defied him, the corrupt lawman had used a rifle butt to beat him.

While on the ground and dodging deathblows, Kern had snatched a knife from the lawman's boot-well and lunged upward, sticking the blade an inch below the sternum and angled into the lawman's heart.

Wide-eyed, the corrupt officer puffed a final shocked breath, before landing flat on his back with blood gurgling from a fresh stabbed wound. As Kern stood at the dead man's side, a puddle of bloody mud oozed at his feet and between his barefoot toes.

Kern no longer cringed at the memory of blood soaking feet and dripping along the knife blade. He kept the knife. It was not like stealing from the dead, which brought bad luck. The knife was already in his possession before the man had died, hence the bad luck rule did not apply. He rested his hand on the bone-handled knife sheathed across his stomach.

Free of foul weather, unclouded skies spanned horizon to horizon. Again, Kern's thoughts focused on the land where east meets west and better times ahead.

Over the wind an arrogant voice bellowed, "What are you waiting for? The sea never gives up her dead! Get over it, he's not coming back!"

Kern spun around, his eyes malice at the sight of Fat Sam. He had killed before and knew he was able to do it again. Fat Sam had taken part in murdering Carl. Here and now, he wanted to introduce his blade to Fat Sam's spongy gut. He had to wait for the right time and place too silence the fleshy waif.

Kern tethered on edge and barely managed to maintain a calm voice. "I'm but saying goodbye. Leave me be, you Fat Baland."

Fat Sam clinched both fists at his sides and glimpsed over his shoulder. Second-mate Caleb was within site, keeping Fat Sam from acting on a pressing desire to thrash Kern. He was unsure what Baland meant in English. However, the tone rang offensive and called for a rigid response. "Watch your mouth, boy! As long as you're standing there, yank-up the mop." As Fat Sam turned and swaggered away, his trousers slid partly down, exposing the upper crack of his horrendous ass.

Kern's shoulders churned, shaking an urge to kill the grotesque Imp and focused on his task. Dragging the mop was a weekly ritual, allowing him time alone to reflect on the past, present and contemplate a future. He steadied himself alongside the starboard railing, took hold of a rope and pulled a mop from over the side.

Kern untied the mop, rang it dry and inspected it. The ocean had thoroughly bleached it white. It was ready for usage the next morning when he was required to mop the decks.

Awestruck, Kern gazed across the vast ocean. He recalled a Dreaming Story told by his adoptive Clan father. Weowie the Water Spirit gave life to the thirsty and cleansed body and soul.

Kern realized his soul needed cleansing of hatred against Balands. The stranger who had sacrificed his life and later Carl had proven not all Baland were depraved mad men.

The amount of water Weowie used to separate the lands was remarkable. Perhaps, Weowie had separated lands to keep people of different skin color from fighting. Given what Kern had witnessed in Kakadu, it was a wise decision.

Kern realized he had done nothing to upset Weowie the Water Spirit, and felt safe for this journey to the land of Baland peoples. His own white skin confirmed he was a Baland on the outside. Although a Baland father had seeded his Baland mother's womb, inside he vowed always to remain Namra and part of the Clan. Countless times, his adoptive aboriginal father had told him, "The inside counted for more".

His Clan father was better at Dreaming Telling than Carl. Yet, Carl had interacted with him on a different level. Their brief talks had given him much to consider. It seemed as of late, he was always fleeing from something or someone. Waves of prejudice from Baland hunters and rolling walls of fire had driven him from Kakadu. Later, lying posters at Limmen Bight had exiled him from a land he loved.

Kern came aboard Lady Beth as a cabin boy, escaping the wrath of Australian Law. After he had befriended Carl, shipmates no longer treated him as part of the crew. Since Carl's death, bulkheads felt incarcerating and leaving no room to run should the need arise. Soon enough, he would run from these thieving and murdering fools.

In the distance, Kern spotted a pair of humpback whales spouting jets of water. In a Dreamtime World, the whales would carry him to where east meets west on their backs. He replaced imprisoned feelings with thoughts of California and gazed across a vast Pacific Ocean.

Sunset streaked colors of burnt orange, yellow, violet and deep purple accented the skyline. He would miss sunsets at sea, amiable rocking of waves and salt air cleansing his lungs. Returning to sea for any length of time was unfathomable. As the sun slipped from view an incredible shade of green flashed across the horizon.

Joyful at the sight, Kern stared heavenward and expanded his lungs to full capacity. Never before had he witnessed such beauty and contemplated the splendor of it all. He wondered, was it possible Carl's soul had requested the Sun Spirit Jindoo paint that special sunset as a gift for him?

Bright faced, Kern whispered, "Thanks Carl, and I'll watch after Bristol for ya. Make sure he gets to his new home at that big old White House ya told me about. Ya have my word on it…" He grinned and finished with a phrase Carl had taught him. "A man's word is his bond without it he's worth nothing."

As the painted skyline faded to dusk, Kern decided the green flash marked a beginning of his new life. Again, he stared at his white skin.

Without a doubt, he was Baland, a white-man and had to try to live as one. He was days away from a fresh start in California the land of opportunity. He planned to find handfuls of golden nuggets shimmering in mountain streams, simply waiting for him to scoop-up.

Kern drew an extended breath of salt air and assured himself of a grand life. After scooping gold from mountain streams, he planned to use his new riches and build a home near the ocean.

Years from now, he would tell stories of his Dreamtime at sea to his children and someday perhaps even grandchildren.

3

Enveloped by darkness, Kern crept backward from the cabin hatchway. He was grateful ocean sounds masked his footsteps. Minutes ago, he had planned to join shipmates for a tin of hot tea. He overheard a discussion whether to keep or dispose of him at sea before reaching port. It hinged on his friendship with Ver Haven and if Kern was trustworthy after reaching the Americas. Their debate was short lived. They decided to hold him for their return voyage to the Far East.

Had their decision gone the other way, Kern suspected it translated into another burial at sea. For now he was safe, however, his shipmates could easily change their minds and toss him overboard to feed the sharks. On past decisions, they flipped like a falling coin. It was best to consider this coin as spinning on edge with heads or tails teetering.

A sudden swish of air pulverized both of Kern's ears, followed by a dual whack on both sides of his head. Between expanding and decompressing air pressure, his eardrums popped. He covered his ears, reeled sideways and expelled a high-pitched wail akin to a tormented dingo.

As his equilibrium failed, dizziness spun him into a swaggering and agonizing dance. Through tear-blurred eyes, he snapped a foggy glimpse of Sam's fat bellied laughter. Unable to maintain his bearings, he was helpless to strike back.

Crewmembers piled from inside of the cabin, knocking each other aside as they cleared the hatchway. Caleb grabbed a hold of Kern and balanced him, then dished a baffled glare at Fat Sam and questioned, "What have ye done to the lad?"

"That wet rat had it coming," Fat Sam defended his actions, then pointed harshly and accused, "The whelp was sneaking a listen whiles't ya were conversing. I caught him in the act of spying and bobbed his ears right good." Proud of his actions, his tone lifted to a fault. "I dare say he won't be sneaking a listen on anyone again. There be none present who'd not done the same!"

Caleb's temper exploded. With a snarling growl, he leaped into Sam's bellied chuckle. Fat Sam stumbled backward and fell to the deck. He moved on top, straddled Fat Sam's stomach and proceeded beating him senseless. As fists pounded away, five crewmembers pulled Caleb from on top of Fat Sam.

Fat Sam's nose and lips washed the deck blood red. His own shrills of pain mixed with Kern's tormented wail, each shattering the peaceful sea.

Caleb shook himself free of crewmates He pointed at the fallen tin and splattered tea. "At my earlier invite, he was coming to join us for the evening!" Then he yelled at Sam, "You fat slobbering simpleton, he is part of this crew!" His attention diverted to Kern. He shoved everyone aside and ordered, "Let me have a look at him!"

Disorientated, Kern's legs and feet flung every direction. Not intending to hurt anyone, one of his bare feet hammered Caleb's ribcage. Nevertheless, Caleb held-fast and forced him to sit against a bulkhead.

A ghost train thundered through Kern's ears, deafening him to Bristol's ferocious barking from below deck. The ghost train chugged louder and louder as if on a collision course with his brain. Although his vocal cords strained, his own distraught howl failed to breach the roaring sound barrier.

Caleb's mouth opened and closed, but Kern was unable hear a word. Caleb pulled a frantic Kern into a crossed arm chest-lock and held him tight. Distraught, Kern thrashed to break free of the dreaded ghost train.

Caleb skirmished to his feet, lifted Kern, kicked at the hatch and clamored, "Someone get that damn hatch open!"

A blur of motion swung the hatch open, accelerating Kern's spinning confusion. Unsure of his fate, Kern fought harder. Caleb held tighter, stepped across the threshold and forced Kern onto a hammock.

Finally, Kern's thrashing and agonizing wail subsided, leaving a sweating fever accompanied by intense episodes of trembling. Throughout the night, Caleb kept Kern cooled using a damp rag. Kern's fevered rambling had kept everyone awake.

***

At daybreak, Caleb moved Kern below deck and into the front-hold near Bristol. For the next two days, Caleb listened to Kern's incoherent sleep-talk. The boy mutterings broke between a strange language and English.

Caleb assumed the strange language accounted for Kern's odd accent. Through interludes of English, Caleb pieced together a story. Kern had rambled about the Australian Outback and tribe called the Narma, and walls of fire, and a dead Magistrate. With each passing day, an air of familiarity with Kern grew stronger. He knew or had seen him somewhere in the past.

A day before the Lady Beth entered San Francisco Bay, Kern's fever broke and he regained his balance. However, he remained unable to hear. Too calm Kern, Caleb freed Bristol from the wire-mesh crate. Immediately, the dog leaped on the stack of burlap bags where Kern rested. Having Bristol to pet had a tranquilizing effect on Kern.

Caleb had sided with Kern and insisted, "Ease dropping was part of a natural behavior for any boy, and should not be mistaken as spying." Generally, among the crew, Kern's presence was accepted.

Since a good cabin boy was not easy to find, La Horn decided Kern's punishment was a denial of liberty in San Francisco, a harsh punishment for any sailor, and worse for a boy seeing the world for the first time. It would be a lesson the lad would not soon forget.

Caleb had hoped when on Liberty in San Francisco, that Kern would abandon the Lady Beth and strikeout for new life in a new land. That hope had faded.

4

As daybreak evaporated morning mist, Lieutenant Crisp trotted up a gangplank leading onto the Lady Beth. Wooden pine boards bobbed and creaked beneath footsteps of seven soldiers trailing behind him. At noon, he expected to begin a new assignment. Orders to search for a missing diplomat did not rest easy with him. He was available that morning and given the assignment.

In the prior night, an office clerk dressed in civilian attire, and spent time at pubs near the waterfront. He pretended to be looking for work and asked a few questions regarding the Lady Beth's command. Beyond La Horn and Forester, Crisp knew nothing of the crew.

Captain Jonathan La Horn was a Frenchman with a nasty scar across his forehead that arched downward across one eye. La Horn had a reputation of holding a grudge for years, and out-of-the-blue serving coldhearted revenge.

La Horn's second-mate, Caleb Forester was a New Zealander of British origin whose smirk left one questioning his sanity.

Crisp's morning duty was easy enough, search for a missing governmental representative named Carl Ver Haven. A witness had reported that Ver Haven had booked passage on a Tea Clipper christened Lady Beth. Their witness was a cattle trader going by the name of Ernie Smit.

Smit had boarded another ship that departed the Hawaiian Islands three days after the Lady Beth. Apparently, Ver Haven and Smit wagered who would reach the mainland first. The Lady Beth was a several days late arriving.

Smit assumed he had won the bet and visited a local army office on Mission Street, hoping to collect his winnings. Lady Beth, fastest of the two ships should have arrived first. A day passed since Lady Beth docked. Mister Ver Haven failed to check-in.

Candid, Crisp extended a fleeting courtesy handshake. "Good Morning, Captain La Horn. I am Lieutenant Crisp," he introduced himself and back-waved at his small contingent of men. He smiled and commenced, "We're looking for a representative of the United States Government returning from China, a Mister Carl Ver Haven. It is known he booked passage on your vessel."

La Horn sighed, "Aye, it is a fine morning for the living." Despondent, he gazed at the deck and shook his head. Without blinking, he stared straight at the baby-faced Lieutenant. "We had a passenger named Carl Ver Haven aboard. I must say he was a fine representation of your government. A chivalrous gent and although a paying passenger, he acted as a crewmember when the need arose."

Despondent, La Horn shook his head and furthered the lie, "Unfortunately, he was lost at sea during a terrible storm. Right before our eyes, a huge swell swept him off the deck." He motioned at his crew. "Near all present bore witness to the fact… Against gale force winds and huge swells, we turned and searched the sea for him but to no avail. The tempest delayed our arrival in San Francisco. If you'd like to read about it, the incident has been noted in the ship's log."

Crisp cocked an eyebrow. Smit had mentioned catching the tail end of a storm while sailing to San Francisco. La Horn's account for a delay was conceivable; however, the man's words rang untruthful. Crisp requested, "Of course we'd like his personal possessions, so his property can be sent to his family."

The request caught La Horn by surprise. He drew a tense breath and exhaled an excuse. "We buried his belongings at sea. It seemed only fitting we paused and gave words for a man who had given his life. Lacking a body to bid departure, we used his belongings, being a field office case and one large trunk."

Crisp refused to buy it and pressed, "Why bury his personal property at sea? That makes no sense whatsoever." Detecting trouble, his men fanned into a semicircle near the helm. "I'd like to hear a reasonable answer." He halted short of accusing La Horn of murder.

La Horn shrugged, "We were distraught at the time, and perhaps should've kept his goods. The deed is done and there is no undoing it." Lightly, he fluttered his fingers and covertly signaled Caleb.

Caleb's right hand met the handle of a Starr .36 Caliber Navy Revolver tucked behind his wide leather belt. His eyes scanned the crew, putting them on notice to prepare for a fight and set a running sail. Part of the crew fanned toward the mooring lines, while another portion inched toward the Lady Beth's jib sails.

Crisp held firm and not giving an inch for lies to gain ground, or for La Horn's crew to stage themselves for a fight and quick getaway. He commanded, "Everyone stay-put! We are going to have a look around."

La Horn's crew halted and eyed their captain for a gesture. Without looking back at the crew, La Horn raised a temporary halting hand.

Crisp ordered his men, "Inspect her from stern to bow."

Agitated, La Horn raised an index finger. He stepped forward and cautioned, "I'd strongly advise against trespassing. This is a private enterprising vessel and under French protection."

"Don't force a confrontation," Crisp warned, his hand drifted onto the butt of a Starr Revolver holstered at his belt. He loosened a flap over the gun holster and insinuated, "You'd yield to this search, unless of course you're hiding something or someone."

La Horn entrenched his position on the matter. "We fly the flag of France on this ship. Again, I insist that we are under French protection. By what laws do you violate our God given Sovereign Rights?"

Crisp snapped, "It's by our authority. You're docked at a United States Port of Entry and subject to inspection at our whim." He motioned outward at distant hillsides encompassing San Francisco Bay. "If you object to our search, the Lady Beth will not be returning to sea." He smirked and bluffed, "It'd be like shooting ducks in a pond, our cannon fire will sink her right here in the bay."

La Horn stiffened and demanded, "Who do you think you are? Some sort of Port Authority?"

Crisp smarted, "Port Authority? That does have a nice ring to it." For a second time, he waved at surrounding hills. "Our boys are growing tired of target practice and itching to use those new Dahlgren Smoothbore long range cannons on a real target."

Crisp altered his tone to nothing short of an accusation, however left La Horn a way out of a confrontation. "Unless you realize this was all a misunderstanding as to our laws."

La Horn gritted his teeth, glimpse at surrounding hillsides and tilted the brim of his cap upward. This was a country on the brink of civil war. It was fathomable California had placed long-range cannons amid her foothills to protect their shores. Losing the Lady Beth to prove a point was fool-hearted.

La Horn spread a grin and accommodated, "Yes of course Lieutenant, this was but a simple a misunderstanding. Go ahead, waste your time and that of your men, but you will find our holds are empty. Our cargo of tea, rice and gunpowder was unloaded last night."

Crisps split his men into pairs to proceed with the inspection.

As La Horn followed two soldiers headed for his private quarters, he cursed under his breath using French. Their cargo already delivered to a warehouse, Crisp would find nothing. Although the Atlantic Ocean was continent away, his stomach churned. This near the Atlantic had risks. Was it a bad omen the army had aboard his ship?

Watchful, Caleb remained near Lieutenant Crisp, noting how the man conducted himself. A young appearance was deceiving. Lieutenant Crisp was cultivated, raised on his wits, educated in the art of war, and likely had field experience. In short, Caleb thought Crisp was older than he appeared and no dunderhead.

Instinct drew Crisp toward the forward-hold. He scrutinized a heavy chain and padlocked securing the entryway. Crisp drew his pistol, pointed it at the lock then looked over his shoulder and inquired, "Need I fire a shot to open it?"

Caleb raised his hands, signifying no resistance and yielded, "Let's not get fool-hearty ruin a good lock." He stepped forward, slipped a key from his trouser pocket and unlocked it. After rattling the chain through the wooden door handle, he stood back and requested, "Please holster that sidearm. There's no need to be working us up any further by risking a misfire and causing bloodshed. We've nothing to hide here." Then, he opened the hatchway and stepped aside.

Crisp holstered his pistol, leaving the flap unfastened, then stepped past Caleb and into the darkened hold. Amid rays of sunlight that filtered inside from open the hatchway, he discovered a boy curled on top of burlap bags labeled rice. He guessed the boy to be twelve or thirteen years old. His gut twisted at his core. Something was not right here. This boy desperately needed help.

A dog inside of wooden wire crate emitted a low growl, warning Crisp to keep a distance from the boy. Slowly, the boy stirred and shielded his eyes from a pouring of sunlight from outside.

"It's just me," said Caleb to the dog as he entered the front-hold. Then he informed Crisp that, "Our cabin-boy, Kern. He's been taking care of our ship's mascot. Sadly, the lad took sick not long ago and has been resting. I'm sure he'll be rested, then up and about before long. Stone deaf, he cannot hear a word said to him but he manages to get-by."

Kern retreated, crawling backward away from Crisp, until a bulkhead preventing him from going any further. Unsure of the uniformed stranger, he eyed Caleb who had proven his only remaining friend aboard ship.

Peaceful, Crisp gestured his hands open. Although Caleb had mentioned the boy was deaf, Crisp spoke. "I mean you no harm, boy." At closer inspection, Crisp noted dried blood on the side of Kern's neck. Cautious not to frighten him, Crisp shuffled Kern's dishwater blond hair aside and noticed the blood had trickled from Kern's ears.

Crisp suspected physical abuse. Perhaps it was an attempt to ensure Kern's silence to a crime. Likely, a witness to whatever happened to Ver Haven. Caleb had refereed to an illness, presenting a good excuse to remove Kern from the ship.

Concerned, Crisp glimpsed over his shoulder at Caleb and stated, "He could be contagious. I am ordering the lad placed under quarantine. That is, until a doctor can have a look at him. Once he's given a clean bill of health, he'll be returned." Without waiting for an answer, he lifted Kern in his arms, stood and turned to leave.

Although this stranger wore a uniform that reminded Kern of the bad lawman at Limmen Bight, his heart told him to trust him. His hands stretched toward the dog crate, and he whispered a monotone dread of separation, "Bristol."

Crisp's eyes flashed wide at the mention of the name. He spun around and stared at the crate. His momentary shocked was masked by shadows inside the dark forward-hold of the ship. His expression had gone unnoticed by Caleb.

Without losing a beat, Crisp included, "I'm placing the dog under quarantine as well. If the boy did come down with something could be he caught it from the dog. " He nodded at soldiers who had joined him inside of the forward-hold and ordered, "Fetch that dog, crate and all."

As the soldiers neared the wire-mesh crate Bristol growled, barked and bore his fangs. The soldiers retreated and stared at Crisp, hoping he would change his mind.

Caleb cautioned, "Be careful, he's a nasty one and known to bite." Then he advised, "Captain La Horn wouldn't approve of taking his prize dog and our cabin-boy."

Crisp nodded. "Yes, you could be right. Perhaps, we should leave them here, and place the entire ship under quarantine as a precaution. Of course there would be an around the clock regiment posted at your gangplank. It may take a few days for a doctor to issue a clean bill of health. Doing-so, would infringe on your liberty ashore and making crewmembers cranky when returning to sea. Be that as it may, I am sure you understand our position, and we do what we must to protect our shores."

Defeated, Caleb raised his hands and granted, "By all means take both boy and dog. Don't let Captain La Horn see you until you're off-ship or he'll throw a fit."

Crisp noted Caleb's objection lacked enthusiasm. Whatever reason, Caleb's feelings for the lad lay beneath a transparent mask. He motioned and ordered his men, "Grab that crate."

As soldiers lifted the crate, Bristol barked and gnashed his teeth against the wire mesh. They watched their fingers carefully to avoiding gnashing teeth and grumbled.

A few minutes later, Crisp stood at the base of the pine planks and looked upward. He wanted to avoid a needless gunfight between the ship's crew and his soldiers.

Crisp decided, reading the ship log had to wait. A living witness was more important. Besides, it was certain La Horn had doctored his log entry concerning Ver Haven's death. Taking the boy and dog was likely a breaking point for La Horn.

La Horn stood at the top of the gangplank, his face tighter than dried leather. His eyes narrowed with a shout, "I am wanting them back in good shape, and no more than a day or two at most because I intend to set-sail soon."

Crisp issued a slick grin. "I'll have a messenger keep you updated on the boy's condition, daily. Again, I am sorry about forcing an inspection of your ship. Given this boy appears ill, and this dog may be a carrier of diseases, you are lucky rest of the crew wasn't infected as well."

La Horn mocked, "Heard tell your country is splitting at the seams. To what side do your men hail? When war breaks loose, will they stand at your side or as enemies against you?"

Crisp stated, "California is a long way from whatever comes between North and South." He turned and walked away. At the end of the pier, they encountered an extremely heavyset man with broken nose and bruised eyes. He felt Kern stiffen at the sight of the man.

"The abuser," Crisp muttered with an immediate dislike of the heavily obese man.

One of the soldiers succumbed to temptation and tossed a rude comment, "Those black eyes make you look like fat raccoon."

Another soldier added further insults, speaking more to Fat Sam than his fellow soldiers. "He must weigh a couple tons. Does the ship lisp to whichever side his on?"

Fat Sam grunted and strutted past them, pitching Kern a mischievous glare.

5

Hands clasped behind his back, Lt. Crisp paced back and forth across the wooden floor, waiting for a doctor to complete her exam. Given Kern's reaction to the heavyset man, he had a suspect for Kern's mistreatment. He hoped Kern had not suffered sexually indignity as well. He heard horror stories of men at sea for too long and rumors of what took place inside dark-holds onboard ships.

Crisp halted pacing and his eyes fell on the boy. Since uttering the name Bristol, Kern had not spoken. However, Kern permitted the pretty lady-doctor to examine his ears.

Crisp considered severe bruises on the heavyset man's face. Was it possible Kern had inflected damage to such a degree? It was unlikely. Another point of interest was La Horn's second-mate, Caleb Forester. Caleb had expressed only mild displeasure at Kern's removal from the ship. Caleb appeared torn betwixt loyalties.

For a second time, Crisp glanced at an amulet that had hung around Kern's neck. The doctor had coaxed it from around the boy's neck at the start of her examination. The imagery was familiar, yet he was unable place where he had seen it before.

Earlier, Doctor Hanna Steadson suggested the inscription on the amulet was ancient Latin, but she was unable to translate it. He wondered if the amulet had belonged to Ver Haven. Slick, he pocketed it and planned returning it to Kern after having it translated.

As Doctor Hanna Steadson continued her examination of Kern, Crisp reflected on events thus far. Early that morning, a cattle trader from Texas named Smit had reported Carl Ver Haven was a passenger on the Lady Beth at the Hawaiian Islands. An hour earlier, Crisp had re-question Smit at pub near the docks.

Carl Ver Haven had told Smit the dog was a gift from China's Emperor for President Lincoln. Smit had mentioned seeing Kern speaking with Ver Haven at the islands. Rushed to leave, Smit departed with a handshake and invited Crisp to high-stakes poker game.

Crisp suppressed a grin as he considered the dog's name. Evidently, Ver Haven had named the dog Bristol as a private joke. Bristol lay quietly inside the crate, having recently returned from fertilizing the backyard. Corporeal Shepherd had a way with animals, when leashed Bristol had behaved for the trip outside and back.

Currently, Shepherd stood behind a kitchen table where Kern sat, waiting for a signal from Doctor Steadson. Kern's blue eyes remained transfixed on the beautiful lady-doctor.

Shepherd raised a metal pot and wooden spoon, and prepared to bang the two against each other. Steadson issued a covert nod to Shepherd. Kern failed to flinch at a clattering of wooden spoon against hollow metal. Kern's love struck gaze remained concreted on the woman.

Crisp had noticed Hanna's elegance as well. He placed personal attraction aside. The mission took precedents over possible romantic involvement. He asked, "Well?"

"That confirms it," Steadson said, her concerned face drawn. "I'm afraid he is completely deaf. Judging by the blood clots, his injury was recent."

Crisp inquired, "Accidental?"

Hanna shook her head. "Doubtful, it was probably an assault from behind catching him by surprise. Last month, I treated a similar injury after a brothel-fight on Seventh Street. One man bashed another man's ears with both hands from behind." Again, she shook her head. "Liquor induced violence never ceases to amaze me. One would think those given to it when drunk would avoid the drink."

"One would think," agreed Crisp. "However, I'm no judge of human character to be making that sort of call." His eyes focused on Kern. "What about his hearing? Will it return?"

Hanna studied Kern for hints of sound recognition. There was none. She sighed. "At this point, I am not certain if his hearing will return. If it does, it will never again be at a hundred percent. If damage is severe enough, it will affect his speech. When speaking, he will sound as if slow witted. It'll be a rough life for him being treated as if ignorant."

Crisp nodded. "Ms. Steadson, you put a lot of ifs in there… But he will be able to speak?"

Hanna turned her eyes from Kern to Crisp. She preferred Doctor Steadson, but allowed it to pass without comment and advised, "After surgery and given time, allowing emotional trauma and shock of near deafness to wear-off, he'll likely remember how to articulate easier pronounced words. Right now, it is not what you think. Deafness of his sort isn't total silence. He is experiencing what sounds like thousands of crickets chirping. At some point, he will become accustomed to it and simply rule it out as background nose. Until then, it will make him irritable. At the moment, he seems to be handling it very well."

Crisp cocked an eyebrow. "Surgery… When and how soon?"

Steadson shrugged. "The quicker the better, I'd like to see the pressure inside of his ears relieved. I have flushed-clean what I could. We'll see if he's improving come morning. If so, maybe surgery is avoidable. If not, I know of a specialist at the new University Hospital who takes on charity cases. I will see him this evening at a staff meeting. I'd like him to look at Kern for a secondary opinion."

Crisp approved, "Sounds fine, I'll leave his medical care in your capable hands." Casual, he added, "If anyone asks, due to a fever Kern and the dog are under a strict quarantine as a precautionary measure."

Crisp nodded toward Shepherd. "Don't concern yourself - the lad will have around the clock protection. Corporeal Shepherd will stand guard in case trouble arises. Shortly, I'll have another guard sent and rotate shifts."

Steadson's nerves rattled at the mention of trouble. "You think whomever did this will come looking for him?"

Crisp waved his hands as if not to worry. "Don't be alarmed. Simply put, Shepherd is not a man to be toyed-with.

Back to the subject at hand, no one and I mean no one except our people are allowed near the boy. Is that understood?"

"I understand," Steadson acknowledged, unsure about having danger left at her doorstep. "Realize, I've other commitments to keep, and won't be here a good part of each day. Given there are only a few woman entering the medical field, the new Medical University takes much of my time. There is a stigma against women doing anything of value with their lives. We are encouraging more women to take that bold step into medicine."

Crisp was unsure how to respond. He had never paid attention as to how many lady-doctors he had met before today. Come to think of it. Steadson was the first he had encountered. If what she had stated was true, she had a hard trail ahead of her. Changing the way people thought about women and their place in the world was not easy. With a pending war in the East, perhaps that stigma would fade. Both sides needed doctors, male and female alike.

Steadson had made it clear she was not babysitting Kern. Crisp instructed Shepherd, "Corporeal, make certain the boy feels wanted by us. Loved as if a son, as if we're all one big happy family and he's now a part of it."

Shepherd snapped a salute. "Sir, yes sir."

Crisp drew a troubled breath and halted short of rolling his eyes. Something in that salute did not feel right. Other than Shepherd was a new man under his command, he was unable to put a finger on it.

Crisp returned the salute. Then he left for headquarters and a meeting with the dog's namesake, Captain Bristol of the United States Army.

* * *

Twenty minutes later, Crisp had walked several blocks and entered the Mission Street Office to file a verbal report. He cupped his hands at waist level and listened.

Captain Bristol stood five feet, seven inches tall. A firm demeanor overcame his height and demanded respect. Agitated, his neck veins appeared on the verge of exploding.

First, Crisp should not have commanded a search for Carl Ver Haven. A lower ranking officer had mistakenly written the order for Crisp. Second, the dog's name struck him as a personal insult.

Crisp was doing his best to rectify the situation. "Sir, I was unaware of your friendship with Mister Ver Haven. I know it seems far-fetched... Perhaps, Ver Haven named the dog after you was a gesture of good intent."

Captain Bristol nodded, "Perhaps… Ver Haven and I go back two decades. He was a good friend and his untimely-death doesn't set-easy with me. He was as surefooted as a soldier can be…"

Unconvinced, Captain Bristol shook his head. "That he fell overboard, I am simply unwilling to accept and find it highly unlikely. Carl had seen stormy seas before. If seas were that rough, he had tied-down to something. He would have put duty ahead of all else and left keeping the ship afloat to the crew. Something reeks and it sure ain't rat droppings on that ship. Sergeant Van Haven's mission was far too important to risk his life."

Crisp became confused and inquired, "Sergeant? I was under the impression he was a representative of our government as show of goodwill toward China. I didn't realize he was a sergeant in the army."

Captain Bristol elaborated, "He was former army." Then he stepped to a back window and looked skyward above an alley. "Sergeant Ver Haven was personally recruited by Senator Douglas and commissioned for a trip to China. Ver Haven spoke Cantonese fluently, making him a practical choice. Where or when he learned the language was a mystery, he never talked about it. He kept his childhood quiet and avoided the subject."

Captain Bristol turned from the window, walked to his desk chair and sat. As he leaned back, the chair squeaked. Reflecting, he clasped both hands behind his head. Fond memories poured forth of a lasting friendship, speaking of his departed friend by first name. "I recall at a social gathering back East, Carl had voiced his views on England and France's Opium Trade in China to Colonel Baker and David Broderick. At the time our then as of yet to be elected President Lincoln was within ear shot and heard everything."

Bristol chucked, holding intact his dignity. "Ver Haven was a Sergeant at the time. Colonel Baker learned of Carl's higher education and jolly on the spot promoted him to Lieutenant. I never got use to calling him Lieutenant."

Bristol smiled. "In humor of course, Carl vowed to get-even with me for not recognizing his new rank. Not long after, he shed his uniform and became a diplomat. After shedding his uniform, Carl was more at peace with himself. Something gave him a higher sense of purpose, but I was never clear as to what."

Captain Bristol exhaled disheartenment, not so much for the dog's name but Carl's departure from the living. "By naming that dog after me, I reckon he got the last laugh."

Bristol leaned forward, clasped his hands on top of the desk and commented, "He must've learned or discovered something onboard and was caught doing it. I would sure like to get my hands on his personal journal. Sure as fog rolls off the Pacific, he kept a written record of what happened onboard that ship."

"Buried at sea with his body I suspect," injected Crisp, grateful Captain Bristol's temperament had mellowed.

Bristol disagreed, "No, if Ver Haven knew his life was in danger, he'd have found a way to hide it. Likely, telling someone where it was case of his demise, someone he trusted."

Crisp suggested, "Possibly, the boy Kern knows where it was hidden. He has relationship with the dog, and appears he befriended Mister Ver Haven."

Bristol looked up from the desk. "Given mistreatment that boy suffered, that theory makes sense. La Horn may have suspected Kern knew something. I believe Carl's journal is hidden aboard the Lady Beth. Keep working on that boy. Get him to tell you where it is. Then have one of your men get onboard and retrieve it. Keep me posted, you're dismissed."

Crisp issued a salute, turned to leave and hesitated. "Sir, about the dog, he is a new breed from Australia. Smit claimed to have seen the breed before, a Queensland Heeler bred for herding cattle. A cross between an Australian wild dog known as a dingo, a Smithfield, and a Highland Collie, the latter two being herding dogs from England."

Crisp commented, "Smit distrusted the dingo part of the breed and thought it too wild for taming. A very protective breed, he mentioned seeing a man's leg nearly tore-off by one of these dogs. Apparently not meaning to, a stranger got too close to the dog's owner. I hate to put the dog putdown. We need Kern's cooperation with this investigation, I'm afraid it'd upset him."

Captain Bristol nodded. "If the dog does prove gentle, he should be given to the President. As you know, Lincoln's children are fond of pets. I would hate to be the one to tell President Lincoln we put-down a gift from China's Emperor because it was vicious. If you do putdown that dog, I am sending you to Washington to personally inform the President." He raised a finger. "One last thought; I want that dog renamed."

Crisp explained, "I'd ask the boy to rename the dog, however as you know he isn't speaking at the moment. As I recall, Kern had uttered the name Bristol with such affection, I doubted he would rename the dog.

Crisp pondered for a moment and inquired, "Sir, I have another question regarding Mister Ver Haven. Did you happen to notice him wearing a piece of neckwear?" He held up his right hand and formed a circle using a thumb and finger. "About this round with a silver chain."

Captain Bristol thought briefly and replied, "I seem to recall he was partial to a certain piece of jewelry. I would have to see it again to recognize it... Why?"

Crisp explained, "Kern had a piece of neckwear that seems a tad pricey for a lad of his age to own. I am guessing he may have gotten it from Ver Haven." Then, he slipped the amulet from his coat pocket and passed it to Captain Bristol.

Bristol examined it and commented, "Looks familiar but can't say for sure. Probably means a lot to the boy, if he gave it to him - let him keep it. Although Ver Haven never had children, he was the fatherly type. Willing to bet he was educating him."

Bristol returned the amulet and said, "One more thing, don't allow your men to start jesting about that dog's name. Last thing we need with a pending war back east is a loss of respect for the chain of command." He tossed an offhanded salute, ending their meeting, "Dismissed."

"Of course," Crisp said, returned the salute and left.

* * *

At the corner of Seventh and Mission, Crisp paused on the boardwalk and waited for a carriage to pass. Subconsciously, he straightened his coat. It was time to get out of uniform.

Captain Bristol had suggested a fair priced tailor on Broadway Street. He had another meeting with Doctor Steadson planned for later in the day, and a freshly tailored suit would leave an impression. He wondered how his men would cater to wearing something other than a uniform.

A week earlier, Crisp had rented a business building near the waterfront. Spearheading their undercover operation near the piers was convenient and placed them near a port of entry for the country. That he publicly conducted a military operation that morning wearing a uniform and had not set well with Captain Bristol.

Crisp found the entire affair of working undercover unnerving. The likelihood of a murdered government representative made matters worse, causing him to cringe. In the East, insurmountable issues divided the country. Even those directly under his command were taking sides. Disarming verbal confrontations between his men was increasingly difficult.

Topping it off, yesterday's paper confirmed an army intelligent report. A wealthy cattleman named, Clifford

Akerland had declared a political bid to become the next governor on a platform that California should succeed from the Union.

If Akerland gained support, it would disjoint the nation into regions, North, South and West. Times were complex.

Crisp longed for simpler days when he fought to free Native Indians from local slavery. He grumbled, "Damn, why had Colonel Montgomery transferred me from Fort Tejon to San Francisco?"

As Crisp stepped off the boardwalk, a mangy mud-soaked dog darted across the street and dodged a horse drawn cart. His thoughts latched on Kern and the dog named Bristol.

6

Awe struck, Kern peered outside a second story window of Doctor Hanna Steadson's combination office and home. His thoughts drifted across the city. It was amazing. This city was far larger than he had imagined. Like giant rock formations but made of wood, buildings reached skyward.

Below, horse drawn carriages rolled on top of iron rails. At both sides of the street, people walked hurriedly on wooden planked sidewalks. They appeared intent on reaching destinations and lost in their personal dreamtime worlds. It was remarkable they did not bump into one another.

Kern wished he were able to hear the bustle of the city. Never ending sound of a thousand crickets chirping their wings was nerve-racking. Deaf for sure, and he planned play mute to match.

Although wearing uniforms, the strangers who had taken him from the Lady Beth acted differently than lawmen at Limmen Bright Australia. Maybe, these Balands wearing uniforms were good people. It was too early to pass judgment, but he decided to remain on guard.

Earlier, he had shrugged at their attempts to communicate through written words. While men dressed like constables had rescued him from La Horn, he had learned at Limmen Bight that lawmen were untrustworthy. His clan never approved of stealing. Stealing was plain and simply wrong. How long until these lawmen tried forcing him to steal?

Stealing and death was in the past. He had made it to where east meets west. Thoughts of untold-riches raised a smile. After keeping a promise to Mister Ver Haven, he planned to find a mountain stream laden with gold. Then he could pay the lady-doctor to fix his ears.

He looked to the soft bed and grinned. Bristol lay resting his head on feather pillow. He had caught glimpses of similar beds at the colony in Australia. He had a distant memory that his birth parents had a bed resembling this one. Bristol was no fool and enjoying comfort while it lasted.

Kern was tempted to join Bristol on the bed. First, there was a promise to a dying friend. Inside the first page of the journal, Carl had jotted down an address and told him, "Most anyone on the street should be able to point you in the right direction."

Free of Captain La Horn, Kern dreaded returning to the Lady Beth for the journal. Part of him wanted to ask those watching him for help, yet he feared authority. Did these constables know he had killed a lawman? If so, how long until they chained and placed him on a ship bound for Australia?

Kern rested a hand on the knife handle sheathed at his side. No, if they suspected he had killed a constable, they would have taken his weapon. Perhaps, distance traveled had freed him of past burdens. He realized time was running out. Soon, La Horn would secure a cargo and return to the Far East.

Carl's journal had to be gotten and soon.

He studied a ledge outside the window. With a guard posted outside his door, the window was his only option. The ledge offered enough foot-space to tight-walk his way to the corner of the building. From there, he could shimmy down to the street.

He did not want to leave Bristol behind, but there was no choice. With luck, he would get the journal and deliver it before sunrise. He would tell whomever he gave it, what happened to Mister Ver Haven and where to find Bristol.

He needed to wait for nightfall and cover of darkness. With time to waste, he laid next to Bristol. The mattress soft against melded around his back and his head sunk into the large feather pillow. Bristol rested his chin across Kern's chest, and exhaled a contented moan.

Kern stroked Bristol's head and whispered, "I'm sure they've got plenty of beds at big old White House that Carl told us about. You just wait and see..."

* * *

Nightfall brought with it a thick wet mist clinging to everything. Within seconds of slipping outside of the window

Kern's hair was soaked, his clothing moistened and pasted against his skin.

The ledge was as slick as an algae covered bolder in a stream. His bare feet allowed enough traction to keep from falling. Three rooms westward, he peered into another window and saw the lady-doctor resting on her bed. With her hands propped beneath her head, she was fast asleep.

Steadfast, Kern grabbed onto a wooden drain-gutter and slipped one leg around the corner of the building. He straddled the corner, one foot on the eastside and the other on the west.

Abrupt, he lost his balance and slipped backward. Frantic, he latched tighter onto the wooden drain-gutter. As his weight pulled the gutter away from the building nails jerked free of wooden siding. Like a weighted tree branch, the gutter tilted downward foot by foot.

His legs buckled as his feet met the ground. He released the drain-gutter, fell onto his back in the muddy street and gazed wide-eyed at the gutter. The gutter sprang upward and bounced several times before bobbing outward at sixty-five degree angle. Unable to hear, he was unsure if his earlier falling yell was silent or aloud.

Unhurt, he scrambled to his feet and glimpsed-up over his shoulder at the windows. Things were not going as hoped. A constable who guarded the bedroom door was peering outside of a window.

"Sure enough, they'd be coming after him," he thought. He focused on the Lady Beth and Carl's journal. As he darted away, his feet sucked in and out of ankle deep mud. Within seconds, he melded into the night mist.

7

Private Muser had lost a key-witness to a possible murder of a government diplomat. There was no denying failure. He tensed and explained, "Sir, Corporal Shepherd lit-out right after him. Couldn't have been but a few minutes behind that youngin. I'm sure he's caught the boy and put an end to any escape plans." As his eyes shifted to his feet, his shoulders slumped.

Crisp noted Private Muser's anxiety. He kept his tone absent of harshness. "Stand at ease." Then he raised an index finger and clarified, "Remember, he's not a prisoner, we're protecting a possible witness to a murder."

Crisp stepped to the window, peered at the ledge and muttered, "Damn, that ledge isn't large enough for a cat to prowl on, let alone a boy. He must've worked in circus and walked a tight-rope."

Muser seized the near impossible feat as an excuse. "Yep, I was as amazed as ya are. Had not I heard him yell, I wouldn't have known."

Astound, Crisp gazed at the wooden gutter sticking outward at thirty-five degree angle. He shook his head. "Well one thing for sure, he must have as many lives as cat. If so, he just used one of those lives tonight."

Muser shrugged. "I would know about cats, sir. Allergic… Cats make my skin crawl, can't stop sneezing around em, either."

Crisp glimpsed over his shoulder and advised, "It was meant as a joke in the face of disaster." Suddenly, the hour struck him. It was after midnight. Firm, he turned from the window and inquired, "Mister Muser, why are you out of uniform?"

Puzzled, Muser looked himself from head to toe. "Given that it's now after midnight, I've been wearing the same uniform since early yesterday morning. I'm sorry, sir. But I haven't had a chance to get on a fresh one."

Crisp grouched, "It's after midnight and that's why I asked. You know full well, no more uniforms… Was Mr. Shepherd wearing a uniform when he lit-out after Kern?"

Muser explained, "No sir. He was wearing black pants, a black knit shirt with a dark blue watch cap. Once he rounded the corner and from under the gas lamps, he blended into the night mist. It was eerie as hell. He was like ghost, there one minute and gone the next. Creepy if'n ya was to ask me."

Pleased, Crisp remarked "Good." Apparently, Shepherd has a decent head on his shoulders. Shepherd was not Crisp's personal pick of men. Not that it mattered. During the past three days, Shepherd had twice proved his worth as a soldier.

Crisp gazed at Bristol who lay inside of his crate. Dog and man's eyes meet. Bristol appeared concerned for his young human friend. He assumed that, Kern planned to return for the dog. Was Kern attempting to retrieve Carl Ver Haven's journal from the Lady Beth? It made perfect sense. In the near future, the Lady Beth was leaving port. Kern had likely realized time was short.

Crisp ordered, "Muser, I want you out of uniform pronto and into civilian attire. Dress as a dockworker out for a night on the town. Grab an empty bottle of rye and trek down to the docks. Find a spot near the Lady Beth and pretend you're passed out drunk. Keep an eye out for trouble. I am betting Kern headed back to the Lady Beth for something."

Muser slapped a salute. "Sir, yes sir."

Crisp's eyes pulled tight. He issued a stiff warning, "Salute me again, and I'll break your arm. Is that understood Mister Muser?"

Muser halted mid salute of acknowledging the order. He stammered for a moment before catching his wording. "It will take some getting use too, sir." He took a beat between words and asked, "Is it all right to use, sir?"

Crisp grinned. "Of course, you're the son of a wealthy family and taught respect from birth. As a child privately schooled, well manners are expected. Don't say sir as if in the army. Use a different tone with it."

Muser's brow puzzled. "My pa's a hog farmer in Ohio, with nine youngins and me being smack in the middle of ma's litter. Money wasn't even dreamed of at home. Farmed our own food and Mason canned crops in the Fall Season, so we'd have plenty of food during winter months. Hell, I spent most of my life farming, slopping hogs, axing firewood, slaughtering hogs and smoking meat in the winter. Ma insisted we learn to read and write. A local preacher's wife taught us readin and writin."

"Another thing," said Crisp. "Drop that regional accent you're carrying from the backwoods. It is poor grammar and I am not about to have you getting us killed. Think before you speak. Choose your words carefully and if you can't, keep your mouth shut."

"Yes em' sir. Iii... I mean yes, sir.

Crisp motioned at the doorway and ordered, "Now get out of that uniform, pronto."

Muser scrambled out the doorway, nearly tripping over his own feet.

Crisp knelt in front of Bristol's crate and said, "Well boy, looks like it is you and me."

Bristol exhaled a low-cut growl.

Crisp smirked, "I'll have no disrespecting the chain of command." Again, Bristol growled. Since Carl's death, Kern was acting as alpha dog, leader of their two-person pack being the boy and dog.

Crisp firmed his voice and thumbed his chest. "Me, I'm the alpha dog around here, you understand that?"

Bristol eased his growl and crawled backward against the rear of the crate.

Crisp grinned, "Much better." He stood and returned to the window. A heavy mist had settled into the Bay Area, reminding him of a childhood trip with his father to London England. Again, he missed Fort Tejon.

In the distance, he heard a woman's shriek cut short as if her life had bluntly ended. He shuttered and commented, "I'd have to say someone is meeting their Maker tonight."

Across the bay, originating on a rocky-point a lighthouse beam filtered through dense mist. A foghorn resonated over the city, adding a forbidding chill to the night.

Crisp recalled Shepherd recently breaking up fight at local brothel and cringed.

Shepherd had moved at incredible speed. A blur of motion, he had laid five strong men to the floor leaving each man maimed for life. Arms and legs broken at the joints, and a nose smashed flat against a cheek.

Crisp stared at Bristol's crate. "If your friend has returned to the Lady Beth, I pity anyone crossing Shepherd's path."

8

Crewmember Madison wandered topside for a breath of night air. Last evening, while drunk he had lost his earnings at a poker table to a slick card shuffling Texan. An hour earlier, a hoard of crewmates returned drunk, obnoxiously loud and shortly thereafter had passed-out. A stench of rye from clothing and breath seeped across their sleeping quarters.

Rudely awakened by their nonsense and foul smell, he was not in the mood to fall asleep again. Awake, broke, bored and nursing a hangover, he was ready to put back out to sea. With authorities watching their every move, La Horn was having difficulty contracting a return cargo. Whatever type of cargo for their return voyage, it had to be legal. It could be days, if not weeks until returning to sea.

Madison exchanged a casual conversation with a fellow crewmember walking patrol along the deck. After commenting on the thick fog, he strolled aft to find a quiet place free of an alcoholic stench.

Madison spotted movement near a starboard side lifeboat. He squinted, trying to see through the foggy mist. The hazy outline of person was visible. Sure enough," he thought, "someone was rummaging beneath the canopy of a lifeboat." He grunted a guess, "That spying brat Kern searching for God only knows what."

As Madison drew a knife sheathed at his belt, a killing smirk lit his face. He darted across the deck, locked an arm around Kern's chest and grabbed his forehead. He tilted Kern's head back for a killing slice and stated, "Never figured you for a turncoat. Guess we were wrong. To think not long ago, I voted not to toss your sorry arse overboard."

Shadows came to life, forming the figure of a man leaping through the fog. Spooked Madison released Kern, stepped backward and gasped, "Holy mother of God!"

An airborne shadow-man wrapped his legs around Madison's back. He latched his hands on Madison's chin and head. Using a sharp twist, he snapped Madison's neck.

Shadow-man shoulder rolled from on top of Madison's twitching body, then stood with Madison's knife in hand as if expecting another fight. Madison laid dead, his head looking backward and against the deck.

Stunned, Kern stood frozen. Things were happening fast. It was difficult to focus. Another crewmember who was standing watch at the gangplank slipped behind Kern and seized him.

As if by magic, a knife was suddenly sticking the crewman's throat. Severed vocal cords silenced his death cries. Grasping the knife handle, he staggered backwards and dragged Kern with him to deck.

Blood spurted onto Kern, soaking his hair, face and shoulders. He had only one thought, escape. He yanked the knife from the man's throat. Then he scampered to his feet and slid into the lifeboat. As he sawed through the first rope, he glimpsed across the deck for shadow-man. Amid a thickening mist, shadow-man was nearly invisible.

When the first rope broke free, the lifeboat angled downward and slammed against the haul, causing Kern to tumble over bench seats and toward dark waters below. At the last seat, he swung around and managed a handhold. While he heard no sounds, he assumed the banging of a lifeboat against the haul had awakened the crew.

Hand-over-hand and feet sliding across fog-dampened wood, Kern grabbed board-seats and laddered up the dangling lifeboat. After reaching the bow, he saw crewmembers roused from drunken slumbers tripping over one another in an effort to clear a hatchway. He caught a glimpse of shadow-man taking a bullet, then diving for cover behind a stack of kegs.

When falling, Kern had lost the bloody knife pulled from the man's throat. Quick, he slipped his own knife from its sheath and cut the rope. With a jerk, the rope snapped free of the Lady Beth. As the lifeboat plunged toward water, he grabbed a hold of a seat and braced for impact.

The boat collided with the surface of the water, sending splashes upward and waves outward. Immediately, he gathered himself from the shock impact and grabbed both ores. Anxious, he stared upward at the Lady Beth.

Shadow-man was back on his feet and attempting to flee. Another bullet jolted him over the starboard railing. Much like shadow-man had appeared from nowhere, he vanished into murky waters.

Crewmembers focused their attention on Kern. Bullets zipped water at both sides of the lifeboat, with one bullet coming dangerously close. Kern braced his feet against an opposite seat. Using his arms, legs and back, he strained every muscle and repeatedly pulled both ores through the water.

As distance grew further and further, bullets fell short. Within seconds, the Lady Beth intermingled with the fog and appeared as if a ghost ship moored to the docks. Taking a few seconds, he paused and caught his breath.

Although unable to hear their voices echoing across the watery night, Kern was certain they were swearing a vendetta against him. Again, he drew both ores deep into the water and pulled hard. Then, he cut the mist with both ores and repeated the process.

Kern considered shadow-man's identity. Who was he? Where had he come from? Was Carl's ghost helping him to retrieve the journal? Maybe his adoptive Namra father's spirit came to protect him? Possibly, his original Baland father's spirit had come to guide him, and found his son in danger.

Kern's adoptive Aborigine Namra father had said, "Spirits often return to protect the innocent." His Namra father explained the spirit of Kern's Baland father had requested him to act as a new father. That was seven years ago, and right after his mother had died. Years ago, tales of friendly spirits had dried his young tears.

A year had past, since Kern completed the clan's ritual for manhood. Considered a young man, he needed to act accordingly. His Aboriginal father would have expected nothing less of him. As he grew older and further from innocence he wondered if spirits of dead friends and family would continue to aid him during troubled times

The bay's mist enveloped Kern beneath a protective blanket, concealing him from demons hunting him. As the Lady Beth faded from view, tension eased and the sound of crickets returned. Without a doubt, he would survive the night and next day as well.

Shadow-man's appearance on Lady Beth confirmed spirits were real. He had many spirits looking after him in the form of his Aboriginal Clan, plus Baland father and Carl looking after him.

* * *

Daybreak failed to shed fortune on Kern's fresh start in the land where east meets west. The night prior, he rowed ashore at desolate stone beach and abandoned his lifeboat. With Carl's leather satchel strapped over one shoulder, he had hiked through brush-thickened foothills. Making travel difficult, thorns and thickets had sliced cuts across his entire body.

By midmorning on the streets of San Francisco, Kern was lost. Fortune took a better turn, when he showed the address inside of Carl's journal to a nicely dressed lady. She had smiled and pointed him a general direction of the address.

He returned her smile and thanked her, aloud. He noticed something about his voice had made her uneasy. Concerned, her brow had drawn tight. Although her mouth opened and closed, he failed to hear a word.

Kern grinned, waved and walked the direction she had pointed. He decided against trying to speak again. Had a loss of hearing had effected his speech or did the wrong words come out? What if he had spoken using a Namra dialect and not known he had done it?

An hour later, Kern stood at the address Carl had written at the front page of his journal. The building reminded him of a constable's office in Limmen Bright. A sign above the door read, Army. Inside men were dressed similar those who had rescued him. Thus far, these uniformed men had proven trustworthy. Before going inside, he wanted to ensure these men were honorable.

Casual as not to draw attention, Kern walked into the alleyway. Keeping his back against a wall, he peaked into a rear window and gasped. Inside, La Horn was yelling and waving a small poster above his head. Harsh, La Horn slammed the poster on an officer's desk. Then, La Horn pointed at Bristol's crate located at a corner of the room.

Kern took satisfaction when the officer refused to give-up Bristol. Two lessor-ranking constables at either side of an interior door eyed La Horn, waiting for their chief to give an order to strike.

Again, a fiery red-faced La Horn jarred his index finger outward at the officer and yelled. The men at the door stepped closer to La Horn, ready to act should La Horn raise his anger another notch. Their lead constable motioned his men to show La Horn the door.

As La Horn was ushered to the door, he continued yelling. Kern ignored the torturous sound of crickets inside his head and imaged La Horn's threats.

Alone in the room, the lead constable sat at his desk and stared at the drawing on the poster.

Kern swallowed a lump in his throat. Sure as could be… There was no denying it. The sketch was of him wanted Dead or Alive for murder in Limmen Bright Australia.

The constable rolled the poster, tied it with a thin rope for easier carrying, then walked to a closet and changed from a uniform and into a business suit.

Sly devil, Kern thought, a dingo in sheep's clothing. He clutched the pouch containing Carl's journal and gun. Keeping that promise of delivering Carl's journal was nearly impossible. If these constables were Carl's friends, maybe in the land where east meets west constables were honorable. Only time would tell.

Kern wanted to be certain the right people were getting the journal. He noticed, the constable slip the rolled poster into inner pocket of his suite coat.

Kern slipped into the shadow of neighboring buildings. Then, he eased along back alleyways for several blocks. He hefted the strap to Carl's bag, securing it along his shoulder and stepped onto a main street. That poster La Horn gave to the constable had tainted delivery of the journal.

Afraid, Kern wondered how long until copies of the poster were tacked to walls and lampposts throughout the city. He needed time to think.

Moving at a quick pace, he trekked away from the hustle and bustle of a large city.

9

Bristol had already learned, Shepherd had taken a bullet in his left shoulder and another had creased the side of his head. The only good news regarding last night, Kern had escaped from La Horn, leaving them a fighting chance of finding him and Ver Haven's journal.

Crisp explained, "Fog was so thick you couldn't be outside without getting soaked, much-less see any great distance. Muser was approaching the berths as Kern escaped using a lifeboat. He trekked southward along the docks, hoping to catch another glimpse of the lifeboat. Luckily, he encountered Shepherd crawling ashore ten piers down from where the Lady Beth was docked."

Crisp drew and exhaled a steady breath, gathering his thoughts. Explaining Kern's escape was easier than the fact two of La Horn's men lay dead. He cocked an eye at Shepherd and shook his head.

Shepherd sat on an operating table while Doctor Steadson dressed his wounds, and jittered as she wrapped a cloth around his chest.

Steadson warned Shepherd, "Sit still or it'll hurt worse."

Shepherd stopped shuffling, gritted his teeth, squeezed the table edge and looked at Crisp and Bristol.

Bristol stared at Shepherd. "Crisp, you handpicked this man. I know nothing about him or where he came from. Montgomery was under the impression you had vouched for him as a fine upstanding solider."

Then Bristol planted both hands on his hips and exclaimed, "Fine and upstanding my arse! We are damn lucky he got away without exposing the entire operation! Who gave him orders killing those men was okay? I sure as hell did not! Do you have anything else to add?"

Crisp cringed, his neck muscles pulled taut.

Captain Bristol's rage lifted with an index finger. "No, I didn't think so. I sure as hell don't recall asking for this mess laid at my desk!"

Shepherd inserted, "Sir."

Captain Bristol snapped his head toward Shepherd and ordered, "Soldier, you are to speak only when spoken too. I've a good mind to remove you from this assignment!"

After a moment of consideration, Bristol asked "Are you an actual solider? You act more like a thief, wearing black and sneaking around in the night fog. That alone causes me to wonder. You lack any type of military respect as sworn by an oath..."

Shepherd shrugged. It was clear Bristol headed down a dark path. He glimpsed at Steadson and changed the subject, "Thanks for seeing to my injuries."

Bristol turned a blank stare at Crisp and commented, "Aside from being polite to the ladies, Mister Shepherd has at least one saving quality. He managed to help that boy escape from La Horn's motley crew. But he is clearly not military, at least none I've had under my command before… I have no desire to know what darkened hole you pulled him from. What the hell kind of Post do you think I'm running here?"

Without losing a beat, Bristol jabbed a finger Shepherd's direction and said, "If he's not regular army already, I want this man sworn-in before sunset! If he claims to have been sworn-in before, make him do it again until he gets it right! Is that understood?"

"Yes sir," replied Crisp.

Bristol's tone lowered, nevertheless, his mind-set remained impenetrable. "Doctor Steadson, you've just been drafted into this man's army as well. I know drafting a woman is unheard of. However, you are in this over your head and there is no pulling back. Your new office will be at the A.R&B building near the piers." Then, he grunted "With soldiers like Shepherd, I'm sure your services will be needed damn near around the clock. Crisp will fill you in on the details."

Still on edge, Captain Bristol gazed at Crisp. "Don't forget that campaign fund raiser coming up in a couple of days at the Grand Hotel for Ackerland. And-by-the-way to make life interesting, Ackerland's stepson recently returned from India.

Also, we need a look at Ackerland's finical records at Shoreline Bank located on Main Street. Think your boys can manage it without killing anyone?"

Crisp assured, "We'll do our best, sir."

Captain Bristol eased back. "Lt. Crisp, your best thus far has not been near good enough. You'll have to do better." Stern, he turned and left, closing the door solidly behind him that it rattled interior walls.

Crisp stared at Shepherd, and ignored Steadson's presence. Since Bristol had drafted her into the group, she may as well hear it. His brow tightened. "Shepherd, did you really have to kill those men?"

Shepherd expressed little regret, his tone flat and matter of fact. "The first one had a knife at Kern's throat. It was him or the boy... As far as the second, he grabbed a hold of the boy and it didn't look good. For simple surety, I figured he meant the boy harm. Besides, sir..."

Crisp sliced an open hand across the air, cutting him off. "You seem to enjoy killing far too much to suit me. Not to forget, Captain Bristol appears a tad confuse who recommended you... This entire time I had was under the impression it was Montgomery. Apparently, I was incorrect on that assumption. I'd like to know who you really are, where you come from, and who sent you, and what you're doing here? And in that order..."

Respectful, Shepherd dropped his pretense. "Not be disrespectful... Do understand I am not taking a vow to '*this man's army*' as it were. I will to tell you this... Like you began in recent days, I have played the part as needed for years. Originally, I came here to escort Carl Ver Haven safely back East. As you know, he is dead... I am going to ensure his killers meet justice, nothing less is expected of me."

There was an edge of finality to Shepherd's tone, giving Crisp pause. Crisp suspected Shepherd personally knew Ver Haven, perhaps longer than Captain Bristol had. It was certain Shepherd intended to carry out a personal vendetta and guarantee justice served. Bristol was right. Shepherd was not regular army. If Shepherd had known Ver Haven, should not Bristol know who Shepherd was?

Shepherd took the silence as a 'no-comment' and continued, "If you'd prefer, I'll clear out and finish things on my own..." He picked his shirt off the table. "It's probably for the best, that way *this man's army* is out of the loop."

Crisp raised a halting hand, "You're not going anywhere yet... Since you seem to be working on our side, whatever-the-hell that side that is, I would as soon have you around and keep an eye on you. As far as you playing a part as needed, you damn well best play the part of a soldier under my command to the hilt. Last thing I need is Bristol breathing down my neck any more than he already is."

Crisp gazed at Steadson and said, "So long as you're now in *this man's army*, you may as well know it all. Lord knows I'm confused enough by myself. A little company among the chaos is welcome." A rap at the door silenced him.

The door swung open and Smit strutted into the doctor's office. His spurs clinking like bells across the floorboards. He tipped his hat brim upward, reviling a brown-eyed smirk. "Don't reckon I meant to barge in on ya-all. Came to ask about that dog, I'd like to buy him - say for a dollar?"

Crisp allowed his frustration to fall on Smit. "The dog is not for sale. The other day, you swore you'd never trust a dog like that on your spread? If I recollect and I believe I do. You said; *That dog should be put down*. Those are damn near your exact words."

Smit's eyes swerved to the floor, searching an intelligent reply. He glimpsed up and grinned. "Change of heart, realized I ought-not judge a book by its cover. Dog was bred to work in the heat, and hardly any greater heat than Texas."

Unintentionally, Smit had planted another burr beneath Crisp's saddle blank. Texans always bragged, they had the meanest steers, the biggest this, the largest that, the worst storms.

Frustrated, Crisp glanced around the room and ridiculed, "As you can see the dog isn't here anymore. I resigned my commission as of this morning. The army took the dog. Once the government sinks its teeth into something, they don't let go."

Then Crisp advised him, "We're a tad busy at the moment. With a war pending back East, shouldn't you be getting back to that spread yours?"

Smit's lean frame flinched at the mention of war. "If'n I were to get back before the fighting broke-out, my sons are likely to join under Lee's Command. With me gone, I reckon they have to look after things at home. After bullets start flying, it keeps em out of harms-way. Having a dog to train would keep me occupied, at least till I see how the war is leaning. About that dog, I'd be willing to go as much as three dollars on him."

Crisp repeated, "As I explained, the dog is gone. Are you deaf or what?"

Smit shifted the conversation. "Read the morning paper?"

Ready to shed himself of Smit, Crisp replied, "No, can't say as I have."

Smit elaborated, "Last night some poor lady got her skull bashed with a hammer. Heard tell her brain was splattered all over an alley. Paper said she was a working girl, if'n you know what I mean. Not that I'd ever pay any woman to bed down with me, no sir." He smarted, "Woman love Texans."

Crisp noted Steadson's face sheeted white at the news of a murdered woman. He warned, "Mister Smit, at the risk of sounding rude there is a lady present."

Smit dodged the comment regarding manners. "Resigned your commission? What happened, afraid of war?"

Crisp gritted his teeth and spelled it out, "If you must know, my father decided to open a branch in San Francisco. Shipping exports and imports to and from the Far East. Seems back East; people are suddenly craving tea again, and Chinese herbal medical remedies are the latest craze. Never know how long trends will last, and I plan to strike while the iron is hot."

"Nice outfit," Smit smarted, "Ya' know what they say; a man's style of clothing can go a long way." He glimpsed at Shepherd's dressed injuries. "What happened to him?"

"The dog took a nasty bite out of him," Crisp lied and pointed at the doorway. "As I've said twice already… We're busy here, if you'd excuse us."

Smit tipped his hat toward Doc Steadson and apologized, "Beg my pardon for commenting on that murdered working gal." Then, he left closing the doorway behind him.

Crisp sighed, spun on his heels and requested, "Doctor, could you leave myself and Shepherd alone for a few moments. We have a few personal issues that need settling. I am planning a briefing at five this evening, if you can make there I'd sure appreciate it. I'll see what I can do about getting you undrafted from *this man's army* after we've located Kern." He lifted a pencil and paper from the table and jotted down the address for her.

Steadson crossed her arms, her eyes swept back and forth between them. "If it comes to locking horns, don't ransack the place. Take it outside where it belongs. You trash my office… Well, let's say whatever you do to each other won't come close to what I'll do."

Crisp handed her the address, yield his palms upward and promised, "It won't come to that." Then, he gave her a lazy and joking salute. He jested, "Dismissed."

Hanna Steadson rolled her eyes and exited the examining room, leaving them at odds with each other.

Before the door had completely closed, Crisp was nose to nose with Shepherd and remarked, "It seems odd that you were dressed the part last night, wearing black at the opportune moment. Care to explain why?"

Shepherd set his shirt back onto the table and adjusted the bandages across his wounds. "I was about leave and explore the Lady Beth's cargo holds, just in case something was missed yesterday. The thought came late at night. Being late, I didn't want to bother you with it. As I was about to leave, the boy took-off. I doubt he was going to ground. He would not leave the dog, unless he planned on returning. Figured, he was going back to the ship for something and planned to return here. When I arrived at the Lady Beth, Kern was there and in trouble. I made another judgment-call and rose to the occasion."

Skeptical, Crisp nodded. "Mmm, so it would appear… Since you are on top of things and this is a sprawling city… Any passing thoughts as where to begin searching for him?"

Shepherd questioned, "He wouldn't stay in the city. He would head into the wilderness where there is room to hide. It'd take a good tracker to find him, provided of course we were able to locate Kern's point of entry into the wilderness."

Crisp frowned. Shepherd had raised a vailed point. Kern's personality was not a city boy. That Kern was a cabin boy meant nothing, other than La Horn had taken him aboard at some-point. Shepherd formed opinions three-dimensionally, looking at the larger picture. He respected that rare quality. He tested Shepherd's thought processes. "On what do you make that assumption?"

Shepherd replied, "Because, he moved like a boy raised among the wilds." Then he snaked a grin. "Like Bristol's ancestors, speaking of course of the dog and not the Captain. Last night, Kern stayed focused in spite of what was happening around him. He was intent on getting at whatever he had stashed inside of a lifeboat."

Shepherd looked at the door and continued, "Not being able to easily retrieve whatever it was, he simple took the lifeboat with him, along with whatever he had hidden inside of it. My guess, he headed into the foothills where he'd feel more at home." His forehead crinkled, suspecting Crisp knew what Kern was after. "What do you suppose was that important he'd risked his life to get?"

On edge, Crisp fanned his index finger up and down. "Before we take this any further, we're back-stepping a bit. First, I need a few answers. Before last week, I never laid eyes on you. Captain Bristol was under the impression I recommend you, while I was under the impression it was

Montgomery. As it turns out, it wasn't Montgomery. Care to explain that lie to me?"

Defeated, Shepherd gestured outward with raised palms. "Bristol was mistaken, Montgomery recommended me." He shrugged. "Typical army, loosing paperwork happens all the time."

Crisp cocked an eyebrow. "Montgomery recommended you? I seriously doubt it… I've known Montgomery for years, and he would have sent me a telegram telling me about you." He glimpsed at the door Hanna had used to leave. "We're alone, so let's try this again… Who sent you?"

Shepherd evaded an answer, "Isn't it enough I saved the boy's life last night? Doesn't that say something about where I stand?"

Rigid, Crisp held his ground. "I've recently learned that it's standing room only in this town. I keep bumping into people in the strangest places. Stand still for too long and you are libel too get ran over. Nor am I sure who can be trusted anymore."

Shepherd advised, "You have to trust someone." He picked his knit shirt off the table. Unexpectedly, a piece of jewelry concealed beneath his shirt fell to the floor. Despite injury, he immediately snatched his amulet from the floor and cupped it, leaving only a silver chain dangling between closed fingers.

Crisp noted Shepherd's amulet was the same size and shape as the one Kern wore from Ver Haven. He decided against requesting to view it. Shepherd's quick reaction to conceal it had answered and raised questions.

Crisp released him from further duties for the day. "I want you to get rested and healed. I'll have Captain Bristol send out a search party of soldiers to scour the foothills."

Shepherd suggested, "Make sure they're not wearing uniforms. I've a feeling Kern had a brush with the law somewhere and doesn't trust men wearing uniforms."

Crisp nodded, having noted Kern apprehension of people wearing uniforms. Shepherd was not a man to allow an injury to stand in the way of completing a mission. For measure he mentioned, "I'm willing to bet Kern went back for the journal," and waited for a reaction.

Shepherd muttered more of a remembrance than a question, "Journal?"

"Yes," confirmed Crisp. "Our dearly departed Carl Ver Haven kept a personal journal. If you do happen across it, at least have the decency to let us read it before you vanish with it. I am sure it contains whatever information you are after. Information important enough, you had to personally escort Ver Haven back East to whomever, and or whatever group you're working for."

Shepherd slipped on his shirt. While tucking shirttails he vowed, "If I do find the boy and this supposed journal, rest assured, I'd return with both. Bear in mind, I am here to aid with your investigation. You simply have to trust me. I am not here to work against you."

Crisp exhaled wavering stress. "As I said earlier, I'm not trusting anyone at this point. Looks can be deceiving… Don't forget, he is wanted for killing a Peace Officer in Australia. Kern could have us all fooled. I'm not sure who's more dangerous you, La Horn, or that boy."

Shepherd stepped to a window and glimpsed skyward. Casual, he slipped the amulet over his head, concealing it beneath his shirt. Steadfast, he turned and inquired, "What about Ackerland? You've yet to meet him."

Crisp groaned. "You're right on that count him included. It's damn sure as hell he's tied into all this. Whatever the hell this mess is turning into." He grabbed his stomach. "My gut is knotted tighter than a thirteen knot hemp rope around someone's neck. Good God, the country falling apart and I've got conspiracies up my to my arse. At this rate, I'll be smothered in trickery before this all ended."

Shepherd shook his head and mumbled, "Trust me, it never ends. As Roman burns, we do what we must to keep humanity from crumbling..." He straightened his shirt, stepped to the door and placed a hand on the knob.

Unsure, Shepherd paused, looked over his shoulder and counseled, "Lieutenant, your life betwixt the shadows has just begun. Your intentions unknown by those you mingle with, you are stepping into unseen raging fire that could easily consume you and those under your command… Don't allow anyone to make you a man with no past, no present and no future."

Then Shepherd stated, "Recently, you must've done something out of the ordinary and unexpected. What was it that caused them to cast you amid a shadowy life?" Without further explanation, he left the young baby-faced Lieutenant alone.

Transfixed, Crisp stood there. He knew what had cast him into this new life. When serving as part of a Dragoon Regiment, and against orders of a superior officer, he had struck out on his own with Hindor, Trick and Ring. They brought an end of Indian slavery at ranch in Northern California.

Crisp wanted to ask Shepherd a similar question. What had driven him into a shadowy life, and for how long had he lived such a life? Evidently, a very long time. Was Shepherd prepped from childhood for the life he currently lived?

While Crisp would never admit it to Shepherd's face, at a gut level he trusted him. It was doubtful an army patrol would find Kern. If anyone found Kern and brought him back safely, it was probably Shepherd. Ver Haven's journal remained in question. Shepherd was likely to deny finding it.

10

An hour later, Crisp stood at a three-story office building. Second and third levels served as living quarters for his men. Their recently acquired building was being retrofitting due to the 1857 earthquake. Carpenters were busy adding to the masquerade by hanging a sign that read, A. R. B Imports & Exports.

Crisp had no idea what the initials A. R and B meant, and planned to ask Captain Bristol about it. Against a brisk late morning wind, he pulled the front of his suit snug and avoided walking beneath a latter used to hang the sign. He was not superstitious but why take-chances.

As Crisp entered the front door, hinges squeaked loudly. His first thought was to have the hinges oiled. No, he decided. Squeaky hinges were apt to alter his men, and or himself whenever someone entered the building.

Upon Crisp's entry into the front office, five men seated around a square pine plank table militarily sprang to their feet. If not for a dead diplomat, missing lad and journal, he would have had this meeting a day prior.

Crisp ordered them at ease, sat on top of a desk and surveyed his men, allowing a minute of silence to pass. In the past, he had fought side by side with three of them. Two newer recruits were too young to have seen battle.

Crisp had read files on each new man under his command, except of course for Shepherd whose file was supposedly in route. He doubted the file would arrive anytime soon, if at all. It dawned on him that Shepherd had never given a first name when reporting for duty. Concerns over Shepherd aside, he focused on those present.

Present were three who had taken part in *The Incident* as the army referred to it. Perchance or warped sense of army justice had kept them together. Fellow officers referred to his men as an Unholy Trio and iced insults spiked with serrated chuckles. It was true that, his core trio was rough around the edges with unique faults. Nonetheless, they were decent and trustworthy men. He eyed each and suppressed a grimacing smirk.

Sergeant Calvert Hindor was of African American decent, not of slaves but African settlers. His lineage in this country transcended 75 years. On numerous occasions, Hindor had proven his worth as a solider. Personality wise, he was cagey to say the least.

Corporal Stanley Ringwald haled from Chicago. He had confirmed his value as well. A love for alcohol often got him into trouble. When drunk, he bluntly mouthed whatever sparked a debate. Even if opposed to an idea or issue, simply for the sake of an argument he took the side no one else dared.

Recently demoted to Private was Trickster, or Trick for short. Crisp had long since forgotten the man's birth name. Where or when the nickname had fallen on the solider was anyone's guess. Crisp suspected it originated at a card game during Trick's youth. Trick possessed an uncanny ability at getting out of tough situations. He originated from Louisiana and freely spoke his views on issues back East.

Thus far, Ring and Trick had served together for three years. Not long ago, they came to drunken blows over the pending war. While they disagreed concerning issues back East, they remained friends. Each chose to remain on the West Coast. The likelihood of them fighting on opposing sides was slim.

Crisp's eyes fell on his two newest men.

Private Jackson Taylor hailed from Alabama. His eyes were dark and shady, his brows met in the middle, his voice bitter and crude. Always at odds with life, he was a powder keg ready to explode and needed only lit fuse.

Taylor was not to be trusted. Yesterday, he had voiced a desire to serve under Lee's command back East. Amazingly, Trick had convinced him running off and joining Lee's army was foolhardy.

Private Clancy Muser was a simple Ohio farm boy trying to make good in life. Young, innocent, ready to meet any challenge.

Crisp did not expect Muser to survive his first field battle. He pictured himself drafting a letter to Muser's parents. With luck, perhaps Trick's natural instinct for survival might pass onto Muser.

"Men," began Crisp and smirked. "While you're in *this man's plain-clothed army,* you are to act as non-military personal. Keeping in mind, you are to follow orders from only Montgomery, Bristol and myself."

Crisp looked left to right at his men and exhaled a tense breath. "As everyone here knows, our nation is splitting at her seams." Stern, he glared at Trick and Ring. "That ain't our concern, we're here and they're thousands of miles away."

Crisp nodded eastward. "The Rockies are our buffer zone from come what may over-yonder. I'll have no more talk about siding with North or South. Anyone breaks that rule, and I will let Hindor publicly whip you arses."

Crisp spoke more to the new recruits. "That your, Sergeant is a Negro best not affect your judgment of him. As Trick and Ring will tell both of you, he has saved their butts from certain disaster and death." Then he raised a finger for emphasized, "more than once I might add. Trust him with your life, because I do. When I am not present, his orders stand. Meaning, if he makes a judgment-call while on a mission you had best heeded it. Even if his judgment call counters previous orders. If he orders retreat from any given situation - Do it. Always remember when in the field situations change, and you cannot wait on new orders. Any questions on that?"

Everyone nodded, shuffled and waited.

Crisp issued their assignments. "Half the day is already spent. Take what's left of it and set the stages for tomorrow."

"Taylor and Muser, I want you to dress as dock laborers. Any day now, the Lady Beth will take on a cargo and you are to help load her. Listen and watch, but under no conditions are you to act on your own. All you're doing is gathering information for use at a later time. Not to fret, Hindor will be within eyes throw of the Lady Beth. Should trouble arise, he'll be there to help. One more thing, keep an eye open for a journal kept by our dearly departed Mister Ver Haven. If you spot it and it's easy to grab, snap it up and both of you get off that ship."

Crisp eyed his Sargent and grinned. "Hindor lose the leg, dress as drunkard, then hang in front of the pubs across from the docks and beg for money."

Hindor stood, stomped his wooden leg on the floor and protested, "Sir, I worked damn hard to buy this leg! I'm not giving it up! As far as begging for money! What do I look like, a common street-bum?"

Defeated, Crisp raised palms and yield, "Fine, wear a suit and tie, and I will give you another assignment."

"That sounds better," grunted Hindor. "I can play to part of reputable business type. What type of business am I into? Anything to do with gold? I've been reading-up on minerals as of late."

"Slave Trader," Crisp sneered with a touch of humor. "Once more thing, you'll have shave your bread to fit the part. Your face already looks like the backside of a grizzly. Being clean shaven will add an air of realism of the role."

Hindor stared at his dark skinned arms and guffawed, "Slave Trader? They'd never believe it!" Then he stroked his bushy beard. "Shave my beard! I've had this beard long before you daddy spermed you into your momma's womb! I will not shave it! And by God and you cannot make me!"

Crisp sunned a twisted smile. "I'd ask you to at least comb those birds' nests from it. However, a nasty smelling beard does fit the part of a drunkard. Losing that log of yours' would be nice touch. You know, pity the old one-legged-darky with spare change."

Hindor retorted, "By God you are insane!" Then he stomped his wooden leg, again. "This leg keeps me mobile." Upset, he waved an arm at the new recruits. "Without I'd never be able to rescue these two pups if the need arises as you so mildly put it! I'll have to keep my leg nearby."

Ring and Trick busted into laughter. Stunned at how their Sergeant and Lieutenant interacted, Taylor and Muser's mouths dropped open.

Crisp eyed Ring and Trick and advised, "You two had best be on speaking terms, I've got enough problems without having to step between your fists again. Last time, I nearly got a black eye and my teeth knocked out."

"We worked it out, sir." Trick jeered, his face spread an open smile. "The South is going to kick the North's asses."

Fists clinched, Ring jumped to his feet and forged, "That ain't how I'm seeing it! The North has far more resources. King Cotton ain't gonna to do nothing to help the South get supplies from England."

Crisp cleared his throat and pointed at the floorboards. "Right here and now, you'd best put your attention in the West or I'll jam my boots so-far up your arses, Doctor Steadson will have to perform an extraction to end your pain."

Trick and Ring simmered their defensive tones.

Crisp maintained a firm voice, "Much better. I realize this stretching it, but you are to act like respectable businessmen. Ring, I want you to get a job over at Shoreline Bank. We need a look-see at a man's accounts there."

Crisp stood walked around the desk, removed a file from a draw and extended it toward Ring. "Here's a file for your assignment, study it."

Crisp cocked an eye at the gambler and instructed, "Trick, I need your Southerness to play-up to a cattle trader going by the name of Smit. Don't turn your back on him he's bound to be deadlier than a pissed-on rattler."

Trick hung his head and griped, "No need to be reminding me about pissing on that snake last year." An afterthought struck gold, he glimmered at Ring and joked, "If my best friend here hadn't been around to suck out the poison, well I might not be around today."

Ring seethed, "As I seem to recall ya waz suppose too return the favor and never did. Damn it, I'm still waiting. Sometimes, I lay in my bunk at night just thinking about it, wondering when you're gonna get around to it. All I've heard are broken promises."

Muser and Taylor sat stunned, unsure how to react, questioning what type of outfit they had gotten into.

Frustrated, Crisp raised both hands and insisted, "Enough sick and twisted jokes. Trick you've got a job to do with that silly Texan, and I don't want you to be causing a fuss with him."

Trick stood, brushed the front of his new tweed pants. "Sir, if ya don't mind me saying-so. You've gotta come to grips with this hatred of people from Texas. Every time Texas gets mentioned, ya damn near blow a cork. What did Texas ever do to ya that caused such a thing?" He scratched his upper legs and grumbled, "Damn, these pants itch."

Rigid, Crisp dodged the hate issue. "Smit hailing from Texas makes no difference. He was asking about that dog, plus he had contact with Ver Haven, and I suspect La Horn as well. Hence, I want him checked-out. Watch yourself, heard he is prone to gambling on anything and everything."

Trickster grinned.

Crisp rocked his index finger at him. "You're not to gamble with that man... And that's an order."

Bruised, Trick pleaded as if denied life-sustaining food and water, "But sir... If'n he's asking for a friendly game of cards, what better way of getting to know a fellow?"

"N. O," Crisp spelled and said it, "No... I've learned there's no friendly game of cards when you're at the table. Hell, you deal the deck lower than a lizard's belly to the ground. Maybe, you could find a job tending bar wherever it is that he's gambling at."

Ring glimpsed around the office, nodded quick a head count and asked, "Where our other new man, Shepherd?"

Crisp explained, "Shepherd was shot last night. Muser was there but missed the gunplay. Shepherd is resting over at Doctor Steadson's place."

Crisp's face pulled taunt. "A word to the wise, don't get on Shepherd's bad side. Last night, he killed two men and without so much as blinking. Everyone here saw him break up that fight the other night at Lizzy's Brothel. We all commented on it, we've never seen a man move that fast in a fight."

Ring asked, "What are you trying to say?"

"Nothing," Crisped waved the question away, "Give him a wide berth and don't be pissing him off. If it comes to killing, best stay out of his way. I'd sure as hell hate to see anyone hurt in the crossfire…"

Trick inquired, "That ain't telling us a whole lot concerning a man who we're supposed to serve with, and not to forget trusting each-others' lives with. You're being a tad vague, sir. And to be honest - that ain't like you."

Crisp raised his palms, letting them know not to press the issue. "Let's leave at this, there's no need to write anyone's folks telling them about it. Stay out of his way. One more thing, everyone keep an eye peeled for that boy."

Crisp removed a poster from an inside coat pocket, then unrolled and passed it around. "This doesn't mean he killed a lawman. It may be a simple case of mistaken identity. Besides, this isn't Australia, and we're not about to hand him over to the British if they come asking."

Crisp cringed. "The idea of penal colonies doesn't set right with me. Hell, Trick, they'd have you at one."

"Hell is right," moaned Trick under his breath.

Crisp thought of the amulets. The one Shepherd had hidden from him, and the one Ver Haven had likely given to Kern. He inquired, "Anyone here read Latin?"

No one answered.

Crisp grumbled, "Didn't think so." He dismissed everyone to change into proper attire, matching whatever each assignment required.

As everyone left, Crisp motioned for Hindor to linger. If his gut feeling was wrong and things took a turn for the worse, someone else needed to know about Shepherd. With everyone else gone, he explained what had happened.

Hindor was not surprised to learn, Captain Bristol was under the impression Crisp had vouched for Shepherd. If and or how Clifford Ackerland tied into this affair was akin to a Chinese puzzle without an easy resolution.

They agreed, there were forces-within-forces working behind the scenes. They had no easy way out of what lay before them. Ties needed breaking and unseen strings severed.

For now, they decided to play the game as Bristol secretly issued orders from another desk at the local Branch Office.

Resolved, Hindor mentioned their recent past. "Sir, speaking frankly, you've an uncanny knack for slipping in behind people and hitting them on their-blindside. Need I remind you, it was our actions that got us into this current predicament. Had not Trick, Ring, you and me pulled that stunt…"

Crisp raised his hands, halting the reminder. "It's in the past, and it worked out for the best. Aside from those we saved from slavery, who is to say what happened out there? The bad guys are dead and buried, and as far as those we saved."

Crisp floated his fingers upward. "Gone as if they've never existed, like smoke in the wind they vanished. I've never seen so many people disappear that fast. There one moment and gone the next."

Hindor flinched. "Those folks were down right spooky if'n you were to ask me. With that woman acting the way she did, I said right from the start something was amiss with those folks. I never saw so-much witchery in my life. I'm not one for burning people at the stake, but damn if she didn't scare me shitless."

Hindor exhaled stress and continued, "Even Trick was spooked and he's got Cajun blood in him. Did you ever listen that rascal spin tales around a campfire about Backwater Bayou Voodoo? Making little dolls that look like real people and cursing em. It is enough to raise the hair on anyone's neck."

Crisp sighed, recalling Trick's wild tales of voodoo among the Bayous of Louisiana. He shook his head. "Half those stories ain't true, he enjoys scaring new recruits with tales of the walking dead. I wouldn't put it past him, once out in the wilds and sitting around a fire with Taylor and Muser, he spins a tale of how that woman changed into a panther."

Hindor took a backward step and pointed at him. "You saw it happen, we all did. It sure wasn't simple trickery doing what she did! No sir, she changed into a wildcat right before our eyes. I swear to God, she wrought black magic straight from hell and the devil."

Crisp remarked, "It was dark. The fire was low and inside of a hole, no one was sure of anything. I'm telling you, the cat was there all along - like a pet."

Hindor rebutted, "If'n you were to ask me, it was a darn big pussy cat to keep around as a pet. Answer me this - why was it whenever she was around the cat was nowhere to be seen; then when the cat paced us along those ridges she was nowhere to be found?"

Again, Crisp dismissed the notion. "Believe what you will, as far as I'm concerned she wasn't a witch." He took Kern's amulet from his pocket and rolled it between his fingers. "If anyone asks, I went to a reading room for research."

Crisp needed to find a book on Latin and translate words on the amulet, or find someone to do it for him.

11

The next morning, Crisp continued his research at the city's two reading rooms, and the Merchant Exchange on Clay Street. He had failed to turn up anything to aid with translating the amulet. Captain Bristol had said it appeared familiar. Had Kern had stolen it from Ver Haven's dead body, or was it a gift from a dying man as a keepsake?

Until proven otherwise, Crisp chose to believe the latter. Reflecting back, when Steadson had exposed Kern's necklace during the medical exam two things happened. Kern was reluctant to give it up, and Shepherd was puzzled to see it around Kern's neck.

Later, Shepherd had concealed his own piece of neckwear. If the two amulets matched, it served further speculation of a broader conspiracy. If so, did it involve the pending Civil Conflict between North and South?

Crisp took a short lunch at a Chinese restaurant and skimmed a morning paper. Engrossed with news, he hardly noticed what he had ordered to eat. News from the other side of Continental Divide had not changed.

Fort Sumter located in the harbor to Charleston had reported it was low on supplies. Likelihood, first shots fired was going to be over that fort. Thus far, Major Anderson had proven wise at avoiding bloodshed. Months ago, Anderson had pulled his troops from Fort Moultrie to Fort Sumter.

Crisp closed the paper, sipped his tea and pondered his next step to uncovering what the amulet meant. Perhaps, asking Liberians and doctors was the wrong approach. Priests had a basic understand of Latin. Crisp knew of a priest to ask, Father Anthony. After finishing his meal, he took a carriage to a livery stable near the A. R & B.

By mid-afternoon, Crisp reached Mission Vallejio. A young Nun informed him that, Father Anthony was visiting a local Native American village and not expected to return for a couple days.

Sheepish, she admitted not having learned Latin. Crisp left a note for Father Anthony to visit the A. R & B office on ninth and collect a donation for the church, then left for town.

Crisp returned his horse Copper to the liver stable then took a rail carriage downtown. He bought a beef sandwich and beer at Portsmouth Square. Trail tired, he sat at an outdoor table to eat. By shear-luck, a street preacher took up giving a sermon near the table.

Over the years, Crisp met street preachers who were highly educated. It was worth shot-in-the-dark. He decided to interrupt him. The preacher paused from his calling for people to repent and looked at the amulet.

Crisp did not catch the preacher's name but he had a basic understanding of Old Latin. Words on the amulet were broken into two parts. A word at the top of the imagery translated as Herdsman. The sentence at the bottom remained a mystery. The preacher doubted language was Latin, and he guessed the language was ancient.

In addition, the preacher had raised an interesting question. Above the man, holding a shepherd's staff was an engraved star pattern. What Constellation was it?

Crisp thanked him with a hefty donation and left. As he trekked toward his office near the docks, he thought about Shepherd man of mystery. Herdsmen written in Latin on the amulet, plus the man's name as Shepherd were to close for happenstance.

Crisp doubted Shepherd was the man's given-birth name. Was it possible, Shepherd had chosen the name as a private joke on others? Did Shepherd chuckle deep inside every time he used the alias? If true, he credited Shepherd for a concealed a sense of humor.

Crisp became suspicious a secret group was at work behind the scenes. Questions needed answering. Did Lincoln know about those who wore similar amulets around their necks? Like a puppet, was a shadowy organization pulling Lincoln's strings from behind the scenes?

Crisp wondered if Captain Bristol shrouded an amulet beneath his shirt. For years, Bristol and Ver Haven were close friends. How close though? If Ver Haven was a member of a secret society, was Bristol a member? If not, did Bristol know the group existed?

Crisp decided, the answer was no. Bristol had questioned who had referred Shepherd to the new unit. Was Colonel Montgomery a member of a secret organization? That seemed doubtful as well.

Shepherd's timely arrival was not coincidental. Were his comments of losing one's self amidst the shadows a reflection of his past? Words of warning as too what comes afterwards?

Crisp pondered what ifs. After this mission was completed what lay ahead for his men and himself. He filed thoughts of a shadowy organization away. He had no proof, at least not until he got his hands on Shepherd's amulet. If similar, he would confront Shepherd on it. Press hard and demand answers.

* * *

Again, Hindor had proved his worth at gathering information. Lady Beth had encountered difficulty securing a cargo for a return trip to the Far East. La Horn had spent the day, scouring warehouses and searching for cargo. With a pending war, not much was going anywhere - except back East. It was unlikely, La Horn wanted to sail around the bottom of South America and into unfamiliar waters of the Atlantic.

When asked where Muser and Taylor are, Hindor described, "Those two boys must've had a contest as to who can work harder. I've never seen two white boys load and unload ships with such keen interest. Soon as we got back, they laid flat on their bunks and haven't moved since."

Hindor tried to appear dignified. "At the moment, Ms. Steadson is attending a gathering of doctors at Pacific Medical University." He spread a grin. "I must say, I do believe she has eyes for you." Eyes glimmering, he handed Crisp the note. "She left a note, probably one of those romantic love poems."

Crisp let the comment go unanswered. It was understandable Steadson was gone for the day. Recently, the university had opened for business and was accepting students. He remarked, "Apparently, the school has offered her a teaching position."

Crisp read the note out-loud, *I will be teaching, whether you still want my services between classes is a matter of scheduling appointments. I am not willing to be drafted. I have a life to live. Best regards, Dr. Hanna Steadson.*

Crisp folded the note and stated, "It was as far from a love poem as words can get. Sure as squirrels gather nuts you tend to pry information out of people, whether it is a need to know or not. You generally trick them into saying whatever. I am willing to bet she turned the tables on you. What did you tell her?"

Hindor assumed a defensive grin, took a kettle from on top of the potbelly stove. Then he poured a tin cup of hot coffee and said, "Assured her absences wasn't a problem." Then he grumbled, "A lady-doctor probing a man's private parts it ain't natural."

Crisp refused comment on the matter.

Hindor moved on to the next topic. "On the upside, about an hour ago Steadson, Muser and you received a private invitation to Ackerland's party tonight." Tight brow, he lifted an envelope from the table and passed it to him. "Sounds like a mighty fine time, a band, dancing and good eats. Why didn't I get an invite?"

Crisp smarted, "Cuz you're colored."

Knowing the answer was not on a cold day in hell, Hindor suggested, "I could pass as a man-servant and slip in through a rear door.

Firm, Crisp sliced his hand across the air. "Forget it. You are needed to hold down the fort here." He slid the envelope into his breast coat pocket. "You'd best get upstairs and wake Muser, tell him to wear his Sunday best for tonight. Make sure he is bathed and clean shaven."

Hindor sighed. "If I have to dump buckets of water on him, he'll be cleaned and ready." Shaking his head, he looked at the floor and grouched, "Damn, I'd like to get some decent eats for a change. Army rations ain't nothing to write home about. There's no way for a decent man to get ahead in this country."

Dog eyed, Hindor stirred pity to the mix. "Even my friends won't help out in a pinch, cuzing I'm colored."

Crisp allowed another remark to pass and inquired, "Any word from Ring or Trick?"

Hindor shrugged. "Nothing yet, want me to send that greenhorn Taylor to find em? Do him a little good to stretch those sore muscles, and keep him limber for another day at the docks."

Crisp shook his head. "No, Ring and Trick are a bad influence. They'd have Taylor off on a misadventure." He pulled a pocket watch and looked at the time. "Bank closed an hour ago. Without a doubt, Ring is boozing it and Trick is snaking Smit out of money in a friendly card game. You know how they are, when fists fly the drunkard backs the card player every time."

Hindor blew swirling steam from atop of his cup, took a careful sip and sighed. "Trick always denies deliberately spooking up trouble. It is no small miracle he hasn't been shot at card table. He's come close more times than I care to count."

Crisp smirked, thinking of the only card game he played with Trick. "Damn near shot him myself once. Trick weaned me of any desire to play the game, again. I haven't split a deck of cards since. Any sign of Shepherd?"

Hindor shrugged, "Nope. He wasn't resting at Steadson's office, and didn't see him come or go here." He nodded toward the stairs. "His gear turned up on the third floor. Could've came and went whilst Muser, Taylor and myself were at the docks."

Crisp noted his relieve aloud, "Since his gear is here, I reckon he'll be back and hopefully with Kern in tow… We may need a witness to nail La Horn's hid to a shed."

"Nearly plum forgot," Hindor reminded himself. He limped back to the table and scooped a sealed envelope from it. "Bristol had a message curried over about an hour ago, sealed for your eyes only." His face scowled. "I've no idea what is says, sir."

Crisp opened it and silently read.

'La Horn has filed a grievance with the French Consulate. The French are raising a stink stronger than a scared skunk. The British Consulate claim the boy is wanted for murdering a lawman in Australia. Be advised we do not believe our witness the boy Kern is the same person suspected of murder in Australia. Expect to meet representatives from both Consulates at tonight's gathering. Handle with care. End message.'

Crisp returned the letter to the envelope, then opened the potbelly stove and tossed it inside. He watched flames devour the message and muttered, "I hate politics."

Then Crisp closed stove door and latched it. Then he said, "I need to blow off steam and will personally fetch our wayward boys. The walk will do me good."

12

Crisp swung through a third set of pub doors and entered Lizze's Brothel, hunting for his two missing undercover soldiers. Distance having separated them from a coming bloody Civil Storm, many in the West appeared uncaring. It was business as usual. The noise level of whores toying with boisterous drunks had no effect on several card games underway.

Crisp regretted not reprimanding Ring and Trick for a previous night of binge drinking and gambling. Through pillars of cigar smoke, he spotted his two strays. Scarcely standing, Ring was propped against the bar with an empty beer mug in hand. As expected, Trick was engrossed in a card game and drinking sarsaparilla.

Crisp was grateful Trick never drank when gambling. Trick always kept a clear head whenever money was involved. Ring on the other hand was a flat-out drunkard.

Over the past three years, Crisp had a collection of flasks appropriated from Ring. At the current rate of confiscation, he figured to have enough whiskey flasks to fill a chest before next year. He cut around the backside of a small crowd gathered near a billiard table and eased himself next to Ring at the bar.

Ring was eyeing Trick's opponents at the table, waiting for someone to accuse another cheating.

Over the racket of a fast picking banjo player, Crisp said "Evening, Mister Ring."

Blurry eyed, Ring swayed a blank stare at him, his words slurred, "Yep, sure is evening. Saw the sunset for myself... I's a witness to it." He raised a beer mug and crackled, "Willing to testify in court if need be..."

Crisp let Ring's drunken humor pass.

Again, Ring eyed the nearest card table where Trick engaged other players in a game of poker. With everything at the table running smoothly, he turned back to Crisp. "I's surprised to see ya joining us here. About damn time you dropped pretense, and showed us that you're human like the rest of us." He swaggered the empty mug over the counter and called, "Barkeep, another for myself and one for my friend here!"

A burly bartender wearing a sweat stained white shirt, lumbered to counter. He leaned across the oak bar, took the mug and glimpsed at Crisp expecting an order for a drink.

Crisp gestured a mild slicing across his throat with covert glimpse at Ring. The barkeep nodded, took the hint and mug without returning. Ring's supply of beer for tonight had run dry. Crisp's next goal was to drag Trick from the poker table without upsetting sore losers.

"Ya may wanna take note," Ring garbled and tapped an unlit cigar between his fingers as if shaking ashes. He leaned close and lowered his drunken voice. "It's a rare moment to witness... Our buddy over there is on a losing streak. Trick could die with his boots off tonight. Shame too, he just bought that footwear yesterday and tossed-out his old pair."

Crisp glimpsed the card table and grimaced. Trick's new riding boots sat dead center on the table next to a pile of cash. He grumbled, "Not his new boots. I will not have him strutting around stocking foot. It is simply not proper attire. He'll look no better than a common street-bum."

Ring's head rolled. "Be that as it may, he's been on a losing streak all night. That gambler from Texas ain't no small piece of work. I dare say he is stacking the deck with underhanded dealing."

Smit's eyes glowed as he doubled palmed a stack of cash across the table and toward himself. Grinning, he stood, leaned across the table and lifted Trick's new boots. He jeered, "This are a tad on the small side for my huge Texan feet. Maybe they'll fit one of my youngins back home."

The bartender strutted past, balanced in his hands a load of full mugs splashing over the rims.

Ring realized he had not had a fresh mug of beer as requested. Determined, he slammed a hand on the bar, rattling mugs from one of it to the other. "Barkeep, where's my beer!" As his fist banged the bar a second time demanding drink, a gunshot melded with an upheaval of beer mugs.

It happened so fast, Crisp was reeling an hour later at the local police station. No one was sure of what happened.

One theory, Ring's first fist slam against the bar was mistaken for a gunshot and caused the gunfight. Another theory, Smit was caught cheating and lay dead with a bullet betwixt his eyes. It was a man seated next to Trick, who drew first on Smit. Either-way, Smit was quicker, shot and killed the man seated next to Trick.

A heartbeat later, Smit and Trick had taken aim at each other. Smit was the lesser fortunate. Smit's bullet nicked Trick's left forearm, which by no means affected Trick's right-handed aim.

As Smit's eyes met dead center, the back of his skull sprayed brain-matter over those behind him. He stiffened and fell backwards to the floor.

Amid the confusion, Crisp had snapped Trick's boots off the table. Then he passed Ring the boots. Drunk, Ring swaggered out the batwing doors with boots clutched to his chest. If Trick was bound for the stockade, it would not be stocking footed.

* * *

Captain Bristol stormed into the local police station and bellowed, "Where are they?" Without a word, Chief Crivitz pointed toward a backroom.

Forehead veins pulsated as Bristol stepped past Crivitz, and entered the backroom, closing the door behind him. Disgusted, he eyed handcuffs around Trick's wrists.

At a low level, Bristol questioned, "What the hell's going on around here? First you lose a witness, and one of your men kills two potential suspects, and this evening one of your men shoots a witness stone-cold dead."

Silent, Police Chief Crivitz slipped into the room, then loomed near the door and listened.

Trick expressed remorse, "Sir, plain as can be it was him or me. Witnesses said - I had no choice in the matter, sir."

Bristol's eyes and nostrils flared, he ignored Crivitz's presence and lashed at Trick. "That excuse's already been used by dozens of men in your same situation! Find another one, because I ain't buying it!"

Chief Crivitz stepped closer, hoping to calm Bristol's rage and assured, "Captain, we've interviewed at least a dozen witnesses. Everyone tells roughly an identical story. Cut and dried case of self-defense, no charges will be filed."

Trick rattled his handcuffs toward Crivitz. "I am ready to go here."

Bristol roared, "Not so damn fast! I am not convinced he shouldn't spend a night or two in jail! Possibly, a few years of hard labor inside of prison walls."

Crivitz stated, "Captain, if you wish to lock him up at your stockade that's up to you, but we're not holding him. The city can't afford to incarcerate soldiers at every turn, which is the reason we turn em over to the military near every time there's a problem."

Bristol conceded, "Fine cut him loose." Dumbfounded, he stared at Trick's stocking feet. "Do I want to ask where your boots are at?"

Trick cleared his throat and glimpsed at Crisp.

Bristol warned him, "Don't be looking to him for an excuse, because he's fresh out."

Ashamed, Trick stared at the floor and shrugged. "I lost them at a card game, I reckon. Not sure, since the hand never played-out. You might say they waz stolen among the confusion."

Crisp injected, "We have his boots at the A R & B."

Suspect, Bristol glared at Crisp. "Ringwald? They are peas from the same pod. I suppose he was drunk as usual but managed to back the gambler as he always does?"

Crisp kept his tone calm and subdued, "I'd rather not say and upset you anymore than you already are, sir."

Crivitz tapped Trick's shoulder and requested, "Let me see those wrists." After unlocking the handcuffs, he winked. "Well solider, I'd suggest you get your boots."

Trick seized the missing boots as excuse to leave and dashed for the backdoor.

Bristol blared, "Get your arm treated by Doc Steadson before it gets infected."

Trick tossed him a sloppy salute and darted outside. Then he slipped on the muddy street and fell flat onto his side. Without losing a beat, he scampered to his feet and was on his way.

Watching the door spring closed, Crisp broke into a suppressed chuckle.

Bristol's eyes flared. "What's so darn funny!"

Crisp stammered, "Trick, ahhh… Nothing, sir." He pulled a pocket watch and noted the time. "I've got to get ready for that party tonight, sir."

Bristol leaned close to Crisp's ear and whispered, "I'll see you there, and make sure Muser doesn't shoot anyone." He eyed Crivitz. "Keep this idiot in the dark."

Stout, Bristol stepped across the room and shook Crivitz's hand. "Chief, thank you for taking a personal interest with this unpleasant affair. Mister Crisp will take care of whatever you need for closure concerning tonight's shooting." Then, he left to prepare a political gathering at the Hotel Regal.

Casual, Crisp headed for the door.

Crivitz called after him, "Wait one moment. I cut your boy a slack and kept him from hanging. I do believe a little cooperation is due on your end of things."

Crisp turned and forced a grin. "Your efforts are appreciated, chief. The army is extremely grateful. You've helped us avoid public embarrassment and lengthy trial. A trial we both know what the outcome was to be."

Crivitz crossed his arms and took a firm stance. "With your arrogant captain gone, I want some straight answers. I do believe the San Francisco Police are due it."

Crisp wondered if Crivitz suspected what Bristol thought of him. He skipped asking and stayed focused on the shooting. "Self-defensive, said so yourself. You can't get much straighter than that. A dozen witnesses agreed to the facts."

Crivitz indexed his finger *no, no, no* and implied, "There was enough confusion among witnesses to hold him for trial. Heard from three witnesses, the first gunshot was fired from the bar, right about where you were said to be standing."

Crisp cleared his throat and said, "My weapon was cleaned last night and hasn't been fired. I can show it to you if you'd like." He reached under his suite coat to pull his weapon from a concealed shoulder holster.

"That won't be necessary," Crivitz said, yet remained unyielding. "For all I know, this Ring fellow you mentioned could have fired the first shot, or you fired it and traded guns with him."

Suddenly, it struck Crivitz that Crisp was not wearing a uniform. "Why are you out of uniform? Army men don't wear anything else, even when out for a night on the town. I'm not buying the story you gave me earlier. The A.R&B as a ligament business venture, and how you and three of your former army buddies are running it? I recognized Trick from previous encounters as an army man. Soon as I notified Captain Bristol we had Trick locked-up, he wasted no time getting down here. Hardly the actions of an army captain if those men recently resigned. Is there more here than meets the eye?"

Crisp grinned. "Chief, I cannot go into detail and discuss military matters. With everything going on back East, there's a lot at stake."

Interest peeked, Crivitz's brow tightened. "They are a number of folk in these parts who want nothing to do with what's going on back East. I pray this had nothing to do with that pending war. Darn that Brown for causing such a stir, I'll be glad once they hang him. Him and his boys have caused this country nothing but trouble in Kansas and trouble is spreading quicker than the Pox between tribes of Indians."

Crisp shook his head. He did not want to lie or give him a straight answer. "Not to my knowledge. I'll keep you posted when I know more. I could use someone around when the dust settles."

A thought struck home for Crisp. If Crivitz believed he was part of the action but from the sidelines, it may ease current tension. If things took a turn for the worse, having Crivitz on his side was a good idea.

Crisp spread a slick smirked and said, "We're involved with an investigation. I'm not sure whom I can trust. Will you be there - if or when I need you?"

An unexpected open invite surprised Chief Crivitz. An army officer requesting behind the scene aid was unheard of. He suppressed an initial shock and replied, "The San Francisco Police would be proud to help with any investigation. But I do need a little more detail to go on, a few tidbits couldn't hurt none."

Crisp apologized, "Sorry… Can't offer any details, simply asking when the dust settles you are going be there for the A. R & B."

Unsure, Crivitz glimpsed the door and inquired, "What about your captain? With police looming in the background of your investigation, ain't he bound to be suspicious?"

Crisp cocked an eye and injected, "What about him?"

Crivitz scratched his head and muttered, "I'm tad confused, here."

"You're not alone," Crisp agreed and reached for the doorknob.

"One more thing, lieutenant," added Crivitz, "I'm having my own bit of confusion lately." He opened a desk drawer, lifted a wanted poster and passed it to him. "British and French Consulates are looking for this boy. He was last reported to have been a cabin boy on a ship called the Lady Beth. This morning, I spoke with Captain La Horn who enlightened me the army took him. This afternoon, Captain Bristol denied knowledge of having sent men onboard the Lady Beth and taking the boy. Have you seen him?"

Crisp unrolled the poster and saw a drawing of Kern. He stared at it and remarked, "Looks mighty young to be wanted for murder. If'n you do find that boy, I'd take my time with him. Heard-tell he's deaf. Being unable to hear, I'd hate to learn he was back-shot because he failed to hear one of your men ordering him to surrender. It'd be headline news in the papers, *Deaf Boy shot in the back by San Francisco Police*."

Then Crisp shook his head. "Sure doesn't sound appealing. Don't forget, there is the new medical center where a lad like him can get help. A better headline, *Deaf boy rescued from the streets by San Francisco Police, gets medical help and hears again*.

Then Crisp proposed, "Think of the positive possibilities for the department and yourself. With positive attention in the papers, you'd be in a good spot to run for mayor in the next election."

Crivitz nodded. "My men'll be careful…" He suspected Crisp knew more than he admitted. "Is this boy part of your investigation?"

Crisp preformed a graceful redirect, casting doubt on the entire affair of Kern wanted for murder. "One does have to wonder what British and French Consulates really want with him. Maybe, he is not actually a cold-blooded killer at all. What if they wanted him silenced, and that whole murder charge was made-up to throw everyone off track?"

Crisp raised an index finger for emphases. "Think about it, why chase halfway around the world for a young pup? What if he saw something they don't want anyone knowing about?"

Crivitz took the hook, line and sinker, bending the rod and wanting more. What lurked behind closed doors at French and British Consulates? He inquired, "Are you saying representatives from Foreign Consulates would lie to the police?"

Crisp jerked the line and set the hook, "Ever met a politician you trusted? I sure as hell haven't."

Enthralled by a potential conspiracy, Chief Crivitz wanted to hear more. "What do ya reckon he knows?"

"If I couldn't answer that, we'd all be happy," Crisp replied, "If one of your officers did locate him, simply for safety sake of the boy, it is best not inform those looking for him. Perhaps, what he needs is military protection. We do have safe houses for these types of situations. I happen to know of a few here in the city where he would be safe."

Again, Crivitz nodded and thought for moment. A safe house for witnesses to a crime was something the city should consider. The city had nothing of that nature. Not wanting to sound behind the times he opted, "Yep, you may be right on that count. If my boys do catch him, I'll be sure and let you know. You could place him under military protection. That is until we sort things out, but you have to keep me in the loop."

Crisp concluded, "Yes, it'd be in the best interest of the boy, not to mention national security." For good measure he mentioned, "My back was itching when I got here, and seems it doesn't itch as bad now."

"My back was itching too," Crivitz agreed, "It was getting so bad, I was thinking of going to Chinatown and buy one of those fancy back itchers made to look like a small hand. Like ya said, my back feels better now."

Crisp slackened the line and allowed him to run with it. "One more thing chief, sums of money has been passing hands. People left and right, bought and sold like cattle and sheep. The fewer people involved the better.

Then Crisp glimpsed around and lowered is voice. "If I were you, I'd keep my men in the dark as much as possible. Safety of the boy if'n you know what I mean. As you heard, he worked as cabin boy on the Lady Beth, and I'd keep an eye crewmembers. Any reason to lock one up, I'd jump on it. Make La Horn's life as miserable as possible, and keep him in port longer. At least until this thing is settled with the boy."

"Of course," Crivitz said, resolved to work with him. "I'll have our sketch artist redraw a new poster and list him as the lost boy of a wealthy family."

Crisp agreed, "Sounds like a good idea. I've a party to prepare for. Again, thanks for your assistance regarding tonight." He left Crivitz holding a false sense of involvement with a mysterious investigation. With Chief Crivitz looming beyond the shadows, it gave him an edge if later needed.

Part Two

Garden Party

13

Crisp, Muser and Steadson arrived at the Regal Hotel for Ackerland's party with VIP passes in hand. They skittered a wide crowd, after which were delayed by hotel guards checking invitations against guest lists.

Upon entry they parted-ways, Steadson spotted the mayor of San Francisco, while Muser headed toward a group of women and tables that surrounded the dance floor. A Mexican band accented the air with festival music. Cheerful couples jammed the dance floor, stepping to the culture of Mexico.

Crisp's love of Mexican music was another reason he had chosen to live in California. Although from the East Coast, he had become a Californian. California had it all, pleasant weather along the coastline, snow in the mountains and vast deserts.

Crisp trotted up a series of cast-iron steps to the top floor, and gazed downward. He smiled and lightly waved at Hanna Steadson. As Hanna mingled from group to group, her dark blue silk gown flowed inches above the hardwood floor. She was fine woman of taste, carrying etiquette with everyone she encountered.

Crisp capped a head-over-heals rush and focused on his mission. Instinctive, he surveyed the circle entryway of the hotel. A spacious lobby converted into a dance area for the night provided room to move.

Counters that normally served as registration for overnight hotel guests, was tonight doubling as an open bar. Finely carved pillars and glass-stained windows rang of wealthy elite. On the top floor and located outside of the three eating rooms, an expansive balcony wrapped the rooms together.

The hotel sat high atop of a hill, offering an impressive view of city street gas-lamps, and during daylight hours a spectacular view of the bay. Because it was a recently constructed building, Crisp believed the hotel would withstand a major earthquake. Since the last quake, architects used stronger supports for building designs. Fancy pillars were thick as hundred-year old Norwegian pines and wrought iron used to construct staircases.

Crisp meandered onto an outside balcony. Amazed, he gazed across expansive flowerbeds and tree gardens lit by kerosene torches. The garden area was roped-off and guarded too keep party crashers away. In the distance valley, gas streetlights from San Francisco sparkled like gold stones amidst a wide river.

Squeaking wheels of an arriving carriage caught Crisp's attention. He stared at a circular drive directly below. Guests were dressed as if fit for burial. Women wore long flowing dresses edged with fancy lacings, and silk scarfs draped over their shoulders. Men wearing white shirts, black pants and suit coats, stood at either side of the garden-way entry, puffing on cigars or smoking pipes.

Crisp returned into the interior balcony, looked down into the ballroom. A large than expected number younger women caught his attention. They were dressed in the latest fashions. He suspected a portion were working girls, hired by Ackerland to please his male guests. It was likely many had hopes of landing a wealthy man at the gathering.

As the band played, Muser danced with a beautiful blonde haired young woman, spinning her like a top and pulling her in close, cheek to cheek. For the son of a hog farmer, Muser had a refined taste in women, not to mention several clever dance steps.

Below and across the floor, Captain Bristol acknowledged Crisp's presence with a subtle nod. He wore full dress-blues, complete with yellow strings around his shoulders, white gloves neatly tucked behind his belt and yellow tassels dangling off a saber hanging at his side.

Crisp was grateful he was not confined to a dress uniform, and was unsure that he would ever fit into one again. Once this assignment was completed, perhaps it was time to resign. Step into the real world of business, and put aside all-pretenses as Shepherd had put it.

Although the hotel interior had plenty of lighting, Crisp saw shadows everywhere. People gathered at corners and spoke at whispers. Businessmen concerned with a pending war back East. It was conceivable they pondered how to profit from mayhem and death at a distance, while remaining safe beyond the Continental Divide.

If Ackerland had his way uniting the country this side of the Continental Divide, any armies coming from the East would not make it through the Rocky Mountains.

From a safe vantage point, Crisp watched military officers conversing among each other. Colonel Montgomery received an invitation but was unable to attend.

Given Colonel Baker's recent quotes in local papers that *California should side with the North,* it was surprising to see him attending Ackerland's party. Presumably, Colonel Baker was filling in for Montgomery.

Crisp noted Steadson gracing steps toward the third level balcony, carrying two crystal glasses of burgundy wine. He permitted himself a pleasing smile. His heart raced. No, he warned himself. Although she was clearly attracted to him, this was not a time for romance.

Steadson's face glowed. "It was nice of you to invite me as your guest." She passed him a glass, then glimpsed over her shoulder at the crowded floor below. "I'm never one to pass on a chance to raise money for the hospital. With the city's wealthiest people in attendance, it allows me to network on the behalf of the university. Fundraising for medical research and health related needs transcend political indifferences."

Crisp guided her onto the outdoor balcony. Together, they absorbed the night horizon. Buoyant, he raised his glass and sniffed the aroma of wine. Pleased, he sipped it and commented, "Ahhh… Another fine Napa Valley Wine."

Again, Crisp sniffed the aroma and amended, "California should market her wines back East. It is a downright shame France has cornered the market. We should be breaking their grip with this new and better product. Maybe instead of shooting each other in war, they'd toast this nation's notable accomplishments."

An unexpected guest rambled toward the outside balcony, spoiling Crisp's moment of admirable taste. Annoyed, he lowered his glass and remarked, "Here comes trouble."

Crivitz was wearing a baggy gray tweed suit that appeared one size too large and hung on his shoulders. He limped on his left side, giving him an awkward gait.

Crisp thought perhaps, Crivitz was once a heavy-set man who recently lost weight and not had a new suit tailored.

Crivitz arrived with a respectful nod for Doctor Steadson. "Evening my dear, I hope my friend here isn't boring you."

Crisp extended his hand. "Chief Crivitz, I'm surprised to see you here." He nodded at Hanna and introduced her, "This is Doctor Steadson."

Uncle-like, Crivitz took Hanna Steadson's hands then stepped back, took a worthy look at her and said, "It's good to see you, again Hanna. It's a shame your father's not alive to witness your accomplishments. He was an upstanding citizen, a fine doctor and decent man. He is missed at my Tuesday night poker game."

"He was a noble man," agreed Hanna, her eyes lowering toward her feet.

Crivitz turned his attention to Crisp. His grin out-shinned the cloud lace moon above them. "After hearing about this get together, I simply had to come. Being Chief of Police for a district downtown, reckoned I ought be here and let the public know I am a respectable and cultured man."

Attentive to surroundings, Crivitz leaned back and peered along the inter balcony. Ackerland stood at the nearby doorway of another room, finishing a conversation with people inside. Beaming, he waved Ackerland to join them.

Perturbed, Ackerland excused himself and stepped onto the balcony. Crivitz either missed or ignored an agitated glare on Ackerland's face and proceeded, "Cliff, I'd like you to meet Mister Crisp."

Ackerland frowned at improper usage of his first name, Clifford as Cliff.

Radiant, Crivitz continued without losing stride, "I recently learned Mister Crisp resigned his commission in the army to open an import and export business near the piers called the A. R & B. He's a good man and I thought…."

Ackerland cleared his throat and extended a political handshake. "Nice to meet you Mister Crisp… I do hope your venture into the world of business meets with success."

Crisp shook Ackerland's hand. "Thank you." Courteous, he bowed slightly and gestured at Steadson. "I'd like you to meet Doctor Hanna Steadson. She's taken a teaching position at the new medical university."

Ackerland lifted Doctor Steadson's hand, kissed the top of it and offered a raised smile. "The pleasure is mine. As far as smarts, I've always thought in-the-over-all scheme of things, women had one-up on us men. We need more women entering the medical field."

Steadson recalled having overhead Ackerland's name regarding an ongoing investigation. She pardoned herself and left Crisp breathing room with Ackerland. After several steps, she decided to take Crivitz along with her. She stared over her shoulder and requested, "Chief would you care to escort me?"

As Crivitz waddled toward her, she grinned at Ackerland and hinted, "A donation wouldn't hurt your political standings within the medical community. However, I'm not one to be pushy on such matters." Then, she rotated an outward palm toward the chief and smiled. "Shall we?"

Crivitz took her hand and said, "Of course madam…" Again uncle-like he intertwined their elbows, led her toward the steps and began telling a joke. As they strolled down the cast-iron staircase, Steadson chuckled at his amble sense of humor.

Ackerland's smile tightened into a lip locked grin. Watching Crivitz lead Hanna Steadson down the iron staircase, his distaste for Crivitz emerged in the form of a soft grunt.

Casual, Crisp injected a comment to learn Ackerland's judgment of Crivitz. "No disrespect intended of the man or the office of police chief. While I doubt he intends it, at times he is bothersome. I tell you, he has the ears of an elephant."

"That he does," Ackerland agreed, stared at them and shifted to the topic of women. "Good God, that Ms. Steadson is a woman of character." His eyes meet Crisp. "She's not the marrying kind, unless of course a man doesn't mind having a woman controlling his life."

Crisp reflected on Hanna's note from yesterday and conceded, "For sure, she does have self-determination."

Ackerland thought for a moment and commented, "Self-determination is a worthy phrase." His hands spread wide as if reading a newspaper headline. He stated, "California, land of self-determination."

Then Ackerland gazed at him and searched for tell-tell signs of a political stance. He inquired, "Has a nice ring to it, don't you think?" Not waiting for an answer he continued, "It is inevitable, war is coming back East. What side do you think will win? North or South?"

Crisp shrugged. "Does it really matter? I simply want to be on the right side when it is over. A man has to make a living. Wouldn't you agree?"

Ackerland nodded, still accessing the man. Unsure what to make of him, he agreed, "Yes, a man does… Perhaps it is for the best if the nation splits into sections. The way we are grabbing territories and depending on how territories divide themselves, we may end-up with fifty or sixty States by the end of this century. Our forefathers escaped from power-crazed kings, barons and noblemen in Europe. All that power could be too much for one President to handle." He glimpsed downward at his guests, ready to move-on and greet them.

"You may be right," Crisp said, resolved to keep Ackerland talking. "It's an awfully huge responsibility for one man. To be honest, I was never in favor of California becoming a State. As far as I am concerned, the Rockies create a nice dividing line between East and West. How North and South divide, I don't really care. My father's business is in New York and far from where any dividing line may be drawn. One of my younger brothers is in Florida looking for the right port city to open an extension of the family business like I've done here."

Ackerland's attention reeled back from the dance floor below. Surprised, he inquired, "Florida?"

By design, Crisp smiled. "If the Union does divide into separate counties, we'd like to have every angle covered. Better for business after the dust settles, providing a favorable position in the marketplace."

Crisp raised his palms and stated, "Not that my family wants to profit in the event this country does go to war. We are simply positioning ourselves accordingly. No matter what comes, trade and commerce will continue." He sighed as if emotionally drained. "But on a personal level, I'd like to see the West freed from lawmakers in Washington."

Ackerland's resolve on the issue surfaced with an established response, "Yes, I understand completely. In the long run, as a separate country we have a greater advantage. Which is why I am in favor of seceding from the Union." His grin widened. "Your suggestion of using the Rockies as a dividing line? It is a thought for later. First, we have to see how California swings on this pending war issue."

Again, Ackerland glimpsed past Crisp's shoulder and toward ground level of the hotel. His guests were gathering near an eating room on the main level and waiting for the doors to open.

Crisp realized he was losing Ackerland's attention. He wanted to leave a lasting impression. "If you don't mind me saying, we do have a widely diverse people living here in California. Our diversity here ought to teach the rest of the world a lesson or two."

Ackerland's interest peaked from the ground floor and returned to Crisp. He asked, "How so?"

"As I see it," Crisp explained, "Diversity is our wealthiest resource not gold. Mining and panning will only last for a time an industry. As a people, we should be looking toward the future. If a man were able to pull our wide diversity together as a rallying cry of sort, he'd be able to do most anything. Having the support of the masses in general never hurt a man's cause."

A modest ruckus on the dance floor below diverted Crisp's attention. Muser had lost the girl during a dance where partners changed hands a number of times. Another man was whisking her across the dance floor and further away from Muser. Clearly, Muser was displeased at the prospect of losing her.

Crisp sensed a fight brewing and wanted to skirt downstairs, grab Muser and haul him outside for a scolding.

"Mister Crisp?" Ackerland said, pulling Crisp's attention back to the balcony.

Crisp forced a smile and apologized, "Sorry, I was distracted for a moment, the dance floor got a tad loud."

Ackerland glimpsed over his shoulder, then back at Crisp with a trifling grin. "Speaking of diversity, there's a variety of fine looking women here tonight." He pointed at the man who had snatched Muser's dance partner. "I see my stepson Richard has found a lady to keep him company. You should consider joining the crowd. Dancing is fine way to meet a woman."

"I don't dance," Crisp replied and faked a hint of embarrassment. In truth, he was worried about Muser and Ackerland's stepson having a fistfight over the girl. With Bristol nearby, there was no chance to make excuses for Muser.

Puppy-like, Muser had sulked into a corner off the dance floor, stood alone and stared at his feet. Crisp hoped Muser remained timid.

Ackerland patted Crisp's shoulder and assured, "No need to be embarrassed. I'm sure there's any number of women who'd be pleased to converse with a fine gentleman of your standing in the community. If nothing else, sit at a table and enjoy a few drinks."

Again, Crisp's eyes drifted to Muser who had left his corner.

Pent-up, Muser was working his way through the dance crowd, searching for his lost love.

Crisp kept the conversation going. "This new branch office for the family business has kept me busy. It doesn't leave room for romance."

Ackerland nodded and unknowingly confirmed ties with La Horn. "Earlier today, I had a Captain La Horn at my office looking for a cargo bound to the Far East. Couldn't help him, I deal mainly with cattle. I invited him here tonight, hoping the poor man may meet someone with a shipment of goods."

Crisp spoke nonchalant, not reveling he had gained valuable information. "Nothing headed that direction. I'm expecting a shipment of Chinese Herbs to arrive any day. Cargo bound for the Far East is increasingly difficult to find. Merchandise going south around the Cape and back East is easy enough to find." In part, what he had told Ackerland was true. For A. R & B to work as front, they needed too actually conduct business. Earlier that day he had placed an order for Chines Herbs with a local shipper.

Ackerland inquired, "Chinese Herbs?"

Crisp explained, "Chinese herbs used for healing. It is the latest craze back East. I'm riding the wave for as long as it's cresting and there's money to be made."

Ackerland issued a standard response, "I understand business does come first. Speaking of which, I must be going. Before I do, please consider attending a luncheon at noon on Thursday of this week. A number of business associates, mainly men of like-mindedness will be attending. It'd be in your best interest to join us and make a few contacts."

Crisp did not want to appear overeager and pondered consideration of the invite. Then he replied, "I'll reschedule my calendar for it."

"I'll have an invitation drawn-up and delivered first thing tomorrow to your office. Ninth and?"

Crisp answered, "Last building on the right if he is coming from downtown. We're located near the piers." He spread his hands shoulder width and said, "Large green and white sign on top, A. R & B Imports and Exports."

"I'll see you at the luncheon," Ackerland confirmed and shook Crisp's hand. "It was nice meeting you, and hopefully your new business venture will prosper here in California."

"It's a fresh new land," replied Crisp, "I'm sure we'll do fine. It was good to meet you as well." Satisfied, he watched Ackerland descend the stairs and meld amid the party.

Ackerland greeted people as he mingled with crowds looking to leave an impression on him. For a man without previous political ambitions, he acted as if a seasoned politician from Sacramento. He was slick and cunning, choosing each word carefully.

Thinking of Chief Crivitz, Crisp smiled. Thanks to an introduction from Crivitz, a glimpse into Ackerland's inner circle of political cronies was possible. Earlier that day, Crivitz had struck him as the type of man who inadvertently blundered. Second thoughts concerning involvement with Chief Crivitz vanished.

With concern for Muser temporarily forgotten, Crisp stepped onto an outside balcony looking for solitude. An invite to Ackerland's business luncheon was a move in the right direction. For the remainder of the party, he only needed to avoid La Horn. Opportunity knocked directly below the balcony when La Horn arrived outside.

Private security guards provided by the Regal Hotel, kept reporters and party-crasher at bay. La Horn shoved his way through the crowd, waving an invitation above his head and clamored, "Get out of my way and let a man of importance through!"

A pair of hefty security guards halted La Horn at the doors and verified his name against a guest list.

Crisp rotated a wineglass between his fingers. He smiled, extended his arm over the railing, aimed and released. Quick, he stepped back from view. La Horn's agonizing howl carried above crowded noises. Over a loud commotion, he heard a security guard calling for a doctor.

Crivitz was returning to the balcony, heard the turmoil, rushed unto the balcony and peered down. Dumbfounded, he gazed at Crisp. "You should see this! Some poor gent is laid flat on his back with a bloody head. I'd best be getting down there and see what happened. Take statements and what-not, don't want anyone thinking I ain't doing my job."

Crisp held his chuckle as Crivitz waddled toward the steps. Without intentions, he had struck two buzzards with one drop of a glass. La Horn and Crivitz would be busy for a short time. Casual, he put both hands into his pants pockets, whistled and strolled down the winding staircase.

14

For the next three hours of the party, Crisp mingled with several of Ackerland's business associates. He enjoyed a lettuce salad with green pepper, black olives and wild onions. An elegant main meal consisted of boiled red potatoes, a choice of vegetables and thin cut strips of prime beef, all fresh from Ackerland's ranch.

Crips topped his meal with a small slice of hot cornbread that melted buttery in his mouth. For dessert, there was German chocolate cake. If forcing anything else down his stomach, he thought it would explode. Yet, he managed a slice of cake.

While the band took a deserved break, a star filled sky drew guests outside. Partygoers lingered beneath kerosene touch lamps and chatted. The garden had beautiful flowerbeds, palm trees, statutes and water fountains. The land of opportunity and gold was the popular subject. A few people ventured short-lived discussions over the pending conflict between North and South.

Tired of mixing among San Francisco's elite, Crisp filtered indoors. A redwood pine grandfather clock chimed the midnight hour. He had hoped to grace Hanna Steadson's presence on the dance floor. It was not to be.

At ten o'clock, Hanna Steadson had implied, "Enough hobnobbing for one night. I've let every money mongrel here know their generous support for the medical school is expected." Then, she promptly deserted the party and caught a carriage ride back into the city.

Two hours later, Crisp felt drained as well. He had done all the socializing a man could stand for one night. It was time to locate Muser and return home. From the center lobby, he spotted Muser three floors up.

As if a lost puppy, Muser was searching for a woman he had met earlier on the dance floor. His soft call echoed into the vaulted ceiling above. "Jane, Jane, Jane… Darling where are ya?"

Crisp rendered a silent assessment of his crew. "I've got an irate captain about to blow a blood vessel, a drunkard, an addicted gambler, a grouchy old man with a nasty disposition, a cold-blooded killer, and a womanizer. Lord only knows what Taylor's personal problems are, but I'm sure they'll surface sooner or later. No one winds-up under my command by happenstance they're dumped on me from elsewhere."

As Crisp crested the top of a spiral staircase, a ruckus rambled from a third floor bedroom suite caught his attention. Paranoid, he darted into the large bedroom. Once inside, his fears proved true. Muser was pounding fist after fist into Ackerland's stepson Richard.

Crisp exclaimed, "What in the hell is going on?" Panicked, he wrestled Muser from on top of Richard and barked, "Get a hold of yourself!"

Enraged, Muser shook himself free. Fists clinched at either side he stepped away and panted, "I was doing my duty as a gentleman." He pointed an accusing finger at Richard. "He's the problem, sir. I had do something, he waz about to violate Ms. Jane." Pleading, he looked at Crisp. "I couldn't stand for it, sir. A woman's honor and virtue was at stake!"

Crisp raised a hand flat toward Muser's face. "I don't wanna hear it." Perturbed, he looked at the large bed and groaned. Ms. Jane lay passed-out drunk, the top of her dress ripped open, exposing her petticoat. Buttons from her dress lay scattered across a Persian rug on the floor. Although Muser was justified protecting Ms. Jane, Captain Bristol was bound to throw a fit.

Richard back crawled into a corner and wiped blood from the corner of his mouth. Before able to say a word, his stepfather stormed into the room.

Ackerland saw his stepson's bloody face. Richard's upper front teeth were gone and his broken nose bleeding as if a fountain. Stone-face, Ackerland glared at the passed-out woman then at his stepson.

Crisp tensed and reached beneath his coat, touching a shoulder-holstered gun. Then he thought better of it and withdrew the thought. Foresight had paid-off when he ordered Muser to leave his sidearm behind at the A. R & B. Given Ackerland's expression, he suspected it was not the first time Richard had taken unfair advantage of a woman.

Before Crisp or Muser was able to inject, Richard attempted to justify the presence of a passed-out drunk and half-naked woman on the bed. "I was only getting me some, pa." Miffed, he shook a closed fist at Muser. "This here tin-horn barged in on us." His eyes appealed for mercy with a simple question, "Ain't that why ya hired all them whores was to keep us men folk happy?"

Brisk, Crisp stepped to the entryway and sealed the coming tempest behind closed doors. When things were looking up, Muser had dragged their investigations into the gutter. Saving him from sentence in a stockade was not going to be easy.

Muser delivered a straight-faced verbal blow, stunning everyone. "Why I didn't realize Councilman Pitt's niece Ms. Jane was a commonplace whore! If you waz to ask me, I thought she'd make a fine wife. Putting a young-man like myself, or your stepson in the right places at the right times."

Then Muser hammered his point, "A position of political influence sure ain't a bad place to be standing, not when laws are being passed effecting trade. Who knows what a little family influence can manage to accomplish? Had I know Councilman Pitt's niece was a hired whore… Well, I'd not beat the shit out of Richard's sorry-arse face! But I thought Ms. Jane's honor was a stake!"

Ackerland's legs wobbled between rage at Richard and fear of an unknown Councilman Pitt. Alarmed, he stared at Muser and questioned, "Councilman Pitt's niece?" Dumbfounded, he gawked at his stepson. "Richard, how could you? I hired twenty-plus working girls for tonight! Wasn't that enough? Couldn't you find one of them on the dance floor? They weren't that difficult to find."

Ackerland threw his arms high and bellowed, "Damn it to hell Richard! If you'd get your arse out of bed before the sun falls, you could have had pick of the litter before everyone arrived." Unsure, he looked at Muser and asked, "I've never heard of a Councilman Pitt. Where is he from?"

Muser tossed a mean glare at Richard whose blood covered the expensive imported rug beneath his feet. Barely holding his wrath and explained, "Had lazy arse Richard had spent time getting know her before attempting to violate her, he'd learned Councilman Pitt was from Portland's southeast side. His niece was down here with her father on a business trip. Her father is the younger brother of Councilman Pitt. This afternoon, Ms. Jane and her father stopped over at Doc Steadson's place. Her father had a corn removed from his toe."

Muser exhaled and gathered air for his next round. "Mister Ackerland, her father learned about your get-together here. Said, he wanted to learn what you had to say about an independent California. Since North and South are at each other's throats, her father being the Councilman's brother and all, he thought for Oregon's sake he outta hear your view on things. In case California strikes for independence when the war broke, he figured Oregon should have options to consider."

"Where is he now?" inquired Ackerland, concerned her father might come looking for his daughter at any moment.

"Ms. Jane's father left the party early cuz his foot was hurting," Muser said and nodded at the bed. "Ms. Jane stayed and told me herself, her daddy liked what he heard. In fact, he stated something to the effect Oregon should consider striking out with California and form an independent nation." Again, he glared at Richard and sneered, "Lookin' like that won't be happening now will it, Richard?"

Crisp was about to inquire what hotel in the city Mister Pitt was lodging, when without a knock Captain Bristol booted the doors wide open and blazed into the room. Five of Regal's private hotel guards rushed into the suite, directly behind Bristol.

"This isn't the army's concern!" Crisp enjoyed protesting at Bristol and continued, "A simple fight between two men over a whore. Nothing that should be concerning you…"

Bristol saw Richard's bloody face and noted Muser's skinned knuckles. He kicked an iron glare at Crisp, waiting to hear an explanation, yet not wanting to expose their undercover operation.

"Mister Ackerland?" Bristol inquired, barely able to drop his ironclad glare at Crisp. "Is everything all right?" He tossed Crisp another burning glimpse. "At the moment, he is not on the best of terms with the army."

Restrained, Ackerland raised his hands. "Yes captain, everything is fine. The entire affair is settled. If you'd excuse us, these two men need to work-out an apology between them."

Bristol scowled at Crisp, his silent message clear. From losing a witness, to killing two possible suspects, to killing a witness and now beating Ackerland's stepson it was not looking good for Crisp and his team. He pressed, "Are you sure?"

"Yes," Ackerland confirmed and motioned the Hotel Regal's men to ease Captain Bristol toward the door.

Once Bristol and Regal Hotel security had cleared the room, Crisp again closed the double doors and slid a lock into place. In unison, Ackerland and Crisp exhaled tension breaths.

Worried, Ackerland looked at Muser and inquired, "Are you new to the Bay Area?"

"Yes sir," Muser answered, considerably calmed and recalling Crisp had ordered him to use proper English.

"Perhaps you're in need of some money?" Ackerland offered a bribe to ensure silence regarding the near rape of a Councilman's niece. "A little something to tide you over until you're situated. Consider it a grant, no need to pay it back."

Muser looked at Crisp.

Crisp cleared his throat. "Mister Ackerland, this man works for me. He's been under my father's employment for years and doesn't need any cash. My father sent him from back East to give me a hand opening the new branch office. You needn't worry about him saying anything..." He passed Bristol's earlier ironclad glare at Muser and suggested, "Do we, Clancy?"

Muser took the hint, cupped both hands at waist level, lowered his chin and yielded, "No sir, I don't need any money, my room and board are covered. The A. R & B pays me a decent wage."

A wave of relief washed Ackerland's stressed face. Ms. Jane began blasting an obnoxious snore. Ackerland and Crisp stared at her, each restraining their chuckles.

Ackerland looked up from his stare and commented, "Captain Bristol doesn't appear to care none for you. He is a man on the verge of a stroke, those veins in his forehead looked as if they're going to bust."

Crisp responded, "Shortly after being transferred here, I resigned my commission. Captain Bristol had high hopes I would take command upon his retirement. Reckon you'd say he's a tad disappointed with me. Putting money before country doesn't set good with him."

Ackerland shifted toward a casual manner, "One man's enemies are another man's allies." He glimpsed over his shoulder at Muser and grimaced. "At the risk of sounding rude, she isn't the marrying kind. Not with a snore that'd wake a sleeping bear in the dead of winter."

Crisp was getting a handle on Ackerland's character as a man with a low regard for women. It was the second time Ackerland had said, *isn't the marrying kind*. He wondered what Ackerland considered as a perfect woman. They had no history on Ackerland's first wife – other than she died soon after marriage in a carriage accident. Richard was a toddler when Ackerland married for a second time. The second Mrs. Ackerland bore him no children of his own, leaving Richard heir to the Ackerland cattle throne.

Muser nodded as if glad to discover her snoring before offering a hand in marriage. "She's got one mean snore. If we were able to harness it – it'd send a fleet of sailing ships clear across the Pacific." His humor raised soft laughter from everyone, including a painful chuckle from Richard.

Crisp promised to fix things before Ms. Jane awakened from her drunken slumber. Stacking the deck in his favor, he promptly sent Ackerland and Richard from away, removing the risk of potential political damage.

Behind closed doors, Crisp and Muser began putting the room back in order. Muser undressed Ms. Jane down to her petticoat and tucked her under the blankets.

Crisp discovered a sewing kit inside one of the dresser drawers began stitching buttons to Ms. Jane's dress. As Crisp sewed buttons, Muser rolled the blood-splattered Persian rug and tossed it out of a window. Then, Muser went downstairs to carry the rug into the underbrush.

Crisp folded Miss Jane's dress and laid it on a chair next the bed. Unsure, he glimpsed around the room. Everything was in order except the missing rug. Sealing their deception required the doors were locked from the inside. It would appear as if she had locked the doors and fallen asleep, save and secure.

Cautious, Crisp climbed out the window and eased himself onto a ledge. Looking down, he recalled Kern's daring escape. He found a greater respect for the lad's courage. Unlike the narrow ledge Kern had used, this one was wider.

Crisp was not risking a full-scale tittering situation, after a few feet he reached another window. He peered inside, expecting to see a male guest with one of many working girls. The room was empty and dark. He eased the window open and crawled inside. Quick, he stepped softly across the room, then paused and listened at the door.

Discreet, Crisp opened a door leading onto the interior balcony. The band had returned from break was strumming a slow dance tune. Sounds of music lured guests from outdoor gardens and back to the dance floor.

Crisp made his way downstairs and melted with the crowd, issuing a number of goodbyes to those he had met earlier that evening. As he neared the main entry to the Regal Hotel, Ackerland gave him a casual parting nod.

Thanks to Private Clancy Muser, they had gained a barging chip for later. Had Muser had lied? Was it possible there was no such person as Councilman Pitt? Why did Hanna fail to mention Ms. Jane and her father had visited her office? Then again, why should she?

Exhausted physically and mentally, Crisp exited the lobby. On the front circle roadway, Muser was waiting with their horse drawn carriage. He eased onto the carriage and sighed, "It's been a long day, let's get on home."

Muser slapped the reins and grunted, "What we just did wasn't right, sir. That gal has a right to know what almost happened. She needs to realize what type of person Richard is, in case they ever got romantically involved."

As the carriage jerked forward, Crisp thought of one thing. Muse had nearly jeopardized their assignment. His tone flattened, "We saved this investigation from another disaster. From what I gathered by facial expressions, this was not the first time Richard acted on lustful illusions. I'm sure Ackerland will whip that boy's arse into next month."

Crisp considered Muser's military file. Nothing had suggested womanizing, fistfights or pathological liar. Often, circumstances kept certain things out of a person's military record. Muser's was clearly a problem child from another command, transferred to avoid whatever headache he had caused.

Crisp needed to know what triggered the transfer. "What happened at Fort Mc Kay?" His inquiry was more of an order than a question.

Muser's face tightened. "Sir?"

"Don't sir me," Crisp continued his military tone. "What happened that got you transferred here? They don't assign winners under my command. What was it that got you consigned here?"

Their carriage had reached a point along the road, where they began a downward decline toward the city. Muser levered the brake on and off, easing the pull gravity on the carriage. He smirked and asked, "You want the plain and simple of it?"

Upset, Crisp clarified "Yes, I want the plain and simple of it. No lies, exaggerations, and or leaving something out that I should be knowing about."

Private Muser's face beamed. "I shared my prize procession with a visiting colonel's daughter." Abrasive, he grabbed his crouch. "It's a gift that's meant to be shared. Before shipping-out, I shared my gift with her again. The second time around, she brought a friend. Which as it turned out was my then captain's nineteen-year-old sister. Me and those two gals got along fine. It was heavenly bliss for all concerned. I've never seen two gals go at it like that… It was…"

Crisp cut him short, "What? You slept with the daughter and sister of two superior officers? Where was your head at?" Then he decided to drop the question. "Never, mind. Forget I asked."

Muser grinned. "Actually, we got no sleep. I'll gladly tell you where my head was at, sir. I waz giving those so-called *Superior Officers* something to think about. After I was gone, I'm sure those gals brought up my name countless times."

Then Muser's conceit notched up a level, "By now I reckon those superior officers are tired hearing those two gals pissing and moaning about my transfer." Cocking an eyebrow, he deadpanned a stare at him and inquired, "Sir, does that answer your question?"

Crisp yanked the reins from Muser's hands, and steered the horses and carriage to the side of the road. After Muser's humble attitude the past few days, it was shocking to see his true nature surface.

Agitated, Crisp exerted his command position. "Don't sir me in that manner because I won't stand for it. I'll knock you silly and have your sorry arse locked inside of a stockade on bread and water for a week."

Traces of rye whiskey on Muser's breath swept past Crisp. Liquor was doing most of the talking. "Okay, I won't call you sir. But what should I call you?" Then he slightingly slapped Crisp's shoulder. "Relax sir, don't be so uptight. You're starting to remind me of old man Bristol. If'n his arse were any tighter, I'd doubt he could fart."

Crisp dismissed further agitation. He stared across the valley and changed the subject. "From here the city looks peaceful. In cities of this size, there are people who prowl like wild cats ready to eat you alive. You'd be wise to remember that."

Suddenly, the shrieking echo of a woman rescinded from the city's lower red light district. Her echoing cry ended suddenly as if put to death.

Muser winced, his nerves rattled. "Did ya hear that? What a God awful sound…"

Crisp exhaled a stressful breath and confirmed he had heard it. "Yes, I heard it." Then, he slapped the reins. After the carriage jerked forward, he returned the reins to Muser and said, "Given what I read in the newspaper concerning a girl in the red-light district last night, I reckon another one met the blunt end of a hammer."

Muser slowed the horses, keeping their speed at a casual walk. He commented, "Yesterday, a carpenter working at the A. R&B complained his hammer went missing. More-than-likely, he misplaced it."

Crisp nodded. His thoughts fell to Shepherd and Kern. Shepherd should have checked back by now. Perhaps, Shepherd decided to keep the journal and Kern. He discarded reconsideration of Shepherd's character, and hoped he had accurately judged him.

15

Kern sat, leaned against a palm tree and fingered through food folded between a large silk-napkin. Earlier and hidden behind a tree, he had watched a man drag a rolled rug into the brush. He resisted an urge to unroll the rug, fearful a dead body lay inside.

At first, he thought the man had seen him stealing food from the hotel galley. However, the man was too busy sneaking around to have noticed him. The man reminded him of those who had guarded his room at the doctor's house. Either-way, the man was gone.

He was growing accustomed to a never-ending singing of crickets. He realized maimed animals did not last long in the wild. A loss of hearing dimmed chances of survival. Yet, he had a strong advantage over other animals, a smarter brain. In addition, spirits of his birth and adoptive aborigine families were looking after him, not to forget Carl Ver Haven as well.

What type of predators lived in this new land, and how to avoid becoming a meal for hungry animal? Large and small creatures could be deadly. Small creatures often had venom. Larger ones had claws and fans. Food was another issue. He planned to watch animals eat before eating himself to learn what was safe and what to shun.

Between mouthfuls of wild turkey and brown rice, he drew swigs from a bottle and washed down the nourishment. The liquid taste reminded him of Jupie Berries from his homeland of Kakadu. When berries were in season, the Namra Clan created juice from the berries and celebrated.

After Kern finished eating, he gazed skyward and thought of his aborigine family. He pondered the sounds of his homeland. Laughter of a kookaburra bird, night bellows of crocodiles and howls of a lonely dingo in the night.

It was a life forever lost. He missed songs around a campfire, missed dreamtime stories about ancient spirits. The clan lived in dreamtime. Amid a new land of confusion, dreamtime was no more. He now lived a nightmare.

Kern decided, perhaps a change of clothing could settle his mood. Uncaring, he discarded his clothing worn onboard the Lady Beth. Stark naked, he dug into the pack and pulled his tattered brown loincloth. That afternoon, he had washed his loincloth inside of a stream and dried it on a rock beneath an afternoon sun.

Again wearing aborigine attire, he curled against the palm tree. His memories ebbed and flowed amidst chirping crickets. He hated the white hunters who had made a sport of killing aborigine tribesmen. He hated La Horn, Fat Sam and the rest of the Lady Beth crew.

Onboard the ship, only Carl and Caleb had expressed any measure of kindness. Carl was dead and buried at sea, murdered by La Horn. Caleb had chosen between him and La Horn, the latter winning.

His biological father and mother remained hazy images. He considered what his life had been if not for their deaths.

Then he mulled what if Baland – white hunters had not driven his clan into the flames of the Fire Season. Tonight, he would have been safely snuggled with a dog, or two dogs depending on how cold the night. The colder the night, the more dogs he snuggled with for warmth. Tonight was a three-dog night. He missed Bristol's cold nose nudging him, missed feeling Bristol's warm fur against him.

Chilled to his core, Kern trembled. In the Australia aborigine languages, no one word described home. Home was land, sky, water, sun and moon. Home was his clan and other clans roaming the outback.

When speaking of America, Carl had used the word home. After long talks with him, Kern came to understand the word home and its meaning. America was homeland of his long-dead biological father. On board the Lady Beth, Kern had trained his thoughts to regard America as his true home.

Kern rugged wild-child of the Australian Outback of Kakadu, who later became a tough street-kid at Limmen Bight, and then a robust cabin boy onboard the Lady Beth melted away.

Distraught he rolled onto his side, pulled his knees to his chest, rocked himself and sobbed using the Namra dialect.

"I want my fathers, I want to go homeland, I want to go land, sky, sun, moon and waters... Namra, Kakadu, Namra, Kakadu, Namra, Kakadu..."

16

As morning broke over foothills along the eastern horizon, Crisp and Hindor sat on a second floor balcony of the A. R & B. Silent Bristol the dog laid at Crisp's feet, his chin resting on his paws. Sipping a tin of hot coffee, Crisp considered the day ahead.

Muser had left an hour ago with the companies' carriage, returning to the Regal with hopes of offering Jane Pitt a ride into the city. Ring, Trick and Taylor were downstairs sponging bathing in the kitchen. Doctor Hanna Steadson had likely spent the night several blocks away at her combination office and home.

Crisp decided against requesting Hanna move into the A. R & B building, although Captain Bristol had suggested it twice. Crisp did not blame her for refusing. What sane woman would consider living under the same roof as this bunch?

Haphazard, Crisp spoke more to himself. "You ever see the army throw more misfits together than this bunch of losers?" He paused and gave it more thought. "It's as if they want us to fail. Doesn't make any sense does it?"

Hindor poured himself a fresh tin of coffee and blew steam away from the cup rim. Careful not to burn his tongue, he took gradual sips. A sandpiper glided past the balcony, squawking. Content, Bristol raised an eyebrow and watched the bird.

Hindor raised the pot of steaming coffee and asked, "Want me to warm your tin?"

Crisp set his cup onto a pine-plank end table. His bladder urged a pressured remark, "No thanks, I'm about ready to wet my pants as it is. Not even sure I can stand and make it to the jake outback."

Crisp sighed and returned to his earlier comment. "I took a mental stock of everyone last night. Make no mistake it is a rough bunch. We don't know enough about our three new guys to trust them. Shepherd straight-up gives me the willies."

Hindor stroked his beard and replied, "As far as I'm concerned everyone in the army is a misfit, present company included. As far as setting us up to fail?" Then he shook his head. "Nah, not likely given all that's going on back East. Put those conspiracies out of your mind… Trick, Ring, Muser and Taylor are here because of special skills regular army men lack. Sure, their skills ain't like most but look at what we're trying to do here. Normal army wouldn't cut it, at least not for this type of work. No doubt, Muser and Taylor got themselves transferred because of problems elsewhere. Then again, I'd dare say most transferees are due to personal conflicts."

Crisp stood, stepped to the railing and looked down. Bristol raised his head, following Crisp's every move. The sandpiper returned, squawking and circling the building for a second time. He considered shooting the bird, simply to end a nuisance but opted not to startle neighbors with an early morning gunshot.

Crisp said, "La Horn and Ackerland are natural criminals. Regardless of the cost to people in their path, they take what they want. Without a doubt, those pair are involved in some type of illegal activity. Ackerland is more-slick about it than La Horn, and he'll be hard one to nail on anything."

Hindor planted both feet onto another chair across from him and sipped from his tin. Relaxed, he stepped back into the conversation. "La Horn and Ackerland having criminal ties betwixt each other doesn't surprise me none. But I seriously doubt Ackerland had any doings with killing Ver Haven. I'd be willing to bet a month's pay, whatever cargo La Horn brought to this country was for Ackerland. Probably, went to another holding company and dispersed from there. Why else would have La Horn asked Ackerland about a return cargo to the Far East? Unless of course, they had business dealings in the past?"

Crisp leaned against the railing and agreed, "I'm not arguing with you on that… With opium trade waning in the Far East, most of those former buccaneers who transported the poison have returned to pirating. If La Horn isn't pirating on the side, I'd be shocked."

"Most likely is," granted Hindor. "I'd like to get a look-see at whatever secret cargo he was delivering here."

Crisp nodded. "La Horn's cargo of rice and tea was delivered a few blocks from here at Golden Bay Warehouses." He took a note pad from his pocket, glimpsed at it and said, "This morning, I'd like you and Trick to find day work there. Inspect those crates that came off the Lady Beth. It's likely, Ver Haven discovered something aboard the Lady Beth he wasn't suppose too know about."

Hindor shrugged. "Could be selling gunpowder, cannons, and cannon balls. North and South are stocking weaponry."

Crisp said, "Sounds reasonable enough, except delivering and selling weaponry isn't against the law. It had to be something else." He paused and pondered aloud. "If there was a cargo bound for Ackerland, even of a legal nature it is possible he didn't want anyone learning about it. There's no telling what Ackerland has planned beyond what he's made public. With Jim Brown's trial pending back East; it is only a matter of time until he is hung. Sure as the sun rises, his hanging will spark a fuse."

Hindor snickered, "Spark the fuse?" His brow tightened and tone gruff. "What the hell are you talking about? That fuse is near-burnt to the powder keg. Brown's hanging, provided he loses in court will be the final spark before the keg blows this nation wide-open."

A paperboy on the street halted his bicycle below the balcony and called upward, "Hey, wanna buy a paper. Headlines are bloody, again. Another woman killed in the red-light district at Nancy May's rooming house. She had her head smashed by a hammer."

Crisp cringed at the news. "Figured as much, heard her scream clear up into the lower foothills last night. Damn awful sound and disrupted a peaceable night."

The paperboy raised a hand to his brow and shielded his eyes from the morning sun. "Folks are saying her skull was cracked open like a melon. Heard tell her brain waz splattered all over the walls. When I dropped off Ms. May's paper this morning, the rest of her working gals were packing and leaving. Scared stiff I reckon. What's a poor fellow like me supposed to do? I am just coming of age, and the way it is going there won't be any women left. They're either dying or leaving town." He waved a newspaper at them and asked, "Ya wanna a paper or not? If not, I've gotta get going."

Crisp tossed a coin over the railing, and the boy pitched the paper upward. He reached over the balcony, nearly missing the catch.

The boy pocketed the change and said, "Thanks mister. Nice catch, you outta be playing ball back East."

Unexpectedly, an idea struck Crisp. As the paperboy was leaving, he waved and called, "Hold on lad, I'd like you to look at a picture for me."

A minute later, Crisp was at the front door and requesting to have the paper delivered daily. He showed him the poster of Kern, minis the torn off part of Wanted Dead or Alive. He inquired, "You have name?"

The boy replied, "Bassett." Leery, he was hesitant to comment on the drawing. "You ain't the law are ya?"

"Nope," Crisp answered truthfully, believing that law meant police and not military. He dug another coin from his pocket and passed it to him. "This might help jar your memory."

Bassett eyed Crisp carefully, judging the suit as a business type of person. He shrugged. "Ya look alright… But ya could be lying about being a lawman. I can't stand em, they're always sticking their noses into other folks' private affairs…"

Crisp glanced up at the A. R & B sign above the door and smirked, "Does that sign spell police?"

Quick witted, Bassett smarted, "I can read some, so don't be playing me for stupid. A. R & B could stand for most anything."

Crisp rolled his eyes. "Well, it sure doesn't spell p. o. l. i. c. e, or s. h. e. r. i. f. f. Back to my question, you seen this lad?" Again, he showed Bassett the drawing of Kern.

Unconvinced, Bassett's eyes pulled tight as if studying the drawing. Skeptical, he looked Crisp in the eye. "You a lawyer? Cuz ya sure ask enough questions." Crisp failed to answer, and Bassett glimpsed at the drawing for a third time.

"Yep," Bassett answered, "Saw him twice. Once yesterday, he was sneaking around behind the army office. That must've been roundabout mid-day. Spotted him this morning when I was running a paper up to the Regal. He was headed-off on a steep trail into the foothills. Heard tell he stabbed a lawman clean through the heart somewhere. I'm steering clear the likes of him. Last thing I need is old Waddles thinking I'm keep'n bad company, again."

"Waddles?" inquired Crisp, guessing it was a nickname for a local policeman or schoolmaster.

Bassett kicked up a jeer. "That's what we call old man Crivitz. If'n ya ever met him, you'll notice he walks like a duck. Quacks like one too if'n ya listen to him talk."

Last night, Crisp had noted Crivitz's peculiar walk and said, "Already met the man. If you were to run and hide in the hills, any place you'd go?"

Bassett's brow crinkled. "You sure ask questions like a lawman or maybe a lawyer. Ya never answered my question about being a lawyer."

"Well, I ain't a lawman or lawyer either," replied Crisp, then swung his arm outward toward the bay. "The boy's my nephew from across the sea… He can't hear and doesn't speak very well either… Hoping he could live a normal life, his ma and pa had him sent here to see if doctors could fix his ears. All this confusion, he's gotten scared and ran-off. He's from a country called Australia from down at the bottom side of the world."

Crisp's attitude shifted and played the sympathy card. "I reckon he's mighty scared with all that's going on. Not being able to hear makes matters worse."

"Mmm," Bassett nodded, pondering what he had heard. "Rumors about him killing a lawman and all, nothing but lies?"

Crisp stated, "Yep, rumors and lies… But he could've seen something important on his way to this country. Maybe, just maybe those people are afraid of what he might tell. Lot of folks are looking for him, important people want him to tell what he saw, and really bad people that don't want him telling."

Bassett's eyes perked. "Yep, there's reward for finding him, hundred dollars. You the one paying the big bucks mister?"

Crisp gasped, "A hundred dollars?" A second later, he wished he had avoided expressing surprise. Reward on the poster was for twenty dollars, and Crisp had not mentioned it to Bassett. His stare fell firm on Bassett. The gig was up.

"Yep," Bassett said, dodging the glare as he thumbed the strap of his newspaper carry-bag higher across his shoulder. "Read it in the paper this morning. I didn't say othing earlier, cuz I wasn't sure about ya. The paper didn't mention who'z putting up the cash."

Cautious, Bassett glimpsed around the area and informed him, "Heard tell the British are putting up fifty and French another fifty. Overheard a couple reporters saying, they didn't print that part cuz it wasn't confirmed. You don't sound or look like no foreigner to me, and him being your nephew, reckoned ya outta hear about who's putting up the reward money."

Pieces were falling into place. Crisp responded, "Those would be the bad guys with friends in high places. Can you image, a bunch foreigners trying to yank the wool over our eyes? Especially when it appears this great country of ours about to dive headlong into Civil Conflict. Sort of makes one wonder what going on?"

Bassett's interest peeked, "Ya reckon the British are trying to take-over California? Force us live under a King or Queen's rule?"

Crisp shrugged. "Hard to say… Could be they thought he heard something he ought-not have, of course my nephew couldn't hear a thing because he's deaf as a bat."

"If'n I was to find him," inquired Bassett. "A young man of my statue could go a long-way in a company like yours?" He glimpsed past Crisp at the doorway. "What is it ya' all do here?"

Crisp eyebrows cocked. Bassett was asking for a job as a counter offer to the reward money. There was no way he'd get Captain Bristol to lay-out a hundred dollars. They needed someone to clean-up after his men, and Bristol would likely go for it as part of their budget.

"Tell you what," said Crisp. "Give me some references, and I'll consider hiring you for cleaning and helping cook meals."

Bassett grinned, shoved an open hand outward and agreed, "Shake on it?"

"First your references have to check-out and no past trouble with the law?"

Concerned, Bassett stepped back and stated, "No troubles worthy of hanging, or jailing for more than a couple nights. Old Man Waddles had me locked-up for a couple days, said I was drunk in public. Haven't touched a drop of rye since. Hell of a headache the next day, and sitting behind bars didn't help none."

Crisp shook Bassett's hand. "Agreed provided that is it, and you're not drinking anymore."

Bassett's face glowed. "Hell this is better than being a cabin boy. Not sure I'd cater to being on the water for months on end with no land insight."

"Cabin boy?" Crisp asked, suspecting it was onboard the Lady Beth.

"Word on the street, Captain La Horn is looking for a cabin boy. I was planning to head there this afternoon and see what it paid. Not anymore, though." He climbed onto a high-wheel bicycle and called over his shoulder, "I'll be back with your nephew tomorrow afternoon at the latest, ya wait and see. Room and board, plus pay, right?"

Unsure, Crisp raised both palms and said, "We'll see after you get back."

Hindor stepped outside at ground level in time to watch Bassett's high-wheel bike tires kick up mud from the street. Seconds later, the boy turned from the dead end road and was gone.

Hindor cleared his throat. "You think that was good idea, sending a boy out to do a man's job?"

Crisp cocked an eyebrow. "He probably has a decent chance of finding Kern. Given their ages are close, they probably think alike. If he's lucky and does bring him home, Kern will need a friend near his own age to buddy with."

Hindor probed, "Home? I hope you're not getting emotionally involved and losing perspective. If he turns out to be guilty of murder, you are in for a big letdown. You hardly know him, and sure as hell ain't kin to ya. Are you getting fatherly feelings toward him? I sure hope not. You'd be losing perspective on these two cases."

Crisp defended his actions, "It was simply a figure of speech." Again, his bladder was urging for quick relief. "Excuse me, I've got hit the jake outback then send a telegram, plus a report to file for Captain Bristol. Have Taylor watch after Bristol. When Kern is back with us, I'd as soon not have him wondering what happened to his dog." He turned, rushed around the building and toward the jake.

Hindor shook his head, "Without me watching after him that young Lieutenant wouldn't survive a month."

17

Crisp exited a telegraph office on Fifth Street, hoping for a quick reply from an Upstate New York premier academy located near Crystal Springs. Crystal Springs, a private academy was better than an orphanage. With Kern safely hidden on the East Coast, murder charges from overseas would fade to obscurity.

As Crisp stepped onto the boardwalk, the telegraph office door banged shut. Startled, he drew a gun holstered under his suit coat and jerked around.

"A tad jumpy?"

Taut, Crisp swung back toward the street with gun in hand.

Caleb's smile defused a tense and awkward moment. Humored, he raised his hands as if surrendering and teased, "Don't start shooting, I've done nothing wrong. At least nothing that you're aware-of, or can prove in a court of law."

Crisp reined his embarrassment, re-holstered his weapon and atoned, "That slamming door spooked me. I do apologize."

Caleb glimpsed at the doorway and concluded, "If I hadn't seen the bang coming, it'd had spooked me too. They should loosen the door-spring before someone gets hurt." Puzzled, he stared at Crisp's suit and commented, "You're out of uniform? Taking a holiday?"

"I recently resigned my commission," explained Crisp increasingly accustomed to the lie with each passing day. He smoothed a portion of his jacket that concealed his gun. "Pressure from home… Simply to keep the peace there, I'm getting involved with the family business."

Anxious, Crisp glimpsed toward the sun. He had a secret meeting with a sergeant from Captain Bristol's office in thirty minutes. Prying information from La Horn's second-mate was crucial. Happenstance rarely presented an opportunity like this.

Happenstance seemed to be in full play as of late. It had set Hindor, Ring, Trick and himself on the trail of Indian Slave Traders. Aftermath of it had put happenstance into play again with their current assignment.

Crisp dared not allow a prosperous occasion to pass unused. He explored why Caleb was at the telegraph office. "What brings you here?"

Caleb stated the obvious, "Came to send a telegram, much like yourself I assume." Then he pocked his hands into his coat and said, "We're looking for a cargo to the South Pacific. Rumors of a pending Civil War has everyone shoring up resources, nothing seems to be leaving port. Makes it tough for those of us who rely on a movement of goods to make a living. You know of anything?"

Crisp decided Caleb's answer made sense. Since La Horn was unable to find cargo in the Bay Area, he would begin checking other ports along the coast. He shrugged, "Can't be of much help locating a cargo bound for the Far East. I'm only importing goods from China for sale here in this country."

Crisp repressed an urge to interrogate him concerning Ver Haven's death. Caleb seemed peaceful and willing to talk but there was not time. He offered convenience, "If you ever want to stopped by for coffee and grub or simply to talk, my office is near the docks. A. R & B Import Exports overlooking pier 32."

Caleb nodded. "How's Kern doing? Holding-out alright?"

"The army hasn't locked him in a stockade," Crisp told the truth before telling a white lie. "Last time I saw him, he was doing fine. Hard to say where the army is keeping him. Not my problem anymore."

Caleb stepped onto the boardwalk and reached for the door. At the last moment, he paused and asked over his shoulder, "How's that dog doing? Heard, the army put him down."

Caleb's unintended revelation confirmed it. The tinhorn from Texas had indeed attempted to secure Bristol for La

Horn. If Caleb stopped at the A. R & B, it was easier to explain the lie now.

Crisp smirked. It was time to let him know the army had one up on them, which may make La Horn anxious enough to make a mistake. He explained, "The dog is fine… As it turned-out, Bristol was a gift for President Lincoln from the Emperor of China. Think of it, years from you can tell your grandkids how you had part in bringing a gift from the Emperor of China to the President of the United States. Sure be something to brag about."

Caleb nodded and avoided telling a lie himself. Unlike La Horn, he rarely tried to cover one lie with another. Lies had a way of tripping the liar. Instead, he offered a partial truth. "La Horn will be pleased to hear Bristol's doing fine. After hearing tell the dog was put-down, he was none too happy."

Caleb glimpsed toward the bay and said, "Best get about business, La Horn's bound to wonder what's taking me." He entered the telegraph office, careful not to allow the door to slam shut behind him.

Crisp stepped off the boardwalk and headed for a livery stable across the street where he had stopped prior to visiting the telegraph office. A stableboy had Crisp's buckskin saddled and waiting.

Crisp rubbed the horse's nose and whispered, "Copper my old friend, we've got a boy to find and I'm counting on you to keep a sharp eye for him." He pulled a carrot from his coat pocket and fed it to him. As Copper enjoyed the treat, Crisp slipped a coin from his pocket and handed it the stableboy. "Dowling, here's a little something for your trouble."

"Thanks mister," Dowling said and patted Copper's flank. "He sure is a nice mount. Bet he's fast as a jackrabbit."

Crisp admitted, "He does alright. Did you pack my saddlebags?" Then he inspected contents inside of the saddlebags.

Dowling explained, "Yep, sure enough did. Dried shanks of beef, some mason sealed goods…" He pointed at the saddle horn. "And three canteens of water."

Crisp checked his bedroll and cinch, and then he footed the stirrup and mounted. He reined backward Copper several steps and said, "I'll probably be back roundabout sunset. Those supplies are in case I don't get back for a day or two. Keep an eye out for us, Copper will need a brushing and grain when we get return."

"Sure-thing Mister Crisp," assured Dowling. "I'll keep my eyes peeled for ya around sunset, ya can count on me." He grinned as he watched Copper trot away then exhaled a breath on the coin and polished it on his shirtsleeve. He inspected it one last time and tucked it into a front pants pocket.

Ten minutes later, Crisp greeted Sargent Forks at an alley behind a pub on a side street off Main Street. Plain clothed and uncomfortable, Sargent Forks fidgeted, pulled a pocket watch and commented, "You're almost an hour late. Bristol's likely sitting behind his desk fuming. He is expecting me with your report. We both know the captain ain't a man to be kept waiting."

Crisp handed Forks a sealed brown envelope and informed him, "Well that's too bad… I was gaining information not in the report. Be sure and tell the old man, La Horn's first mate sent telegrams to other ports looking for a cargo to the Far East."

Forks was steaming but agreed, "Fine, I'll inform Captain of it. Don't be late next time or send one of you flunkies instead of coming yourself. Trick is under the mistakable impression I owe him a dollar over a couple of dice tosses. I swear those dice were loaded, and he ain't getting othing from me until I look at those dice up close. You ever send Trick in your place – he won't be coming back a whole man."

Crisp advised, "I'm not getting betwixt the two of on it. Nor would I mention it to the old man if I were you. Bristol would have both your hides tacked to a shed for gambling."

Forks hated dressing in civilian clothing. Since Forks had insulted Trick, tossing him a snide remark seemed fair play.

Crisp smarted, "By-the-way, civilian clothing doesn't suit your demeanor" He reined Copper back onto Main Street.

***

An hour later, Crisp located a footpath behind the Regal leading into the foothills. He dismounted, knelt and searched the ground. He discovered a discarded silk napkin used to hold food. Perhaps, Kern had taken food from the hotel.

Luckily, it had not rained overnight. Three sets of footprints were visible. The oldest footprints were bare-feet boy, probably Kern. The boots likely belonged to Shepherd who had not checked that morning. The third prints were a pair of worn boots too large for the person wearing them, and likely belonged to Bassett.

Crisp decided he should have made it clear to Shepherd to periodically report or send a message as to his whereabouts. With luck, he hoped to find Shepherd, Kern and Bassett together and returning the city.

Crisp pulled his pocket watch and tipped it toward sunlight for easier reading. He had twenty-three hours until Ackerland's luncheon. Not near enough time to search the foothills. He grumbled, "Damn."

Command had its disadvantages. Often, Crisp felt removed from the action. Determined to do what time permitted, he remounted Copper and reined onto the tight trail. As Copper hoofed upward, Crisp ducked a low hanging tree limb.

18

Hindor stood guard outside the warehouse office of Golden Bay, located near the main barn doors leading outdoors. Inside the twelve by twelve-foot interior office, Trick rummaged through manifests inside of a file cabinet. He glimpsed into an open indoor window used to pass paperwork back and forth. Trick intently focused on his task and rushing him was pointless. He glimpsed around the barn, taking stock of the facility.

There were plenty of unoccupied crates and empty stacks of burlap bags. Whatever cargo that came from the Lady Beth was long gone. A lack of cargo leaving the country meant day laborers worked shorter hours. Twenty minutes earlier, the business owner sent laborers home for the day.

With nothing to do, office personnel left for an extended lunch break across the street at Annie's Pub and Grill. Hindor estimated they had another ten minutes to locate records disclosing what had happened to La Horn's cargo.

The warehouse timber was old and rickety, Hindor was surprised it withstood the last earthquake. Perhaps a lack of structural support allowed the barn to roll with shaking ground during the last quake. Again, he glimpsed into the indoor window. Trick was lost amid a drawer of paperwork, muttering file names as he fingered his way through folders.

Hindor gazed upward and watched a rat scurry across a rafter directly above Trick's head. He flinched and commented, "Given rice and grain are stored here, one would think they'd have a couple cats guarding against mice and rats."

Trick looked over his shoulder and inquired, "What was that? Is someone coming?"

"No, just a rat..." Hindor answered. "Hurry-up in there, we're about out of time. They're bound to be back at any given moment. With old man Bristol steaming over everything else, last thing we need is to be dragged into Crivitz's office for breaking and entering."

"Found it," Trick announced, then turned with a manifest in hand and agreed, "Let's get out of here while the get-n's good..."

As office personnel returned from Annie's Pub and Grill, Hindor and Trick slipped out of a backdoor. As Trick eased the backdoor shut, hinges squeaked. He mumbled, "If Crisp keeps sending us on these types of missions, I'm gonna start carrying a can of oil and lock picks again."

In route to the A. R & B, Hindor pondered the 'again' part of lock picks. Although he had served three years with Trick, he knew little of the man's past prior to army life. He heard rumors a judge offered Trick two choices, prison or the army.

Hindor prodded, "What do you mean by again?"

"Again, what?" Trick replied half-listening and reading through the stolen manifest, pausing at each page and memorizing addresses.

Hindor reworded his question, "Back at the warehouse, what did you mean by carrying lock picks and oil? Is there something Crisp and I ought to know about your past? There was rumors that I had personally laid to rest, if any of em were true..."

Trick ignored an inquiry of his past and shifted their conversation. "Cargo went to three different locations. The Lady Beth was loaded with rice, tea and gunpowder. Rice went to a company called Morgan Grains located at the northern part of town. Tea went to Chen's Tea Shop downtown. The gunpowder was delivered to a place called River Mountain Suppliers."

Hindor shook his head and said, "Yep can see it now. Come daybreak, Crisp will have us looking for day labor at each of those places. One thing for-sure, between army pay and day labor we'll be saving-up money."

Trick announced, "I'm calling the job at Chen's Tea Shop. As you know, I've got this thing for Chinese women, can't get enough of em."

"Long as we're calling jobs, I'm taking River Mountain Suppliers. Maybe, I'll hear rumors of a big strike somewhere.

Ya know I'm fixing to retire soon, and I was thinking of panning."

Trick chuckled, "Yep them streams are glittering with nuggets. You'll be weighted down with gold in no time flat. All ya have to do is avoid bandits along the way back down mountain passes. Given of course ya actually find the shiny stuff and it's not fools-gold."

Shocked, they halted dead in their tracks. They hardly believed their eyes. At the front doors of the White Pines Hotel, Muser was escorting a fine looking lady off the boardwalk and toward a hitched carriage. Muser had their arms lovingly locked at the elbows.

Astounded, Trick muttered, "Will ya look at that… Our young fellow misfit Private Muser has found himself a respectable lady friend. Guess the wondering as to how Muser ended up with us is over." He spread a smirk. "He's a man after my own heart, a womanizer"

Hindor partly explained, "Womanizer is right and I am willing to bet that's Ms. Jane. Crisp filled me in this morning on her. Now, we need to put a handle on Taylor's issues. Of course, whatever we learn will have to be played-up, simply to keep those our new boys on their toes. Teasing newcomers is the only right and makes em feel accepted."

Trick's lips curled upward. "I couldn't agree more. Reckon we need to get started straightaway and spoil Muser's roll in the hay."

Hindor suggested, "Maybe we oughta send him off to Morgan Grains and line-up a hard day of work for tomorrow?"

Fully intent on doing that very thing, Hindor did not wait for a reply. He stepped toward the hotel and waved. "Hey, Muser! We've been hunting high-and-low for you… Then by shear chance, there you are."

Muser missed intended sarcasm and introduced, "This here is Ms. Jane, niece of Councilman Pitt from Portland. Been showing her around and letting her take-in the sights."

Trick walked toward the carriage and cynically muttered, "Yeah, I'll bet you've been doing that very thing…"

Hindor cut Trick's mutter short with an elbow into his ribs.

Trick stepped back and redirected his demeanor. "That's a mighty fine thing to be doing Mister Muser. Earlier, Crisp was inquiring as to your whereabouts. I'll be sure and let him know you're not lying dead in an alleyway."

Ms. Jane extended her hand. "I am pleased to meet you both. I'm truly sorry to have taken Clancy from his work. Had I know, I would never have imposed on him to show me the city."

Hindor and Trick glimpsed at each other and chimed, "Clancy?"

Uncomfortable, Muser excused himself, "You have to pardon us, but I need to get Ms. Jane to a dinner engagement. She's meeting her father in China Town." He helped her into the carriage and walked around behind the buggy.

Quick, Hindor and Trick tagged along side of Muser. Trick, grabbed a hold of Muser's shirtsleeve and tugged him a couple steps from the carriage.

Trick whispered into Muser's ear, "Clancy, if you're not careful those soft baby blue eyes of yours' will be your undoing. Not that I'm one to be talking… But hitting the hay with a Councilman's niece? Come-on and think about it for a few minutes. Consider the consequence of your actions… That'd dump a heap of trouble at our feet."

Childlike, Muser stared at the street and kicked a road-apple aside. Sheepish, he looked up and grinned. "I am only ensuring she has a memorable time in San Francisco. Didn't ya read the morning paper? There was another hammer bashing last night. Besides, I'd hate to hear she was bashed upside the head by a robber."

"Don't be leaving her a bundle of joy to recall you by," added Trick, then he patted him on the shoulder. "Get-on-out of here… But be at the A. R & B by midnight or Hindor will have you peeling spuds for a week straight."

Muser stopped himself short of saluting and promised, "I'll be back with time to spare." He climbed onto the buggy, eased the hand brake off and slapped the reins.

Stunned, Hindor and Trick watched Muser and Ms. Jane's carriage rambled away. Tick commented, "I thought he bowered our rig? Ain't that one of those fancy rentals from down the street? Think he charged use of that carriage to the A. R & B?"

Hindor cocked an eyebrow and said, "Now that ya mention it, it does look like one of those expensive rental rigs. One does have to wonder. Considering the dirt pay the army gives us, how can he afford to rent such a nice rig? If the A. R & B is billed for it, Crisp will dock his pay until the cost is covered. Or Captain Bristol will have Crisp's hide tacked to a barn."

Tick mulled over possibilities awaiting Muser for misuse of army funds. Heat for having shot the Texan would shift to Muser. Then again, there was likely to be additional killings before this Kern, La Horn, Ver Haven and Ackerland affair drew to a bloody conclusion.

Trick wagered his odds for misfortune. Misuse of army funds was nothing compared to killing a person the army wanted to question. Whenever a shootout happened, blame always pointed at his smoking gun.

At mid-afternoon with a couple beers settling inside of their stomachs, Trick and Hindor approached the rear of the A. R & B office. In the backyard, they spotted Taylor. Perplexed, they concealed themselves behind a eucalyptus tree and spied from a distance.

Taylor was fiercely banging nails into a board spread across a pair of sawhorses. Eyes glossed, he was intent on hammering whatever frustrated him into the board. Nail by nail, first a slight tap setting the nail into position and remarking, "This is for being a bitch," followed by a thudding blow of the hammer driving a nail into the board.

Taylor tapped another nail into place and said, "This is for being a man-hater," followed another hard swing of the hammer and slamming the next nail through the board. Another nail tapped into place was followed by "This is for loving another woman" was succeeded by another whack of the hammer.

Cautious, Hindor and Trick backed-away, until blending among the broad shadows of a lilac bush. Without a word passing between them, they decided to leave whatever strange ritual was taking place alone.

Trick and Hindor glimpsed each other's drawn face. Their thoughts converged on nightly hammer killings. In unison, they assured themselves "Our luck ain't that bad."

When returning from a covert mission, standing order was to use the backdoor. Given Taylor's state of mind, they opted for the front door. Aside from the dog Bristol greeting them at the front door, the building was empty.

Tail wagging, Bristol paced at the rear door and wanted outside to relief himself. Trick leashed Bristol and slipped out the front door, avoiding contact with the mad-nail-banger in the backyard.

19

At midnight, Crisp finally returned to the livery stable. Dowling was gone for the night, so he unsaddled Copper and refilled both grain and hay bins. As he brushed Copper, he skimmed the day through his mind. Beating through brush and dense forest had proven fruitless. Still, it was better than sitting at the office and doing nothing.

Footprints had vanished onto a rocky trail that led deeper into the foothills. Adding to his misery, the rocky trail divided a number times to narrow paths too hazardous for a horse.

He was tempted to call for Shepherd and Bassett's names. For security reasons, he had decided against it. It was possible that La Horn had sailors searching the area, and or bounty hunters were within earshot of an echoing shout.

Tired and saddle-sore, Crisp exited the livery barn and gazed skyward. A slight breeze had shifted night fog against mountain bases giving the Bay Area an unusual panoramic view of the night heavens. He pulled Kern's amulet from his coat pocket and rubbed his thumb across the imagery. He had yet to determine what star pattern was above the shepherd's head. A sailor may recognize it, but asking Caleb was not an option.

Suddenly a high-pitched wail of terror pierced his moment of solitude. He assumed another woman of the night had lost her life to the Hammer Killer. He scowled and stared toward distant foothills. He was worried for Kern and Bassett, and questioned himself for having sent Bassett to search for Kern. Had a pressing desire to complete the mission caused bad judgment?

***

Kern lay inside of an abandoned trapper's cabin, curled at corner of the rickety building, wrapped in a tattered blank. A promise to a dying friend weighted him. He hugged Ver Haven's leather carry-bag to his chest and sighed. His deaf ears had missed the roar of a cougar from directly behind the cabin. However, his alert eyes captured a blur of motion as the cat leaped through a broken window.

The huge cat crouched and extended her front claws into the wooden floorboards. Kern inched his knife from its sheath at his waist. Then, he lay motionless and prayed the predator did not consider him a meal or threat.

Kern's ploy at playing dead failed. The cat snarled and sprang forward. Ready, he rolled and swung his knife into the cat's side. As he rolled, the right side of his upper arm snagged a jagged nail protruding from a wall. Shocked, he missed the feel of cat claws nicking his ribcage.

Injured, the cat swaggered toward the same window used to enter the cabin. Her attempt to leap outside floundered. She thudded onto her side, her weight shaking cabin floorboards. Panting, she coughed a snarl at the man-child who had inflected her fatal wound.

Kern crawled backward into a corner and eyed the demon spirit sent to kill him. His arm and right side stung worse than a scorpion bite. He used one hand to apply pressure on the arm and the other against his left ribcage. He trembled, waiting for the spirit-possessed creature to regain her strength and finish him.

Again, the cat snarled and tried leaping out of the window. For a second time she rumbled backward to the floor, causing lose floorboards to expellee a thin dust cloud. She exhaled a conclusive snarl before yielding whatever immoral spirit that had possessed her.

Abrupt, the cabin door banged open rattling interior walls. An agony of cat scratches slowed Kern's reaction time. Painful, he crouched onto his feet, unsure he was able to fight again.

A small person busted into the shack, swinging a small pistol back and forth searching for a target. The stranger missed Kern's presences and cautiously approached the dead beast.

Kern concluded this person had summoned and controlled the beast. There were good and bad forces at work, each fighting over Carl's hand written book. Good forces wanted the book to reach the right people, and evil wanted the book destroyed and him dead.

During Fire Season in Kakadu, Kern had learned first-hand that good does not always win over evil. His clan the Nirama wiped off the face of the land by evil white-men. Again, good had lost to evil when Carl was murdered.

Kern's heart turned to parents that he barely remembered. His broken heart turned to fury. This evil presence needed expelling from his presence. Tense, he clutched his blood soaked hands. Pain of stinging claw wounds dissolved against a pressing desire to vanquish evil from his presence. His rage sprang into bold action.

Bassett spun around but too late. Kern was on top of him, pounding savage fists. Failing, he attempted to deflect blow after stunning blow. Forgetting Kern's deafness, he yelled "Hey, Kern! I'm here to help ya!"

Nose to nose, locked in hand-to-hand combat both teenagers twirled across the floor, kicking and punching. Bassett's black-powder shot derringer spun across the floor. Upon impact with a wall, the derringer discharged and sent an iron ball slicing inches of air between their faces.

They shoved each other away and slithered into opposite corners. They eyed one another, each not eager for round two of the fight.

Desperate, Bassett broke the silence. "I know ya can't hear a damn thing I'm uttering. But ya gotta believe me, I'm here to get ya back home to your rich uncle." He cringed, regretting having said rich uncle. Was Kern a lip reader? He decided it was too dark for lip reading and discarded the notion.

Bassett stared at the knife sticking from the dead cougar's chest. When Kern struggled against the cougar, was he injured? Kern appeared drained and sluggish. Fresh bruises from Kern's fists came into bear. He wanted to offer help, yet he was uncertain of Kern's reaction.

Puzzled, Bassett felt the wetness of blood on his clothing. Fleeting, he patted himself from head to toe. Relieved, he found only bruises from Kern's fists. If Kern died, there would be no reward of a job from Kern's wealthy uncle.

Small cabins dotted the foothills, and Basset considered it lucky to have found this shanty. Having come this far, only to see money bled away was intolerable. As Kern slipped into unconscious, his head slumped to one side.

Cautious Bassett stood, spread his arms wide as a peaceful gesture and crept across the lose boards. Kern's blood had smeared across the floor, making walking difficult. Kern had lost a lot of blood and losing more with each passing second.

Bassett moaned, "You sit tight there, I'm coming to help ya. Don't be jumping on me again like ya did, or I'll have to get rough with ya."

Bassett knelt at Kern's side and sighed. He grabbed a tattered blank and ripped it into strips. He tightly wrapped pieces around Kern's chest and halted the flow of blood. With Kern's bleeding under control, he stepped outside and gathered wood.

Minutes later, Bassett was sparking a fire inside of a stone fireplace. After a strong fire was burning, he returned outside and fetched water from a nearby mountain stream. Using an old pot, he boiled what was left of the blanket strips.

Cursing, Bassett cleaned Kern's wounds and changed the temporary tattered bandages. "Damn, don't be dying on me – you're my ticket to easy street."

With bleeding was under control, Bassett knelt backward and stared at the cloth bandages. He pleaded, "We're supposed to become best of friends, and spend your uncle's money chasing after rich girls. We've got fancy dancing parties to attend, and I am counting on you to teach me to dance. We're going be the best of friends, ya wait and see."

20

Crisp entered the restaurant for the luncheon, wearing another new lightweight gray tweed suit. He decided against wearing the same suit worn at the garden party. Wearing the same suit risked consideration as a one-suit man rubbing shoulders with men of wealth and influence. Earlier that morning, he dipped into savings and had it tailored.

His thoughts leveled on those directly under his command. Each had their assigned tasks for the day. Hindor was in charge of dispensing and supervising assignments. Secured with Hindor at the A. R & B office, he strolled across the foyer. Puzzled, he noted the restaurant was nearly void of people. Being noon-hour, the place should have been pack with people waiting for a seat. Staff had arranged several tables to form one large eating area.

A quick head count put ten men seated at the tables. Two young Asian men wearing silk black suits were pouring tea into cups. Stir-fried rice, beef and vegetables scented the atmosphere. An unusually loud meow caught his attention, halting him in his tracks. Staring at him was a fluffy and overweight white cat lying on a pillow inside of a wooden box.

Ackerland stood and waved Crisp their direction. "Mister Crisp, over here… Don't let that old cat bother you, she's harmless and simply saying welcome to Father Ginn's Rice House."

As Crisp neared, Ackerland pulled a chair from the table and suggested, "We saved you a seat next Albert." He nodded toward each man and made an introduction, "Gordon, Fredrick, Samuel, Thomas, Philip, Blake, Theodore, and of course Abe not to be confused with the current president." The comment raised laughter from around the table.

Crisp shook Ackerland's hands with a casual greeting, then sat and slid to the table. He looked at those seated and said, "Thanks for inviting me here. I look forward to getting to know each of you."

Ackerland inquired, "Mister Crisp for the life of me I can't seem to recall your first name. Forgive me, but my thoughts the other night were elsewhere." Chuckles rumbled across the tables with several of Ackerland's friends commenting on the garden party.

Crisp smirked. "Crisp is my name, I've no last name, per-say. My parents wanted each of their children to have a unique identity. My father is Worthington Ellsworth from Upstate New York."

Stumped, Ackerland's brows raised. "That would make you Crisp Ellsworth?"

Crisp offered a glimpse into his childhood. "My father decided against allowing his children to use his last name. He wanted us to make it on own merits without the family name pulling favors. It kept folks from befriending his children as a means of getting close to him. That oddity kept my youngest sister from an attempted kidnapping. Confused kidnappers grabbed the wrong girl from school."

Albert gasped. "My word... What happened to the girl they took by mistake? After the kidnappers realized their error, was she returned safely?"

Though a hurtful memory, Crisp elaborated, "We'll never know for sure, her body was never found. Her parents could not afford the ransom. It was too late by the time anyone contacted my father. Rumor had it the kidnappers realized their mistake, slit her throat and dumped her body into the river. Shame too, as my father was willing to pay for the girl's release."

Gordon shook his head. "That is a shame, and sounds as if your father is a good man."

Thomas added, "Why not tact a last name behind the first, it'd make life a lot easier?"

Crisp raised his palms and shrugged, "As far as last names go, my father relented later in life. I was already in the military and choose against using his last name. My younger brother was injured racing thoroughbreds and unable to have children." Everyone gathered at the table, lowered their hands and cringed.

Crisp smirked. "After our father realized there'd be no one to carry on the family name, my decision left him none too pleased. At that time in my life, I figured the military was a career. Turns-out there was more of my father in me than I realized. It's all business now…"

Then Crisp assured, "After the business is up and running full steam, I'll tack Ellsworth behind Crisp. But first, I'd like to prove him right. His children are bred to make money and do not need the name Ellsworth for it."

"Excuse me," Blake stood and leaned across the table to shake Crisp's hand. "Blake James Cunnings, president for Shoreline Bank at fifth and main. Clifford was telling us about you, however he didn't elaborate as to what type of goods your company was bring here from the Far East."

Crisp nodded, recalling the bank as the same Ackerland used. He had yet to gain information concerning Ackerland's bank accounts. Daytime bank security was tight, and as a result Ring was having difficult accessing records. Perhaps, a midnight break-in at the bank was called for.

Crisp remained on subject, "We're importing Chinese Herbs used for medical purposes."

Abe's interest peeked. "Opium?"

Crisp waved the opium inquiry away, but silently noted Abe's interest with the drug. He explained, "We're importing tree bark, spices, plant roots, fish oils for medical use, and incense for meditation. The market back East has a craving for Chinese Imports. I suspect it is one of those passing fads, and intend to cash-in while the iron is hot. Even after the craze has ended, I'll likely keep the A. R & B office up and running. I enjoy my life here in California."

Crisp raised his teacup and grinned, "Spices and tea are continually in demand. I'll always have a marketplace to sell goods. I am considering a California farm product that hasn't gained popularity back East. If presented to general public properly, I'm sure it'd turn into a positive cash flow."

Ackerland's interest peaked, "Farm product?"

Humored, Crisp shook a finger. "Not saying as of yet, don't want anyone beating me to the punch on it. It is a venture I'd like to pursue away from family influence, sort of a make on my own type of deal."

Several agreed with Crisp's decision to keep his endeavor veiled. Small talk subsided as waiters lifted fruit bowl appetizers of grapes, strawberries, blueberries and diced melons from the tables and set lunch into place.

Crisp was certain he would never forget the meal. Tender beef tips melted in his mouth. The rice had a flavor of its own, accented with green peppers, tomatoes, wild onions, and other vegetables.

Their meeting adjourned with Crisp learning little about Ackerland's business ventures. There was chitchat concerning the situation back East, however, none appeared to take sides with North or South. Everyone was neutral.

None had mentioned California leaving the Union. Unmarried men at the luncheon talked about women they had dated and considered dating. Crisp suppressed a raised eyebrow when someone had mentioned Hanna Steadson.

Crisp did not consider the luncheon a waste of time. Ackerland had brought him partly into his inner circle. He had made contacts to use at a later time and place. Met Ackerland's close friends and pegged each one into a keyhole as to who was who, and what function each served amid Northern California's elite.

Thus far, the day was a good one. If Shepherd, Bassett and Kern showed at the A. R. & B, it would bring perfect closure to the day. Crisp pondered swinging past Shoreline Bank and checking on Ring's progress then decided against it. If Blake spotted him, it would appear he was over anxious to become part of their inner-fold. Instead, he headed deeper into China Town to check on Trick.

21

Near sunset, Trick and Crisp caught a ride on a horse pulled trolley car. Standing room only on the trolley, they avoided discussing what Trick had learned. Other passengers were preoccupied with speculations concerning the Hammer Killings. A favored theory concerning an identity of the Hammer Killer was a carpenter gone-mad.

Occasionally, someone mentioned tensions back East, but it seemed a taboo topic. Regardless of where and whom, it was like treading hot coals and the subject quickly changed.

Crisp noted how uncomfortable Trick was concerning the topic of the Hammer Killer. He wondered if Trick had a suspect in mind. Trick was never one to turn someone into the law for a minor offense. Murder was another matter.

Crisp had seen this behavior from Trick in the past. Last year, Trick refused to say who had fired the fatal shot that killed an Indian slaver. After they stepped off the trolley, Trick suggested they return to the A. R & B, skipping an earlier suggestion of catching a drink at local pub near the office. Not the norm, it was another step out of character for Trick.

Crisp was unable to nail Trick down regarding the Hammer Killer. His gut feeling, Trick suspected someone. After a fifteen-minute walk along dried mud streets, they arrived at the A. R & B, where Hindor and Muser were preparing supper.

Hindor had Muser peeling potatoes. Where Taylor had gone-off was anyone's guess. Hindor had allowed Taylor the night free. Surprising everyone, Trick went straight to work in the kitchen dicing onions and carrots for stewing.

While Trick and Muser kept busy at kitchen duties, Hindor motioned Crisp upstairs to their preferred balcony for a cup of coffee. Crisp slid out of his boots, sat and kicked his stocking feet up onto a wooden footrest and aired his aching feet.

After a long sip of coffee, Crisp inquired about Shepherd, Kern and Bassett.

Hindor shook his head. "No signs of any of em… For all we know, Shepherd has Kern and they headed for parts unknown. Lord only knows what happened to that newspaper kid. Wouldn't surprise me none if'n he signed up with La Horn as the new cabin boy. Trick, learn anything yet?"

Crisp shook his head. "No. As far as scaring up information at the bank, Ring wasn't alone long enough to look at banking records." His eyebrows pulled tight, Ring's absence had missed him earlier.

"Where's Ring? You know damn well because of that shooting, he is barred from having free time for a month. I hope you didn't allow him to venture inside of any pubs?"

Hindor followed Trick's earlier manner of keeping something from him. "Don't rightly know at the moment, sir." Which was not a total lie, he had sent Ring to tag behind Taylor at a distance. He needed to learn what their new recruit did with his free time before springing suspicions to Crisp and Captain Bristol. Since he did not know where Taylor was headed, he had no idea where Ring was at.

Crisp cleared his throat. "Damn it! You, Trick and Ring are keeping something from me, and if othing n't part of the plot it's only because he's new. I strongly suspect it has something to do with the Hammer Killer. Now out with it!"

Uneasy, Hindor shuffled and replied, "Speaking of the Hammer Killer, you're friend Chief Waddles stopped-by to speak with you."

Crisp eyed him tight. "Have a little respect for the man's office, his title is Chief Crivitz. I've never seen an insulting name spread so fast off the streets." He exhaled a sigh. "What did he want?"

Hindor shrugged. "Seems to think we can be of aid with his investigation into whoever is killing those working-gals. He wanted one of our boys to dress as a woman and work the streets in the red light district. Damn, I am half-afraid to send anyone. Some poor lost soul out looking for a woman is bound to be disappointed once he discovers the pluming is wrong. I am afraid, he'd likely shoot whoever was assigned the duty. Crivitz seems to think we owe him a favor. I dare not ask what favor he has done for us or is about to do. You know how Captain Bristol feels about local law enforcement. *Bunch of wanna-be tough men, not good enough for the army*. Bristol has said it enough times, I have it memorized and that was a direct quote."

Frustrated, Crisp shook his head. "We simply don't have the manpower to spare. What'd you tell him?"

"Not much," said Hindor, "only that I'd have to consult you first." He chuckled. "Having thought on the matter, Clancy would look mighty fine dressed as woman. A man would have to yank off his dress before he'd learn Clancy was a man. At that point, Clancy would likely be shot and killed. I can almost image the letter you'd have draft to his folks, explaining why their son was dressed as woman of the night."

Crisp rolled his eyes. "I suppose we could spare Taylor for a couple nights. Seeing how he's not seen any real covert action, it'd be a decent way of testing him undercover."

Hindor stiffened at mention of Taylor setting a trap for the Hammer Killer. Then he tipped his chair onto its hind legs and almost fell backwards. The chair thumbed back onto all fours. Apprehensive, he cleared his throat but withheld comment.

Crisp pointed a finger and demanded, "Damn it, now I'm certain you're keeping something from me. Maybe not about the Hammer Killings but damn sure it's about Taylor."

Then Crisp raised their past. "This reminds me of the time as to who fired the shot that killed an Indian slaver. I sure as hell won't stand for being-kept in the dark, again. I don't want any more surprise visits from an irate Bristol when things go amiss with Taylor."

"Said it before and I'll say it again – No one is sent to us by chance," Crisp recapped, "he screwed up somewhere along the line. When it comes down to covering for each other's foul-ups, you boys are sneaky."

Hindor stood and said, "I don't know nothing about anyone or anything. All I've gotta say is wait and see what tonight brings and come morning we'll know more about Taylor." He turned and left the balcony without explaining further.

Crisp pitched remaining coffee from his tin over the railing and grumbled, "Damn it to hell, I swear they'll turn my hair gray before its time." He grabbed his lower stomach. "Ah, they're already given me ulcers."

22

Shepherd stood alone inside an abandoned cabin. Amid scatter moonlight filtering through holes in the roof, he raised a lit candle and surveyed the floor. Dried blood puddles left clear evidence of two separate struggles. Someone had fought a cougar that lay dead at a corner of the cabin. There was evidence of another struggle between two smaller framed people, likely teenagers.

Shepherd was certain barefoot tracks belonged to Kern. A second set of tracks appeared to be someone wearing oversized shoes with worn-out soles, probably another teenager.

Shepherd dug a steel ball from a wall, and assumed it was a shot fired at the cat. Judging by blade width and depth, a knife wound in the cat's side was a killing stab. He was certain Kern had lived in the wilds, somewhere. It was doubtful Kern coward and fought back, inflecting the fatal stab.

Someone had torn skin and left blood on a lose wallboard, either dodging the cat, and or in person against person fight. The cold potbelly stove had fresh ashes, a half-day old at most.

Branches along a footpath leading toward the cabin snapped and popped under the weight of people approaching. Shepherd stepped back into the shadows, stooped and drew two knives, one from each of his boot-wells. He had expected unwelcome company.

A pair of bounty hunters entered the cabin, laughing between shots from a bottle of rye. Their fur coats humped their shoulders, making them appear larger than life.

Shepherd issued no warning. One knife flew, followed by the second one. Target number one staggered backward into a wall, and slumped dead to floor into a seated position, the knife sticking from his chest. The second knife caught its target high in the shoulder. The bounty hunter grabbed a hold of the knife handle and pivoted for the doorway to run.

Shepherd was right behind him, snatched the hunter's fur coat and yanked him inside. Then he tossed him to the floor, and jerked his knife from the man's shoulder. Without a word, he sliced the man's throat and silenced pleas for mercy.

Shepherd wiped his knives clean of blood against one of their fur coats and shook his head. Society was better off without these cutthroats. That afternoon, he had encountered them at mountain stream refilling their canteens. He had remained hidden and eased dropped. Laughing, they discussed murdering a miner and his family for gold nuggets. Then they argued whose gunshot had killed the miner's daughter as she fled. After filling their canteens, they looked at wanted poster of Kern. Clearly, the wanted *alive* portion of the poster was not an issue.

Shepherd blew out the candle and stepped across the cabin to leave, a floorboard creaked beneath his feet. Creaking floorboards were common for old cabins however, this board called for attention.

He squatted and used a knife to pry the board lose. Inside a crawl space, lay leather bound book and gun. A quick confirmed the gun was unloaded and not fired recently. It was Carl Ver Haven's gun.

Shepherd relit a candle and sat, crossing his legs. Emotions swelled as he fingered through pages. He slowed at the last few pages and began to read.

'Today, I boarded the Lady Beth, a fine Tea Clipper. It is a shame that in my lifetime sailing ships of this sort are replaced by steam engines. There is something about nature's wind moving a man across vast bodies of water that sets a troubled soul at ease.

Captain La Horn is a man not to be trusted, and I strongly suspect these men were once Buccaneers, and later pirates on the High Seas. I keep my personal belongings nearby at all times, save of course for my clothing trunk and field office as both being too large to tote around with me. The cook is somewhat to be desired. I fear yielding to hunger and eat what he serves or die of starvation.'

Day-two on the Lady Beth, Kern the cabin boy is a quick and eager learner. I've decided to pass the time teaching him to read and write. His accent is unusual and I've yet to place it. Not quite Australian, nor is it English or French. I fear he's on the run from his short lived past. Then again, aren't we all on the run from ourselves, if not physically than mentally.

Shepherd glimpsed over the next few pages, noting Carl's life had fallen into a pattern of walking the dog above deck, teaching Kern to read and write, and preparing his own meals against the cook's objections.

Day twenty-five onboard the Lady Beth, I caught a deckhand named Fat Sam slapping Kern's face. Before I was able to intervene, La Horn's first mate Caleb was on top of it. Fat Sam backed away, fearful of Caleb. As each day passes, my fears are being confirmed. This crew were Buccaneers and later Pirates. I am concerned for the boy, Kern. Worried they'll influence him badly. I've decided to fill his head with tales of life in America, this in hopes he will leave the Lady Beth after we reach port in San Francisco.

With no kinfolk to look after him, I'm sure it'll be a difficult life for him in America. A rough start in America is better than what he'd have with this motley crew. Given how well manned Kern is, he had a decent upbringing somewhere along the line. Where remains a mystery...

Slowly, over time he is opening up to me. He speaks of Water Spirits, Sun Spirits, and such as that. He's a complex puzzle beyond easy answers. Given he speaks of spirits as if an American Indian, perhaps he was raised by a native tribe somewhere in the South Pacific. I am leaning toward Australian outback.

If I were to ever settle down, marry and raise a family, I pray my own children would be of similar disposition to Kern. The dog is barking again at a rat. The ship is infested with rats.

Shepherd noted blood stained fingerprints on the next few pages, his suspicion validated by the next entry. Kern was there, helping in the final days of Ver Haven's life, a friend to the end…

Having been tortured for days seeming without end, I've lost track of time. A few days ago, Bristol alerted me to something sealed inside of a tea crate. Opium, known as black tar. I've seen its devastating effects on the people along China's coastlines.

China's Emperor had given the dog as gift for the President of the United States, and being as I learned at the Hawaiian Islands, Abraham Lincoln won the election, hence Bristol will be his. A vengeful sea rages outside, we are riding against twenty and forty foot swells.

I'd likely be dead had it not been for the tempest outside. Kern has proven my only ally onboard. He sneaks me food and water, plus my journal so that I may log my dying days. I grow tired and weaker with each day, and my dreams are vivid.

During waking hours, a sense of I teases me. My time to depart this earthly body is nearing. The means of torture used against me was beyond any sane man's ability to conceive. Bamboo shoots jammed beneath my fingernails continue to irritate me. Three broken fingers makes writing difficult, however, I must do so. Before we encountered the tempest, the cook broke my front teeth at the roots and probed a thin wire to the open nerve endings.

I have never experienced such pain and feared my heart would explode. I have entrusted Kern with delivering my journal to a trusted friend, Captain Bristol in San Francisco. I pray the lad is able to smuggle it off the ship without being caught.

Once Captain Bristol reads these last few entries, he will send soldiers to rescue the dog for President Lincoln, and ensure La Horn is brought to justice.

This will likely be my last and final entry. One may think that a man would express great words of wisdom on his deathbed, the sort of words able to move other men's hearts. I can think of none, it has all been said before.

I pray to God above to forgive me of transgressions against others. Should I have strayed against His will for my life, I pray for His pardon…

I look into my own heart and realize all are wicked – only that some do not act upon passing thoughts. May God forgive me for short-fallings and countless times I've gone astray. Should His judgment find me wanting and undeserving of His grace, then it would be just cause to cast me aside…

Any Earthly belongings I leave to Kern, the money in my bank accounts, locations known by Ms. Clare Shepherd. I'd like to rest in peace, knowing he's using the money for a proper education. Based on my recommendation, Ms. Clare will look after the boy and see he's raised right.

She's been known to take in strays and lives in Denver. A barkeep at Tony's Restaurant in Denver knows where and how to find her.

Consider this as my last will and testament. There are so many people whose lives have touched mine and my life has touched theirs. I cannot begin to list and thank them. If anyone who knows me well enough, realizes I have not forgotten them.

Jasper, if anyone comes looking for me it is likely you. I care deeply for you as father would a son. I have no way to perceive where, and or what is transpiring as you are reading this.

It is almost a given trouble is afoot, and a life needs saving. You know what must be done. You have traveled far from home. A passage of heart is before you – embrace it. Look to the future and take the path. I close with but a name of Carl Ver Haven.

Shaken, Jasper Shepherd closed the book and stood. His feet spread shoulder width, he clutched the journal and tears trickled from his eyes.

Silent, Shepherd vowed Kern would have a decent life, as he had had with Ms. Clare. She was a noble, fine and upstanding woman, and of good humor. She had a boundless love for God and others.

Shepherd pulled a 'wanted dead or alive' poster from the pocket of a dead bounty hunter. The he stepped to the potbelly stove, used the candle and lit a flame to it.

Ceremonial, he offered words of hope, "Kern your past matters not, a new life lay before you, look to the future and step onto the path."

He tossed the burning poster into the stove and watched flames consume it. Then he stepped outside, and slipped into the darkness behind the cabin.

Back at his horse, he placed the journal and gun into his saddlebags. The journal was important, and needed closer scrutinizing before shown to Crisp. Then he was taking it with him when leaving.

Carl Ver Haven's journal belonged with other artifacts gathered and hidden by the Herdsmen. Historical records of societies through several centuries documented by men, women and children who had lived through it.

Shepherd mounted his horse and road off into the night. Behind him, small traces of smoke twisted from the cabin's chimney.

23

Ring leaned against a gas lamppost and waited for Taylor to leave a Pub & Grill. So far, Taylor's life away from the A. R & B was boring. An hour ago, Taylor tried on a number of new hats. Although Taylor had clearly favored a flat top gambler style of hat, he failed to buy it.

Ring thought the hat looked good on Taylor and was surprised when he declined to purchase it. Earlier, he had watched from distance as Taylor pissed and moaned when paying for a new suit. Taylor was several days late buying it. Two days ago, Crisp had ordered everyone to buy a suit, shirt and tie, then provided an allotment but required a receipt. Luckily, Taylor had not needed to don a suit and tie. During a surprise inspection, Hindor had called him on it.

Ring decided, Taylor needed a lesson or two on losing-up. Unsure of style, the private was fussing about the smallest of things, buying a hat, suit and boots. Now, he was unable decided what to order from a one page menu.

Ring grumbled in conjunction with his stomach. "What's taking so-long to place an order and eat? This boy's starving me at a distance." He pulled his pocket watch. Taylor was inside for thirty minutes.

Ring tossed his shadowy pursuit aside, crossed the street, pulled his jacket collar along the side of his cheeks and shielded his face from view. Between shadowing his face and the heavy fog, it would be difficult for Taylor to recognize him.

Casual, Ring strolled past the grill and glimpsed into the near empty Pub & Grill. Aside from a waiter wiping tables, the place was vacant. Ring cursed, "Damn it all to hell, he gave me the slip that sneaky little bastard! He is not as dumb as he lets everyone think he is. Hindor ain't going to like this one bit."

Ring turned into a side ally and darted around back of the Pub & Grill. He squatted, studied recent boot prints and recognized a slight wearing on the inside heel of a boot. Sure enough, Taylor had slipped out the back door.

Ring spent the next three hours searching high and low through layers of fog amid the city's lower districts. It was time to accept a verbal thrashing from Hindor. Defeated, he convinced himself not to buy another flask of rye before heading on foot to the A. R & B.

Once Crisp discovered their suspicions, Hindor was bound to receive a far worse verbal thrashing. Ring had no desire to be within earshot after Crisp learned of Taylor's hammering in the backyard.

Instinctive, Ring reached into his back pocket for a flask that was not there and muttered, "Crisp you've cost me a small fortune in tins. Leaving a man nothing to cut a chill, it just ain't right."

A high-pitched scream emitted from a darkened side street. Ring froze stiff, a shiver crept along his spin and across both shoulders. Quick, he pulled his gun and dashed into the side street. Between night fog and near total darkness, it was difficult to see. Someone was hovering over a body with a raised hammer and ready to deliver a killing blow.

Ring was certain it had to be the Hammer Killer. His blood delivered adrenaline at an accelerated rate through his body. Was it Taylor or not? It was the waking hour of truth.

A silent approach would have allowed an element of surprise. A split second decision meant life or death for the victim. The killer and victim were to close for a safe shot. Perhaps, simply yelling police would scare off the killer and save her life. He raised his weapon, aimed and shouted a lie, "Halt police!"

The killer dropped the hammer, raised a pistol then pivoted and popped off a shot. The bullet struck a wall behind Ring and sent splinters flying.

By the time Ring re-aimed, Hammer Killer was on the run. He ran to the downed woman and checked her life signs. Blood spewed from her forehead but she was still alive.

Ring raised his voice and called, "Help! Help! Help! There's an injured woman back here!" An Asian man arrived at run, coming off the main street. Ring was unsure if the man understood English and decided it did not matter.

With each passing second, Hammer Killer was making good an escape. It was time to give chase. Ring said, "Stay with her, I'm going after the Hammer Killer."

Ring took off the general direction Hammer Killer had ran. The alleyway was long and narrow. Hammer Killer had a good head start. Ring possessed an advantage, he had stumbled drunk through these streets and alleyways countless times. The next major intersecting street was Mason. Ring hinged a bet, he was a faster runner.

Ring's feet pulled and sucked mud as he pushed himself harder and harder. Yards ahead, amidst fog and dim light that poured from hotel windows was Hammer Killer. For a third time, Ring aimed and this time fired. Without losing stride, Hammer Killer glimpsed at him.

"Bastard," Ring cursed, "You'll go for an unarmed woman, but when it comes to facing another man, you turn chicken and run." With Hammer Killer insight, there was no stopping the chase.

Ring's heart pulsated. This was it. He would end Hammer Killer's reign of terror. He was unsure what drove his legs faster. Was it a desire to know if Taylor was a killer of whores, or it was a stranger? While he gained ground with each passing second, Mason Street was within the killer's reach. He dared not aim and fire, fearing it would cost him valuable seconds and possible harm an innocent bystander.

Hammer Killer hesitated at the intersection, unsure of what direction to flee. Then, turned left and fled toward the bay. Ring held his pace, right behind him.

Hammer Killer darted into a dead-end alley and scampered over a fence. Ring scrambled over the fence as well, and stood frozen on the other side inches from the largest dog he had ever seen. Hammer Killer was nowhere in sight. The dog lunged forward. Suddenly, a chain stopped the beast short of biting Ring's leg.

The dog backed away and lunged forward for a second time, his chain pulling lose from a post.

Ring took off at a run, the dog nipping at his heels. Frantic, he reached the next fence and started pulling himself over it when the dog's teeth sank into Ring's leg and dragged him down.

On the ground and at dog level, a fight between dog and man began. Between gnashing fangs, Ring pulled his gun and fired pointblank against the dog's side. The dog's yelp was short and quick. The dog swaggered backward and fell dead.

Ring back crawled away and leaned against the fence. His arms and legs bled and soaked his clothing. He tried to stand and fell face forward into the mud. The dogfight had drained him of energy. He had lost the chase. The Hammer Killer had escaped.

Ring did not want to be found lying there. The A. R & B did not need another bad incident. This new undercover gig was the best assignment he ever had. He raised himself and struggled his way over the fence. Exhausted, he tumbled onto the next street a bloody mess from head to toe.

Footsteps halted directly above him.

Ring expected someone had heard the dogfight and gunshot, and help had arrived. Through blurred eyes, he caught a glimpse of Hammer Killer loathing over him.

Shocked, Ring recognized the Hammer Killer and gasped, "It's you?"

The hammer came down, cracking forged metal against skull bone.

24

Chief Crivitz stepped carefully around the dead dog and commented, "One thing for sure, both man and dog put up a good fight. I'd tend to think your man chased the Hammer Killer this far and ran into the dog."

Crivitz nodded toward a cracked fence post. "From the looks of it, if the dog hadn't broken that chain Mister Ringwald would've had the killer last night, and our local working gals would have slept better."

Then Crivitz sighed. "It appears after he shot the dog, he managed to climb the fence, and the Hammer Killer was waiting in the shadows."

Crisp glanced eastward, his thoughts rested on Ring. An early morning sun was burning away remnants of fog. Normal city-foot traffic made it impossible to track Hammer Killer. Besides, onlookers had spoiled tracks in the alleyway. He looked at Chief Crivitz and asked, "What are you going to do about Kay Yang? You and I know he didn't do it."

Crivitz shrugged. "For the time being I'm holding him, and not against his will. Early this morning a lynch mob started gathering outside the jail." He shook his head and grumbled, "I swear that mob has to have someone running around and recruiting people. Their numbers are getting larger by the hour."

"Kay Yang didn't do it," affirmed Crisp, "he was helping."

Crivitz confirmed, "Kay understands he is not a suspect. If not for him, she would have died last night. As it is, she is still unconscious and doctors ain't giving her much hope of ever waking again. She took a heavy blow to the forehead, the hammer broken clean through her skull and into her brain."

Crivitz's brow tightened with a question, "What's your Captain going to say about this?"

Crisp glimpsed at distant foothills and wondered about Kern, Shepherd and Bassett. He prayed they were faring better than Ring had last night. Solemn, he turned his attention to the matter at hand. "I'm not sure what to tell you.

Far as I know Ring was simply out for a night on the town. Weather never stopped him from going out for drink. From what it appears, he was looking for a little comfort to warm himself, when by shear chance he happened upon the Hammer Killer in action."

Crisp did not want to say more, not until he had spoken with Hindor and Trick. Crivitz felt responsible for having asked for their help. There was no reason to rub salt into an open wound. Last evening, Hindor had dodged this issue of answering Ring's whereabouts. It was certain, that Ring was not out last night on his own accord. Hindor had sent him on a covert mission of some nature.

Crivitz stared at the dead dog and stated, "Maybe asking for your help wasn't a good idea… I'm sorry to have dragged you into this. You don't have to cover for me with your captain on this, I'll shoulder blame on it. I doubt Mister Ringwald was drinking, he didn't smell of it."

Crisp glimpsed into Crivitz's eyes. The Chief was truly sorry for requesting the A. R & B boys help with a murder investigation. The deed done, and there was no undoing the damage. The A. R & B was down a good man. Ring was a difficult man to replace.

"No," Crisp said, "It's not your fault. He did what he did because he loved this town more than most. By virtue, he cared about the lives of innocent people… It went against his grain not to do something. If he took to chasing after the Hammer Killer last night, he did out of a sense of justice."

Crivitz sighed. "I betting he saw the killer's face."

Crisp failed to reply. In route to the scene of the crime, he had visited the hospital. The Hammer Killer had left Ring at Death's door. Bandages around Ring's head gave him the appearance of an Egyptian mummy. Dog bites had inflected severe damage; Ring's legs had enough stitches to patch a quilt.

Kay Yang had provided a description of the first person on the scene that fit Ring. Shortly afterwards, Ring was discovered by a carriage driver. Crivitz added one, plus two and equaled it was Ring who had chased after the killer.

Crisp believed Ring had paused to aid the woman after he frightened off the killer. Seconds later, Kay Yang must have arrived. Ring left the woman under Yang's watchful eye and gave chase. No matter what type of ground was beneath Ring's feet, he was surefooted at a dead-run. Although the Hammer Killer had a head start, Ring's long legs would have narrowed the gap.

Crivitz remained concerned and commented, "I saw a couple reporters interviewing the carriage driver who found your man. I won't be able to keep the papers out of it. I'll tell them Mister Ringwald worked for you and happened on the scene. Let them know Kay Yang is innocent and helped the woman as any God-fearing man would do."

Crisp shook his head and advised, "No don't say Ring worked for me… He worked at Shoreline Bank as a clerk."

Before Crivitz was able to inquire as to why Shoreline Bank, a patrol officer on foot arrived at the Mason Street side of the fence.

The patrol officer peered over the fence and announced, "Chief, the woman is dead. She died about twenty minutes ago, and that mob outside the jail is getting ugly. They want a quick trail and hanging. A number of folks are carrying signs with Kay Yang's name and calling for his hanging."

"I'm on my way," replied Crivitz, then looked to Crisp and said, "Fine, I understand. After I'm finished speaking to reporters, Ring will be a hero as will Yang. You mentioned the other day the army had safe houses. I hate to impose, but do you have a place where Mister Yang could lay low?"

Crisp pondered it for a moment and said, "I've a place in mind, one of the missions outside of town. I know a priest, who will see that Yang has a roof over his head and fed until this thing blows over. I'll send a couple of my men by later this morning to fetch him. Be ready with a bait and switch for the mob."

Crivitz inquired, "Bait and switch?"

Crisp explained, "One of my boys will pull up around back and load Yang into a canvass wagon and get him out of town."

Crivitz agreed, "Sounds like a plan. Let me know when you're ready." Solemn, he headed toward the jail and an angry mob ready to hang poor Kay Yang for the Hammer Killings. The public wanted a speedy end to the killings and justice, whether the right man hung did not matter.

***

Hindor and Trick had searched the A. R & B from top to bottom. Taylor and his gear were gone, deserted the army and possible miles away. Crisp was not pleased to learn, Taylor had angrily hammered nails into a board in the backyard. Hindor had no easy answers.

Easing tension, Crisp assigned Hindor and Muser to rescue Kay Yang from the mob.

Trick was an emotional wreck. His best friend balanced between life and death at University Hospital. Doctors were unsure Ring would awaken. He was worried if the newspapers printed Ring was alive, the Hammer Killer would come and finish the job.

Crisp agreed Ring needed protection and sent Trick to the hospital. Aside from protection, someone needed to be present, if and or when Ring awakened.

Bristol the dog laid at Crisp's feet as he drafted a report for Captain Bristol. Crisp wrote to the point, keeping the note as short as possible. It appeared Private Jackson Taylor had deserted for parts unknown. He thought it best not to inform Captain Bristol of Taylor's odd behavior in the backyard.

How to inform Crivitz of Taylor's demeanor was another matter. Hindor having assigned Ring to spy on a fellow enlisted man was unnerving. One had to trust those under his command. Distraught, he read his report aloud.

Taylor has deserted to parts unknown. Given his knowledge of our operations, he needs to be found ASAP. We need to know what happened at his last Post prior to transfer. Did he get into trouble? If so, what type of trouble? Who did he chum with? I recommend sending someone in person to ask direct questions, someone who will not accept a runaround from Taylor's former commanding officers. I suggest Sargent Forks as best suited for the assignment.

It appears last night, Ring stumbled onto the Hammer Killer, and put his life on the line in pursuit of justice. His condition is critical. Doctors have said it is unlikely he will live. Will keep you posted on his condition at the University Hospital.

Crisp folded the letter, slipped it into an envelope and tied it with a thin string. He wanted to have the Ackerland, La Horn and Ver Haven affair concluded before informing Bristol of Taylor's odd behavior. Between now and then, Captain Bristol would have fits of rage regarding a deserter.

Meanwhile, Crivitz had a suspect as the Hammer Killer, Private Jackson Taylor…

Crisp growled. "Damn it to hell, nothing every goes easy for those under my command. It is like I am cursed…"

Crisp looked down at Bristol, "Well buddy, it's up to you to look after the office while I'm gone."

Lonely, Bristol raised his head and offered a dropping gaze. Crisp petted the dog's head, and left for another secret rendezvous with Sargent Forks.

25

Mentally drained, Trick stepped onto the first floor of University Hospital. Down the hall and posted at either side of Ring's room stood two statue-like uniformed police officers.

Trick forced a smile and stepped toward them. "I'm here to sit with my friend, excuse me." Then, he reached for the door, only to have them step shoulder to shoulder and block his path.

One of the officers raised his palm outward and warned, "You're not going in there… Orders, sorry."

Frustrated, Trick tossed his head back and explained, "Look, I'm his friend and he needs me. Step aside or else."

The officer smirked. "Or else what, you're going try and fight your way in there? If so, think again… We're not standing here because we're harmless kittens. After we've finished mopping your sorry arse across the floor – you'll be staring at bars for a long time. Judge Mc Henry doesn't take kindly to someone forcing his way past protective custody."

Near defeat Trick replied, "Ring and I've been the best of friends for years, and it's not right keeping me from him. If you checked with Chief Crivitz, I'm sure he'd okay me to see him. Hell, my sitting there may even help him recover quicker and he can tell us who the Hammer Killer is."

The officer asserted, "Chief Crivitz was explicated on the matter. Aside from two doctors and three nurses who are treating the victim, nobody but nobody is allowed in that room, and that included the Angel of Death." He nodded at the front doors and dictated, "Hit the planks outside."

Trick clinched a fist tight, and then thought better of creating a fracas inside of the hospital. He had to secure clearance to visit from Crivitz. Blaming Crivitz for extreme security measures to protect a witness was pure foolishness.

Trick pondered a comparison and stomach sank. These two officers made a mockery of the job done watching after Kern. When it came to keeping an eye on a witness, those at the A. R & B were like bumbling clowns. When returning, he thought it best not to be on their bad side. Simply to leave a good impression, he apologized.

Once outside, Trick paused and considered his next move. Hindor and Muser were busy rescuing Kay Yang away from a lynch mob and did not require assistance.

Trick stepped off the boardwalk planks and crossed the street. There was plenty to do. Kern needed finding. Ackerland's bank records given close scurrility and La Horn's whereabouts checked.

In addition, Chen's Tea Shop needed investigating. The bank was nearest. It was time to stop act like a dunce and get results. His earlier mental exhaust was suddenly gone. Energetic, his mindset focused on a list of daunting tasks.

* * *

Muser reined an open buckboard wagon to a halt behind the jail, engaged the brake lever and commented, "This is a better idea as far as I'm concerned. A canvass wagon would've drawn suspicion."

Hindor smirked. "Yep, just don't be trying to take credit for it, the idea was mine." He stepped off the buggy and onto the muddy alleyway. He patted the top of a pine coffin and smirked. "I'll head inside and let em know we're here and fetch help getting this coffin inside. With luck, we'll be on our way within a few minutes."

Periodic shouts from a mob gathered in front of the jail raised Muser's level of tension. Hindor glimpsed over his shoulder and grumbled, "These white folks ain't much different than some I've met with hatred for colored folk."

Muser shook his head and observed, "Nah, that ain't true at all, no sir. Doesn't matter what the color of his skin is; brown, tan, black, white, orange or green, so long as they have someone to blame. These folks are hell-bent on seeing a hanging for those killings. It makes them feel more secure when tucked into their beds at night."

Hindor grunted and rapped lightly on the door. Muser was right. Whoever took blame, guilty or innocent; they wanted the Hammer Killings brought an end. If the wrong person hung for it, maybe the real killer would count his blessing and relocate to another city. He grumbled, "Damn mob mentality."

Cautious, an officer opened the backdoor a few inches and glimpsed around. Seeing only Muser and Hindor, he opened the door wider.

Hindor stepped back to wagon, patted the coffin and said, "Here to pick a dead-man."

Moving quick four officers slid the coffin from the buckboard and carried it into the jail. In less than three minutes, they had sealed a nervous Kay Yang inside and loaded it back onto the buckboard.

Unexpectedly, a portion of the mob shifted toward the alleyway, shouting accusation of using the coffin as a means of sneaking the Hammer Killer outside.

A number of guns came into play on both sides, each holding their fire. Before Hindor, and Muser had a chance to attempt and defuse the situation, suddenly someone from the mob yelled, "Hey, Shoreline Bank is going up in smoke!"

A few blocks away, windswept billows of black and blue smoke drifted against the foothills. The mob's attention migrated toward the bank. Their devotion refocused and clamoring about their savings going up in smoke, they took-off at a run toward the bank.

Muser seized the opportunity and slapped the reins. As the wagon jerking forward, Hindor hobbled alongside and repressed an urge to curse Muser for leaving him afoot. If nothing else, Kay Yang was on his way to safety.

Two blocks later, Muser reined to a halt long enough for Hindor to huff and puff onto the buckboard.

Hinder exploded, "If not for rescuing an innocent man from a lynch mob, I'd pistol whip ya for leaving me afoot like that like!"

Muser chuckled, "Well, we ain't out of town yet." Several blocks away, billows of black smoke darkened the skyline. He grumbled, "If'n that is indeed the bank, we're not getting Ackerland's finical records, and Crisp is gonna have a fit over that fire." Then he teased, "Your bright idea using a coffin didn't play-out too well did it."

Hindor grunted under his breath, "Not long ago, I seem to recall you were trying to take credit for the idea."

Muser ignored the comment and observed, "You guys always have this much trouble. Does near everything turn upside down on a regular bases? I've never seen so much go wrong for a bunch of people in life. It's like we're working against the devil himself."

Hindor sighed. "Could be we're working for the devil and don't know it. Remember you are part of our little charade and it is upside down for you as well. Not to forget, the army put you with us for a reason, and after the other night we've got a decent handle on your womanizing." Then he pointed toward a side road leading out of town. "Let's get our butts out of here and into the countryside. Sure as can be, hammered inside of that coffin Kay Yang is working-up nasty sweat."

Muser cringed, "Don't be using that word hammer, it gives me the willies."

* * *

Trick stepped from a side door of Shoreline Bank and glimpsed around. Beyond a gather crowd of onlookers, the formation a bucket brigade was starting to pull water from a nearby horse trough. Not wanting to cause serious damage, he had built and lit several smoke bombs. Within a matter of minutes, everyone would realize the money was safe.

He shoved his way through the crowd. With each step, a precious second ticked away. With a wet bandana tied around his nose and face to protect his lungs from dense smoke, he prayed not to be mistaken as a bandit.

A wooden box clasped between Trick's hands was overflowing with files and paper. An on looker reached for the box and said, "Mister, you're damn brave to going inside that inferno and get these bank files."

Trick held onto the box and coughed, "Done as much as a man can do. Hurting something fierce, smoke has scorched my lungs raw." He stepped around crowds of onlookers and set the box onto a buckboard wagon, along with other boxes of files taken from inside of the bank.

One of Crivitz's men grabbed a hold of Trick's arm, yanked the bandana down and said, "Do you work for the bank?"

Trick faked a cough and lied, "Had to save these bank files. Don't want people saying they lost more money in the fire than they actually did."

The officer swallowed the story, "I understand."

Then Trick requested, "Can you keep an eye the buckboard and files? My lungs are burning, I've gotta get some fresh air" Before the patrolman was able to answer, Trick looked at the crowd and commented, "Lot of people getting underfoot there."

The officer stepped toward the crowd and ordered, "Either pitch-in with the bucket brigade or get out of the way! There are people needing access to the building with water!"

Trick stepped to the front of the buckboard, lifted one small box and slipped away. With Ackerland's banking files secured for the A. R & B to inspect, he chuckled under his breath and dodged a group of angry people coming from the direction of the nearest jail.

After the file box was safe at the A. R & B, Trick planned to check on the Lady Beth and ensure the ship had not set-sail. From there, it was onto Chen's Tea Shop for a little spying.

26

Dog tired, La Horn sat at a table inside of his quarters. After a knock at the hatchway, he exhaled a puff of smoke from his pipe and called, "Enter!"

Caleb entered and passed him a telegram. Discouraged, he notified him, "Nearest cargo bound for the Far East is in Seattle, a shipment of pear and apple seeds for Japan. An orchard in Japan is hoping to cross pears and apples. They want to create a new fruit and call it a pear-apple. Their cargo will be ready for shipment in three weeks, which gives us plenty of time to reach Seattle. However, we have only two days to give them an answer. I'm ready to set-sail and get out of here, tonight."

La Horn grumbled, "I hate Seattle. Every-time I've been there it does nothing but rain." He leaned back, drew on his pipe and exhaled a cloud of smoke. "I'd sure like to get my hands on that wet-rat Kern. He has caused us a nasty heartache, and there is that reward money in Limmen Bright to consider." His brow tightened. "I swear he reminds of someone, I simply can't put my finger as too whom."

Caleb declined response and glimpsed at the deck. There was debt to repay. After seeing a wanted *Dead or Alive* poster at Limmen Bright, leaving Kern at the mercy of the law was unthinkable. He stared outside of a porthole at foothills surrounding the bay.

Tight brow, La Horn leaned forward and asked, "Something bothering ya?"

Caleb turned from his gaze and said, "No, just wondering what became of him is all. As far I'm concerned, I'm pleased we're shed of him." He eyed La Horn for a hint of vengeance.

For La Horn, the reward money for Kern meant nothing. Once onboard and out to sea, Kern was as good as dead. America was vast and remaining to enact a vendetta was foolish. It was clear La Horn was willing to risk losing a cargo in Seattle to get his hands on the lad.

La Horn faked a sigh as if using his better judgment. "Send a telegram we'll be there in three weeks. That should allow us time to linger here. Hopefully, we can secure a cargo in San Francisco and avoid going further north."

Caleb nodded and left without saying a word. Outside, he headed for the gangplank. Lingering in San Francisco for a cargo stunk worse than a pile of fish-guts. When it came to outright meanness, La Horn had the market cornered.

As Caleb trotted down the gangplank, boards creaked under his weight. He stepped onto the pier and stared upward at La Horn's quarters. Crisp had finical resources. Would Crisp help Kern escape a far distance away?

A number of times, Caleb had eased dropped on Ver Haven and Kern's conversations. He had heard Ver Haven's advice to flee the ship after arriving in the Americas. Perhaps, Ver Haven had the right idea and not simply for Kern.

Caleb stood at a threshold in his life, he needed only to step away and never return. A fresh start, freed of past crimes in a new land where no one knew his name or face. However, leaving was a major decision. He did not want to act on a whim. He had been a sailor most his life.

What would he do on land? Farm labor or work as a ranch hand. If unable to find work, would he again turn to crime? He turned from the Lady Beth and trekked toward the telegraph office, stepping around mud puddles.

An hour later, Caleb swung past the A. R & B offices on his way back from the telegraph office. From a distance, the place appeared deserted. His footsteps across the pouch raised barks from a dog inside of the building. Evidently, Bristol was working as guard dog. He decided not to inform La Horn, Bristol was alive and well at the A. R & B.

Caleb pondered whether to leave a note pinned to the door or not. Thinking from an unlawful perspective, he decided against it. A note was physical evidence. Something was not right with this business. Why would a military man like Crisp leave the army with a Civil War brewing? Crisp did not strike him as the sort of man who bailed if things got tough.

As Caleb stepped away to leave, the door creaked opened a few inches.

Surprised La Horn's first mate was at the door, Trick explained, "The boss ain't around. Can I do something for ya?"

Worried, Caleb glimpsed toward the piers. He was risking a crewmember seeing him. He looked back at the man and said, "The other day, Crisp invited me for a cup of coffee. Had a little free time and figured I'd take him up on it. I'll come back tomorrow." Ready to leave, he stepped off the porch.

Trick smirked. "Don't be quick to leave, not when we've got the best South American coffee beans in San Francisco. I'd be more than pleased to warm us a pot. Hell, I've got a lunch on its way from May Ling's Rice House, and more than enough to share." His smile broadened and he opened the door.

* * *

Inside, Bristol backed-away and growled until he saw it was Caleb. Trick squatted and petted him. As Bristol's tail fanned back and forth, Trick remarked, "He sure likes you. In general, dogs are a good judge of character. I'd have to say you're not all bad." Then he extended his hand and introduced himself, "Most folk call me, Trick."

Caleb noted a hint of smoke had scented Trick's hair and clothing. A hasty washing had left traces smudged soot from a recent fire. Earlier when leaving the telegraph office, he heard that Shoreline Bank was ablaze. At the time, billows of black smoke in the distance confirmed a building was on fire. An hour later when leaving the Lady Beth, pillars of black smoke was nonexistent. If there was indeed a fire, it was a small one. He wondered if the fire a diversion.

Caleb was certain, Trick was not among soldiers who had boarded the Lady Beth and taken Kern. Sure as fish swim the oceans, Trick was military but wearing street clothing. There was more to the A. R & B than meant the eye.

Caleb decided against informing La Horn of his suspicion, knowing it would only serve La Horn another excuse to enact revenge against Crisp. He excused himself, "I've the afternoon free and don't want to waste it. Was planning on exploring western culture and hunt for tattoo parlor."

Trick pointed toward the bay and explained, "Three blocks due south, same street we're on is Joe's Tattoo Parlor. Can't miss the place, big old sign hanging out front, has faces of pirates painted on it." He grabbed a feather pen from an inkwell and piece of paper off a desk. "I can jot down a message for Crisp."

Caleb raised his hands and shied from leaving a message. "I'll stop back at another time." He noticed a large pattern of dots the paper and remarked, "Studying the stars?"

Trick ran with it, "Me and buddy are always testing our knowledge of it. He left me this one yesterday, I have to connect the dots and name the star system. I can't seem to figure it out."

Caleb took the paper and feather pen. He connected the dots, returned the paper and pen. He said, "It looks like the Herdsman, also known as Bootes."

Then Caleb squatted, stroked Bristol's head and said to the dog, "You be a good boy for these people." He stood, stepped to the door and said, "Again, thanks for your time and the suggestion of a tattoo parlor."

* * *

Caleb walked to the Shoreline Bank and mingled among a crowd of onlookers. Billows of smoke had faded, leaving traces of soot on windowpanes. The building was undamaged by flames. There was never a true fire. Had Trick set up a diversion? If so, why? He recalled seeing a bank draft on La Horn's desk from Shoreline Bank and wondered if there was a connection.

Caleb's thoughts fell to Clifford Ackerland. Ackerland was a slick politician who had a criminal mindset. He gazed at distant foothills. He stood at the western threshold of a country torn at the seams and poised for the bloodiest war in history.

Over the years, he had seen countries tattered by inter strife. America possessed vast resources. Men elected by voters had a backing of the people. It would be a long drawn-out and bloody war.

Caleb stared at nameless faces amid the crowd of onlookers at the bank. These people lived far away from the heat of any fighting that laid ahead, save, secure and able to ride out the war a distant. He placed aside ideological ponderings and left the crowd to explore California's vast cultures. He planned to stop at Joe's Tattoo Parlor for a new tattoo on his right forearm, art to serve as a reminder of San Francisco and Kern's new life.

* * *

Chief Crivitz stood alongside a buckboard loaded with bank records and watched Caleb stroll away. Shortly after the Lady Beth had docked, the Hammer Killings began. Caleb did not strike him as a man given to bashing heads of working-gals.

The Lady Beth crew was a rough bunch, involved with several knockdown drag-out fights at local brothels. They had his men pulling double shifts to pick-up the pieces.

He wished for a quicker means of contacting other Ports the Lady Beth had visited. Had there been hammer killings at the Hawaiian Islands?

"Damn to it hell," Crivitz grumbled. If not for Trick, he had been able to ask the gambler from Texas if there were killings at the islands.

Crivitz headed toward the docks, leaving a suspect fire that caused no lasting damage. He planned to compile a list of ships that had visited the Hawaiian Islands prior to arriving at San Francisco Bay. Poke a stick into enough holes and a rat was bound to dart from inside of one.

Part Three

Chilled Souls

27

As Bassett fed wood on a small campfire at the mouth of a cave, sparks kicked into the night air. A gentle breeze swept traces of smoke into the cave, finding an exit somewhere deeper inside of the mountain.

Abandoned pots, panning-tins, canteens and empty whiskey bottles lay scattered across the cave floor. Rust on pots and panning-tins left the impression this little sanctuary had gone unused for a long time.

Bassett stared at his new friend who wore nothing but a loincloth. Local natives had enough sense not to dress-down this time of year. Crisp had not told him everything about his nephew or had outright lied.

Bassett was not about to lose his prize possession, Kern. Returning him to the city was a decent shot at a better life. He stared at his oversized shoes pulled from a dump outside of the city. A long-term job was better than reward money.

On his list to buy was pair of new boots. Then, he planned to buy new pants and shirts. If not for bounty hunters roaming the area, they would have returned to San Francisco hours ago. They had doubled back and avoided contact with everyone.

Outside, overcast night skies dusted large fluffy snowflakes across rugged ground, boulders and tree branches. Other than bitter cold, it was a beautiful evening.

Kern's warm breath misted upon each exhale. As if watching his soul exhaled from his mouth, his eyes widened. It took several seconds before realizing the mist was his warm breath mixing with cold air.

Bassett chuckled. He was grateful that Kern was unable to hear the laughter. Apparently, Kern had never lived in a cold climate or seen snow before today. Puzzled, Bassett watched Kern dart outside and gaze skyward. Within seconds, Kern was dancing amid feathering snowflakes.

After a couple minutes, Kern returned inside of the cave and warmth of the fire. He pulled a small cloth pouch from his leather carry bag. Then, he spread a fine powder from inside of the sack onto a flat rock and wet the powder with water from a canteen. Using an index finger, he mixed into a fine paint like paste.

Ritualistic, Kern used the paste to dab five white dots along his forehead, followed by two white lines alone each cheek. Completing the process, he ran one line down each shoulder and arm, finishing with three lines arching across his chest.

After Kern finished painting himself, he stepped back outside. Amid falling snow, he knelt and leaned back, then raised his arms and palms upward. Monotone due to his hearing impairment, he chanted using the Namra language.

Stunned, Bassett remained at the mouth of the cave and watched. It was the first time he had heard Kern speak, and this was more along the lines of singing. He had seen Indians practice ceremonies but none like this one. The language was unlike anything spoken by local tribes. Sure-as-can-be, Crisp had lied or held-back information. This kid was not normal. What self-respecting white boy would wear paint like an Indian and chant?

Bassett realized he was witnessing a rarity. He scooted nearer the fire, warmed his hands and spoke aloud to himself. "For-sure that boy ain't from these parts. He's calling on spirits, or thinks the spirits are trying to communicate with him by dropping snow from the clouds."

* * *

Late afternoon the following day, Kern lay belly flat next to a redwood and alongside of Bassett. In the valley below, a large encampment of armed men were busy going about their tasks. Groups of pup tents dotted the landscape. Rope corrals prevented horses from having free roam of the valley.

The encampment reminded Kern of white hunters who had massacred his adoptive family. Slick faced, Bassett nudged him, then pointed at the nearest group of horses and said something.

Kern wanted to play stupid, however he understood Bassett's plan to steal horses. When rescued by the white stranger from the hunters, it was at a dead-run on horseback. That horse was a graceful beast, willing to serve its master. This was different, and he envisioned falling off the beast. He shook his head and grunted disapproval of the plan.

Bassett mouthed, "Chicken". Playful, he tucked both thumbs under his armpits flopped his arms and clucked.

Stiff browed, Kern was not amused.

Bassett shrugged, "I sure as hell ain't walking out of these mountains, not when there're a couple horses for the taking. With so many, they're not gonna miss a couple scrawny ponies." He groaned, "Hell, ya ain't hearing a word I'm saying, I don't know why I bother… Only question of importance, will ya wait here while I snatch us a couple ponies?"

Bassett motioned for Kern to wait. Then he started to belly crawl away, until Kern grabbed his ankle and yanked him short of leaving. Upset, he stared at him and motioned, "what?"

Kern pointed at the late afternoon sun and grunted.

Bassett realized Kern was correct. He rolled his eyes and said, "Yep, you're not as stupid as ya play yourself to be, you've got stealing down pat. Been so long since I've done it, simply forgot my better judgment of night cover is all."

Basset mimicked a rope around his neck and advised, "Just so ya know, in these parts they hang a man for stealing a horse. Figured ya oughta know what we're up against, if'n we're caught. I'm figuring they hang a man anywhere for horse thieving and ya already know the risk. But don't ya worry none, cuz I'm not getting us caught."

Bassett gazed skyward. It was another couple of hours before dusk settled. After stealing a pair of ponies, night riding was going to be difficult. Between potholes, tight mountain trails and darkness, they had to take their time. Unless the men below had posted sentries, slipping a couple horses from one of the corrals should not be a problem.

Kern shivered and sat cuddled against a tree. In the valley below campfires flames licked back and forth as if inviting the boys to share its warmth.

Suddenly, directly behind them a gruff voice asked, "You boys lost?"

Bassett turned and sighed. Behind them stood a man wearing a bearskin overcoat with a rifle resting across his arms. Kern noted Bassett's attention had diverted and looked. Unsure how to start the lie, Bassett played along, "We wasn't sure your camp would welcome us."

Considering it, the man's brows pulled taught. He readjusted the rifle across his arms and replied, "Reckon that sounds fair enough. You boys best come on down and warm yourselves. It's not a fit night to sleep without a fire nearby."

Bassett stood. He brushed dirt and pine needles from his clothing. He agreed, "Warm fire sounds fine to me, and maybe a hot meal."

The man eyed Kern wrapped in tattered wool blanket and wearing nothing but a loincloth beneath it. "Come on boy, you too."

Bassett advised, "He can't hear. Deaf and near dumb. Has hardly uttered a word in days, and even then I'm not sure he was saying words, it was more of a chant." He thumbed his chest and said, "Name is Bassett," and nodded at his friend. "This here is Kern."

Fifteen minutes later, they warmed themselves near a blazing fire. The grizzly man who had brought them down from the mountainside instructed a cook bring them warm bowls of venison, carrot and potato stew. Members of the encampment eyed them with suspicion.

Kern felt his acceptance was colder than mountain air. Again, these men reminded him of the white-man hunting party whom had murdered the Namra Clan. He was certain these men had murderous hearts as well.

Kern had a growing dislike for them, and sensed they cared nothing for him. At least he and his friend had their fill of food and warmth of a fire. If they had stayed another night in the cold, he thought they might freeze to death. He gazed skyward.

Dark clouds sporadically obstructed his view of a crescent moon. Cold white fluffy flakes trickled downward. Frozen ground beneath his feet felt as hard as stone. Seasons here were different from his former life in Kakadu.

One of the men approached the campfire, tossed each boy a wool blanket and dropped a canvass pup tent at their feet.

Grateful, Kern gave him a thankful nod then stared at the tent and poles.

The man asked, "You know how to set up that tent?"

Bassett assured, "Sure enough do, mister! And we're mighty grateful to ya for bringing it and these here blankets."

28

The next morning Kern woke and discovered Bassett was busy helping with chores around the encampment. They had turned his wanna-be-friend into a messenger running from one area of the camp to another. Uncertain, his stomach twisted. His skin was the same color as theirs'. He was Baland on the outside. However, their filthy hearts were not as his.

Oddly, Kern missed the uniformed officers whom had rescued him from La Horn. Perhaps, he had misjudged those officers. If he had returned to the Lady-doctor's home with Carl's hand written book, none of this would have happened.

Kern's pressing urge to shed himself of these people grew stronger. It was time to move-on. Steal a horse was wrong, besides, the risk of being caught taking one was high. There would be no horse to ride. He had to strikeout on foot and set-right his misjudgment of those who had saved him.

With the A. R & B building in his thoughts, Kern began trekking westward and out of the encampment. Sooner-or-later, he would find the ocean Water Spirit Woowie had used to separate peoples of the Earth. From there, he planned to walk northward to San Francisco.

Kern had not gone far, when the grizzly old man who had found them last night grabbed his arm. He decided against struggling. He planned to play stupid and confused. Maybe, they would loosen their watch on him and he could slip away under the cover of night.

He believed they wanted their armed presence kept secret. Carl had mentioned this country was ripping apart, and edging toward a bloody civil conflict. He doubted either side of the pending war knew of these men. This was a third addition to the fray that was going to surprise everyone.

At midday, they chained Kern to a post like an animal. Bassett gave him a warm bowl of venison, potatoes and carrots. Kern understood a line was drawn and Bassett stood on the wrong side of it.

Bassett expressed a sympathetic shrug. "Damn it all to hell, I tried my hardest to help you out of a tight-spot. These folks have been teaching me things… Stuff, I never knew I cared about. Living here in the west is the best thing that happened to me… Most folks don't know I came from Saint Louis. I am plum happy to be on this side of the Divide. I'm better off here… If'n I play my cards right, once this war is settled and California has struck out on her own, I'll be setting right-nicely."

Bassett glimpsed over his shoulder at the main tent, then back at Kern. "Don't worry yourself none, cuz I ain't told them about your rich uncle. They haven't seen a newspaper from San Francisco in days. I know ya can't hear a word I'm saying, still I feel it right to say something. Ya have to understand… Only reason you're strung out here like a dog cuz ya tried to leave this morning."

Kern didn't need to hear a word. Bassett was making excuses. His wanna-be-friend had chosen sides. Kern felt he had no bearing on the outcome of war, and that neutrality had him chained. He hated chains. La Horn's chaining of Carl, Bristol's chaining at the A. R & B building, and now his own chaining to a post.

Bassett muttered, "Don't know why I bother." He turned and headed toward the main tent. In the distance, he noticed a rider approaching from the west. Captain York was expecting a courier with a message from San Francisco.

Bassett paused and warmed himself at a fire near the main tent, watched and waited. He wanted to know everything happening inside of the camp, and carrying messages ensured it. After Captain York read whatever the courier had, it was likely messages needed delivering to other parts of the encampment.

* * *

The rider dismounted, passing the reins of his horse to another man and entered the command tent without pausing at a nearby fire for warmth.

Inside the main tent, York drew a sip from a flask, then pulled back and snorted. "Damn, I don't where this comes from… But it sure as hell has kick to it." He passed the flask to the courier. "Here Charlie you've earned it, take a couple swigs. But I'm warning you, it has nasty bite."

Charlie took a swig and hacked a cough, then passed a satchel to York.

York smirked. "I warned you it had a kick." Then, he pulled a stack of papers and newspaper from the satchel. As Charlie drew another sip from the flask, York's eyes widened at the drawing of Kern in the newspaper.

York was stunned and exclaimed, "That pup out there must be a son of the devil himself! He's wanted for murdering a lawman!" He looked up from the paper. "Killing a lawman, he must have balls the size of a steer."

Charlie's brow pulled taught. "Excuse me, sir? I've been gone for near-on two weeks. Who are ya talking about?"

York explained, "Old Grizzly found a couple youngin's spying on us from the foothills. At first, we thought they were a couple lost pups. The light haired one was dressed as if he'd been living with injuns, wearing war paint and nothing but a couple rags covering his front and rear. Darkened skinned as if he had been sun bathing. Strangest thing, since we're on the downside of winter here. I reckoned he wasn't from these parts. Turns-out I was right."

York's index finger trailed a newspaper story. "This here explains a lot. He is a foreigner from the downside of the globe." Concerned, he looked up from the paper and said, "Don't be telling anyone about the reward for him. I'd sure hate to shoot a deserter trying to cash-in on reward money."

Astonished, York shook his head. "Awfully damn strange, why the French and British want this kid and posted a reward Dead or Alive. That treaty with China's Emperor has a lot of business interests in Europe upset over loss of profits. They were making money hand over fist in the opium trade. Simply to be rid of potential trouble, I have half a mind to bury him six feet down. On the flip side of that coin, we could use him as bargaining chip with French and British."

York pondered for a moment and commented, "No need to be telling Clifford Ackerland we have this murdering kid. Ackerland would make a rash decision and regret it later. And don't be saying anything to anyone as about this either."

Charlie agreed, "I understand, sir." He tapped his belly and asked, "I'd like to get my empty stomach settled and bedded-down. This cold snap has me drained."

York nodded. "You made great time, take a couple days off and relax."

Charlie took another swig from the flask and hissed, "It does have nasty bite." Then he offered the flask back to York.

York raised a hand and said, "Keep it for yourself. I've had enough of it." A chilling skirted though the tent flap and ruffled the tent roof. He pulled his collar tight around his neck and remarked, "It's mighty cold for this time of the year. I'm surprised we're not under a foot or more of snow."

"Ground is frozen enough to hold it," Charlie commented, then he took another sip and wiped his mouth. "Thanks for whiskey. It's a strong batch of whatever it is."

York lifted a casual salute, "Dismissed." After Charlie had left, York returned to skimming the newspaper. He read mention of a ceremony at Fort Tejon and smiled. The army had no idea as to what was coming.

York stood, walked to a potbelly stove and poured a fresh tin of coffee. He studied a map spread across a table, sipped his coffee and stared at a red circled marking the location of Fort Tejon.

York expected a large number of the army's enlisted men would desert at the first sign of trouble. Another portion would join the Cause for an independent California. Remaining troops would die fighting, or be captured, or flee the territory.

A cold burst of air rushed in behind one of York's men. "Sir," announced Cole. "A few miles south of here, there's a column of army regulars cutting through Gutman's Pass, twenty plus men on horseback. They are remnants of a Dragoon Patrol. We captured their scout... Aside from his name simply as Cricket, he ain't saying much of anything."

York frowned. "What's a patrol doing this far off the beaten path?" His thoughts fell on the boy chained outside. Was it a search party for Kern? This unexpected patrol needed containing. He ordered, "Bring their scout here I'd like personally question him."

Minutes later, Cole returned with a short wiry man and two guards. York scowled at the handcuffs around Cricket's wrists and asked, "Is that really necessary?"

Cole injected, "He may be a small tike, but he smacks a powerful left jab." He rubbed his sore chin and winced. "His fists are quicker than a swarm of pissed-off hornets."

York trusted Cole's judgment. Cricket was wearing buckskins, topped with a battered tall silk hat. He was not Indian, however, dressed and carried himself like one. The prisoner was a mountain man hired as scout and tracker by the army. One thing for sure, Cricket would not yield any information willing. Not that it mattered. The army patrol was too close for comfort but easily dealt with.

York expelled a tone of authority, "There's no-need to know your given birth name or where you are from. I ask only out of common respect before dealing with you in a proper manner. What's an army patrol doing in the area?"

Cricket shrugged, saying nothing.

York grunted, "Much as I expected. Having two mutes cross our path in one day isn't possible." He motioned at the tent flap and instructed Cole, "Take him a couple miles away from camp. No gunfire, we don't want those soldiers tipped-off. Slit his throat and bury him."

As an afterthought, York stated, "Be quick and clean about it, I don't want him suffering a loss of dignity in the face of death."

York debated whether to have Kern dealt with as well. No, he decided the boy had future value. Why did the English and French want Kern dead or alive? Murdering a peace officer was not a decent explanation. Why post a reward this far from where the murder had taken place, especially for a boy Kern's age?

"Sir," Cole inquired, "Is there something else?"

"As of yet, no" said York. "Take care of this man, and have a guard posted near that boy chained at the pole." A premonition wrenched his gut. Trouble was in the wind, twirling a dust cloud around that deaf mute boy.

After Cole and Cricket had left, York hosted his gun belt from the table and strapped it on. Then, he grabbed his rifle from near his bed. Although he had cleaned it last night, a habit formed during the Indian Wars seized control. He was unable to keep himself from inspecting it. He exited his command tent and into a chilling wind.

York peered skyward. A nasty storm was brewing. He stared at a guard posted near his tent. "Have units one through four met me by the corral. Tell them to be armed and ready to ride."

Within a matter of minutes, York had one hundred men riding out of the camp at a fast trot. He took lead point to show his men, he was not afraid of battle and setting an example.

Frozen ground beneath beating horse hoofs failed to kick up a dust trail that might have given away an element of surprise.

29

After a hundred men on horseback thundered from camp, Shepherd collapsed his telescoping lens and commented, "That lad sure has a habit of falling into the worse situations."

Minutes earlier, Shepherd had watched a mountain man ushered from camp by two armed men. Although a large percent of the camp was gone, rescuing Kern in broad-daylight was risky. He debated the importance of two armed men and their prisoner. No doubt in his mind, anyone with enough willpower and ability to gather this many men had a political agenda.

Shepherd pulled his coat collar against his neck, shielding himself from the wind. In the past, he kept things unreported to authorities. This outfit fell under a different category. It needed reporting to Crisp and Bristol as soon as possible.

Shepherd assumed the outfit was part of a vast secret network with sufficient funds to support an endeavor of this size. It was decision time. Save the mountain man's life and follow the small army or rescue Kern?

Hardened snow crunched beneath Shepherd's feet as he slipped beneath towering redwoods and trekked toward his horse. The prisoner being taken away from camp was about to die. Rescuing the mountain man made sense. If nothing else, he had been inside of the camp and able to provide information. He made a decision. Save the mountain man, then rescue Kern.

* * *

The two men from the camp, leading their prison complained loudly about cold weather and failed to hear any sounds. Cricket on the other hand, passed a guarded glimpse toward the pines. Swift and without warning, a knife sliced end over end from the cover of trees.

The first man staggered several feet, desperately grabbing at the middle of his back but not reaching a knife stuck between his shoulder blades. Dumbfounded, he toppled face forward into the snow and exhaled a dying gasp.

Baffled, Cole halted in his tracks and gazed at his fallen comrade. He spotted the knife and realized his comrade lay dead in spreading pool of blood-crusted snow. He swung around and drew a gun from its holster but too late.

Cricket sprung like cat, taking him down to the ground. His thin hands grasped around the Cole's throat. Using his grip around Cole's neck, he hammered Cole's head against the rocky path.

By the time Shepherd arrived, Cole lay dead as well. Instinctive, he cocked the hammer of his pistol, raised it and asked, "Your move. Friend or foe?"

Relieved and hands raised, Cricket stood slow and easy. His voice was quiet and steady, "Depends on your next move." He waved both hands with fingers spread wide. "Taking into account you saved me from a throat slicing, I'd say you're a friend. Most of my friends call me, Cricket."

Shepherd pointed his gun barrel at the ground, yet kept the hammer cocked. His thoughts divided between Cricket and the group of horsemen that had rushed from camp. It dawned on him the riders had not bothered taking supplies. There was not much time until they completed their mission and returned.

Uncaring, Shepherd kept his voice flat. "I don't have time for chitchat. What brings you out at the forefront of a blizzard?"

Cricket noted the man's stone cut eyes. While this man had saved his life, he was as likely to kill him for reasons beyond easy explanation. Here stood a man who had secrets buried within secrets. Although clearly not part of York's group, this man was beyond reasoning with.

Cricket explained, "I'm scout for the army, guiding a group of reassigned Dragoons on a worthless patrol to keep them out of trouble. Sort of a training exercise as it were."

"Training exercise?" Shepherd remarked and shook his head. "Given what I saw ride out of the camp, their training days are over. At least a hundred men bent on hellfire left that camp of mercenaries. At the speed they were riding, they are not afraid of blowing their horses. I reckon their target must've been close."

Cricket gasped. "Good God, those boys don't stand a snowflake's chance in hell. We had only seventeen men on that training patrol. York didn't strike me as the type of man who'd send unseasoned men into battle."

"York?" questioned Shepherd.

Cricket dispensed with his raised hands and clarified, "I reckon you correct on that assumption of mercenaries. York is their captain from what little I was able to gather about that outfit. Well organized, well fed and trained to work as a group."

Careful and watching for a reaction, Cricket retrieved guns from both dead men. He checked the weapons for load and tucked each into the waist of his pants. Then, he pulled his coat tight against a snarling wind and said, "We've gotta get going and do something. You coming along? Sure could use an extra fighting man, and from what I've seen you're good at whatever it is you do."

"No," Shepherd dismissed the notation along with any desire to help an army patrol. "I've got more important things to attend too." Then he un-cocked his gun's hammer yet kept it hanging at his side.

Cricket was astounded. Against better judgment, he inquired, "What the hell could more important than saving an army patrol of seventeen men?"

Candid, Shepherd re-cocked the gun. "You're alive because I needed information, nothing more and nothing less. I strongly suggest you consider your life saved as a prelude between heaven and hell. What is my best route into that encampment without being seen?"

Cricket sighed. "There ain't one. They have guards are posted everywhere." He stared off in the distant direction of the army patrol was riding.

Shepherd warned, "Bear in mind, if you're bent on dashing to the rescue of that patrol, you're going to die and there won't be anyone alive to report what is happening out here."

He paused for effect. "Give it some thought, what's more vital? Making tracks to the nearest fort and report there's a private militia out here that is up to no good, or throwing your life away trying to save a small patrol?"

Cricket pleaded, "Any chance I can talk you out of your horse?"

"Not a chance," said Shepherd. "You can ride double with me toward their camp. Slip off before they see us, sneak into their herd and steal a horse."

Cricket response was silent. He turned and ran off, vanishing among the redwood undergrowth, ready to give his life trying to save the army patrol.

Shepherd shook his head and stepped back into the forest. Then he mounted his horse and eased onto a trail leading toward the camp. A direct approach was best. With so many men gathered at one place, they would never expect it.

Once inside the main camp, Shepherd planned to play a member of whatever private army this was and rescue Kern. With such a large number of men, it was possible no one would question his arrival. He was simply another face among a sea of them.

* * *

A few minutes later, Shepherd led his limping horse into camp, using the same trail the riders had used to leave. He dismissed a few suspect glares with a disappointed grumble, "Horse took lame."

Earlier, Shepherd had tucked a small pebble into his horse's hoof pad. Later when he removed it, there would be no serious injury to the horse.

Shepherd checked his horse inside of a rope corral nearest to Kern. He noticed many of the corralled horses had the same brand. The letter A inside of a triangle. As he removed the pebble, he glimpsed at Kern. Kern appeared cold and in need of warmth. Moving steady, he shuffled his saddle to a dabbled gray and led the horse toward Kern.

A guard halted him and inquired, "I don't recall seeing you around here before. State your name and business."

Shepherd noticed Kern had recognized him but had kept from expressing it. Smart lad, he thought. He addressed the guard, flat and uncaring. "York sent me to take care of the boy."

Again, Shepherd stepped forward leading the gray. Then he handed the reins to the guard and instructed, "Hold my mount while I…"

The guard asked, "What do you mean, take care of the boy?"

Nasty, Shepherd's lips curled. "What do ya suppose happened to that idiot of an army scout? We simply let him go free? Give it some thought…"

Kern's eyes widened, seeing someone behind Shepherd.

Shepherd swung around, reaching for his pistol but halted and raised both hands.

Bassett stood, legs spread, a rifle butted against his shoulder and stated for the guard's sake, "I've seen you back in San Francisco, mister. What are ya doing here? We don't welcome your kind around these parts. No, sir… Last week, I saw you wearing an army uniform."

Shepherd cocked an eyebrow. "You're mistaken boy, I've never been to San Francisco in my life. Lower that weapon, before you accidentally shoot someone." His ploy failed.

The guard raised and cocked a pistol. "Like I said mister, I sure as hell don't know you from Adam. I ain't yielding this chained pup until I hear from Captain York his-self." Using his free hand, he double fingered a sharp whistle.

Within seconds, twenty men surrounded Shepherd, with their guns pointed. They bore no markings of rank, no uniforms. One of the older men ordered him, "I know it's damn cold but layer by layer strip down to your long-johns."

As Shepherd reached for his coat buttons the older man warned, "Take it slow and easy, using two fingers at a time."

Distance gunfire erupted, echoing through the valleys and canyons. Only a few of the men glimpsed in the general direction of the gunfire. The majority maintained their focus on Shepherd.

Abrupt, the wind fell silent as if a door had closed. A light snow trickled from an overcast sky, accenting increasing sounds of far-off gunfire.

* * *

Three miles and two canyons away, Cricket lay on a rock overhang and slammed his fist against frozen slate stone. In the valley below, the Dragoon army patrol circled into a tight group and fired toward unseen targets concealed amid forested hillsides. Within minutes dead, dying and wounded Dragoons lay across frost covered grass, and their horses stampeded to safety.

* * *

After the firestorm had ended, York and his men rode into the carnage for closer inspection. He circled his buckskin horse around a wounded young army officer and sneered, "I'll ask once peaceably, after that we'll beat what we want from you. What brings out here to the middle of nowhere?"

The lieutenant pressed a bandana against his gunshot shoulder and slowed the bleeding. He refused to answer and deliberated his situation. Who are these people? Where did they come from? It made no sense. Any Civil Conflict was beyond the Continental Divide. Are these people bandits? He had never known bandits to travel in numbers this large.

York grumbled, "No answer? Before this night is through you'll learn new meanings of pain and pray for death." He glimpsed at his men and ordered, "Winston, take ten men and fetch their wayward horses."

"Franklin," continued York, "Have your men slit the throats of everyone near dead, including the ones you think are dead. I want no second guesses as to who is dead and who is not. Those alive and worth interrogating, are to be stripped naked and tied across the back of a horse. First one that gives you lip, make an example and slit his throat."

As York's men went about their tasks, he again turned his attention to the officer and demanded, "Your name?"

The officer replied, "Lieutenant Brocker… When you are done beating us and we have told you nothing because there's nothing to tell… It is clear you intend to murder us."

No reply was necessary. York's cold expression answered.

Lieutenant Brocker wanted to claim, the army would search for them, and there would be hell to pay for slaughtering them.

As if reading Brocker's mind, York interjected "Don't bother me with trivial threats." He motioned westward at gathering dark clouds. "There's a nasty storm bearing down on us, and you're pathetic patrol won't be missed for days. By the time anyone comes looking, you will become another mystery, a minor footnote in the history books. In a hundred years no one will care that small patrol of men vanished, never to be seen or heard from again."

* * *

On a distant rock ledge, Cricket belly crawled backwards until concealed beneath the undergrowth of a low hanging pine. He was on foot with a spring snowstorm an hour or less away from blasting through foothills and valleys.

As the stranger had suggested, Cricket decided to return to the fort and report. Before the storm bore down, he planned to travel a few miles and wait it out beneath a cliff overhang he had used in the past.

Surely, his commander at the fort would understand. It was a difficult choice. There were simply too many men to fight alone. Going against a private militia and rescuing prisoners was an impossible feat.

As a light snow began to fall, Cricket slipped from beneath the pine and stood. Several yards away, an escaped horse from the patrol slowed from a gallop to a walk.

Cricket pulled his coat tight and assured, "Hey there buddy. God-sent, you got here in the nick-of-time. Don't go running off on me, now. We're part of the same group, you recognize me from riding with that patrol."

The horse made no effort to shy away. Cricket gathered the lose reins and checked the cinch strap. Then he swung up onto the saddle, patted the horse neck and said, "We best get a move-on before we're spotted."

As Cricket reined his newly acquired horse toward nearby foothills and the safety of a cliff overhang for the night, he thought about the man who had saved his life.

What was the stranger doing there? Why was he spying on York's private army? Whoever he was, he was not there by choice or chance. There was a boy chained to a pole outside of York's tent. Perhaps, the boy was the stranger's son… If true, it explained the man's intent focus, allowing nothing to distract him.

30

Inside of Doctor Steadson's combination home and office, early morning sunrays cast beams through windows and across kitchen floorboards. Gathering his thoughts, Crips walked to the front window and stared outside.

Hours prior to daybreak, a spring storm had blown-in from the Pacific, flooding streets and bringing San Francisco to a standstill. Downtrodden shopkeepers were shoveling mud off boardwalks in front of their businesses. A number of horse buggy remained sunken axle deep in mud. As horse pulled forward on the rig, several men propped two-by-fours beneath rear the rear axil and leveraged upward.

Crisp returned from the window, finished pouring two cups of coffee, sat at the kitchen table and passed a cup to Captain Bristol who was dressed in civilian clothing.

A day ago, Bristol's anger conceded to concern. Shepherd had failed to return with Kern and Ver Haven's journal.

Crisp decided against informing Bristol, he had sent Bassett to look for Kern as well.

Bristol passed Kern's amulet back to Crisp. "Like I said the other day, aside from having seen Carl Ver Haven wearing it, I've never seen another one like it." His brow tightened. "You say Shepherd wore one exactly like it?"

Crisp nodded. "He went to great lengths to conceal it. Had he not dropped it, I have not seen it at all. How well did you know Ver Haven?"

Bristol sighed. It was a question he should to feel comfortable answering. He had known Carl Ver Haven for twenty years, and thought he knew everything about the man. If Carl was a member of a secret society or shadowy organization, it did not rest easy with him.

Casual, Crisp pressed onward, "Sir?"

Bristol groaned. "I must say – I do resent being questioned in this manner. You are doing a damn fine job of making me feel suspect of wrong doing."

Then Bristol shook his head and waved the comment away. "Notwithstanding, I do understand. One of many reasons we selected you for this assignment, no one can pull the wool over your eyes. You question everything and everyone, as if you are carrying an unresolved issue with authority from childhood... I'm surprised you joined the army."

Crisp assured, "Sir, I don't suspect you of any wrong doing."

Bristol sighed. "I knew Carl for years, and thought I knew everything about him. Until today, I never gave his honor and dedication to duty a second thought. Carl's childhood was a mystery. He spoke three, maybe four languages fluently. I never questioned what a man of his education and ability was doing in the army. Some folks are drawn to duty and put aside personal ambitions."

"I've seen it a number of times in my career," Bristol continued, "men with enough smarts too run a large business and for whatever reasons decide to serve their country… Given all that's happened in the past couple years…"

Unable to finish, Bristol altered his flow. "I wonder if anyone person ever truly knows another. We hide secrets deep inside of ourselves, buried beneath layers of flesh and bone. If Carl had a secret life away from the army, it would be a shock to say the least."

Crisp believed Bristol had answered truthfully and said, "Shepherd's arrival at the same time Ver Haven was reported as missing is downright odd. Not to forget, the means at which he used to join our investigation. It is possible there are forces at work behind the scenes at high levels of government. With a war pending back East, it would explain a lot."

Bristol nodded. "I agree with you on that note. But I don't see Carl," he paused and reworded. "Carl loved this nation and would never have done anything to cause harm. It went against his grain."

Crisp rotated his cup from hand to hand and exhaled a thinking breath. If there was a secret society, it was more complex than a pending Civil Conflict. Perhaps a society centuries old, passing from one generation to the next. As time passed, gaining new members and strength.

Bristol's brow tightened. "I've seen that look before on your face. Last time I saw it, you and the boys struck out on your own and brought an end to Indian slave trading at those ranches." He tapped an index finger against the side of his head and probed, "Crisp, what's going up there?"

Crisp was surprised Bristol had spoken on a first name bases. Since Carl Ver Haven's death, Bristol's normal mood was off-kilter. Was the captain unconsciously trying to tap a new friendship? A captain's life was lonely, always in control, never allowed to expose a tender side.

Crisp smirked. "Nothing, I am simply pondering what we know thus far. I am thinking we are dealing with two separate groups. Those allied with Ackerland's bunch know nothing about whatever secret society Ver Haven and Shepherd are part of… For Shepherd it resolving the Ver Haven matter, he could care less about Ackerland. We're lucky the Lady Beth hasn't left port as of yet."

Bristol commented, "I'm puzzled as to why La Horn hasn't left port… I heard rumor, he filed a complaint against Chief Crivitz. Something about twenty-five percent of the Lady Beth's crew behind bars at any given point, mostly for public drunkenness and fighting, and other minor offenses such as spitting on the boardwalk."

Then Bristol chuckled. "If Crivitz actually arrested a man for spitting, he's bending the law to damn near breaking it himself."

Crisp grinned. "Crivitz has a strong sense of seeing justice served, even if he's not the one to issue it. I'm sure he's doing his part behind the scenes to delay La Horn's escape hanging for murder."

Bristol's brow tightened. "You let Crivitz in on our investigation?"

"Not exactly," explained Crisp, "I let him know about my last assignment, boarding the Lady Beth and mentioned Carl Ver Haven's untimely death. The army was trying to gather evidence against La Horn. Apparently, he took his own initiative from there." He cringed for effect. "I image Crivitz is waiting to hear from you before he eases back on Lady Beth's crew."

Bristol tapped his fingers on the table. Earlier, he had read Trick's report concerning Ackerland's bank holdings and transfers of funds. There was nothing out of the ordinary. Ackerland's holdings and investments were immense along both coasts and points in between. As far as the cattle industry, Ackerland used the phrase cattleman in title only. Ranching was a small portion of Ackerland's income.

Crisp stood, walked to a window and gazed into the backyard. La Horn would not leave with part of his crew behind bars. How long could Chief Crivitz keep arresting crewmembers on minor charges? Was justice to miss this one? Was this an incident where justice needed acting upon outside of the law?

Crisp wanted to conclude their meeting on a positive note. He turned and smiled, "What exactly does the A. R. & B stand for?"

Bristol dodged the question and stood. "As far as Chief Crivitz, tell the duck to keep the pressure on." He left without waiting for a reply, closing the door behind him.

Crisp chuckled, "The duck?" Was there anyone who did not think Chief Crivitz waddled like a duck? Crivitz had peculiar ways. One of which was forbidding Doctor Hanna Steadson to treat Ring. In addition to teaching at the new Medical University, Hanna Steadson was a skilled doctor.

Crivitz had permitted Trick access to Ring's hospital room, however not Hanna. It was strange. With Ring in mind, he exited the backdoor.

* * *

Trick's dreams rose and fell, mixed with truth and fiction, and inserting dialog where memories had faded. He crouched low in the desert night, back-to-back against Ring. Again, the panther's roar echoed throughout the canyon, making it near impossible to get a bead the cat's location. Two nights of traveling across barren rock-lands was wearing on them.

Ring looked at Trick and whispered, "You're the Cajun, how's she doing it? There's gotta be something we can use to defend ourselves against black magic. Shooting off bullets in the dark won't do nothing, except give away our position."

Trick shrugged. "Heard silver bullets can stop a shape-shifter dead in their tracks." As an afterthought he joked, "You wouldn't happen to be toting any?"

Ring grunted, pulled a flask from his rear pocket and offered, "Care for swig? Warm your innards right nice and take this dessert chill out of ya."

Trick backhanded the flask away and advised, "You best keep a level head out here, or I'll knock it clean off your shoulders."

Ring jested, "We could always build us a small fire and melt down a couple of your rings for bullets. I have a ball molder in my saddle bags."

Trick dismissed the notation and grumbled, "Where the hell is Hindor and our beloved young Lieutenant Crisp. If not for Crisp's sense of what's right and wrong with society, we'd not be facing this witchery."

Amid pitch-blackness of canyon walls, a large mountain cat roared. Still crouched, Trick cocked the hammer of his pistol and used his free hand to steady himself.

***

Crisp eased the door closed behind and glimpsed at Ring lying near death. He stared at Trick who was asleep in a chair beside the bed with his hand holding a pistol.

Crisp shook his head and stepped softly to a window. The room reeked of medicine. Fresh air was good for both dying and living. He parted the curtains and slid open the window. A breeze swept into the room, ushering in fresh air.

Trick jumped from the chair so quickly it tipped backward and banged to the floor. Waking from a nightmare and unsure of reality he crouched low, cocked his pistol, aimed toward the source of wind and fired.

Crisp twisted and dropped to the floor seconds before a bullet shattered window glass. Staying low, he flipped his hands outward and called, "Trick, it's Crisp! Hold your fire!"

Trick squinted against daylight, redirected his aim toward the voice and demanded, "Who's there?"

Again but softer Crisp called, "Trick, it's me… Crisp, hold your fire."

Two police officers swung the door open and busted into the room, their weapons drawn and ready.

Abrupt, Trick swung his aim at them.

Crisp yelled, "Trick it's okay, you're not there you're here. It was a bad dream."

Trick lowered his weapon and un-cocked the hammer. Squinting, he glimpsed at Crisp who was slowly standing.

Crisp assured Ring's police guards, "Everything is fine, he just woke-up and was spooked from a nightmare. I'm sorry."

Both officers shook their heads, grumbled and exited the room, closing the door behind them.

Crisp suggested to Trick, "Beyond any reasonable doubt, you need to head back the A. R. & B for food, a bath and rest."

Trick stood, spread his hand flat and objected, "I'm fine. I can wait here forever if need-be. Someone needs to be here incase the Hammer Killer tries to finish what he started."

Crisp's brow tightened. He pointed at the door and stated, "What do you think those two are for, to look pretty? They about the meanest and biggest peace officers I've ever laid eyes on."

Crisp sighed. Trick needed his mind taken off Ring's condition. He eased the pistol from Trick's hand. "Much as I hate to pull you away from here, but your services are needed tonight. I'd like you rested and ready before hand. I'll spend the day with Ring, and if he wakes-up I'll send for you straightaway."

Trick objected, "I realize what you're trying to do here. But it ain't needed, I'm fine. Besides, his doctors told me the voice of a friend could pull him back from the brink of death. I've was going over old times with him and must've dozed off is all."

Crisp suspected Trick had fallen asleep rehashing *The Incident* that had gotten them transferred from Fort Tejon. He stared at the shattered window and an idea came into focus. He said, "Tell you what, since you broke the window head over to the A. R & B, grab an extra window from the shed, come on back here and fix this one. Long as you're there, wash-up and shave, you look terrible. After you've cleaned, you may feel relaxed enough to lay-down on a soft bed. If so, send one of the carpenters here to fix the window."

* * *

A thirty-minute walk in crisp morning air had cleared Trick's mind. At the A. R & B, carpenters were busy hammering new shingles on the roof. A third hammer stolen from one of the carpenters at the building had made them edgy. He sent one of them to the hospital to fix the window.

Midday, because of hammering overhead, Trick relented on attempts for sleep. He left the A. R & B and roamed to the nearest pub. Crowds were gathering inside for card games and billiards. Several patrons recalled the shooting a few days ago and tossed him cold stares.

Not in the mood for games or stares, Trick left using the backdoor. Outside, he encountered one of the Lady Beth's crewmembers expelling a stomach load of rye into the alley.

Two days ago, Crisp had pointed-out the man from a distance. "His name is Fat Sam. I strongly suspect he's the one who bashed Kern's ears and caused him to go deaf."

Fat Sam bent at his waist and braced one hand against a corner of the building for support. Then he heaved another spray of rye from his stomach.

Trick decided Fat Sam was a decent size punching bag and compressed a vengeful heckle. Swift and hard, he raised his foot and connected the point of his boot beneath Fat Sam's ass and against the scrotum.

Fat Sam bellowed an agonized wail, stumbled forward and fell to the muddy dirt face first. Trick pranced around Fat Sam, driving his boots into Fat Sam's ribs and face. He yielded to the man's cries for mercy, stepped back and gawked at his bloody boots then at Fat Sam.

"Damn," grumbled Trick, "I spent an hour cleaning these boots this morning, and look what you've gone and done."

As Fat Sam choked two teeth from his mouth, he gazed at the man towering over him. He was unable to recall having met him before, and had no idea what inspired a vicious attack. Trembling he lost control, pissed his pants and moaned, "What devil sent you?"

Trick leveled his pistol at Fat Sam's head, then stuck a bloody boot against Fat Sam's mouth and ordered, "Since you made the mess, lick it clean."

Defiant, Fat Sam shook his head.

Trick cocked his gun, danced his boot in front of Fat Sam's bloodied face and smarted, "It's do or die buddy, your choice."

Fat Sam leaned forward and licked Trick's boot, smearing the blood on it.

Trick ordered, "Stop, you are making it worse." He jeered, "Hell, I should've shot ya from the get-go."

"Halt there!" a man's rough voice commanded from behind them. "Drop the gun and raise your hands!"

Trick raised both hands, keeping his gun cocked and ready. He turned and saw a young army private. The private was short and thin, had a pointed nose and beady eyes.

Young and foolish Trick thought. He sneered, "Mind your own business, rat-boy. This here is an unofficial, justified beating. This man here was trying to make a play for me, if'n ya know what I mean. He wasn't taking a polite no for an answer. Lower that weapon, I was simply teaching him what no meant in plain and simple English."

Fat Sam crawled onto his hands and knees. Hoping for salvation, he stared at the young private. Blood oozed from his nose and mouth. He tried to speak, however was only able to mumble an incoherent garble.

Rat-boy said, "Looks like he's learned the meaning of no. He doesn't appear fit to put a struggle. I can take it from here."

Trick yielded, "The fight was over before it began. If you want a stab at him, feel free." He stepped aside, un-cocked and holstered his weapon beneath his new suit coat. Then he teased, "The man's given to a foot fetish. You may wanna offer him your boots." He glimpsed at his boots and gripped, "Giving all that blood, he's liable to ruin your nicely shined boots."

Rat-boy declined, "No thanks, wasn't sure what was what until I saw you're a respectable businessman. Sorry to have interfered." Then he departed the area, leaving Trick alone with Fat Sam.

Trick nudged Fat Sam with his boot, shoved him over and said, "I've lost the mood, we can finish this later, maybe a day or two from now." He spread a wicked grinned. "What ya say, two days from now, same back ally?"

Unable to answer, Fat Sam laid there, groaning and moaning.

Trick warned, "I'm not the only one looking to kick your fat arse to death. Not saying as to why either… You'll have to figure that one out for yourself." He turned and left, feeling better for having worked his frustrations out on beating a crewmember from the Lady Beth.

31

Physically battered, Shepherd sat tied to a chair inside of York's tent. Untied and one second alone was all he wanted to send York to meet his Maker for eternal justice. Three beatings had not yielded a word from him. Since York had failed to inquire about Carl's journal, Shepherd assumed they had not searched his saddlebags.

A rap at the tent flap shuffled York's attention to unfastening the flap ties. A cold burst of wind ushered a flurry of snow into the tent. A pair of York's men tossed a young army lieutenant through the tent flap and to the ground.

York shook his head and grumbled, "Again, Lieutenant Brocker who is this man?" Earlier, a quarter-way into his second beating Brocker began speaking freely, giving whatever information he knew. The patrol was simply on a training excursion. However, York remained unconvinced Brocker did not know the other man's name or mission.

In broad daylight, the stranger was bold enough to ride into the camp. In addition, Charlie and another man had failed to return after disposing of the army scout Cricket.

Outside, a raging ice storm prevented York from dispatching a search party for the missing men. He hoped Charlie was riding-out the storm somewhere with a fire to stay warm. He doubted it, and assumed his men were dead at the hands of this stranger and buried beneath a snowdrift.

Thus far, the stranger had endured beatings and said nothing. No words of defiance ventured from the stranger's mouth, only morbid chuckles wicked enough to raise phobic hairs on York's neck.

York ordered one of his men, "James, spread a blanket and get our Dragoon friend into a submissive posture."

As if having done it countless times in the past, James spread the blanket onto the ground, then dragged Brocker to it and lifted him onto his knees.

James slipped a bone-handled bowie knife from his boot-well. Then, he wrapped one hand around Brocker's forehead and tipped his head backward. With the blade tight against Brocker's throat, he eyed York and waited.

York stared at Shepherd and proposed, "His life spared for two simple answers. Your name and why you came for the lad?"

Shepherd cocked a brow. This was shear foolishness. He opted for a chance at saving the young army officer. "My name is Shepherd, and as far as the lad goes… I was just happening past when I saw him chained to that pole. I reckoned a boy his age couldn't have done anything bad enough to justify being chained outside in the cold."

York raised a finger and snapped, "You are no bounty hunter, and that ain't likely your real name. As far as seeing the boy chained to a pole, sure it's possible. Your concern for his wellbeing ain't shear chance, I suspect you came looking for him. You happened upon us, because you were searching for him. You failed to answer my questions with truth."

Cold as the ice storm outside, York looked at the two men who carried Brocker into the tent. "Put Mister Shepherd face to face with the Dragoon officer."

The men lifted both chair and Shepherd. Battered beyond physical resistance, Shepherd offered no struggle.

York nudged Shepherd and inquired, "Why is this boy important to you? If you're a lawman, we'd have found a badge pinned to your chest. Who are you working for, the French, the English?"

Shepherd was tired of York's game and spoke directly to Brocker, "Death is an escalation of life. You will remain an earthbound prisoner free of memories. An uninterrupted journey through the Ages, I bid you farewell unto your next life. Choose it well."

Everyone, Brocker included drew baffled stares at Shepherd. York became harsher and remarked, "You're condemning a man to death, and have the nerve to give him an enigma? Good God, what the hell sort-of man are you? I've come across a number of lunatics in my day – but mister you're in a league of your own." He glimpsed at James and said, "Give him the bath and we'll see if it has any effect."

James tiled Brocker's head as far back as possible. One hard pull of the blade nearly separated Brocker's head from his shoulders, leaving it dangling in place by spinal bones and James' hands.

Quick, York stepped away from erupting blood. Blood hemorrhaged across Shepherd's face, shoulders and chest, and splattered against tent walls.

York barely contained his contempt. James had over-cut, causing a loss of aiming of blood. The technique was simple enough. Aim and slit Brocker's juggler vein and drench Shepherd in hot blood. Perhaps, Shepherd's comments to Brocker had infuriated James beyond normal restrain.

York's operation required men like James Stunfield for particular chores. Unsanitary chores, he excluded his regular militia from performing or witnessing. Warring was bad enough without taking home memories of extracting information from uncooperative prisoners.

When the war back East was in motion, York believed it was to become a long drawn-out affair. He wanted to avoid long and draw-out in the West. As he stared Shepherd in the eye, his gut twisted. Clearly, he had taken this man too lightly. Shepherd was unimpressed by the blood bath. It was time for a break and wait for blood on Shepherd's face, shoulders and chest to cake dry.

York told James, "I'm leaving you in charge, save additional beatings for later…" His eyes shuffled to Brocker's body. "Have your buddies drag Brocker's body into a snowdrift for the time being. We'll dispose of it properly before daybreak."

Then, York exited the tent and into the storm outside. Charlie's tent was empty and offered a place of solitude, where he planned to clean Brocker's splattered blood from himself.

***

After James's comrades had dragged Brocker's dead body outside, he stared at Shepherd and hissed, "York is right, you are a lunatic... When the time comes, I'll enjoy killing you. You'll be one less nut for the world to worry about."

A sudden cold gust flipped the tent flaps inward. Grumbling, James strolled to the entrance and tied the flaps shut. Suddenly, warm air brushed against his neck. Wide-eyed, he turned and gasped, "How the..."

Shepherd clenched his right hand around James' throat. Then he snapped James' neck and stated, "I have no parting words from this lunatic for you."

James fell limp to the dirt floor, his arms and legs twitching a death dance.

At the sound of approaching footsteps from outside, Shepherd stepped to one side of the tent entrance. A pair of hands reached into the tent flap and loosened the ties. The men, who had disposed of Brocker's body entered and froze in place. Stunned, they gazed at James' dead body.

Shepherd cleared his throat, causing them to swing-around. His actions were a blur of motion. First, he slammed the butt of his palm against one man's nose and driving it into the brain. The man was dead before hitting dirt.

Second, Shepherd spun around, elbowed the other man's larynx and silenced a gasp for help. The man grabbed his throat, dropped to his knees and gagged for air.

Soundless, Shepherd stepped closer, seized the front and back of the man's head. A quick twist wrought an end to the man's physical existence. Outside, a hard wind beat against the tent.

Shepherd glimpsed at himself from head to toe, drying blood caked his long johns. Moving fast, he stripped both men to their bare skin and laid the clothing on York's cot. He searched York's belongings, stealing a flask of brandy, then York's notes and maps from the tent walls.

After cleaning himself of blood, Shepherd switched long johns and dressed, he rolled remaining clothing and stolen items into a blanket. He checked his navy revolver for load, strapped on his shoulder holster and put on one of York's heavy fur coats.

Shepherd straddled the overstuffed blanket-roll over one shoulder and grabbed a spare fur coat. He paused at the tent flaps and collared the coat upward against his neck. Unsure, he glimpsed at the three dead men. Dragging three bodies outside and into a snowdrift was an unacceptable risk. He drew a warm breath and stepped into the blizzard.

Outside, ice laced winds lowered visibility to twenty feet. Shepherd eyed a buckboard and darted to it for cover. Curiosity caught the best of him, and he slipped a peek beneath the buckboard's tarp. It was loaded with kegs of gunpowder and boxes of dynamite. He whispered, "La Horn's cargo?"

Shepherd snickered. On second thought, perhaps there was time for tomfoolery. Silent, he unloaded one large barrel of gunpowder and two small ones. Then, he snatched a coil of fuse and several batches of dynamite.

Minutes later, Shepherd had rolled a powder keg into York's tent and laid a small roll of dynamite on top of it then lit a long fuse. Leaving the tent, he swung by the wagon and grabbed a smaller keg of gunpowder. Then lit a long fuse on a stick of dynamite and laid beneath the cover.

Against gale force winds, Shepherd trekked toward the tent where Kern was prisoner. He was grateful there was only one guard. From behind, Shepherd stabbed the guard in the neck and dragged the body out of sight. Seconds later, he slipped into the tent.

An interior guard stood and demanded, "Halt, who goes there?"

Shepherd spotted Kern wrapped in blanket and lying near a potbelly stove. He maintained a casual demeanor. "I was sent to relieve you. There's a bowl of hot deer stew waiting for you at the chow tent." He rubbed himself warmer and glimpsed at Kern.

Kern recognized him, however played it smart, not giving away the jest and remained wrapped inside of the blanket.

Shepherd continued, "Worst weather I've ever seen for this time of year. York must have a screw loose to keep us pigeonholed here like this."

"Got that straight," replied the guard.

Shepherd nodded at the guard's fur coat and pushed, "Ya going or not, I'm only here to relieve ya for supper. Ain't got all night, there's a card game going-on, and I aim to win back my losses."

The guard grabbed his coat and grumbled, "No reason to get edgy with me. Give a fella a chance; I wasn't expecting any relief for at least a couple of hours."

The guard was halfway into his coat selves when Shepherd struck, using a jab first to the throat followed by another blow to the left temple. Stunned, the guard swaggered to his knees and tumbled onto his side, dead.

Kern sat upright and stood allowing the blanket to drop to the dirt floor. Dressed with only a loincloth, he appeared more Native American than white.

Shepherd reached outside the tent flap and pulled his blanket wrap inside. He laid the blanket next to Kern, unrolled it and pointed at the clothing. Swift, Kern grabbed a pair of pants.

Shepherd stopped Kern from sliding into the pants, then pointed a pair of long johns and said, "Long johns first or you'll be freezing out there."

While Kern dressed, Shepherd fetched the powder keg from outside the tent. As before, Shepherd laid a roll of dynamite on top of it and lit a long fuse. They were seconds from leaving when Bassett busted into the tent, complaining about the wind.

Without hesitate, Kern bounded forward and drove fist after fist into Bassett's face. Shepherd pulled Kern from on top of Bassett.

Shepherd held Kern tight and grumbled, "When it comes to controlling emotional upheavals, you've got a lot of learning to do."

Shepherd and Kern gazed at Bassett. Kern had knocked Bassett unconscious. Shepherd was grateful Bassett's chest rose and fell. Bassett was missing a front tooth and his nose lay smashed to one side. Shepherd wrapped blanket around Bassett, then hoisted him over one shoulder.

Kern cocked a puzzled brow as if to ask why save him. Shepherd answered, knowing Kern was unable to hear. "He's too young. There may be hope down the road for him to change."

With Bassett in tow, they headed into the blizzard. They paused at the first empty tent and tossed an unconscious Bassett inside.

Earlier, while being moved from one tent to another, Shepherd had noticed wranglers herding horses toward a boxed canyon for the protection from the storm. He picked Kern up as if a young child. Seconds later, they vanished amid blowing sleet and snow.

Shepherd had planned to reach the canyon before the fireworks started. First explosion was York's tent, sending tent poles and personal belongings to the wind. Moments later, the second tent blew. The howling ice storm drowned cries and yells from the encampment. A full minute later, the wagon detonated shaking the ground beneath their feet.

Shepherd halted at the sight of movement ahead. A few yards away, a man running from the boxed canyon dashed past them. Shepherd and Kern's presence concealed by wind swept waves of sleet and snow.

***

Five minutes later and nearly frozen, they approached the boxed canyon. Again, Shepherd lifted Kern and carried him. Shepherd yelled above the wind, "Hey camp, hold your fire! York sent me to checkup on ya! Found your partner laying near frozen to death in drift. That fire sure looks inviting, we're coming-in."

Shepherd carried Kern into the mouth of a large cave. Two horses stood at the front entrance, kept warm and close for a usage if needed.

Before the sentry noticed Kern was not their partner, Shepherd aimed his pistol and said, "I've had enough killing today to last a lifetime. Don't be mistaken, taking one more life won't make a difference at this point. I'd strongly advise against making a move."

The sentry raised no fuss. "Not a problem here, mister."

Shepherd asked, "You have a name?"

"Ronald," the sentry replied, "Tell ya what, I was figuring on cutting-out once this storm broke. Come daybreak, we could ride out of here together. Ain't no one coming back here tonight, not in this storm."

Shepherd chuckled. "It's an offer hard to refuse, however we've got pressing matters. As you might understand, storm or no storm, we've got hard riding to do. Slow and easy, unbuckle your gun-belt."

Ronald unfastened his gun-belt and allowed it to drop to the cave floor. Shepherd, bound Ronald's hands and feet, and then he dragged him near the fire.

After several minutes of searching through a pile of saddles, Shepherd found his saddlebags. Carl's journal was secure inside of it. Apparently, his earlier fresh horse was among the other horses taken to the canyon, which explained the reason his saddlebag went unsearched.

Shepherd took his time saddling two horses, the cold hike had physically drained him. He was in no hurry to battle Mother Nature's wrath but they had no choice. It was a matter of time until York sent men to check on the herd.

Shepherd lifted Kern onto a Bay horse, then grabbed two burlap sacks of grain, tied them together and hung the sacks over the saddle horn of his stolen horse.

After securing food supplies and canteens, Shepherd mounted the Buckskin horse had started his journey riding. Then he reined around, glimpsed down at Ronald and advised, "If you're smart, cutting out from this outfit would be wise. After York figures out we've escaped, he's bound to send someone up here to check the herd. If you're planning to cut and run, you should do it sooner than later. With all the bodies I left lying around, they'll assume you're dead and buried in a snow-bank. They won't realize you've deserted."

Ronald raised his tied hands and shook them.

Shepherd suggested, "Leaving you tied allows us time to make it into the storm. Unless you'd rather I toss your rifle and pistol into a snowdrift outside?"

Ronald replied, "Nah, there's no need for that. It'll take my time to break free of these ropes. Even then, I ain't crazied enough to venture into that storm. I'll be heading out come daybreak. If'n anyone shows I'll tell em I was alone all night with no visitors."

Shepherd warned, "They'll do a headcount on the herd."

Ronald shrugged, "We're likely losing a few horses because of the storm and wild critters." Then he stared at Kern. "The boy showed up with bruised eyes and that nose gash, we didn't do it. I never cared for the way they treated him. Chaining him outside in the cold didn't set right with me and lot of others as well. And some of us are complaining about the weather."

Ronald shook his head and continued, "I signed up to protect California, and maybe give us a shot at true freedom. Figured it was none too good for Californians having politics thousands of miles away. With men like York in command, I'm not sure what's right and what's wrong anymore. If we need men like him to free ourselves, maybe the cost is too high."

Silent, Shepherd nodded. It was good to learn a percentage of York's men were no longer true followers. He reined his mount outside and into the sleeting blizzard.

Kern's horse followed without a nudging.

On their way from the canyon, Shepherd liberated four spare horses from the herd.

32

On foot, Kern and Shepherd navigated thick pine undergrowth, tugging four horses on lead-ropes behind them. This trail was not as dangerous as the last one, where a horse had slipped along a narrow ledge.

Kern had watched his friend turned wide-eyed and gasp as a horse had fallen to its death in a canyon below. Although deaf, he imagined haunting neighs of terror amid winds from the night blizzard. He shook free of the memory and focused on the narrow deer trail. They had put nearly five miles behind them and the boxed canyon.

Kern had wanted to remain near the warm fire inside of the caved. Wanting to lose no additional time, La Horn had sailed back into a storm. Again, storm or no storm there was a need to keep moving. Armed men from the camp were searching for them.

Kern wondered if there was an end to the ice storm. Pine forests offered minimal relief. Icicles the size of porcupine quills blanketed their clothing. It was nothing like the Firestorms of Kakadu. Flames of the Fire Season were far more deadly than cold winds and frozen rain.

Kern looked over his shoulder at Shepherd. These men were different from those who wore uniforms at Limmen Bright. They had shed their uniforms and dressed in normal street clothing. Thus far, they had proven trustworthy…

Kern questioned himself. Why had he failed to trust Carl and delivered that handwritten book as sworn. It now lay hidden beneath the floorboards of rundown shack. Carl's book was forever lost, a promise broken to a dying friend. He had crossed several small mountain ridges and had no idea where to find the rickety cabin.

Breaking free of low tree limbs, they reached an open area and a vacant mining cabin. Within minutes of stabling their horses inside of a large shed, Shepherd had a fire glowing inside of a stone fireplace of the cabin. He placed a kettle packed full of snow near the edge of the flames. They needed nourishment. He slipped back into his thawing coat and stepped back into the storm, leaving Kern warming himself near the fire.

Outside, Shepherd secured the door closed and collared his jacket against wind driven sleet and snow. He waded through knee-deep wet snow to a woodshed.

Their four horses stood bunched together for warmth. He unsaddled, grained and brushed the horses. Then, grabbed their two saddles, sets of reins and blankets and headed back for the cabin.

* * *

Kern opened the door a crack and peered outside. Freezing rain stung his face. Shepherd had been gone for an hour, maybe longer. Blowing snow prevented him from seeing the woodshed. He assumed Shepherd was checking on their horses. Perhaps one of the horses was injured and needed tending?

Suddenly, Shepherd was at the door. He stepped inside and placed their gear near the fireplace. Then he fabricated a smile, spoke slow and mouthed each word, "I'm sorry about losing those horses on the trail."

As Shepherd diced dried shanks of meat into a pot of melting snow, Kern spread their gear closer to the fire to dry and watched him.

Shepherd added dried beans into the water and stirred. Kern's easy-going temperament gave him a sense of family. For the first time in a decade, Shepherd felt at ease with his surroundings. As the meal cooked, Shepherd arranged their bedding near the fire.

After eating their fill, Shepherd slid a chair near the firelight and pulled Carl's journal from inside of a saddlebag. It was never his intent to excite Kern.

At the sight of the journal, Kern's eyes came to life and he leaped to his feet. His monotone voice broke between a foreign language and English.

Shepherd noted Kern's monotone sound was as Doctor Steadson had explained. A loss of hearing effected Kern's speech – however the foreign language was another matter. He was unable to place an origin for it.

Shepherd pulled a blanket from near the fireplace and motioned Kern to sit. He sat on the chair and reflected on his own childhood. Carl had taught him to read and write. The process was probably similar by learning to read names first.

Shepherd pointed at Carl's name and the word friend. Then, he pointed at his chest and said, "Friends."

Kern comprehended that Carl and Shepherd were friends. He spoke monotone using English, explaining what happened onboard the Lady Beth to Carl Ver Haven, switching to the strange language only when excited.

Most of it, Shepherd had already learned from Carl's journal. La Horn had ordered Ver Haven's beatings. Learning how La Horn and his crew had disposed of Carl's body was new information.

An hour later, Kern dozed asleep near the fireplace and curled beneath a bedroll. Shepherd dipped a quilt into an inkwell and began on the next blank page where Ver Haven had ended.

My name is Jasper Shepherd, friend of Carl Ver Haven. I was orphaned at age ten. At age eleven, Carl saved me from the streets of Detroit and temporarily became a surrogate father, taking me to Denver. That chapter of my life is recorded in the pages of another journal. I am in procession of this journal, and write only to follow this to a conclusion and log when justice is served for Carl Ver Haven's murder.

Kern, the lad Carl wrote about earlier is with me. After Carl's death, Kern suffered an injury to his ears and has become deaf. Hopefully, his deafness is temporary.

Recent history, after the Lady Beth docked at San Francisco Bay, a young Lt. Crisp boarded her in search of Carl Ver Haven. He discovered Kern held inside of a forward-hold and rescued the lad, along with a dog named, Bristol.

Secretly, Kern returned to the Lady Beth for this journal to keep a promise to his friend, Carl Ver Haven. Had not I followed him, the lad would have been captured or killed.

I pray that his deafness is temporary. For an unknown reason, he fears men wearing uniforms, which I suspect is the result of a bad experience in Australia.

Carl had noted Kern was likely from Australia. At former penal colony, I suspect Kern encountered a crooked magistrate. Given the foreign language he uses intermittently, a good portion of his childhood was spent among Native Aborigines in Australia.

I believe that Kern was afraid to pass this journal to Captain Bristol because of the uniform worn by the man. A fear too often justified. Had he given the journal to Captain Bristol, all this would have all ended long ago.

Fearful, Kern chose to run away which brings us to this stormy night. We are hiding from a private militia bent on what I am unsure. Perhaps force California to secede from the Union as Civil Conflict in the East rages. A shame, since California has recently obtained Statehood. This is the worst blizzard I have witnessed. The storm is God-sent, as it keeps the private militia from searching for us. Come daybreak, we will have to move-on.

My plan is to deliver Kern to a Lady-doctor by the name of Hanna Steadson. I am praying his hearing can be restored. While Kern's hearing is restored, justice will be served for Carl's murder.

As Carl believed and I accept, Kern was predestined to become a Herdsman and keep Untainted Historical Records. I plan to bring Kern to my beloved adoptive mother, Ms. Shepherd in Denver. Kern will be raised as another soul to record history as it unfolds.

Once justice for Carl Ver Haven's murder is completed, other missions will be placed on hold. Bringing Kern into the Fold takes precedence.

***

Shepherd and Kern continued traveling, pausing only for a couple of hours to graze and water the horses. An hour earlier, they had reached lower flatlands and warmer weather.

Taking a break, Shepherd shuffled their saddles to spare horses. Beneath their feet, wet grasslands soaked their boots. He wanted to allow their horses additional grazing time, however when leaving the foothills he had spotted three riders following them.

Shepherd doubled checked cinches on the saddles, then grabbed lead-ropes to their spare horses and mounted his fresh horse. Above them, early morning stars faded against a brightening blue sky.

Shepherd nudged his mount alongside of Kern and said, "Since leaving that cabin you haven't said a word. Because you can't hear does not mean I am deaf too. You didn't have to stop talking to me."

Saying nothing, Kern offered him a simple shrug.

Shepherd grumbled, "So-be-it, once again you're both deaf and mute. Though I know better, I'll live by that lie until you're ready to talk again."

A westerly wind shuffled tall grasslands as if waves of water. By days' end, Shepherd planned to have Kern safely at the hospital.

It was certain, French and British governments had past dealings with La Horn. Something they preferred to keep out of the public eye. International politics made a trial against La Horn likely void of impartiality. Another matter bothered him. Why had La Horn used them to up a reward for Kern?

Shepherd glimpsed toward the foothills. The three riders were gone, and he certain they were watching from a distance. Perhaps following to learn where he was traveling.

33

Crisp exited at front doors of the hospital, paused, glimpsed over his shoulder and sighed. The A. R & B had enough on their plates without adding the Hammer Killer. After Ring was attacked attempting to save a woman, he and his men were dragged into it full-steam ahead.

Ring had gained consciousness, however he remained incoherent. He was thinning badly. If he had remained unconscious for much longer, starvation and dehydration would have claimed his life. He was having trouble speaking and recalling things, even the names of friends were difficult to recollect.

In the past, Crisp had lost men under his command. This was different. It was personal. Ring was under his command for years and considered family. He turned at the sound of approaching footsteps and forced a grin. "Good afternoon, Chief Waddles." Immediately, he realized a slippage of the tongue and apologized, "I'm sorry, chief. It's just that…"

Crivitz raised a halting palm. "I hear it all the time, don't allow it to bother you. Most everybody has name-calling and things said behind their backs. Some-stuff you hear so-often, you pick-up on it without realizing it." Casual, he punched a lighthearted sting. "Ever wonder what your men say behind your back?"

Crisp had no desire to confirm what he suspected when not present. He changed the subject. "Security around Ring is tight. Hanna stopped-by to check on him and was denied entry into his room."

Firm, Crivitz shook his head. "She's a recent addition to your little group, and I'm not allowing any suspects near the victim. That's final until the Hammer Killer is captured."

Astounded, Crisp cocked an eyebrow. "What? You think a woman is responsible, let alone a fine respectable doctor, a woman whose upbringing is beyond rebuke... Never in a hundred years would I even raise a doubt as to her character. I am surprised because you have known her for years."

Abrupt, Crivitz cut him off. "I've learned in this business, it's too often the most unlikely of suspects who commit crimes of this nature. Everyone in the city without sound alibis is suspect until the perpetrator is behind bars and awaiting trial. Sound alibi being, I or one of my peace officers had a person in their line of sight at the time of a killing. You, Trick, Muser and Hindor are accounted for."

Crivitz was half a step from entering the hospital when he halted and warned, "Keep an eye open for a local reporter from the San Francisco Examiner, a Joachin Miller. He is digging into like a prairie rat. He already knows Ring has friends at the A. R & B. Since there have been no additional Hammer Killings, rumors are rampant and pointed his direction. Some folk are speculating our injured witness may in fact be the killer."

Crisp cringed at the mention of a reporter digging into Ring's personal life. Reporters in general are nosey. Curiosity would get the best of Miller. An investigation of the A. R & B could create a nightmare beyond resolution. He said, "Thanks for the heads-up."

Smooth, Crivitz nodded at a row of buildings across the street. "Speak of the devil. Here comes Miller from over-yonder, and he's pulling a tablet of paper from his pocket. If'n I were you, I'd make tracks."

Crisp spotted Joachin Miller approaching at quick-footed clip. Slow as not too draw unwanted attention, he stepped off the boardwalk and left.

An hour later, Crisp was at the A. R & B, sipping coffee and listening to Hindor rant and rave. Hindor was not pleased with the fact Taylor had supposedly gone East to join the growing number of Confederate Troops.

Hindor explained, "There's rumor running around, Trick attacked a crewmember of the Lady Beth." Concerned, he reminded Crisp that Shepherd, Kern and Bassett had failed to return. By his standards, he considered them as missing in action.

Hindor calmed his demeanor, "Making matters worse, Ackerland sent one of his henchmen here today." Perturbed, he pointed at a sealed envelope on Crisp's desk and grunted, "Left a secured message for you... You're getting damn chummy with those scoundrels, and it's making me downright edgy."

Crisp ignored Hindor the Grouch, picked up the envelope and opened it. *Mister Crisp, another luncheon is planned for tomorrow. Same place and time. Look forward to seeing you. Sincerely, Clifford Ackerland.*

Crisp folded the letter and placed it back onto the desk. He clasped both hands behind his head and leaned back in the squeaky chair. He allowed Hindor's comment, chumming with the enemy to remain unanswered. The A. R & B was an undercover operation, and they had to maintain appearances.

Today was a normal business. A shipment of Chinese herbs had arrived that morning at a nearby warehouse. Their buckboard needed to be loaded and the shipment relocated to the A. R & B. Then boxes unpacked, sorted, and repacked into smaller boxes for shipment to the East Coast.

They were shorthanded because Taylor had deserted to join Lee's army back East, and Ring was in the hospital. Crisp decided work would shut down Hindor's energy to complain, and take Trick's mind from Ring's medical predicament.

* * *

An hour later, Crisp, Hindor and Trick were at Golden Shores Warehouse loading boxes into a buckboard. Crisp glimpsed at Trick who was absorbed with lifting a heavy box and suggested, "Trick, keep your back straight and lift with your legs."

Trick grumbled using Cajun slang. Then he nodded past Crisp and said, "Here comes, Mister Sabaston owner of this fine warehouse we're in."

A large, broad, stocky man approached and waved. "Greetings, I'm Sabaston and owner of the Golden Shores Warehouse. I do apologize for being late, but I had to finish shoveling mud from the boardwalk at home. If you'd wait a day, I could have a crew here to help you load."

Crisp wiped his hands on his pant legs. Smiling, he shook Sabaston's hand. "With more rain clouds looming off-shore, we couldn't wait for anyone to arrive and help us load."

Sabaston stomped mud from his boots and gripped, "Can't say as I blame ya." He looked over Crisp, Trick and Hindor. "Didn't catch what outfit you're working for? I can have the paperwork and bill for storage in a few minutes. Your boss will have to come in person, sign and pay in cash before anything is allowed to leave the building."

Crisp informed him, "We're from the A. R & B, and I am the boss," then patted his left front pocket. "Cash at hand, bring over the paperwork, I'll sign it and we'll be on our way after this wagon is loaded."

Sabaston grinned. "The boss man himself doing manual labor, must be an inspiration for employees." He stared at Hindor and commented, "I don't cater to slave labor around here. Every man is free as far as I'm concerned, and made in God's image. An honest day's work equals and honest day's pay, no matter the color of his or her skin."

Hindor lowered a box he was lifting, placed both hands on his hips and injected, "I was born free and will die as such if need-be… I've worked for this man for years, and he's never stiffed me a day's wages!"

Hindor was unrelenting, "That you dare think of me as having been a slave is damn right insulting! I'll have you know my folks immigrated to this country like your forefathers! For someone to think my parents were netted and taken here against their will makes us into something we're not. I'll have you know, I've had some upper-level schooling. My reading is writing is better than most white-folk I've met."

Tricked thumbed at Hindor and jested, "Hell, he pays this darky more than me. It's white slavery is what it is!"

Sabaston commented to Crisp, "Cantankerous work-crew, you've got there. It's the sorriest can of worms I've opened in weeks." Then he surrendered both hands. "Forget I said anything."

Crisp suggested, "It's best to ignore them, they're both a tad touchy. We're down three good men at the moment."

Sabaston inquired, "Read the news this week? My wife is afraid to let our daughters walk to the streets in broad daylight. She packing a derringer and escorting our girls to and from school. I keep telling her, the Hammer Killer strikes at night and kills working gals. Maybe he caught something from one of them and is enacting revenge."

Trick twitched at mention of the Hammer Killer.

Crisp suggested, "Let's get the paperwork out of the way and billed paid. We've a lot of work that needs finishing before sunset. It will take us another trip after this one to get everything. An overloaded wagon will sink to the axles in mud betwixt here and the A. R & B."

Before Crisp followed Sabaston to the warehouse office, he glimpsed over his shoulder and said, "Even out the load while I am gone. We're headed off and unloading, then coming straight back here and finishing the job."

* * *

After Trick and Hindor finished evening-out the load, they drove the buckboard to the main entry doors. Hindor shouted toward the interior office, "Hey, remember we ain't got all damn day!"

Sabaston stared out the office door and commented, "Grouchy old man isn't is he? How do you manage to keep him on as an employee? I'd had fired him a long time ago."

Crisp shrugged. "He's a hard-worker, trustworthy and takes incentive when work arrives. Straightaway, he puts men to work and gets the job done."

"You coming or not?" Hindor shouted for a second time. "We've got work to be doing and can't sit around waiting on your yapping mouth to tire!"

Crisp glimpsed out the door and yelled, "Hold your horses! I am finishing up business here!"

Sabaston advised, "Once the war breaks-out, it could lockdown ports back East. You want to get your goods sorted, re-boxed and re-shipped as soon as possible. For the right price, I could call-in a few extra men, and have your cargo loaded and delivered by sunset today."

Crisp cringed. He had not contemplated the outbreak of war shutting down ports along the Eastern Seaboard. It was certain that navel blockades were already sailing into place. He negotiated a delivery price, then joined Trick and Hindor on the buckboard.

As the buckboard sloshed through ankle deep mud and toward the A. R & B, Crisp grumbled, "That man drives a hard bargain, but we'll have our goods delivered before sunset."

Trick formulated the project of sorting and re-packing. "I figure it this way, first we unload crates into the front office, unpack and sort from there. Then move the goods into the kitchen area for re-packing into smaller crates and labeling."

"If'n business gets to good," grouched Hindor, "We'll have to build a storage barn and hire actual workers, or we won't get our missions accomplished."

Crisp agreed, "That's a nice thought. Lord knows our cover needs to be above reproach of watchful eyes, like reporters putting their noses into our private affairs."

Trick's eyes widened. "Reporters as in the likes of Joachin Miller from the Examiner? He stopped the A. R & B right-after sunrise and was asking questions about Ring."

Crisp exclaimed, "What! Why did you fail to inform me of it? A reporter isn't someone to take lightly. They dig and dig until they've got a deep enough hole to bury a person."

Trick was nervous and explained, "He was asking if Ring had a history of past heroic deeds. Said that he's gonna write a full page spread on Ring as a man of the hour. Don't be worrying none cuz I didn't say much. Only, Ring was hard working, decent man, looking to better himself in this new State of California. Miller came asking questions of me, because he'd seen me leaving Ring's hospital room and followed me here."

Crisp inquired, "Followed you? While that nosey reporter may not intend to do so, he may discover our undercover operation before we get rolling with it. We've got things planned you boys ain't even dreamed."

Hindor was offended and stated, "Boys? Watching your language around me, you know damn-well I find it offensive."

Crisp muttered, "It was simply a matter of speech. These past couple of months you taken this race thing too far. You are making more of it than it is between us. Drop it before I start thinking you have taken to a hatred of white-folk. Next thing I know, you'll start a secret society of colored-folks wearing hoods and burning things as a means of getting even for years of oppression."

Hindor grumbled, "Once the war is settled and coloreds are freed to roam as we please, there are bound to be a lot of upset white-folk. Hell, half of the coloreds in chains won't know what to do once they're freed of shackles. Wearing hoods and such sounds more like something white-folk might start doing afterwards. There will be a gap between white and colored for generations. Causing we're freed, doesn't mean we'll be treated any less different than now."

Crisp decided Hindor was to far-removed from the pending conflict back East. It crawled beneath Hindor's normal disposition of a likeable grouch and it worse. It was only a matter of time until Hindor snapped at the wrong person, ending with a shooting or lynching.

Again Crisp, considered Hindor's request for a transfer East and allowing him to join the fight. For years, Hindor gripped and complained how white society treated him. Denying him access into pubs, and denied usage of a jake behind stores and hotels.

* * *

It was midnight when Crisp, Hindor and Trick had exhausted themselves sorting and re-boxing orders. With slightly over half the orders packed and labeled, they retired upstairs for the night. Bristol lay at the center of the house, guarding the building, its contents and those asleep upstairs.

Shortly after daybreak, Crisp woke to Bristol's sharp barking followed by a banging at the front door. Wrapped in a blanket, he staggered to the front door, dodging discarded nails across the floor from opening crates last night.

Crisp cracked open the door and saw Crivitz outside. He motioned at Bristol and ordered, "Quiet down, he's a friend."

Crivitz entered and announced, "Well, this comes of no surprise, the Hammer Killer struck again. Figured you oughta know. If nothing else, it lifts suspicion from Ring." He looked at empty crates stacked around the room and remarked, "Busy night?"

Sore and dog-tired, Crisp nodded. "We're nearly done sorting and repackaging. Need to get orders filled and shipped East before things take a turn for the worst. Heard at the warehouse blockades are forming up and down the eastern seaboard. "

Crivitz agreed, "I read they're already starving out the boys at Fort Sumter. If your goods do manage to make port, you'll be fortunate if you shipment isn't seized by the military on either side. Especially if the goods are considered too have any sort of medical value."

Crisp raised both palms. "The A. R & B is strictly a wholesale business for suppliers across the country. A. R & B goods are headed for New York City. From that, point goods will be shipped by land to Washington, Boston, Pittsburgh, Cleveland, Chicago and Detroit. Suppliers are responsible for final packaging and selling of goods to stores across the eastern seaboard and mid-west."

Crivitz rubbed his chin. "Is this business leaving you anytime for other things?"

Crisp cocked an eyebrow, yet withheld comment. Graceful, he dodged further discussion on the issue. "I'd offer you a tin of coffee, however, I'm allowing the boys and myself a day to sleep-in. We worked into the wee hours of the morning." Mostly for effect, he covered his mouth and yawned.

Crivitz took the hint and replied, "I wanted to let you know about the killing last night. I'd tell our local paperboy to leave a newspaper at your door however, he seems to have vanished."

Crisp faked a smirk. "Yeah, I paid him in advance too." He shrugged off a loss of money, "So much for trying to help a young man's commerce, he stiffed me a fifty-cent piece."

Crivitz left with a simple, "Good-day to you" and closed the door quietly behind him.

Bristol eased from the shadows and inspected the air with a couple of sniffs, then trotted to the backdoor and waited.

Crisp followed and stepped outside, then chained Bristol and walked to the Jake.

After feeding Bristol, Crisp lit the stove and warmed a kettle of water. A second wind had taken hold, there was no sense going back to bed. His thoughts turned to Kern, Shepherd and Bassett.

34

Exhausted, Cricket's horse staggered into a Calvary Encampment. He looked around, noting no one had challenged his arrival. "New recruits," he grumbled. This Detachment was a training mission for what lay ahead. Plans were in motion for soldiers from California to ship back East for the pending war. These boys were young, foolish and careless.

Without having sentries questioning his arrival, Cricket suspected they would not last long in fields of war. Starved and cold from a night of riding, he strolled to a campfire and snapped a tin cup from the nearest recruit.

The recruit stood and shouted, "Hey, what the devil! Get your own damn tin!"

Cricket tossed him a stern glare that backed him onto his sitting stump. After a sip from the near empty tin, his face soured. Abrupt, he splattered the remaining contents onto the ground. Griping, he poured a fresh cup of coffee from a kettle heating on a boulder alongside of the fire.

After a sip to warm his innards, Cricket glared the recruit whose tin he had seized and ordered, "Get me plate of hot food from the chuck-wagon." Then he glimpsed at another recruit and said, "As for you, go fetch your commander! Tell him Cricket is here and in need of a fresh mount."

Hesitant, both recruits lingered a moment.

Firm, Cricket raised his voice. "Soldiers, I may not be wearing a uniform, but that doesn't mean squat! Do as you are told and do it pronto!"

Both recruits stood frozen, unsure what to make of this strange white-man dressed in Native American clothing.

Again, Cricket raised his tone, "Justice is passing us-by like a windswept ice storm! We've got damn near twenty dead soldiers to avenge! Now move!"

As both men darted off too completed their given assignments, Cricket shook his head. "What's this army coming too? Sure ain't what it was back in the day."

Cricket spotted a chair near one of the tents, dragged it closer to the fireside, sat and commented, "All the comforts of home." Casual, he kicked feet on the boulder near the fire.

A voice behind him injected, "Good to hear my camp meets near you needs. We try to ensure our guests are comfortable as possible."

Cricket's brow tightened. He had not heard anyone approaching. Too tired to stand and without looking over his shoulder, he waved the person forward and said, "I ain't budging an inch. Step into my view because I'm dogged, beat and drawn-out from fighting man and ice storms alike. I am not sure what's colder; wind-driven sheets of ice or the hearts of men…"

An older army officer stepped near the fire and in front of Cricket. Then he knelt, picked up a stick and stirred the coals. As the fire smoldered back to life, he stood and turned. Laid-back, he slipped off his riding gloves. His face stone weathered from years of service crinkled. "The hearts of men are colder than any ice storm I've encountered. I image you've learned that long ago and the hard-way."

A smile cracked Cricket's dried lips. This seasoned officer had an understanding of serious situations. Aching from his long journey, he stood, shook the officer's hand and introduced himself, "Name is Cricket, I was riding scout for a small group of Dragoons. With othing better to do, we were riding a worthless patrol to keep them out of trouble at the fort."

Cricket sighed, "As it turned out, our patrol wasn't so worthless after-all. A private militia controlled by a pompous ass going by the name of York bushwhacked us." He cocked an eyebrow. "Ever heard of him? By the way he was running things, seemed like old army to me. Hell, he wouldn't come out to face us in battle. Long-range rifles cut our boys to shreds in minutes. Other than bushwhacking, he ran his outfit tight as a seasoned commander. "

The officer introduced himself, "Captain Gregory Long from Fort Tejon." Haphazard, he grinned and glimpsed around the camp. "We're training new recruits and getting them ready to ship back East should the need arise to help the North."

Long looked around his encampment and continued, "These foolhardy boys haven't a clue as to what warring is about. A war between the States is bound to be long, drawn-out and bloody. Come next winter, those alive after their first few battles will be huddling around fires, wishing they were back in California and enjoying milder weather of home."

Cricket watched new recruits dragging their feet as they went about morning chores. Training was one thing, actual battle another thing entirely. No solider was truly ready for waging war. It was during the heat of a fight, true warriors came alive. He had seen it dozens of times. A solider everyone expected to stand fight runs away, and another expected to turn-tail and run rises to the occasion.

Long returned to the matter at hand. "I'm sure you've a lengthy story to tell. Come with me to my field office where we'll be more comfortable." Then, he turned and walked toward a large canvas tent at the far side of the encampment.

Cricket set the barrowed tin cup on the chair, leaving it for the recruit and followed. It was clear that Captain Long's heart had no desire for involvement in a conflict between the States. A recruit he had sent off to fetch a plate of breakfast trotted up alongside of him.

Excited, the recruit asked, "You're Cricket? I mean really him, the man his-self in the flesh?"

Baffled, Cricket took the plate balancing it as not to lose his biscuits, eggs and slices of pork. "I'm not sure what you've heard about me boy, but it's all rumors and lies. If you'll excuse me, I've got a meeting with your captain."

Cricket withheld an urge to tell the recruit to get packed and ready to ride. It was their commander's place as how to handle the situation and issue orders.

Twenty minutes later, Cricket was downing a second plate of breakfast. His stomach splitting inside, he wiped his mouth and finished. "Like I was telling ya, it was this stranger who helped me escape. If not for him, I'd be staring skyward my eyes froze-open until late Spring thaw."

Cricket wiped his mouth and continued, "One thing for sure, he wasn't part of York's bunch. I've come across a few men in my lifetime whose nature was beyond the rest of us. He'd kill to simply to keep a secret and not bat an eye doing it. Willing to bet he vanishes like a ghost, here one minute and gone the next. He'll leave us scratching our asses and wondering what the hell happened and why."

Long shook his head. "Not sure I want to turn over whatever rock he crawled from under and get stung by a scorpion. From what you're saying, doesn't sound like he was there by chance." Then he rubbed his beard stubble and thought aloud, "Not by chance but perhaps not on purpose either. It could've been destiny putting him there at the right time and right place."

Cricket smirked. "If destiny put him there to save my sorry arse, maybe I've not been living as bad as some say. Could be there is hope for me, yet. Maybe, the Good Lord has seen fit to give me a chance at redemption."

Long allowed the reply to pass. He was not speaking as to destiny having saved Cricket, although destiny had used him to carry news of the private militia.

Long suspected that Cricket was right. There was a higher power at work here, putting men in the right places at the right time to keep this country from going the wrong direction. Ignoring something destiny had dropped into his lap was perilous.

By mid-day, Capitan Long had a written report in route by carrier on horseback to Fort Tejon. Cricket had rested and was preparing to guide a large patrol to York's encampment. He expected to find only evidence of where York had bedded down his men for hiding. If cunning, York had relocated his militia.

35

Their plan of reaching the city a day ago had come and gone. Throwing off trackers, Shepherd had returned to the lower foothills. Yesterday, they had traveled in the general direction of Fort Tejon. At sunset, they had ridden up and down shallow mountain streams and brushed over hoof prints when leaving water.

After nightfall, they swung around and rode toward San Francisco, again crisscrossing mountain streams. Shepherd snagged a rabbit in a trap. He had inspected the rabbit's liver for sickness, found spots and discarded the fresh kill. At midnight, they had set a cold dry camp. Without risking the glow of a fire, they ate dried shanks of meat and canned beans.

Two hours prior to daybreak, they headed westward along narrow trails. Near noon, they cleared foothills and reached a long stretch of flat grasslands. Their efforts to throw-off York and his men had failed. York had men posted throughout the area, keeping watch for them.

At a full run on horseback, Shepherd stared over his shoulder and tugged the lead rope of a spare horse. Kern was keeping pace with another spare horse trailing on a lead-rope as well. In the distance behind them, a dust swirl drifted toward the base of the foothills.

Shepherd wanted to reach the city outskirts before York's private militia closed the gap. With two extra horses, they had an advantage on the militia. He had faith in his own skill at jumping horses at a dead-run and riding bareback. Kern was another matter. While Kern no longer held the saddle horn, his balance on horseback remained questionable.

Kern glimpsed over his shoulder and saw what had drawn Shepherd's attention. His heart skipped a beat as Shepherd switched horses at a full run and rode bareback.

During their last break, Shepherd had placed extra bridles on their spare horses. After Shepherd successfully changed mounts, he snapped his saddlebag back from the tired mount and released it. The tired horse darted away at an angle and slowed to a tired trot.

With no rider to urge the horse onward, her energy faded to a downtrodden walk. Her head hung, nostrils flared and her body was soaked with steaming sweat.

Shepherd reined alongside of Kern and took the lead-rope of their last spare horse. He dropped back allowing Kern to pull ahead. After Shepherd rearranged the spare horse to his left side, he pushed his own fresh mount alongside of Kern.

With one hand gripped on the horse's mane, Shepherd squeezed his legs tight around his horse. Secured, he leaned over, snatched Kern from a tired mount and hefted him in front himself. Riding double slowed Shepherd's fresh horse, allowing York's men to gain ground on them at a faster rate.

Kern's tired horse darted away kicking up dried mud. Yards behind them, the exhausted horse slowed and joined the other discarded mount.

Shepherd tugged their second spare alongside of them. Amazingly, the horse cooperated as having done this type of thing before. He smirked at Kern as if to say enjoy the thrill. He held tight around Kern's chest and urged their mount onward.

Kern gritted his teeth and suddenly had to pee. There was no easy-way of shifting from riding double and onto their last spare horse. It was shaky at best, however Shepherd managed shuffle him onto the spare horse.

The outskirts of San Francisco lay a few miles away. City streets would be bustling with foot and horse traffic. Vanishing amid crowds of people was second nature for Shepherd.

***

Shepherd's horse stumbled into a pothole and fell. He rolled across the ground, easing his impact against the hoof-hardened dirt road. He scrambled back on his feet, hoisted his saddlebag and slung over one shoulder.

Kern pulled his mount to a halt and reined around. Silent, he stared at the fallen horse. A lower front leg bone protruded outward and blood soaked the dirt road forming a puddle of darkened mud. The horse's head tossed back and forth and released agonizing cries mute to Kern's ears.

Shepherd slid a pistol from its holster, cocked the hammer, aimed and fired ending the horse's agony.

Hearing a muffled pop reflective of a gunshot, Kern's eyes widened. As smoke curled from the gun barrel, he wondered if he had actually heard it or it was his imagination. Was his hearing returning?

Shepherd motioned Kern to slide further back on the horse. Then he jumped in front of Kern, and dropped the saddlebag across the horse's withers. Concerned and cussing, he stared eastward at a raising dust cloud from approaching riders.

Kern was unable to hear a word Shepherd had said. Perhaps the sound of a gunshot was nothing more than a trick of his mind. At the horizon line, York's men were gaining ground. He locked his arms around Shepherd's waist and held-on.

Shepherd pivoted their remaining mount toward the city. Then he heeled forward, putting the horse into a run, kicking up dried mud behind them.

Kern grabbed a last glimpse at the dead horse. The horse's muscles jittered so strongly its hoofs appeared as if prancing. Riding double and running was straining the animal. They He felt their remaining horse beneath them struggle with the weight of two riders.

They were losing ground to York's men, and putting the animal at risk. Kern counted the toll of horses. It appeared another horse would die, and this one of exhaustion.

Kern considered the cost of his survival. Independence was no longer an option, and may never have been in this strange land. As San Francisco came into view, a warm feeling of home swelled from within.

Home was a term Kern had learned from Carl Ver Haven. It was a confusing and foreign emotion. His adoptive Aboriginal Clan's conception of home was broader. They existed in Dreamtime. Earth, sky and water was home for the

Clan. These Baland were his true people and lived in real time, not Dreamtime. When or where his perceptions had changed was unclear. Had his perceptions had simply evolved?

Again, Kern slipped a look over his shoulder. Behind them, riders emerged from a dust cloud, slapping their reins across their horses' necks. Worried he turned forward, wanting to warn Shepherd. Ahead was a bend in the road.

As they rounded the bend, Shepherd leaned near their horse's neck, and Kern couched tight against his back cutting wind resistance as much as possible. They passed a horse drawn carriage at breakneck speed, sending the driver and passengers jolting with fright.

As they neared the heart of the city, their fast hoofed flight dropped to a steady trot. Men on horseback and carriages clogged the road. Shepherd passed whenever possible, however passing was not an easy feat.

Their mount's foaming mouth and nostrils blew hot vapor. Steam rose from their horse's sweat soaked body. She was blown and unable to go further without dying.

Shepherd rode straight into the nearest livery barn, then eased Kern onto the ground and slipped off the exhausted horse. Then he patted the horse's neck and said, "Thanks, you've earned a long rest." His pants were sweat-soaked from the horse and stuck to his legs. Kern's clothing was in the same shape. They needed a hot bath and change of clothing.

A stable-boy arrived and patted the tired animal. Stern, he scolded them, "What were ya trying to do? Kill the poor thing?" He slipped the bridle from the horse's foaming mouth and secured a lead-rope around its neck. He explained, "It'll cost ya extra for me to walk this animal down until she's cooled-off." Then he stared at Kern as if recognizing the face.

Shepherd slipped a coin from his pocket and pulled the stable-boy's attention away from Kern. "Here you go, kid." He tossed him the coin and said, "It's a fifty cent piece. If anyone comes asking about us or that horse, you found it wandering outside."

The stable-boy grinned, rolled the coin, then pocketed it and nodded. "Sure thing, Mister, whatever ya say is fine by me." He tipped his head at the tired mount and noted the brand. "She's branded... You work for Mister Ackerland?"

Shepherd glimpsed at the horse's rear flank. As if not giving it a thought he commented, "No, she was a borrowed mount. An hour or so, someone will come looking for her. I'd hate for them to find her this ragged." He tossed the stable-boy another coin. "Here's my appreciation for keeping her out of sight. Walk her down then get her brushed, watered and fed before they find her."

The stable-boy stared at Kern for a second time and lead the exhausted mare away. Disgusted, Kern pulled at the sweat soaked fabric of his pants and stared at Shepherd. Sour-faced, Kern pitched his nose and shook his head.

Shepherd smirked and said loud enough for the stable-boy to hear, "I know of a place a few blocks away." He shuffled the weight of his saddlebag across a shoulder and headed north. Bathhouses lay a few blocks to the west but they trekked north. If the price was right, he assumed the stable-boy would sell them out.

After three blocks, they cut west and circled wide for several blocks. Shepherd recognized two of York's men leaning against a hitching post across from the army office Captain Bristol used. Just as well, Shepherd thought. With the army office watched by York's men, it was an excuse to delay Kern's temporary return to the army's care.

Twenty minutes later at the Hotel Hispa, an elderly Chinese woman greeted Shepherd and Kern. When Shepherd had first arrived in San Francisco, he had spent two nights here using the assumed name of Jeremy Golding. Those two a days allowed time to spy on Crisp and Bristol from a distance before assuming army clothing and beginning the assignment.

Shea smiled, "Mister Jeremy it's good to see you've returned." As she looked them from head-to-toe, her brow crinkled. "It appears you've both neglected taking care of yourselves. I'll have my daughter draw a couple hot baths." She turned and clapped her hands together several times.

A Chinese girl near Kern's age appeared from the back of the hotel kitchen. She wore an apron splashed with the makings of a meal. She gazed at their customers, noting Kern's light blue eyes and sun stained blonde hair.

Shepherd gave her a simple nod. He recalled the story Shea had shared with him at an evening dinner. Shea's husband had died of a fever on a ship coming from China. Shea had not known she was pregnant at the time.

Shea's daughter was a constant reminder of their perilous journey from Mainland China and of hard-times left behind for a new life in a land of opportunity. She held up two fingers and spoke Cantonese to Min.

Min offered Kern a pleasant smile and left to draw two hot bathtubs.

"Ms. Shea," said Shepherd. "As always, you're a step ahead of me. We're not planning to spend the night, just a quick soaking and our clothing cleaned."

Shea eyed Kern, shook her head and commented with broken English, "Those not his clothing. Not fit right. I tailor him new pants and shirt, and be done before you leave. Cost not much, we could negotiate price after you see him wearing cloths. I have a new material from a young man named Levi. Good strong pants, last him long time."

Shea's eyes brightened with an added thought voiced as a suggestion. "Maybe you need new pants and shirt? Take longer though, can have finished after you've rested and eaten."

Shepherd agreed. A change of clothing helped avoid York's men. He asked, "Do you have any hats? One that's good for the city and traveling long distance on horseback."

Shea shook her head. "Not here but I know of man who sells hats. He has shop four blocks away. I send Min to fetch you hats. You pay first for hats, he want money up front, no credit. You no worry, Min very good at picking suitable hats.

Will look very good wearing pants, shirts and hats, maybe new coats too."

Shea eyed Kern and commented, "I read paper, French and English are looking for him. No good, I no like them. Brother in China addicted to opium. You both safe here. He get dressed like city-boy, no one recognize him. Maybe dye and cut hair after bath, make him look different. You get hair trimmed and shaved too?"

Shepherd told her he would consider haircuts when soaking in the tubes. Then he thanked her, dug money from his saddlebag and passed it to her. Minutes later, Shepherd and Kern's aching muscles were soothing in separate hot tubs of bubble-scented-water.

Kern stretched his legs, leaned back and fought to remain awake. Several times, his eyelids drifted shut. Not awake and not asleep, his mind wandered across the ocean Weowie the Water Spirit had used to separate lands and peoples. Tears trickled from his eyes. He slid behind raising foam from the bubble bath and concealed his emotions.

Shepherd was tired as well, yet stayed watchful. It was certain York's men would not give up their search. He sighed as Kern's head vanished behind a mound of foam. He whispered, "Don't be drowning on me."

Shepherd began formulating a plan. First, they needed a solid night of rest. Here they were out of sight and safe. After ear surgery, Kern would spend a couple nights at the hospital recovering. While Kern recovered, he was free to enact retribution for Carl Ver Haven's murder. Then, he would return and inform Crisp of his plan to send Kern far from foreign consults.

Shepherd glimpsed at his saddlebags draped over the back of chair. There was no need for Bristol or Crisp to read Carl's journal. Crisp was intelligent, easily connected dots and drew solid conclusions. Crisp had questioned Carl's amulet. Although Carl had not revealed anything by his writings that directly mentioned the Herdsmen, it was best to keep the journal from prying eyes.

Carl Ver Haven's journal belonged at the Herdsmen's Archives in Colorado. A mission easily completed when he brought Kern to Clair Shepherd's home.

Shepherd leaned back and wiggled his toes above the water line. Again, he pondered spending time with Kern at Clair's home and relaxing for a few months.

During that down time, he could teach Kern reading, writing, reasoning skills and self-defense. After his departure for another mission, Clair Shepherd would continue teaching Kern.

36

Midmorning and dressed for a business meeting, Crisp left Hindor and Trick to deliver small crates to a shipping yard. He stepped onto the boardwalk paused and bathed in the sun, before heading for the restaurant and his luncheon with Ackerland.

He crossed the street, sidestepping puddles of moisture gathered inside of hoof prints. Another day and streets would be dried and dusty. A ringing bell of a horse drawn trolley diverted his attention from dodging puddles. Moving quick he hopped skipped a number of puddles, then jumped onto the trolley and paid a fee.

***

Caleb blended among crowds of people on the boardwalk. Earlier that morning, he had discarded his normal seaman garb, bought a brown tweed suit and bowler hat. La Horn had grown suspicious of the A. R & B and wanted Crisp followed. Supposedly, Crisp had resigned a military commission.

Caleb shook his head. When searching the Lady Beth, Crisp had given an impression of a career military. With a pending war, a resignation failed to fit Crisp's mind-set.

While Caleb was inclined to agree with La Horn concerning the A. R & B, he had not voiced it. He wanted to return to open seas and see this port fade behind them. As far as he was concerned, La Horn was pressing their luck by delaying their departure for Seattle.

Authorities locating Kern ahead of them was not their only risk. How long until, a crewmember in a drunken stupor at a pub, recounted sea-stories of treachery, murder and tossing a body overboard?

Caleb sidestepped off the boardwalk and avoided a woman twirling a white umbrella laced with pink. He thought her a woman freshly in love, and the world around her gently passing-by unnoticed. His memories drifted back to a woman he had once loved, long ago in Canton near Hong Kong. An

Asian beauty with a loving heart large enough to accept him for what he was.

Caleb darted across the street, cut through an alley and ran up another street. Spotting the trolley, he smiled. Crisp had not jumped off. However, keeping pace was not easy and required running. If not for the trolley stopping for an elderly woman, he would have lost it.

Distracted by memories of love lost, Caleb nearly missed seeing Crisp dart across an intersection and entering a restaurant. A huge clock on a bank wall chimed the noon-hour.

Caleb's stomach reminded him that hours had passed since his last meal. A hand-rung bell caught his attention. He stared through the crowds and spotted a small figure of a man waving a dinner bell above his head.

The man made no effort to call people, allowing the bell to speak his message. Caleb glimpsed at the restaurant and noted a closed sign posted on the doorway and commented, "Humph, a private meeting of sorts."

A minute later, Caleb was standing in a line waiting at the lunch-cart. A flat griddle cooking vegetables and tidbits of beef, accented the air. As Caleb's stomach growled, he stared at the front door of the restaurant. Was it possible Crisp had spotted him and slipped out of a backdoor?

"What you have Mister?" The man asked with a thick Cantonese accent. "You try special today, beef and vegetable on fried bread?"

Without thinking, Caleb turned and replied using fluent Cantonese. "Forgive me for my attention was diverted. I'll take whatever you're quickest at preparing."

For onlookers it was an odd thing hearing a white man speaking a Chinese dialect while the Chinese cook replied using broken English. "O-kay, I make you a quickie special. Only take a minute or two at most."

Caleb read a sign listing prices. Far from home, he thought. Unlike Hong Kong, there was no bargaining here with the merchant. He laid a couple of coins on the table cart. Then he noticed the pricing sign included the man's name.

"Philip?" Caleb asked then changed to the Cantonese dialect. "You've traded your birth name for English?"

Philip smiled and answered using English. "No, Philip is a Bible name. Name change was better. Fresh start in new country; I am a better man now. The past is gone, washed away by the Blood of the Lamb."

Again, Caleb looked at the restaurant, then back at Philip and stayed with the foreign dialect. "One cannot run from his troubles, you take your luggage with you everywhere."

Philip wrapped the sandwich in thin paper and said, "Yes, luggage always present but remains packed. The man I was is always there, haunting me. I leave him packed away. God gives me strength to overcome."

Philip looked at the restaurant and warned, "Nothing but low-lives at private luncheon, they plot and conspire wickedness. They have earthly wealth but are poor of heart and soul."

Then Philip shook his head, "Money and possessions means nothing when death comes. Only a kingship with God's Son Christ matters. They think none notice their conniving ways. Many of us see and know their hearts are wicked. They say one thing and do another. Bible teaches; *By their works you shall know them.*"

Caleb forced a grin. "Neither God, His Son or Holy Spirit would give me the time of day. I am far removed from Their graces. If there's a hell, I'm deserving of it." Then he stepped away to leave with lunch in hand.

Philip called after him, this time using a Cantonese dialect. "As long as you have breath there is a chance for redemption. You need only to call upon Him."

Caleb agreed with a nod. There was nothing to say. He had heard it before. Missionaries flocked to the Far East, converting any who would listen. Religion came in all forms, depending on the person's needs.

Casual, Caleb strolled toward the restaurant. Something Philip had mention regarding a private luncheon. He had assumed Crisp was attending a secret meeting with army officers. According to Philip, it was a gathering of wealthy business leaders. He paused at a large glass window and looked inside.

Crisp was at large table with businessmen. Everyone was chatting, eating and drinking. Apparently, La Horn was wrong. Crisp had left the army for a business life. Perhaps, Crisp's offer of someone to talk with was a gesture of goodwill and not pressing for information.

Hot sandwich in hand, Caleb stepped away from the window and headed toward a bench across the street. After Crisp finished his meeting, he planned to continue following him. If nothing else he would report, Crisp was not a threat.

An hour and half later, Caleb was again trailing him.

Rushed, Crisp went straight back to his office. Once there, he was in and out within minutes, wearing riding cloths. From the A. R & B, he walked a couple of city blocks to a livery stable.

Caleb moaned. He hated horses and preferred sea-winds as a means of travel. As he dug into his pockets for money, he searched the streets for another livery stable where he could rent a horse. "Damn," he grumbled, not another stable within sight.

Ten minutes later, Caleb watched as Crisp mounted a large Buckskin horse and ride toward the countryside. He waited until Crisp was out of sight, then strolled to the livery stable and stared several horses inside of a corral.

A dark haired boy asked, "Can I help ya mister?"

Caleb smiled. Aside from hairstyle and color, the boy reminded him of Kern. "Name is Wilber Wilson, I was trying to catch a friend and saw him riding off. He is too far away for me to catch-up. Did he happen to mention where he was headed?"

Sheepish, Dowling grinned. "He told Copper they were going to the Mission."

Caleb asked, "Who's Copper?" Then he stared past Dowling the direction Crisp had ridden.

Dowling said, "His horse, mister. Most everyone talks nice like to their horse, especially if they want get anywhere. Ya don't ride much do ya?"

"As little as possible," Caleb replied and pulled money from his pocket. "If you're quick with getting a horse ready, maybe I can catch-up to him." He passed Dowling the money and said, "While you're getting a mount ready, I'm headed to the jake and will be right back."

Minutes later, Caleb stepped from an outhouse located behind the barn and sighed. Dowling was tightening a cinch on a black mare with a white star on her forehead. He finished tucking his shirt and muttered, "Pure foolishness, a man riding on a wild beast makes no sense." He forced a smirk and approached Dowling and the horse.

Dowling patted the mare and introduced, "This here's Martha. She's one of my favorites, nice and gentle. If'n ya fall off, she will stop and wait for you to get back on." Then he gave Caleb a receipt for deposit and rental of the horse.

Caleb mounted Sara and said, "Thanks lad. My friend has a head-start, so I'd best get going." He stared the direction Crisp had left and patted his rented horse's neck.

"He's headed for the Mission outside of town," explained Dowling. Then he pointed. "That road leads straight there. Ya can't miss the place. It has a large bell-steeple and nuns all over the place." He grinned. "There is a herd of goats keeping the grass short in front of the place. You'll come across a vineyard about a quarter-mile before ya reach it."

Caleb thanked him again, and reined the mare toward the outskirts of the city. Dowling sounded as if he had developed a friendship with Crisp. It was probable, Dowling would mention someone had rented a horse and followed. He had second thoughts about renting a horse from the same stable.

As Caleb crested a hill, a loud whistle sounded from the piers. He stared over his shoulder and toward distant piers. After a second blast of a ship whistle, he noticed steam dispersing into the air. Steam powered ships would change whom ruled the high seas.

Again, Caleb considered leaving the Lady Beth for a fresh start and fairer weather. Perhaps there were ways to avoid becoming a land-lover. His thoughts focused to life onboard a steamship.

37

Kern stood in an ally at the corner of a general store and waited for Shepherd. He rubbed his new clothing and thought of how he had reflected in a mirror at the hotel. Bruises near his eyes were fading, but the cut across the bridge of his nose remained evident. They had cut his hair and dyed it black. He looked like a young respectable young-man dressed for courting a young-lady.

Earlier, Min appeared to have taken a fancy to him. Her long flowing black hair had glistened in the sunlight. Brightly colored clothing with bird designs woven into the fabric accented her natural beauty. Her words unheard and meaning unclear.

After the lady-doctor fixed his ears, Kern wanted to return and ask her to repeat what she had said to him. He tipped his new brown gambler hat back, glimpsed along the smelly alleyway. He thought of the livery stable where they had left their only surviving horse. A stable-boy had acted as if recognizing him.

Kern wondered if like Limmen Bight, there were posters of him Wanted Dead or Alive. However, he had not seen one poster of his face tacked to a lamppost.

Again, Kern scanned the main street. His teeth gritted with a low-cut grunt. Not far away was his archenemy, the turncoat Bassett. From a distance, Bassett's bruised eyes and swollen nose were evident. Bassett's black and blue eyes reminded him of an animal he had seen in the pine jungle.

The creature was at a small mountain stream washing food. The small animal was tan with a bushy tail that had black circles, and a black fur like a mask.

Kern had reached for the creature however, it had hissed at him. He had pulled back and had thought it better left alone. Avoiding the turncoat Bassett was another good idea.

Shepherd appeared from around a corner of the building, leading off the main street. At fast clip, he headed toward Kern and the alleyway.

Bassett squinted toward the alleyway. He spotted Shepherd and yelled, "Hey, there over here!" His arms waved wild, motioning for a contingency of York's search party to give chase.

Shepherd glimpsed over his shoulder, recognized Bassett and took off at run toward Kern. He was surprised when Kern took a bold stance and refused to budge.

Kern refused to allow temptation pass-by and sneered at Bassett. Then he folded his thumbs under his armpits and raised his elbows. He imitated a chicken in the same fashion Bassett had done to him two days ago.

Bassett's temper flared, and he darted alongside the general store and toward the alleyway. Again, he yelled, "They're over here!"

Shepherd grabbed one of Kern's fluttering elbows, dragged him along and muttered, "Damn, kids… This ain't no game of Hide and Seek we're playing."

Kern relented on mocking Bassett and followed Shepherd, crisscrossing city streets. At the first intersection, they recognized three of York's men at a distance. At a second cross street, two additional men on foot joined the chase.

Kern was uncertain, if Shepherd was grumbling cuss words or simply grumbling but his lips were moving. Either way, Shepherd was upset but stayed focus on eluding their pursuers.

A few minutes later, a bank clock chimed the three o'clock hour. Shepherd and Kern found a temporary hiding place inside of an empty warehouse. Shepherd was surprised York's men had not fired a shot. It was possible York had ordered them taken alive for questioning, and shots fired would draw unwanted attention of local law enforcement.

Shepherd had no desire to lead York's men to the A. R & B and Crisp's undercover operation. With Kern's innocents in question, dashing into a local law office was not a good idea. Captain Bristol's army office came to mind. He gripped his saddlebag and sighed.

Stashing Carl Ver Haven's journal was out of the question. The journal was hidden twice all ready, first in the longboat, then a second time beneath cabin floorboards. Shepherd considered another hiding of it was pressing their luck, and the journal could become lost forever.

Distracted by thought, Shepherd failed to notice Kern had slipped to the back of the barn. A scuffle drew his attention toward the rear entrance. Growling like a wild animal, Kern drove fist after fist into Bassett's face.

Shepherd yanked him off Bassett. He drew his gun, cocked and aimed it at Bassett.

Monotone, Kern hissed, "I'm not done!"

"No," Shepherd said and shook his head so that Kern understood. He released his hold on Kern's upper arm, and he pointed at a coil of rope hanging on a gate to an empty stall. He felt ill at ease. Kern had broken another long silence by expressing rage.

Shepherd had gagged Bassett's mouth with a bandana and tied him with the rope. Again, he heard Kern's monotone voice.

Kern yelled at Bassett, "You cause trouble for others!" Then, he kicked Bassett in the ribs.

As Shepherd dragged Kern away for a second time, Kern switched languages. Still monotone, he was speaking directly to Shepherd as if pleading to continue beating Bassett.

"Boy," said Shepherd, "I understand hate and how it eats at a person's soul. You can't allow it to tear you apart like this. It'll make you into a person were not born to become." It was useless. Kern was unable to hear him. He forced him to sit on the dirt floor, pointed a stern finger and mouthed loudly, "Stay put!"

Shepherd lifted and lowered Bassett into an empty large wooden shipping box. He found a nearby lid and returned to the box. Bassett raised his head and stared at him.

Shepherd warned, "Be advised if you're smart, you'd stay clear of him. He has a strong hatred for you. I am leaving you alive solely to give you a chance to grow-up and make something of yourself. Don't prove Kern right by turning out bad."

Shepherd lowered the crate lid onto the box, then turned and waved Kern to stand. He said, "Time for us to move-on."

Gradual, Kern stood then stepped toward Shepherd and Bassett. As Shepherd lifted his saddlebags from the dirt floor, Kern gave the wooden box a solid kick and followed him to the rear barn door.

* * *

Lying on his back, Bassett kicked the lid off the box. He peered over the box edge. They were gone. He jerked and struggled to break-free of the ropes, but found the ropes secured tight. He glimpsed at the vast empty storage barn. It would take time to break-free of the ropes.

Upset, Bassett grumbled through his gagged mouth. "Kern you bastard this ain't over between us! Not by a long shot! Don't think I didn't notice those new duds you're wearing. Ya've gone and done good, and plum forgot about me! I'm gonna kill ya, even if'n I have to back-shoot ya! Then I'll be the one wearing your new pants and shoes!"

38

Caleb knelt behind a row of leafless grape vines out of season. Earlier, he had tied his rented horse to tree behind a small hill out of sight. Not much was happening. Crisp had spoken with a young priest and shown him what appeared to be a coin. The priest looked at it, shook his head and handed it back to Crisp.

Crisp re-pocketed the chained coin and thanked the priest with a monetary donation. Afterwards, the pair sat and chitchatted for an hour. After Crisp checked his horse's cinch, he thanked the priest again and rode toward the city.

Not rushed, Caleb stayed crouched and backed away. He planned to allow Crisp to gain a half-mile leeway. Pondering the chained coin was pointless. It could be any number of things. By outward appearances, Crisp had resigned from the army, having luncheons and donating to a local Mission.

As Caleb approached, his horse lifted her head with a mouth full of grass and chewed. Careful, he side stepped a pile of manure and grouched, "Stinking animals."

Caleb slid his foot into the stirrup and swung onto the saddle. The soft voice of woman called from behind, "Do you want to see a priest?"

Caleb turned and saw a nun standing almost alongside of him. She was thin and pale, her face wrinkled and weathered. He found it unnerving she had managed to sneak on him without a sound.

She offered, "Come and see a priest, he can guide you with confessing your sins."

Caleb reacted, "If I talked to God, it will be one on One." A smirked crested his cheeks, "My sins are so great no priest could bear to hear them, not without carrying around guilt the rest of his life."

"You emotions have raisin to the surface," replied the nun, her tone unsettling. She clasped both hands at waist level and spoke as if knowing his entire life, "You ponder a change. In some cases, change is good."

Caleb noticed two stubs on her left hand where fingers should have been. Although a nun, she had endured terrible hardships. He was no able longer to look at her and glimpsed westward at the distant horizon.

She assured, "While you still have breath there is time to repent and start anew. You need not a priest to do so."

Caleb's breathe tensed. Twice in the same day, he had similar words. Was it a warning of danger ahead in his life? It was eerie. He turned from gazing at the horizon to say goodbye. She was gone, vanished in the blink of an eye as if having never there.

Caleb flinched. He stared across an open meadow leading to the Mission. Even a person in the prime of life was not quick enough to have darted across it and out of sight. It was unsettling.

A southerly breeze ushered warmth across Caleb's face and rustled overhead leafs. He reined toward the road and whispered to his horse, "I am done following people for the day."

Caleb no longer cared if he caught-up with Crisp. He wanted to put several miles between himself, the Mission and vanishing nun as fast as possible.

39

Without turning, Shepherd reached behind him and pressed Kern tight against the back wall of a pub. Across the street from Captain Bristol's office, two men stood at a hitching post. He pulled a small telescope, focused on horse brands and muttered, "Ackerland's brand, must be York's men watching the place."

Shepherd discarded an earlier notation of bringing Kern to the A. R & B. Reaching the A. R & B or hospital was nearly impossible. York's men patrolled streets and alleys, searching for them. Kern needed protection, and the army had plenty of manpower and guns.

Shepherd eased his gun from its holster and checked it. He touched Kern's shoulder and nodded toward Bristol's office across the street. Silent he pointed along an alley, walked two fingers – after which he palmed two fingers.

Shepherd and Kern walked two blocks along the alley, moving casually and not drawing attention. Another pair of men stood at a distance, watching the backdoor of the army office. Abandoning the alley approach, they cut across the street and approached the army office from the side. Unless foolish, York's men would not open fire on a crowded street.

Shepherd and Kern kept on the inside of sidewalk traffic and as close to buildings as possible. Kern opened the front door of the army office and entered with Shepherd close at his heels.

A young private behind a large pine desk, stood and inquired, "How can I help you?"

Shepherd informed him, "I'm here to see Captain Bristol."

"Who should I tell him is here?"

Shepherd had a near photograph memory of faces, and he failed to recognize the young private. The army regularly shuffled men from assignment to assignment. However, he decided it best to lie, "Tell him his nephew from back East is here, Arron."

The solider stepped into Bristol's back office for a moment, then returned and pulled the door within a few inches of shut. He informed them, "He'll see you now." As he stepped aside, he calmly slid his right hand near his gun.

Nonchalant Shepherd eased between him, Kern and the doorway. He recalled a full-length mirror on the back wall of Bristol's office. The door was ajar enough for him to view the situation inside. York's men were brazen and had seized control of the building.

Bristol sat at his desk, scowling. Behind the door stood a man with one pistol pointed at Bristol, and a second ready for Shepherd and Kern to enter the room.

There was no space for error. Shepherd pulled his pistol and slammed himself into the door at the same instant. His first shot ripped through man's neck in front office.

The door slammed into York's man inside the main office, knocking him aside and causing one of the two guns to accidentally fire. A bullet whizzed past Bristol's head and thudded into the wall behind him.

Shepherd busted into the room and preformed a rolling tumble, avoiding the man's speedy recovery. He aimed and fired. A bullet blasted into the man's shoulder and sent him reeling backwards, dropping one of two guns.

Shepherd was almost back onto his feet, when a bullet ripped through his side. Stunned, he swaggered around. There was another gunman, whose reflection was unseen in the mirror. A second bullet sent Shepherd to the floor, gasping for air.

Bristol was already in motion, pulling a hidden gun from beneath his desk. He aimed and fired. A bullet exploded from the front of the second gunman's head and splattered brain-matter across the walls.

Confused, Kern stood frozen at the door. Although muffled, he had heard each gunshot. He saw Shepherd go down, and witnessed the office shoot the man who had shot Shepherd.

Bristol stood, his gun aimed at Kern as if ready to fire.

Kern raised both hands and played mute.

The gunshots had drawn attention of nearby police outside. High-pitched whistles resonated in the distance.

Bristol lowered his gun and stated, "Good God, boy! We've been worried sick about you!"

Bristol waved Kern into the room. He rushed to Shepherd, pulled a bandana from around his neck and pressed it to Shepherd's chest wound. He assured, "Help is on the way."

"Yeah," replied Shepherd between gasp for air. "I hear them coming. You have to protect Kern." His strength was fading and within seconds, he lost consciousness.

Bristol opened the front of Shepherd's shirt and applied direct pressure to both gunshot wounds. He notated an amulet hanging around Shepherd's neck. It was identical to the one Crisp suspected had belonged to Ver Haven. Laying several feet away, Shepherd's bulging saddlebags likely held Ver Haven's missing journal.

40

Sore from a long day of riding, Crisp swung out of the saddle at the livery stable. After leaving the Mission, he had ridden along a few foothill trails, hoping to spot Shepherd, Kern and Bassett. He looped a lead-rope around Copper's neck and slipped off the bridle. After hanging the bridle over the saddle-horn, he began losing the cinch.

A cheerful Dowling greeted him, "Evening Mister Crisp." Then, he took Copper's lead-rope and inquired, "Did your friend Mister Wilson catch-up to ya on the trail?"

Crisp cocked an eyebrow, "Who?"

Dowling replied, "Willard Wilson. He left a few minutes behind ya. Unless you were pushing Copper, he should've caught up to ya, or at least run into each other along the way back."

Crisp asked, "What did he look like, any scars or tattoos?"

Dowling shrugged. "None that I saw. He was dressed in a real-nice suit and tie, and one of those new hats that have a rounded top. Small brim hat like that ain't worth nothing out in the sun. I don't rightly care about fashion myself, and wouldn't spend money on a hat unless it served a purpose."

Was Ackerland having him followed? Crisp planned to take precautions in the future. If Ackerland was having him followed, did he suspect anything?

Dowling continued, "I rented him Martha, she's nice and tame. He sure didn't seem to care none for riding a horse."

Crisp nodded, "Hmmm." Ackerland's boys would not be afraid of riding a horse. Perhaps one of La Horn's crew had followed him. He said, "Thanks for the heads-up. Has he gotten back yet?"

Instinctive, Dowling looked at the corral. There, unsaddled was Sara, still sweating. He griped, "Damn it to hell, he never asked for his deposit back. What am I suppose too do with it?"

Crisp stared at the tired old mare and suggested, "I doubt he'll be coming back for his deposit. If'n I were you, I'd put in the bank, that way if he does come back for his money, you'll still have it. If he fails to show in a few weeks, I'd call the money yours to keep as a tip. Maybe invest in a pair of new boots, cloths or hat."

Dowling agreed, "Yeah sounds like a good idea. That way the money is in the bank if or when he comes back for it. Seems strange a man wouldn't ask for his deposit back. Must be nice not too have a care in the world about money."

Sudden rapid gunfire from the direction of Bristol's office ended their conversation. Without a word and moving fast, Crisp re-bridled Copper and re-secured the cinch. Then he swung onto the saddle and heeled Copper forward.

Fanning dust and dodging flying dirt, Dowling stepped clear and exhaled. "Damn, give a guy a chance to get out of the way!"

It was only a few blocks to Bristol's office, and more than likely the gunfire had nothing to do with the army. Crisp's stomach was knotted, his throat tight. Copper dodged people in their path without a need for reining. Above the sound of Copper's flying hoofs, he heard police whistles.

Crisp slowed Copper to a trot, then a steady walk as they rounded a corner across the street from Bristol's office. Local police were already pushing back crowds of onlookers from the front of the building. He gasped, "Oh my." He fought an urge to heel Copper through the crowd.

"I'm a doctor!" shouted a man, carrying black handbag. A small contingent of local law enforcement parted a path through the crowd and allowed him access. A second later, another single gunshot echoed from inside the office.

The doctor staggered backward out of the door, dropped his open handbag onto the boardwalk. He fell backward, his waist and legs angled upward on the boardwalk, his torso hitting the dirt. A small pistol fell from his left hand onto roadway. The gunshot sent crowds of onlookers scattering for cover. From a safer distance, crowds regrouped and gazed at the dead man.

Captain Bristol stepped from inside the office, a smoking pistol at his right side. He glimpsed down at the dead man, then at the crowds. His voice boomed, "I've had about enough of your people! Keep the hell away from here! And you know who I'm talking too! So, don't go thinking I am shouting as these mindless gawkers! Go inform you bosses we are coming for them, and there's going to be hell to pay!"

Bristol caught a glimpse of Crisp on horseback and drew a tense breath. Clearly, Crisp's luck was in full force when it came to stirring the kettle. Things were heating up. The iron was hot and it was near time to strike.

As a buckboard rolled to the edge of the boardwalk, Crivitz arrived and halted it just short of running over the dead body in the street. Ten Calvary men wearing Dragoon uniforms shoved their way through the crowds.

Bristol nodded, speaking softly to them. He was not allowing anyone access inside who he did not recognize. All but two of the Calvary men entered, the remaining two assumed a post at either side of door with rifles ready for action.

Crisp eased Copper backward a few steps, until standing between two buildings but still facing the army office. A voice from behind startled him.

"Don't turn around, it's me Rabbit. Captain sent me."

Crisp drew a breath. Rabbit was a friend who had missed the stunt that had placed Ring, Trick and Hindor out of favor with the army. Recently, Rabbit insisted he should have been with them and chasing after Indian Slave Traders.

Rabbit kept his voice low, "I've got a message for you. The boy is okay, however your mystery friend was hit twice. Doesn't look good for him but he's still breathing. We've got the journal and the old man is looking it over now."

Then Rabbit stated, "Unless they transfer me back under you command, I'm bailing on the army. There's no one I trust more than you."

Silent, Crisp nodded. When transferred, he had left a large number of good men behind. Rabbit was one of them.

"Don't look back," Rabbit warned. "There's folks looking this direction. I am out of their line of sight, and now yours too."

Crisp did not have to look back. Like a bunny in the brush, Rabbit had vanished among darkened alleys crisscrossing main streets. Rabbit was a good man and worth having under his command.

Crisp decided it was time to go as well. He needed to get Trick or Hindor at the docks to keep an eye on the Lady Beth. He heeled Copper forward and said, "Come-on boy, there's nothing more here to see."

41

After Crisp returned Copper to the livery stable and Dowling's care. He trekked back to the A. R & B. In the main office area, he flopped on his chair, slid out of his boots, leaned back and kicked his stocking feet on his desk. Hindor and Trick were likely visiting Ring at the hospital.

The bottom floor of the office was unusually warm. Hindor was not one who tolerated a mild chill in the air, and had left the potbelly stove banked with wood and low airflow.

Crisp pondered recent events. Shepherd was shot and in route to the nearest doctor or hospital. Kern was under protective custody of the army. In addition, someone had spent the better part of a day following him. Who had shadowed him and why? It could easily be a lackey of Ackerland, or someone from the Lady Beth crew. Either-way, Crisp knew he was suspect of not being whom he claimed.

Disappointed, Crisp slipped the medallion from his jacket pocket, inner-looped the chain through his fingers and studied the imagery. Father Anthony was unable to assist him with a translation beyond what the street preacher had done. Latin words, The Herdsmen. It was falling into focus.

"Herdsmen," Crisp muttered, deciding it was the shadowy organization's name. A slight rap from the backdoor announced guests. Whomever it was, failed to wait for someone to open the door. Two sets of footstep crested the kitchen floorboards.

Crisp swung his feet off his desk, set the medallion on the desktop, slipped a gun from his drawer and onto his lap. A few seconds later, there was a rap at the archway leading from the kitchen area into the front office. Whoever had arrived was taking care to announce their presence as not to alarm him.

Crisp invited, "Enter."

Rabbit entered, ushering Kern in front of him. "Sir, Bristol wanted the boy brought here. He suggested that I fill-in for Ring being you're short-handed at the moment. Though, I'd as soon make it a permanent assignment."

Crisp opened his desk drawer, returned the handgun to its place and stood. He smiled, "Good to have you onboard. I'll put in a request for your transfer and make it official." His attention turned to Kern. "I am glad you are back safe and sound. You're among family here – this place is your home."

Kern glimpsed around, searching for the dog. His face flexed concern. He wanted to ask about Bristol, however doing it would expose his mute act as a fraud.

Crisp shrugged and guessed, "If you're looking for Bristol, he's not here. The army has him under lock and key, hidden from everyone. I'll see what I can do about arranging a visit for you."

Puzzled, Rabbit's brow tightened. "I was told the boy was deaf and mute. If not, there's lying or misunderstandings going on between commands."

Crisp explained, "No misunderstanding on his deafness. Even if he can't hear, I figured talking will help him feel at ease and lets him know we care."

Then Crisp eyed Kern from head to toe and commented, "Those pants, shirt and hat are new. Apparently, Shepherd took good care of him. Other than bruises and cuts, he looks none the worse for wear." He thought of the newspaper boy, Bassett. "Anyone see another boy with Kern?"

Rabbit shook his head. "No sir, Shepherd and Kern showed up alone at Captain Bristol's office. Old man Bristol figured Shepherd knew folks was pursuing em. It was the reason they didn't come here. Shepherd didn't want to risk exposing operations here at the A. R & B."

Crisp nodded. Shepherd, man of mystery was not half-witted. While Shepherd was not directly a part of the A. R & B team, he was unwilling to jeopardize the operation. He inquired, "Any idea as to who was chasing after them?"

Rabbit shrugged. "Shepherd wasn't able to tell us anything. He lost a lot of blood and passed-out. Bristol said it wasn't bounty-hunters upset at losing a chance for a reward on Kern. These boys operated with military precision, taking the office before anyone knew they were under siege. Bristol requested a photographer come and shoot pictures of the dead bodies. I image, he's hoping someone will recognize em."

Crisp sighed. It was a long shot. Bristol was right. If someone did know one of the men who attempted to silence Shepherd and Kern, perhaps they could trace a path of origin to whoever had sent them.

Kern stepped around Crisp and sat on top of the desk. He spotted the amulet and palmed it. He had thought is lost or stolen. Carl had given to him and it was his to keep. He slipped the chain over his neck.

Crisp watched Kern drop the amulet beneath his shirt and smiled. Then he asked Rabbit, "You know Doctor Hanna Steadson?"

Rabbit answered, "No, can't say as I do. Hanna? A lady-doctor?" He spread a grin. "She can check out the privates of this private anytime, provided she's good looking enough that is."

Crisp allowed Rabbit's comment to pass without rebuttal. Rabbit was all-talk and no play. Crisp instructed, "Her office is near twelve and Santa Fe. She has a sign swinging on a pole near a hitching rail. Go and tell her, we have Kern and need her to come here, ASAP. He needs his ears looked at straightaway."

Kern's eyes widened as Hindor and Trick entered the room. Stepping into the room was a dark-skinned man with a bushy hair and beard. Was it real or imagined? Here across the waters was a tribe-man.

Thrilled, Kern jumped to his feet, darted across the floor and hugged Hindor. Tears streamed down his face. Babbling to Hindor, he broke his silence using a foreign tribal language.

Dumbfounded, Hindor took a quarter-step backward.

Crisp ordered, "Hindor hold your place, allow the boy to get whatever off his chest. Nodded as if you are understanding every word and make it look good. I've seen photos of Australian tribes and they could pass for African. For all we know, he could've been raised in the wilds of

Australia, and he's mistaking you for a friend of the family or distant kinfolk."

Hindor brows crinkled, he was unsure if Crisp had insulted him or not. He peered into Kern's teary blue eyes, and his heart melted. The boy was unloading a heavy weight. It was unfortunate he was unable to understand the language. He put his arms around him and patted his back.

Kern's babbling slowed to shorter sentences.

Crisp placed a hand on Kern's shoulder. Gradual, he turned Kern from Hindor and mouthed each word. "You're among friends here, Kern." He looked at Hindor and said, "He has things he's got to do. I'm going to take care of you, okay?"

Crisp glimpsed between Trick, Hindor and Rabbit. "I believe he speaks and understands perfect English when the mood suits him. Until Doctor Steadson has one of her friends fix his hearing, we won't know for sure. For all we know, he can read and write better than most folks."

Trick said, "We saw Doc Steadson at the hospital."

Crisp said, "Rabbit change of orders. Get him cleaned-up and take him to the hospital. Any of the nurses should be able to help you find Doc Steadson."

Rabbit waved Kern toward him. "Come-on boy, we've got get ya ready to see those doctors." Kern followed Rabbit from the room and into the kitchen area.

Crisp cocked an eyebrow at Trick and Hindor. "I don't care which of you, but someone needs to get down to the docks and learn when the Lady Beth plans to set sail. La Horn's losing money by staying. I'm surprised she ain't sailed into the wild blue horizon already."

Bewildered, Trick shook his head. "I've known some twisted folks in my life but La Horn's stench rises above the rest. Sure as fire burns in hell, he's only staying because of that boy. His twisted mind is bent revenge. If ya don't mind me saying, his first mate Caleb doesn't seem to have a mind of his own to speak of. He asked about the boy and dog on numerous occasions."

Trick rolled his head and continued, "Almost forgot to mention, Caleb was here looking for you. A few minutes before he got here, I was trying to figure out what star pattern was on the amulet. I had it dotted onto a piece of paper. He told me it was the pattern for Bootes, also known as the Herdsman."

"Makes sense," commented Crisp, "I think Caleb is riding the fence on this entire affair, more or less stuck in situation."

Trick agreed, "He saw me roughing up a couple of his hard-nosed crew, and didn't do squat to stop me. Hell, he simply strolled past as if nothing was going on, and I had two of his boys spreading puddles of blood from broken teeth and noses."

Crisp groaned, "Trick, you've got a wagon load of pent-up hostilities. Taking it out on Lady Beth crewmembers isn't what I call as the up and up. You're supposed to be buddies with them, learning what you can."

"I'll hobble on down the docks," Hindor offered, hoping to relieve tension between Trick and Crisp. Then he sided with Trick, "Can't rightly say I haven't had a desire to bang a few heads. The Lady Beth's crew are easy targets. With nothing to do, they're drunk most of the time."

Crisp conceded, "Trick go fetch Bristol, and sneak him into the hospital. It'd be good for Kern to see him, again."

Trick asked, "Why sneak old man Bristol into the hospital. Who's he hiding from?"

Crisp moaned. "Not the old man you goof, the dog… He's over at Bristol's office."

Trick jested, "The dog has his own office?"

Defeated, Crisp threw his arms upward and replied, "Whatever, just get the job done."

Hindor reminded Crisp, "Those are famous last words. Remember what happened the last you said, *get the job done*? All hell broke loose and lots of guilty people died."

Crisp moved onto another topic. "So you both know about it. Someone tailed me to the Mission and back. I've no idea who it was. Maybe one of Ackerland's people, maybe not."

"That shootout at Bristol's office, speaking of the man and not the dog," Hindor injected humor to Trick's joke. "I image it has to do with how Kern came back to us?"

Crisp informed them, "Shepherd was shot-up, badly. From what Rabbit told me, he's at the hospital. Shepherd and Kern must've run into something out there. No telling what it was."

Trick advised, "With Kern speaking in tongues to Hindor, we didn't get a chance to mention it. We spotted a couple of hard-nose cowboys across the street. I think they are watching the place."

Crisp grumbled, "Figures... On your way out, let Rabbit know. He's good at giving people the slip."

Then Crisp thought for a moment and said, "I'm headed off to a pub near Bristol's office and try to speak with one of his office boys. I need a face to face meeting with Bristol." He slid a feather pen from the inkwell, took a piece of paper and began to write.

Being watched. Must arrange a meeting, I need a look at the journal. Hospital tonight, there is a janitor's closet on the first floor.

Crisp slipped the paper into his pocket, looked up and noticed that Hindor and Trick were still there. Frustrated, he asked, "What you two waiting on? For hell to freeze over?"

Without another word, Hindor and Trick left.

Crisp sighed. It was tiresome waiting for something to break or happen. Forcing a few hands in the game was risky. His father had a motto, given enough rope the guilty will hang themselves.

42

Rabbit sat on a bench outside the hospital and waited, boredom was getting the better part of him. Tolerant, the dog Bristol lay next to him on the boardwalk. Kern had spent a few minutes with Bristol before Doctor Steadson and another physician took him inside for treatment.

Rabbit glimpsed at Bristol, his own memories vivid of childhood dogs on the family farm. Bristol sniffed the air and stood, then tugged on his leash toward a side alleyway that ran along the hospital and growled.

Rabbit tugged on Bristol's leash and mumbled, "Take it easy boy, Kern should be out of surgery in an hour."

Bristol eased back from a steady tug on his leash.

Rabbit stroked the dog's head and assured, "Don't fret none, you friend will be fine. I'm willing to bet a week's pay he will be hearing your bark before too long." He saw Captain Bristol approaching and dressed in civilian clothing.

As Captain Bristol stepped past them, he gave a casual nod, covertly acknowledging their presence.

***

Once inside the hospital, Captain Bristol strolled past the reception area, then along the hallway. He turned a side corridor and glimpsed back at the reception area. No one was watching. Earlier, he had left his office in uniform, carrying civilian clothing inside of a saddlebag. He had entered a friend's store, changed clothing, and slipped through a side door and back onto the streets. As an army captain, he found the concept of dodging watchful eyes discomforting.

Several yards into a secluded corridor, Bristol paused and opened a door. A small window high on the wall, allowed enough outdoor light to see. His nose crinkled at the strong order of cleaning supplies. Buckets, mops, sponges and cleaning chemicals were stacked onto shelves.

Crisp stepped from behind a wooden rack filled with towels and said, "Thanks for coming. I wanted look at Ver Haven's journal."

Bristol pulled the leather bound journal from inside of shoulder strap carry bag and informed him, "When attending to Shepherd's gunshot wounds, I confirmed his amulet was identical to Ver Haven's." Then he passed Crisp the journal and said, "I read the last few entries. Some of which were added by your friend, Shepherd."

Crisp opened the journal, stared at Bristol and said, "Really?"

Bristol informed him, "Shepherd is an assumed name that's he used since childhood. I doubt he recalls his birth name anymore. He mentioned his first name is Jasper, which may be his real first name but hard to tell. At first, he came to see why Carl had failed to check-in. Appears he has turned this affair into a vendetta. Given what I read, he'll crisscross the globe to enact it. Once healed, he will make certain La Horn is a dead."

Crisp shook his head. "Shepherd won't stop with killing La Horn; he'll torch and sink the Lady Beth along with everyone onboard. He's smarter than most and able to think beyond everyday soldiers."

"Solider?" Bristol's comment smacked of sarcasm. "That young man was never a solider, at least not in this man's army. He crawled from some darkened hole. He didn't come right-out and admit in those pages, but what I was able to gather, he is part of a secret organization of some-sort. It means Car Ver Haven was part of the same group. It gives me the willies thinking Carl and I were close friends, and I knew nothing about the Herdsmen. Whoever these Herdsmen are, they sure as hell ain't regular army. As far as smarter than an everyday solider? Shepherd's smarter and slicker than most generals I've met."

Crisp withheld further expansion on Shepherd's state of mind. Instead, he paged backward through the journal, and listened as Bristol ranted.

"I've enough evidence right there in your hand to hold La Horn for trial. La Horn will be swing from a hangman's noose in a couple weeks, if not sooner. At this moment, I've got

Sargent Forks rounding-up twenty-plus men to board the Lady Beth."

Suddenly, the janitor's closet door swung open, Bristol and Crisp drew their guns and aimed at the doorway.

Rabbit yielded his hands upward with the dog's leash wrapped around his right wrist and announced, "It's me, Rabbit... Don't shoot."

Bristol and Crisp lowered their weapons.

Animated, Rabbit explained, "Sorry to bust in like this, but all hell's broken loose. Kern's been kidnapped! There's nurse and doctor laying-dead with their throats slit ear to ear!"

At the same instant Crisp and Bristol said, "La Horn."

Crisp ordered, "Rabbit, strap that dog to Shepherd's bed and find Sargent Fork! He is in the process of rounding up a group of men to board the Lady Beth to arrest La Horn and the entire crew. Get everyone down at the Lady Beth's birth and board her, guns blazing if need-be."

At skidding run, Rabbit turned and vanished among hospital corridors with Bristol the dog scampering alongside.

Crisp exited the closet at a run, leaving Captain Bristol trailing behind him. Within minutes, they shoved their way through a crowd of onlookers and into the room where Kern was treated.

Crisp expected to find Hanna Steadson's throat slit and lying dead in a spreading pool of blood. He exhaled a sighed relief. Hanna was not among the dead. Instead, he saw a nurse and doctor he had never met. A bloody bone handle knife lay near the bodies. Embedded on the handle were jade snakes. He recognized the knife from having seen it strapped on La Horn's side and announced, "It is La Horn's knife."

Chief Crivitz waddled through the crowd and probed, "La Horn's knife?"

Crisp pointed at the knife. "Chief, right there is your evidence. We have a contingent of men on the way to the docks. They've kidnapped Kern!" He stared at Bristol and asked, "Are you coming along for party this time around?"

Crivitz knelt by one of the bodies, picked up the knife and slipped it into his pocket. By the time he stood and turned, Crisp and Captain Bristol had disappeared.

"Damn," grumbled Crivitz. Shepherd was missing, and now a double murder. These army boys had some explaining, even if it meant locking Captain Bristol and Crisp into cells to get answers.

* * *

Two blocks from the hospital, Crisp paused and waited for Captain Bristol to catch-up. Panting, Bristol held his side and acknowledged, "I'm getting to old for this horse crap. My heart is about to give out, you head-on without me."

Crisp turned and ran at full speed. Five minutes later, he joined Trick at an empty birth. The Lady Beth was gone. Defeated, they stood silent.

Crisp calculated their next move. They needed a ship to chase after the Lady Beth. He eyed ships docked nearby. Two piers over, a new steam engine powered ship rocked back and forth. He ordered Trick, "Once Rabbit, Fork and company get their slow-sorry arses here, we are seizing that steam engine. La Horn can't be far ahead of us."

Trick injected, "He's headed for Seattle. I bumped into Rabbit towing that dog behind him in front of the hospital. He told me what happened. He should be along shortly with help." Then he groaned, "Boarding the Lady Beth at sea won't be easy."

Crisp's brow tightened. Rabbit had failed to follow orders and leave Bristol with Shepherd. Bristol was a good line of protection for a seriously injured man. If Rabbit were joining the A. R & B, he had best start obeying orders.

Trick advised him, "I see what you're thinking about Rabbit and that dog, and it ain't so. Rabbit told me Shepherd was missing." He turned toward the city skyline and spotted a covered Calvary wagon. "They're almost here." He raised both hands and yelled at the driver. "Get your sorry-arses moving!"

The driver slapped the reins, putting both horses into a trot. A minute later, the wagon-driver reined to a halt alongside of them. His Dragoon uniform appeared too small for his larger frame.

Trick stated, "About damn time, you regular army boys were about to get left behind and miss-out on all the action!"

As the driver stared at them, a silly smirk brightened his face. Trick grunted, "What so damn funny you idiot? There's a boy's life depending on us, and justice waiting to be served!"

Suddenly, ten rifles protruded from beneath the covered wagon. The driver's smirk faded with a warning, "Slow and easy, lay your guns at your feet and climb on into the back. There's someone inside who wants to greet Mister Crisp. Not that your friend here isn't welcome, but since he's here – he's more or less invited as well."

Leaving their guns on the dock, Crisp and Trick parted the back curtain of the wagon. Crisp drew a step back into Trick and gasped, "Oh God, no…" Ackerland lay tied, gagged and beaten. Dried blood spotted Ackerland's expensive wool suite, his lower lip split downward to his chin. Ackerland's bruised eyes were swelling closed.

"Crisp," a shadowed voice spoke from deeper inside the wagon. "I've should've figured it was your nose sticking into this. You can't seem to leave me alone." His voice changed direction. "Driver, do you see anyone else out there?"

"Nope," the driver answered.

"Get on aboard," the voice commanded, "Or we'll cut you down where you stand, makes no difference too me."

From the corner of a nearby pub, Captain Bristol yanked Hindor back into hiding. "That wagon is pulling a ton of weight. It is loaded with armed men. If we go in there, they're dead."

Hindor jerked himself away and asked, "How the hell do you know what's inside that covered wagon? Not unless you put those men inside of it?"

Offended, Bristol shook his head. "You boys are too caught-up in conspiracies. Grant there are conspiracies out there, but I sure ain't part of one. Only thing I'm conspiring is how to rescue Crisp and Trick, and not to forget Kern, and bringing La Horn in for trial." He pointed at shadows beneath the wagon. "If you've taken a moment before storming off and getting everyone killed, you'd seen tell-tell shadows of rifles sticking from inside that covered wagon."

Unsure, Hindor and demanded, "If those boys ain't part of La Horn's crew, who the hell are they? Ackerland's ranch hands dressing like army boys?"

Abrupt, Bristol's brow tightened. "It was staring us in the face all along."

Hindor watched the wagon jerk into motion and grumbled, "Whatever was staring us in the face is now rolling out of here."

Bristol said, "I'm taking a horse from the hitching post outside the railing. Odds are; they're headed for Ackerland's spread north of here."

Hindor planted both hands on his hips and demanded, "What about Kern and La Horn?"

It was a tough decision, however Bristol said, "Priorities, Sargent. If my guess is right, this entire affair is coming full circle and right into our laps. Ackerland is tied into whatever private army shot the hell out of my office. I am betting La Horn was carrying gunpowder and opium for Ackerland. It is possible Ackerland was using money from selling opium to finance a private militia."

Bristol shook his head and said, "Ackerland fool that he is, was nothing more than a front-man and didn't realize it. We got too close and spoked someone. Our true opponent is inside of that wagon and seizing control. You boys shook loose nails from their shed and it is falling apart on them."

Baffled, Hindor kept the issue divided. "What about La Horn? Sure as the sunset sets in the west, he's gonna kill Kern, and get away with killing Ver Haven too."

Bristol detailed, "Not by a long-shot. We know where the Lady Beth has set-sail, and La Horn takes his time with revenge. You ever witnessed a steam driven ship on open water? They are fast." His brow tightened. "I know Taylor skipped to parts unknown. But where the hell is Muser?"

Hindor shrugged and without giving it a second thought replied, "Hell if I know. Last I heard he was running with a Councilman's niece."

Bristol nearly exploded, "What?" Then he bellowed, "I don't want to know about it – not a damn word of it! If I don't know, it's not my problem! It lands squarely on Crisp's shoulders and not mine! I don't know anything about anything!"

43

Sally Sue pressed herself against a man and giggled. Rum tainted breath, she whispered into his ear. "Like I was saying on the street, I'll have you shivering with pleasure. Most of my customers are repeats. Like them, you'll be coming back to me time and again, bragging to your buddies about me."

Again, Sally Sue tried to peer beneath the wide brim hat and teased, "I bet you got a beautiful set of eyes."

He brushed her hand away from his hat-brim. A heavy early evening mist clung to her nightdress, chilling her. She wrapped a neck scarf around her throat and shivered. "Let's find us a room and workout this chill with some bodily contact." She smiled. "I keep you warm, you keep me warm."

Determined to seduce him, she stepped closer and reached outward to wrap her hands around his waist. Suddenly, she realized he had led her into a darkened alley. Drunken, she swayed back and forth, and pondered her location. The Hammer Killer had not struck in days, and likely moved-on to a new feeding ground. She slurred, "This isn't the way to the hotel." She tugged at his arm and tried pulling him toward main-street. "Over this way," she insisted and tugged at his arm for a second time.

He stood firm and pulled a hammer from his waistline.

Horrified, Sally Sue's eyes widened. Her scream ended with a blunt echo lost amid a rolling night mist. She slumped to the muddy alley, dead before hitting the mud puddle at her feet.

***

Three blocks away, Crivitz hosted his dress above ankle level and ran toward the shortened scream. He reached the alleyway and groaned. Sally Sue laid dead, her forehead crushed by a hammer blow. Weary, he gazed beyond the alleyway and saw nothing. Again, the killer had eluded capture.

Saddened, he drew a whistle from his purse and blew short, sharp notes. He knelt, lifted Sally Sue onto his lap and begged forgiveness from her blank death-stare. "I'm sorry, but this killer isn't an easy one to catch. Your killer started this spree as a means to end frustration. Now it is a mission to rid the world of working girls. He sees you as a sickness. In truth, the killer has a sickness with no easy cure."

His words caught in his throat. Sickness and cure hung there, staring at him as if intertwined with the night mist. He had thought it before and denied the possibility of it. His list of suspects had narrowed to less than a handful.

A patrolman arrived and called into the dark alleyway as if afraid of encountering the Hammer Killer and not live through it. "You in the alley, this is Officer Wentzle. I'm coming in!"

Crivitz laid her back onto the ground. He wiped tears from his eyes, stood and turned. Wentzle took several steps backward and gasped, "Chief Crivitz?"

Crivitz raised a stern finger and ordered, "Not a word to anyone. I've been dressing like this for the past two nights, hoping to catch the Hammer Killer. One word about this, and tomorrow it is your turn to put on a dress!"

Wentzle surrendered palms upward. "Yes sir, you've my word on it. I heard the scream, came running and founder her laying here."

There was no reason to remain. Crivitz hosted his dress above his ankles and waddled into the mist, vanishing between buildings. Earlier, he had heard the army commandeered a steam ship, giving chase after the Lady Beth. It would take hours for them catch the Lady Beth at sea. La Horn was an army problem. He had a killer to catch.

He had narrowed his list of suspects for the Hammer Killings. Moving his investigate forward, he did not want to do so wearing a dress and makeup.

44

Crisp and Trick sat comfortable on cushioned wingchairs inside of Ackerland's expansive ranch home. Having grown up amid wealth, Crisp was not as impressed as Trick. Large Redwood timbers stood tall holding squared ceiling beams in place. Constructed at either side of the living room were huge stone fireplaces.

Paintings of cattle, horses and landscape adorned the walls. If nothing else, Crisp credited Ackerland with taste for the landscape paintings. He glimpsed at Ackerland and groaned.

Ackerland lay stretched out on a couch across from them. His injuries were not life threatening. Unless their captors decided otherwise, he would live.

Crisp expected them to decide otherwise in the near future. He had no idea who was leading this private army. Earlier when dragged into the cover-wagon, they had blindfolds tied around their heads. Again, he tried to put a face with the familiar voice inside the wagon and failed. Nearby armed guards prevented him from asking Trick if he recognized the voice.

Trick grinned, tipped his head toward glass cabinet and suggested, "Looks like some mighty fine whiskey there. All I was saying, a friendly came of cards to pass the time and maybe a few drinks to mellow everyone."

Slow, Trick stood and spread his hands as show of peace. "You've got us mixed up with this no account Ackerland fellow and it's a flat-out mistake. We've nothing going on with him."

Ready to bounce the butt of a rifle against Trick's head, one of the guards stepped forward. Someone at the top of the stairwell ordered, "Herman, stand-down. We need them able to talk during integration."

Crisp glimpsed upward, only to catch a flitting glimpse of the unknown man as he disappeared behind log pillar. Clearly, there was a meeting in process inside one of the upper bedrooms. Perhaps, deciding Ackerland's fate for putting them at risk of discovery.

Crisp wondered what happened to ranch-hands, Ackerland's wife and stepson Richard. There were no signs of anyone. Except for the men who held them at gunpoint, the ranch was void of people. There were no cooks, no ranch-hands, and no wife or children.

Trick's mindset was near that of Crisp's, and assumed they planned to kill them. He cast aside concern for speaking in front of their guards. He nodded toward the balcony. "I can tell by the look on your face that guy upstairs sounded familiar."

Crisp responded, "He does, but he is to chicken-shit to show his face."

"Could be he's butt-ugly," injected Trick, planning to drag guards into a conversation. "Women see him and run the other-way. Unless of course he swings the other-way, in which case men probably run the other direction as well."

"Yeah," agreed Crisp, "Could be he swings the other-way, and wears dresses late at night when no one is around."

Herman defended, "He's more of a man than either of you."

Trick raised his eyebrows and mocked, "You been down his pants and compared yours to his? Hell, I make both of you look like schoolboys. Wanna make a wager on it?"

At first Herman's mouth dropped open, and he took a full two-steps backward. Angered, he stepped forward and, again raised the butt of his rifle to strike Trick's head.

Another guard jumped-in, blocked is comrade's path and warned, "Don't let him yank your chain! You heard the order! Don't beat on them until integration."

"He's begging for a beating," Herman griped and glimpsed at his friends. "Tell everyone he was making a break for it, and I had to do something."

Another man near the front window announced, "Riders coming, two of them."

Herman stepped to the window and ridiculed, "Well Bernie, pull that fancy spyglass and take a look-see at who it is."

Bernie slipped a spyglass from his back pocket, elongated it and peered into the lens. "Can't say for sure, but looks like that jackass son of Ackerland, Richard. More-than-likely, he's riding drunk with one of the ranch-hands Ackerland has babysitting him."

Bernie looked over his shoulder at Herman. "That boy is a good reason to outlaw inbreeding. Cousins marrying cousins ain't right in my book."

Infuriated, Ackerland sat upright and his face flushed red. "He's my stepson, and his mother wasn't my cousin."

Herman laughed, "What did you say? His mother was your sister… Wouldn't that make Richard both son and nephew?" He slapped his leg and chuckled, "Wait, I get it now… That grotesque woman you called a wife, was once your mother before you married her. If true, it would make that jackass Richard your little brother?"

Bernie wanted to end personal drama and stated, "Herman, shouldn't you be upstairs and telling them about our arriving guests?"

Grumbling, Herman relented and trotted upstairs.

Crisp noted arriving riders had guards distracted. Once Richard and his friend arrived, there would be a moment of transition. Trick and himself had too either make a play at escape, or set the stage for additional melodrama.

York descended the stairs with Herman trailing behind. He paused at the window and placed a small wooden box on an end table. Unhappy, he stared out the window.

Outside, Richard and his friend were tying their horses to a hitching rail. York ran his index finger along a thick scar across his cheek and turned toward Crisp.

Crisp recognized him, smirked and sneered, "York, I figured you'd be back East and sticking your nose into affairs out-there. What are you doing way-out here? Too many shady business dealing send you slithering across the Continental Divide?"

York ignored him, turned to his men and ordered, "Let them come inside, keep it low-key until their relaxed." He turned to Herman and said, "Stop irritating the prisoners. Ackerland is a bloody mess. I don't want our hand tipped. Get him a blanket and hat to cover himself."

Herman tossed a blanket and hat on Ackerland. He said, "Make it look convincing."

York stared at Ackerland and warned, "Remember your wife is in the barn with everyone else. Don't be exposing your nasty face, keep it under your hat and pretend to be asleep."

As the front door swung open, Ackerland did as told. He laid-flat and shielded his bruised face with a hat. At the last moment, he pulled a blanket over his bloodstained shirt.

Richard and Taylor stumbled inside, drunk.

Richard announced, "This is the place, home sweet home." He paid no attention to men standing around the room. His stepfather had numerous hired hands, most of whom he had never met. "Pa," he called to Ackerland who appeared to be napping. "Wake-up, I've brought us a new hired hand. Met him camped at the far-side of the ranch overlooking the Pacific."

Suddenly, Taylor recognized Crisp and Trick. He edged toward the doorway. Herman blocked his path and said, "Don't be in such a rush, not unless you're afraid of hard work."

Wide-eyed, Trick stood, pointed at Taylor and proclaimed, "He's the Hammer Killer!" His accusation caused a flurry of reaction. York and Bernie pulled their weapons, fanning back and forth between Crisp, Trick, Richard and Taylor.

Ackerland sat upright, the hat falling from his face and onto floor. Taken-back, Richard gasped at the sight of his stepfather's damaged face. Herman dropped the point of his rifle against Taylor's temple and ordered, "Move and I'll drop you here and now!"

"Everyone stand-still," ordered York.

Bernie took Richard's pistol, slid it behind his belt and shoved him against a wall. Confused, Richard glimpsed back and forth between his stepfather and York.

York glared at Trick and stated, "Don't play me for a fool. There was another killing last night." He nodded at Taylor. "This pup isn't the Hammer Killer, not if he was camping out here last night."

"I don't what's going on here," said Taylor. He pointed at Crisp and Trick. "Those two ain't business men, they're army. Whatever's going-on here, I'm on your side, not theirs."

Trick pointed at Taylor and suggested, "Herman check his saddlebag and you'll find proof of what I'm saying."

Herman shouted, "Shut-up, I am tired of your gambling mouth!"

"Check his saddlebag," instructed York. "We need to learn who he is."

Steady, Herman lowered his gun and pulled Taylor's sidearm from his belt. Then he took a saddlebag from Taylor's shoulder and dumped the contents onto the floor.

Herman examined the contents and found a shaving kit, gunpowder horn, shell balls, bag of nails and an old hammer. Unsure, he stood, stepped back and gasped, "I'll be damned, he is the Hammer Killer!"

York discarded Herman, "Not likely." He stared at Crisp and stated, "Crisp, your thinking is more twisted than a cuspiss vine. You had something planned for Ackerland, hoping to get him to fess-up. Well, I got news for you, it ain't working."

Then York stepped to the end table, opened the box and removed a bone-handle sliver derringer. He examined the gun as if a fine piece of art. Lamplights sparkled from its polished barrel.

Casual, York approached Ackerland and explained, "I recall when we first met. You showed me this derringer and bragged how it belonged to your daddy. How he had it built special for your mother to carry. I'm sure it means a lot to you."

York aimed and fired. The shot planted Ackerland's head against a pillow, and the back of his head splattered brain-matter across the couch. He tossed the derringer on top of Ackerland's body and turned toward Crisp.

Richard screamed, "Pa!" Then he dashed forward, his face torn between grief and rage. He lifted Ackerland's limp body from the couch, shook him and called, "Pa I'm sorry… I'm sorry, this ain't my fault." Raging shock seized his reasoning skills. He jumped to his feet then leaped hands stretched outward toward York's throat.

Another gunshot, this one from Bernie's rifle sent Richard sprawling across the wooden floor. Agonized, he curled into a fetal position, pressing both hands against a gut-shot and wailed.

Having heard gunshots, Muser and four well-dressed men exited the upper study. They gazed at the bloodbath below. One of the men yelled, "What the hell York! We didn't sign-up for killing our own!"

York replied, "In for a penny in for a pound!"

Another of the men answered, "What the hell is that supposed to mean? I am speaking for everyone; we are pulling our support for this endeavor. We are leaving here with our cash."

York stated, "Have it your way!" Then he ordered his men, "Kill them! His men raised their guns and fired toward the balcony. Gunfire erupted from two sides, bullets raining down and flying upward.

As Muser dove to one-side, a bullet ripped through his left shoulder. He pressed tight behind the pillar and looked along the balcony. Other than himself, only one man on the balcony had survived the volley of gunfire. The man had a hand pressed against his neck, hoping to stem blood pumping an artery wound.

Muser did not expect him to live for long. He pulled a pistol from a shoulder holster, cocked the hammer and drew a painful breath. His shoulder was aching and blood soaked his new suitcoat. He laid the gun down, pulled a bandanna from his pocket, jammed it into the bullet hole and slowed the bleeding.

Below, York lowered his smoking gun and glimpsed across the room. "Damn," he grumbled. His attention had only diverted for a few seconds. Crisp and Trick had vanished, and two of his men lay dead.

York ordered, "Spread-out and find them! They can't have gotten far."

Taylor eased himself toward the front door.

Herman aimed at Taylor and cautioned, "Don't even think about!"

York stated, "If he tries to make a break for it, shoot him. Don't waste ammunition. Make the first shot count, up close and personal."

Richard moaned, and side crawled toward the couch where his stepfather sat dead. He gasped, "Pa, pa, pa… Don't fret, I'm coming."

One of York's men asked, "Want me to finish him?"

York sneered, "He got on my nerves every time he was around, let the bastard suffer and bleed-out."

45

Trick and Crisp dashed through a backdoor in the kitchen and ran to the nearest barn. Trick parted the barn door a few feet and slipped inside. Crisp stepped in behind him and out of sight. Aghast, they began batting an army of flies buzzing their heads.

Beneath scattered rays of sunlight filtering through small holes in the roof, lay twenty or more dead people heaped one on top of another. At the top of the heap laid Ackerland's wife, her body twisted at an unnatural position.

Crisp muttered, "When York said Ackerland's wife was in the barn with everyone else, he wasn't kidding. He must have had everyone killed when he took Ackerland into town to get us. He simply wanted to avoid having this many people to guard." He turned from the grotesque display and said, "I had a couple of run-ins with York at the military academy. Years ago, I passed on a chance to place a bullet between his shoulder blades."

Trick's face pulled tight. "Whatever it was he did, I'm sure this pales in comparison. You're not one for back-shooting someone. Don't be blaming yourself for this. York needs to pay for what he's done here, and you've got no argument from me."

Trick and Crisp heard the cocking pistol of a gun hammer from behind, but not soon enough. York aimed and fired, the bullet sent Crisp tumbling onto the pile of decaying bodies.

Trick dove into a shoulder roll, coming up face to face with York, his boot knife drawn and ready. Without hesitation, he stabbed into the ribs and jeered, "Surprise, surprise, surprise…"

York reeled backward taking the blade with him, it sticking upward through his ribs. Trick pounced forward, knocking York's feet from under him. Locked in a life and death struggle, Trick and York rolled across the straw covered dirt floor, landing partly on top of a manure pile. Struggling for breath, York grabbed for his fallen sidearm.

Trick planted his left knee against York's right forearm. Then he yanked his knife from York's chest, poked it tight against the man's throat and advised, "Let go of the gun."

Gasping for air, York released his pistol.

Trick grabbed the weapon, stood and checked it for remaining shots. There were four shots left. He closed the cylinder, cocked the hammer and aimed.

York pressed a hand against his wound and inquired, "You gonna to check on your friend? He may still be alive?"

From on top of the body pile, Crisp stated, "Don't fall for it, I'm fine. We need us a couple mounts and right quick. He's got too many men at the house for us to take them all. We have to settle for taking him prisoner. If nothing else, we have the head of the snake. Without its head, the body will squirm for a time before dying."

From outside, gunfire erupted toward the house. Both front and rear barn doors swung open. Abrupt, eleven Calvary men barged inside. "Don't fire," called Hindor to the soldiers with him. "That man aiming the gun is one of ours!"

Trick grinned. "Nice of you to join the party, not that Crisp and myself didn't have the situation under control. But a little help is always appreciated at times like this."

Hindor lifted an injured Crisp onto his feet and moved him away from the pile of dead bodies. He asked, "What's going on inside the house. How many innocent people inside?"

Trick injected, "Depends on who you wanna call innocent. Taylor is in there, and was alive when we escaped. Muser, I ain't sure about. He was there too. I'm thinking he may be dead but hard to tell at this point. Not sure if Muser was selling us out, or a prisoner, or what."

As a fierce gun battle waged outside between those inside of the house and the Calvary, Trick tied York and gagged him. Then he stuffed a bandana into York's knife wound. Tick's thoughts rested on Taylor and Muser. Was Taylor the man who put Ring in the hospital? Had Muser turned-coat on them?

* * *

Inside the house, bullets shattered windows, spreading a rainbow of stained glass across lower rooms. Muser kept tight against the balcony pillar and evaded attention of York's men. As gunfire from the main living room lessened, he lay flat and scooted across the floor to the railing. Out of ten men that York had guarding prisoners, only two remained alive.

Muser smiled, aimed and back-shot Herman. Avoiding return gunfire, he rolled several feet. A bullet impacted the wooden railing and sent splinters flying in every direction.

Bernie slid down in front of the couch and shoved Ackerland's body away. Using his foot, he jostled a nearly dead Richard aside. He called up toward the balcony, "Hold your fire up there." He stared at Herman and shook his head.

Herman reached a bloody hand outward. Blood gurgled and foamed from the corner of his mouth. His right lung was collapsing and drowning him.

Bernie spat at Herman's hand and muttered, "You've always been a worthless no-account in my book. Always talking about inbreeding, I was starting to think you are inbred yourself. From the looks of it, I reckon you'll be having a family reunion hell before too long"

Gunfire from outside ended, followed by someone calling for everyone inside the house to surrender. A moment later, flaming arrows crashed through glass windows.

Again, Bernie called up to the balcony. "There's blood dripping from where you were laying. I know you've lost a lot of it. You probably ain't got much time left. I need higher ground for a look-see outside. I'm coming up!"

Muser replied, "I ain't wounded that bad! Come up here at your own risk, I am loaded for bear!" He waited a couple minutes, then inched belly down toward the railing. Among the dead lay Taylor, his blank eyes gazing at the ceiling.

Muser noticed the hammer near Taylor's body. If Taylor was camping nearby last night then he was not the Hammer Killer. As dusk bedded the night, flames licked upward along window curtains and walls. He cussed, "Damn they're burning everyone into the open."

***

Outside, Captain Bristol stood with Trick and Hindor. Crisp laid in the back of a buckboard, an army doctor cutting a bullet from inside of his shoulder.

As gunfire from behind the house erupted, Bristol said to Trick and Hindor, "We ran into a Calvary contingent on the way here. Their scout had a run-in with Shepherd and lived to tell the tale. They were tracking a private militia, same people we were after. We've got the house surrounded, no one is escaping."

As flames consumed the roof, glass from an upper bedroom shattered. Muser waved a white towel and yelled, "I'm coming out!" He pulled himself over the window ledge and fell on to a pouch roof. Then he rolled downward across its slop. He fell to the ground, landing with a thud.

Trick, along with a several Calvary men braved the heat of the fire and ran across the yard. Muser needed the benefit of a doubt. He yelled, "Hold you fire, he's one of ours!" Although, he questioned the statement, nothing was as it appeared in games of deceit.

As Trick arrived, two soldiers carried Muser away from the heat. They hosted Muser on the buckboard and next to Crisp. Trick said to the soldiers, "Thanks boys. I need a moment alone with my friends."

As the men stepped away, Trick climbed into the buckboard and whispered to Muser, "Crisp is in no condition to be asking, so I'll do it for him… You've got some explaining to do."

Trick noticed Bristol was headed their direction. He encouraged, "Be quick about it, old man Bristol is about on top of us. Our stories have to match."

Weak from a loss of blood, Muser nodded. "I was having lunch with a couple of Ackerland's people and they asked me to join them here. We swung by the A. R & B for Crisp but he wasn't there. I found a letter stuck in the door-jam for me."

Concerned, Muser's eyes tightened. "Miss Jane left me a note. She's returning to Oregon. I tried to chase after her but

Ackerland's people told me it was too late. She already booked passage on the Lady Beth and it sailed."

Trick inquired, "What about Taylor?"

Muser stared at the burning house and informed him, "Dead and charred." Then he grabbed Trick's hand and assumed, "If La Horn learns who she is, he's probably gonna hold her for ransom. The thought of those sea-rats having their way with her, I can't stand it." His pleaded, "We've gotta get up the coast and save her."

Captain Bristol halted his clipped pace at the wagon.

Feeble, Crisp reached back with his good arm, tapped Trick and said, "Tell him about Miss Jane, we gotta do something."

Bristol demanded, "Tell me what? Your buddy has been having his way with a Councilman's niece? I already know about it and don't want to hear any details."

Trick explained, "Sir, it's the details you need to know. Before Muser was able to stop her, Miss Jane booked passage on the Lady Beth."

Bristol stood firm, his body tensed.

Trick decided not to tell him about Taylor's charred body inside of the house. It was information Bristol could read later inside of a final report, hopefully a few days from now.

Bristol stated, "There's not much we can do at the moment, except pray. Provided Rabbit did as Hindor ordered, there is a steam engine loaded with troops and chasing after the Lady Beth. Those steam ships are fast, they'll catch her before she reaches the Oregon Coast."

Bristol motioned at a tied-up York and said, "I'm stunned he's still alive. With your group around, the guilty generally don't make it to trial." Then he shook his finger and offered an offhanded complement, "When this undercover operation was conceived, I warned the powers-that-be; you boys wind-up in the middle of everything. You'd get the job done but don't expect it to be pretty."

46

Kern wiped a wet rag across Shepherd's sweaty forehead. Dried blood had caked bandages wrapped around Shepherd's chest. Miss Jane sat chained across from them. The Lady Beth had barely cleared San Francisco Harbor before La Horn had secured her inside the front hold, and murdered her father right in front of her.

After clearing the harbor and amid open waters, Kern assumed Miss Jane's father was weighted and tossed overboard. They had spent several hours alone inside of the forward hold, before La Horn and Caleb returned.

Kern wanted to remove itching cotton-balls from his ears, but did not do so. At the hospital, a doctor had a raised a halting hand followed by two fingers after inserting the cotton-balls. He was unsure if two fingers meant two hours, or two days before removing the cotton-balls. Hearing muffled voices, he stared at La Horn.

La Horn paced back and forth in front of Caleb. "If it weren't for that damn Treaty of Nanking, we'd still have a lucrative opium business in China, and we'd not be resorting to kidnapping."

La Horn stared at Miss Jane and commented, "Being a related to councilman she ought to bring a hefty price." He rubbed his hands together. "I told you we'd come out ahead on this. Bide our time and fair-winds would blow our direction. Caleb, you worried for nothing."

In Caleb's opinion, fair-winds had long since diminished. After the army showed looking for Ver Haven, the Lady Beth should have sailed north searching for a return cargo to the Far East.

La Horn tossed his hands upward, his face brightened at the prospect of a hearty ransom. "Politicians in every country are as crooked as any true fairing pirate. Hell, most politicians put kings, queens, barons and monarchies to shame." He gazed upward at the hatch and moaned, "Sooner or later, the boys will be wanting turns with her." He inquired, "You wanna her first before she's ruined by everyone else?"

Caleb faked a smile and answered, "Oh yeah, but I'll be having my way with her for a couple hours or more. Seeing how you had me busy following people in San Francisco, I wasn't able to plant myself inside of a decent woman. You know how much I dislike whores. You never know if your snake will get sick afterwards and drip green slim."

La Horn chuckled "Let the boy have a piece of her too. He may as well get some pleasure before…" He halted short, unsure if Kern was able to hear him or not. "Well, you know what I mean." Then he trotted up the steps, pushed open the hatch and vanished into an early morning sun above deck.

Jane assured Caleb, "I won't stand for rape like a common woman of the night. Before having your way with me, you'll to have to put a knife to my throat and slit it first!"

Caleb unbuckled his pants and stepped forward. His desired outcome exploded at full volume. Jane exhaled a series of ear shattering screams.

Jane drew back and pleaded, "Please, God nooo!" She closed her eyes and continued heightened shrieks of terror.

After Caleb refastened his belt buckle, her continuing screams kept La Horn believing nothing had changed. Then he looked at Kern and Shepherd. Kern had his hands covering his ears to stifle Jane's high-pitched sheiks.

Satisfied Caleb said, "So it's true, the doctors flushed your ears clean and you can hear again." He nodded at Miss Jane who had calmed herself and was listing.

"Kern?" asked Caleb, "you want to ride her for a-while?"

Kern lowered his hands from his ears and shook his head.

Caleb grinned and observed, "In sync with your father, he danced between right and wrong. He confused the hell out of me. I was never sure what direction the wind blew him. He was bad as a man can be one day, then honest and upright the next."

Kern's eyes pulled tight. Although his hearing was not at one hundred percent, he had heard him. It was an odd twist of fate. Among the first words he heard, beyond muffles involved his Baland father.

Kern had thousands of questions. How did Caleb know his father? Did Caleb know who had killed his parents? Maybe, Caleb could tell him if he had living relatives and where. If so, he would no longer be an orphan.

Shepherd raised himself into a sitting position. Then he leaned against a support beam and insisted, "Stop scaring the boy. It is decision time. You have to decide the difference between right and wrong."

Caleb discarded Shepherd's speech of right and wrong. Words spoken by Kern's father remained etched in memory.

At some point, you'll have to decide the difference between right and wrong, and take a stand. As long as you're drawing breath, ain't too late for a change of heart, always remember that. Somewhere along the line, you'll stand at a dividing point in your life. Hoist the jib and set sail for better shores.

A herd of heavy footsteps thundered above deck. Caleb listened to the voices of his crewmates. In the distance, he heard the sound of a steam engine driven ship. A short burst of a steam whistle reverberated. Jane Pitt was about to speak when Shepherd motioned her silent.

Caleb stared at her and pondered the sudden ruckus above deck. The Americas were uncharted waters for the Lady Beth and most of her crew. How Americans reacted to foolery and kidnapping on the High Seas was anyone's guess.

For reasons only known by La Horn, he generally avoided sailing across the Pacific to the Americas. Often, Caleb suspected this part of the world held bad memories for La Horn. Memories not associated Northern America but something further south, in Mexico or South America.

This entire affair of bringing opium and gunpowder to San Francisco was a bad venture. La Horn was right the Treaty of Nanking had damaged the Opium Trade. With a pending civil war, gunpowder was in demand in the Eastern United States. Potential earnings from the delivery of weapons were vast.

Instead, La Horn kept their hands in the Opium Trade, and now another kidnapping.

Caleb gazed at Jane and shook his head. She was not taken by masked men at knifepoint, no blindfold had covered her face while onboard ship. Many people knew she had boarded the Lady Beth.

Caleb moaned, considering an out of their current dilemma. After the British had granted amnesty in exchange for transporting opium, beginning this illegal affair was idiocy. Even if La Horn had no plans to return to the Americas, they were again hunted men.

With the Treaty of Nanking in effect, the British had no future interest in keeping the Lady Beth crew out of trouble. Britain was no a position to offer amnesty for crimes against another nation. Kidnapping of a politician's niece was foolishness.

Cannon fire boomed, followed by a large splash across the Lady Beth's bow. The above hatch flew up spreading a wide beam of sunlight into the darkened hold.

"Caleb," bellowed La Horn, "We need negotiating power! Grab that bitch chains and all, and haul her up top. Haul Kern up here as well and put a gun to his head! That ought to scare them into backing-off."

47

La Horn shouted commands, "Lower those jib sails and slow us down! Let em think we're coming to a stop! Stay at your posts and be ready to re-hoist our jibs at my command!"

Then La Horn leveled his spyglass toward the steamship and exclaimed, "There are twenty or more soldiers onboard and three cannons on deck!" Another cannon ball shot across the bow and splashed in to the water. He exhaled a stunned gasped, "Don't they understand we are holding hostages?"

Caleb arrived above deck with Jane Pitt in tow. Fat Sam grabbed Kern's arm and dragged him across the deck.

La Horn spun around and ordered, "Caleb, chain her to a railing and lower her over the aft side. We want her hanging in plain view of our adversaries. It should cause them to think twice about firing at us again!"

Caleb groaned but followed orders as he had done since he was Kern's age. "Ms Pitt," he whispered, "Don't fret none you'll get out of this alive." After securing her chains around a railing, he loosened her wristbands and said, "Hold tight until I signal you." He lowered her over the edge until dangling a few feet above the waterline.

Desperate, Jane Pitt grabbed the chains above the wristbands and stared at Caleb. Her eyes begged him to end the nightmare.

Caleb leaned over the railing and assured, "Again, don't fret Miss Pitt, you'll come out of this alive. Can you swim?"

Jane Pitt nodded.

Caleb advised, "I loosened those wrist-irons, when the time is right you can slip free. Don't do anything until I give the say-so, or your friends aren't getting out of this alive."

Wind ushered her petty-coat upward and across her face.

Caleb stood upright and stared at the ship's bow and took a running count who among crew would side with him. If this went sour, La Horn would hang him for mutiny.

Silent, a wounded Shepherd belly crawled up the steps from the forward-hold. Stiches were breaking losing and blood sipped through his chest-wrap. He fought darkness closing in around him. He raised a muzzle pistol Caleb had given him minutes ago and aimed at La Horn.

At sound of cocking gun hammer, La Horn spun around and pressed a knife against Kern's throat. He warned, "I'll slit his throat ear to ear, and still have the woman to bargain with."

Shepherd shouted, "Let him go La Horn, this is between you and me! You're paying for what you murdering Carl and countless others. Nothing's standing in my way of killing you, and that includes the boy." He kept his face firm, hoping he was able to shoot La Horn and not harm Kern.

La Horn asked, "How about the woman? I could kill her first simply to prove a point!" Then he ordered, "Caleb, let the sea have her!"

Caleb turned, peered overboard and spoke to Jane Pitt. "Enjoy your swim." He unsecured her chains from the railing. He held on for a moment, feeling the weight of her body at the other end. Within seconds, she had shaken free of the wrist-irons and clasped onto the chains. She stared at him and waited for a signal.

Caleb gave her a cryptic message, "If you happen upon Poseidon let him know who sent you!" As if uncaring, he released the chains and gazed aft. As expected, the steam engine slowed hoping to save her.

Caleb stared at Shepherd, Kern and La Horn. While the steam engine searched rolling waves for Miss Pitt, La Horn commanded the crew to raise all sails.

Caleb pondered La Horn's miscalculation that the steamship had pursued to save Jane Pitt. He shook his head. They had not delivered a ransom note for Miss Jane Pitt's safe return. It was unknown she had been kidnapped. Their pursuers gave chase for another reason. He assumed the army had given chase for Shepherd, Kern and justice for murdering Carl Ver Haven.

Trembling, Shepherd was growing weak from reopened wounds. He was dying where he stood, on his feet fighting to the last breath. Blurry eyed, he re-aimed at La Horn. Part of him wanted to leap overboard and rescue Jane Pitt. She was gone, drifting far below the reach of a surface dive. She was drowning, if not dead already, her body shark food. It appeared that, Caleb moved like the wind and switched sides at his convince.

Caleb halted at La Horn's right side. Helpless, Kern remained caught in La Horn's tight grasp, a knife against his throat. Years ago after Kern's father had jumped-ship, Caleb's promotion to first-mate was a natural progression.

Caleb's memories of Kern's father rose and fell, amid recollections of his own lost childhood. Two decades ago, La Horn and his motley crew had boarded a merchant ship for shady business dealings along China's coast.

La Horn had met in secret with British Naval Officers concerning the opium trade. The British had planned to colonize China. In theory, with China's youth addicted to opium, Britain would encounter little to no resistance to fight colonization.

At the time, La Horn was in need of another cabin boy and had seen Caleb above deck. As he negotiated amnesty for past crimes in exchange for running opium along China's coast, a crewmember from the Lady Beth had abducted ten-year old Caleb Hefton from the merchant ship. Within months, Opium Trade along China's coast was a booming business.

Caleb doubted anyone missed him on the merchant ship until the next morning. By then the Lady Beth was long gone, and his untimely disappearance considered as a young boy having fallen overboard.

Excited as any boy facing adventure, Caleb had discarded his last name Hefton and joined the Lady Beth's crew as cabin boy. His parents and grandparents were Christian missionaries in China. After both his parents died of yellow fever, his grandparents had decided to send to a private school in England.

With the passage of years, Caleb's grandparents who had placed him the merchant ship from Hong Kong to England were long since dead. They had certainly blamed themselves for sending a boy on a long journey alone.

Caleb's words and actions came from a place vaster than the ocean beneath them. He slid a knife from his belt and took a half step back. He glimpsed at Kern and said, "Kern it was La Horn who murdered your father."

Baffled, La Horn loosened his hold on Kern and stared at Caleb. His lips pulled tight, his brow crinkled. Abrupt, Kern rolled from La Horn's grip. As if timed by Kern's departure from La Horn's grasp, Caleb stepped in closer.

Silent, Caleb stabbed the blade inward at La Horn's sternum and stated, "You are at an end of causing misery in other people's lives. I am dispatching you to hell." Then he angled the blade toward the heart and twisted it.

Bewildered, La Horn staggered backward. He grasped a knife protruding from his chest and stumbled to his knees. His mouth dropped wide and his face expressed betrayal.

Caleb leaned forward and yanked the knife free. As the crew rushed forward, he raised the bloody knife and ordered, "Everyone stand-fast! This is between La Horn and me!" He scanned the crew, searching for tell-tell signs of anyone willing to help La Horn. Awe swept as if ocean waves had suddenly brought their lifestyle to an end, crewmembers stood steadfast and waited.

Then Caleb raised a foot and shoved La Horn onto the deck. He announced, "La Horn was not thinking clearly, he created our current predicament! As by laws of the High Seas by which we live and die, I am now captain. I dare any man to challenge me!"

Hands pressed to his chest, La Horn swaggered back onto his knees. As spurts of blood gushed between his fingers, his eyes asked an unspoken question… Why? Unsure, he gazed at Kern. Reality had struck home. Was he was Edward's son. Suddenly, the resemblance was clear. How could he have not seen it before? Had Caleb known when accepting Kern aboard the Lady Beth in Australia? In effect, Caleb had saved Kern from gallows in Australia and enacted vengeance for Edward's death.

Caleb noted puzzlement in La Horn's dying eyes. He exhaled a deep breath. "I am a freed man, and your chance for redemption is at an end! For all that you've done, may your soul burn in hell for eternity!"

Then Caleb swung his blade across La Horn's neck. La Horn fell backward against the deck, his body shook violently as it yield his ghost to a Higher Judgment than what man was able to offer.

Caleb stared at Kern. "I will not harm you, even if means my own death."

Kern darted across the deck, then knelt and lifted a barely conscious Shepherd. Speaking monotone, Kern gazed at Caleb and broke his silence. "Who am I?" Tears streamed along his cheeks and he repeated, "Who am I?"

Caleb smiled, "Your name is Kern Elder, your father was a merchant sailor from the State of Maine, and your mother was a forced British colonist from England for crimes. You are the son of a great man and God-fearing woman. You've done right by them by taking the side of decency."

As new Captain of the Lady Beth, Caleb turned to his crew and commanded, "Lower the sails and prepare to disembark passengers then onward to Seattle for cargo."

* * *

An hour later, Shepherd lay on a bunk inside one of the steamship's private cabins. Kern and Jane Pitt stood at his side, watching and waiting for him to awaken. Fat Sam, Cookie, and five other former Lady Beth crewmembers sat chained below deck and awaited return to San Francisco for trial regarding the murder of Carl Ver Haven.

Jane bent over, lightly kissed Caleb and said, "Thanks for saving my life. "

Unable to speak, Shepherd opened his eyes and shook his head. Caleb deserved credit for having removed the pins from her wrist-irons. Pleased at the turn of events, he turned his head against a pillow and gazed at a porthole. It was a clear day and calm seas amid wicked hearts of men.

Kern squeezed Shepherd's hand. "You are my shadow spirit, a protector of innocent children."

Before disembarking the Lady Beth, Caleb had informed Kern, "Your father once mentioned an older brother by the name of Bain Elder. As I understood it, Bain lived here in California. A year ago, he was a passenger on the Lady Beth from Hawaii to Australia. Last time I saw him, he was setting foot in Australia in search of you. La Horn didn't know Bain was Edward's older brother. I figured it out but kept it a secret from La Horn and Bain, thinking it was best for everyone."

Caleb had provided Kern a physical description of Bain Elder. Kern realized his uncle Bain was the stranger who had saved from the Baland Hunting party, and later rescued him from walls of fire. Bain had given his own life that Kern may live.

Like a dark cloud, death seemed to circle Kern's life. First his parents, second the Clan, then his uncle Bain, and friend Carl Ver Haven. Today death circled his friend Shepherd.

Tears streamed down Kern's face. He whispered, "No more dying, no more, no more. You have to stay. I don't want to be alone again…"

Shepherd gave Kern's hand a solid squeeze and painfully spoke. "I ain't going nowhere. We've got a long trip ahead of us. A place you'll be safe from harm, and far removed from this coming War Between the States."

Tired, Shepherd closed his eyes and he dreamed of living amid the shadows.

48

Crisp, Trick and Captain Bristol stood inside of hospital corridor. Wearing civilian clothing, Bristol tapped a large envelope across his hand and said, "You boys sure stirred up a hornet's nest. But I am not sure we've reached the bottom of that snake pit."

Crisp adjusted his should-sling and said, "What we know so-far is all there in the report. Not that any of us are sure how it all came together. Ackerland is dead, the organization he was part of us is in shambles. It's too bad about York..."

Bristol nodded. York never made it from the Ackerland's ranch to the city. A large contingent of York's men, estimated at fifty had surrounded ten men assigned to bring York to the city. The ambush had raised the death toll.

Ten additional soldiers killed in action, and their bodies in route to Fort Tejon for proper burial. This affair was far from finished. Bristol believed as States in the East fought a public war: States and territories in the West would fight a secret war to remain a part of the Union.

Trick gazed down the hallway and toward Ring's hospital room. Ring was expected to live another day at most. Emotionally lost, he glimpsed at Bristol and Crisp. Suddenly, a gunshot lacerated quiet hospital corridors.

Trick had no question as to the origin of the shot and ran to Ring's room. He was first to arrive and busted inside. A street lamp shed light onto the main floor where a dead body laid face down, bleeding from a single shot to the head. He rushed to Ring's bedside and lifted a smoking gun from his friend's hand.

Ring rolled his head, stared at Trick and muttered, "I reckon it was you who left that gun under my pillow. As it turned out, I needed it." His eyes met the ceiling and appeared to see beyond it. Heart felt, he gazed upward and prayed, "God forgive me, cuz I am coming home." As his soul departed, his eyes closed and he passed into a breathless sleep.

Trick sat on the edge of the bed, hugged Ring's lifeless body, and rocked back and forth. His best friend was gone. He wept as never before, tears releasing years of hard living. He vowed that secrets Ring carried to the grave forever buried with him.

Crivitz eased past Bristol and Crisp at the doorway. Then he knelt, rolled over the body and muttered, "I was right all along, the Hammer Killer was a woman of High Society." He pried a hammer loose from between her dead fingers and stood. He stepped aside, giving Bristol and Crisp a full view of the Hammer Killer's lifeless body.

Crisp gasped, "Doctor Hanna Steadson!"

Dumbfounded, Bristol stared the dead Hammer Killer. He passed Crisp's report back to him and commented, "Given what just happened, I imagine you want to amend a few things before I read it."

Stunned, Crisp took the envelope and simply nodded.

49

Crisp joined Trick, Hindor, Muser and Rabbit at Ring's graveside. Crisp laid a bundled of lilacs at the headstone and said, "Sorry doesn't began to…" He stopped short, unsure his words meant anything. The deed was done, Ring was gone.

Trick commented, "He loved the smell of lilacs, I'm sure he appreciates it, sir. Right now he is looking down and wishing us the best."

Crisp gazed at mid-afternoon clouds. There was nothing more to say. His thoughts fell to what Chief Crivitz had told him concerning Hanna Steadson's father. Two years earlier, her father had contracted a venereal disease from a prostitute and died.

Crivitz had suggested her motive at first was revenge. As her thirst for vengeance grew darker, her rationale for killing grew stronger. He had theorized Hanna was attempting to rid San Francisco of what she considered a sickness.

Hours ago, Crisp had finished letters to the families of Ringwald and Taylor. The A. R & B had paid a high price bringing the Hammer Killer and Ackerland's group down.

Making matters worse, Shepherd had vanished with Kern and Bristol the dog. Bristol was fuming, having discovered his office safe open with one item missing, Carl's journal.

Trick sighed and stated what everyone present felt. "I'm skipping the hanging of those who killed Mister Ver Haven. I am through with this entire affair. We've got better things to be doing than gloating. York is out there and recruiting men."

Crisp placed a hand on Trick's shoulder and agreed, "York won't be an easy man to catch. We've got our work cut-out for us." Sad, he pulled a newspaper from his coat and showed them the headlines.

Shots fired at Fort Sumter. War has broken out.

Trick muttered, "God is judging this beloved nation for wrongs of slavery. I pray when it's over, this nation is able to recover from His judgment."

Hindor injected, "I believe your right, God is shaping this nation into a land where everyone is treated equal. It is not a war simply to free slaves. It is to free our way of thinking and looking at things."

* * *

Miles away, Shepherd and Kern reined their horses to a stop and turned. They gazed downward from foothills above the city. San Francisco was fading to memories. Bristol darted back and forth in front of them.

Shepherd patted a saddlebag with Carl Ver Haven's secured journal inside. Then adjusted the bandage wrapped around his chest. He grinned and said, "We've a long ride before we reach home. After we're rested there for a few weeks, we'll get Bristol to his new home in Washington."

They reined their horses eastward and rode into a canyon trail that cut through the mountains. Pleased with freedom from cages and chains, Bristol trotted between the horses.

Kern stared at Bristol and mimicked Shepherd. "You've a long way to go until your home at that big old White House Carl told us about. I promised Carl and I am promising you too, I'll make sure you get to your new home."

"For those lost of Eden, the Heavens await your arrival"

Copyright revised 2012©
Casper Parks all rights reserved

14062002R00170

Printed in Great Britain
by Amazon.co.uk, Ltd.,
Marston Gate.